Acclaim For the Work of PETER BLAUNER!

"One of the best books I've read in a long, long time."
—*Stephen King*

"Gripping…convincing…richly imagined…A harrowing, compelling read."
—*New York Times*

"Even the most seasoned mystery authors will be hard-pressed to write a better novel…It may very well be the crime novel of the year."
—*USA Today*

"A taut psychological thriller with [an] ending you'll never see coming."
—*Time*

"Riveting…Blauner has a fine ability to pile crisis on crisis…He builds a palpable sense of heartbreak and menace."
—*People*

"His portrait has a complexity that few authors could achieve."
—*The New Yorker*

"Raw, savvy…a mystery with satisfying moral heft."
—*Newsweek*

Rosemary ducked through the ropes to begin her promenade around the ring with the Round 10 card. Her sequined red swimsuit was riding up her butt again and giving her a wedgie in back. Her arms ached from holding the giant card and the hot lights were melting her makeup.

She looked over at Terrence's corner and saw his trainer kneading his shoulders. Terrence kept glaring at her.

She crossed one foot in front of the other and felt the muscle stretching from her hip to her thigh go as taut as a fishing line. She hoped she'd shaved high enough so there wasn't any pubic hair showing at the bottom of her outfit.

She was coming up on Terrence's corner. He was looking right at her now and his eyes narrowed a little. She wished she could climb out through the ropes right there. She had an eerie feeling like he was about to jump off his stool and come charging after her for the way she'd set him up.

When she was directly in front of him, he said something to her.

"You and me after this is all over, bitch," he said. "We gotta go another round..."

CASINO
MOON

by **Peter Blauner**

A HARD CASE   CRIME NOVEL

A HARD CASE CRIME BOOK
(HCC-055)
May 2009

Published by

Dorchester Publishing Co., Inc.
200 Madison Avenue
New York, NY 10016

in collaboration with Winterfall LLC

*This book is a work of fiction. Names, characters, places, and
incidents either are the products of the author's imagination or
are used fictitiously, and any resemblance to actual events or
persons, living or dead, is entirely coincidental.*

ISBN 0-8439-6117-1
ISBN-13 978-0-8439-6117-1

Cover design by Cooley Design Lab

Typeset by Swordsmith Productions

The name "Hard Case Crime" and the Hard Case Crime logo
are trademarks of Winterfall LLC. Hard Case Crime books are
selected and edited by Charles Ardai.

Printed in the United States of America

Visit us on the web at www.HardCaseCrime.com

Acknowledgments

This is a work of fiction about Atlantic City. Though some institutions depicted in the book are real, the characters and events are not.

I would like to thank the following people for their help: Bill Tonelli, Suzan Karpati, Robert Flipping, Lou Toscano, Glenn Lillie, Shannon Bybee and the rest of the staff of the Claridge Casino-Hotel, Mary Jean Arriola, Tim Voigt, Gay Talese, Vin Czyz, Steven Smoger, Larry Holmes, Thomas Hauser, Ferdie Pacheco, Joe Sayegh, Alia Sayegh, Gail Marrandino, Doug LeVien, Iggy Pop, Robert Lacey, Paul Solotaroff, Pat Pileggi, Dave Lewis, Otto Penzler, Kate Stine, Wayne Kral, Michael Siegel, Dominick Anfuso, Carl Sifakis, Roger Gros, Bobby Fox, Chris Smith, Pat Dodd, Bobby Czyz, Steven Griffin, Casandra M. Jones, James B. Harris, Joanne Gruber, Dan Tyre, Gleason's Gym, Mark Pfeffer, Fran and Barry Weissler, Fran Kessler, and, of course, Peg.

As always, Arthur Pine and Lori Andiman have been in my corner. And I would like to give special thanks to Richard Pine and Clare Alexander, two champs who were willing to go the distance.

Some people never learn to be good.
One-quarter of us is good. Three-quarters is bad.
That's a tough fight, three against one.
—MEYER LANSKY

In dreams begin responsibilities.
—W.B. YEATS

1

As the colors in the sky faded, the red casino lights along the shore came up to replace them. Slowly, dozens of seagulls began to circle the glowing sign on top of Trump's Castle, like bits of paper caught in a cyclone.

I was watching from the parking lot of a club called Rafferty's, on the other side of Gardner's Basin. It was a short boxy car-battery of a place with a blue neon Schaefer sign in the window. I'd stop by once or twice a week in those days to help total up liquor receipts and invoices. But on this night, my father had called me to a special meeting and I knew it wasn't to count any invoices.

I lingered outside awhile, trying to think of a reason not to go in. I checked my Filofax three times, hoping I had the wrong night. But there it was, 7:30 p.m., June 3. A little stretch of pink showed under the dark skirt of the night. I saw a light cross the sky and thought it might be a shooting star. But before I had a chance to make a wish, it turned into a plane and went blinking off toward Philadelphia. There was no sense putting off the inevitable. I buttoned my jacket and went in to see my father.

Inside, the club was what my old man would call a real *fugazi* kind of joint. Smoked mirrors on the walls, a plush red carpet that would've looked right in either a brothel or an airport lounge, and a glittering disco ball hanging from the ceiling that might've seemed hip in about 1977. The club was officially closed that night, but that ball was still going around.

My father was sitting in a booth near the back, talking

to Richie Amato and a guy named Larry DiGregorio, who had a carting business over in Brigantine.

As soon as I saw Larry sitting there, my head started to throb and my heart began to race. I knew he was in some kind of trouble with my father's crew. He was a nice, mild-mannered guy with a slight stammer. I'd known him since I was a kid. Always fastidious. Never a hair out of place on the steel gray helmet of a wig he wore, and never a stain on his crisp white shirt. He had absolutely no chin, though. His neck pretty much began at his mouth.

Driving over, I'd been praying that he wouldn't come tonight. But with him already sitting there, nursing a beer next to my father, I wasn't sure what I could do. I'd hoped to get my old man alone to talk him out of this craziness.

"Look who decided to show up," said my father.

"It's the Great Pretender," Richie chimed in.

My father—who was actually my stepfather, if you want to get technical—was named Vincent Russo. He was sixty then, but he moved around like someone twenty years younger. His muscles weren't the kind you got from lifting weights, but from ripping open shipping containers with your bare hands. His face was a record of every beating he'd ever caught in a police station or a prison yard without breaking down and giving someone up. When he smiled, he showed rows of broken, snaggled teeth on the top and bottom. He was the most loyal man I'd ever met. If he liked you, he'd take a nail through the heart for you. If he didn't, he'd never rest until he got you around the neck with chicken wire.

He'd been my real father Mike's best friend until Mike disappeared. After that, Vin came in and took care of my family. He courted my mother with Black Label scotch and chrysanthemums and played war games and boccie with me in the backyard. In the fall when it finally dawned on me that my real father wasn't coming back, and the whole world seemed strange and frightening, Vin was the one who took me by the hand and led me back into the schoolyard. When bullies taunted me about losing my old man, he'd stand outside the fence and stare at them with eyes like ball bearings until they slunk back to their dodgeball games. He raised me like I was his own flesh and blood and looked after my mother when she started taking pills and stopped being able to tell the difference between her dreams and real life. I knew he loved me, but in the last few years I'd realized I didn't want to be part of his world.

"You're late," he said in a voice like a manhole cover being picked up. "You were supposed to be here a half hour ago."

"I ran into traffic on the Expressway. I think one of these buses turned over that was carrying old people to the casinos. They had it backed up all the way to Camden."

"You could've taken the White Horse Pike. You would've been here in five minutes."

"I didn't think of it."

"You didn't think of it because you didn't want to think of it," my father said.

Larry DiGregorio raised his beer glass to me and smiled. I turned away quickly and caught sight of myself in the mirror behind the bar.

I've been lucky enough to inherit my real father's high cheekbones and dark eyes, but tonight my suit was letting me down. A blue silk double-breasted Armani knockoff that cost three hundred dollars at the Italian Dimension on Atlantic Avenue. It was a kind of clean-cut *GQ* look I was going for. None of that Italian Stallion bullshit, with all the chains and cologne. Bells and smells, I call it. But in the nearest pillar mirror, my suit made me look like a thirteen-year-old taking his great-aunt Doris to her seat at a wedding.

"No respect, no respect," said my father, taking out a comb and trying to smooth back the wild shock of gray hair that was always jumping from the top of his head.

The other two laughed and tilted back their beer mugs.

"Sit down a second, Anthony, you look like sh-sh-shit," Larry DiGregorio said.

I could barely look at him, knowing what was expected of me. I remembered Larry taking me with his son Nicky to a Phillies game when we were kids. I can still see him climbing over the people in the next box, trying to get us a foul ball hit by Mike Schmidt. But he was too slow. Afterwards, he was so depressed he could barely talk to us. Even as a kid, I felt sorry for him.

"I don't know, Larry," I said, rubbing my fingers together and trying to figure a way out of this. "I don't know. Lot of stress these days, lot of stress. I oughta have my head examined, starting a contracting business in the middle of a recession."

"Recession!" Richie smirked like he'd never heard a word with more than two syllables before. He spent all his time reading *Muscle & Fitness* and the *Physician's Desk Reference*, looking for different combinations of steroids to try.

In that picture *The Ages of Man*, Richie's the second one over from the right. His chest was so pumped up it looked like he'd swallowed a two-hundred-pound barbell. A single eyebrow ran from one side of his forehead to the other like a hairy railroad.

"Yeah, recession, Rich." I looked at him. "You ever hear of that? You oughta pick up a newspaper for once in your life."

My father jabbed a gnarled finger at my white oxford

shirt. "And if you'd listen to me, you wouldn't have to worry about no recession. I'm trying to get you to do some work so you can get the button. But you can't even keep an appointment. I tell you seven-fifteen, it's almost quarter to eight."

"Hey, Vin." Larry put a hand on my father's arm. "He's here. That's all that matters."

"That ain't the point," said my father, slapping the table with his palm. "I'm trying to get Anthony to be a man and accept his responsibilities."

Some people's families want them to be doctors. Others would like them to be lawyers. Mine wanted me to be a gangster. To my father, the greatest thing a man could be was a made guy in the mob. To be able to walk into any bar or restaurant and have other men fear and respect you, and even pick up your check. He'd worked hard all his life and wound up the underboss in a scrubby local Atlantic City crew. But he had greater aspirations for me. He thought I could become a capo or maybe even a consigliere with one of the major families.

He couldn't understand that what I wanted more than anything was to be legitimate. I'd grown up around the Cosa Nostra, I'd lost my real father because of it, and I'd had enough. I didn't want to spend every night of my life staring at the ceiling, wondering if a rival crew was going to have me whacked or if the cops were going to arrest me. I wanted what most people with some college education want: a bigger house, longer vacations, the love of my kids, and a shot at doing better. But my problem was that at the age of twenty-eight, with a wife and two children to support, I was struggling to make an honest living. I hadn't had a decent contract for my concrete business in over a year, even though I was hustling around the clock. To my father, the way I lived was a disgrace. Only suckers worked nine-to-five.

"Listen," he said. "If I could get you in with Teddy, you wouldn't have any more worries in your life about providing."

Teddy was my father's boss. His *capodecine*. A three-hundred-pound engorged pig, who always wanted half of whatever you made. I remember him stealing pancakes off my plate when I was a kid.

"If I lived like you and worked for Teddy full-time, I wouldn't make any real money anyway," I said. "I wouldn't even have a name."

"What're you talking about? I have a name."

"Yeah? Ever have a car leased in your own name?"

"Why do I need that? I got four or five driver's licenses."

Across the table, Larry was sipping his beer and using the handkerchief from his breast pocket to wipe his mouth, oblivious to what was about to happen.

"Ever live in a house that didn't have someone else's name on the lease?" I asked my father.

"No," he said. "And I never paid no taxes either. So what does that tell you?"

He turned to Larry and jerked his thumb at me. "You see, he thinks it's beneath him to be part of a crew."

"Well, Vin, the young generation d-doesn't have the same priorities as we did." Larry stroked the part of his face where a chin should have been. "The F-family doesn't mean the same thing to them."

"That's because they don't understand all the sacrifices we made."

Larry shrugged as my father rubbed his nose with his forearm. "Look, V-vin. They're never gonna t-t-take him anyway. So what're you gonna do about it?"

"That's right," I said. "I can't be made because I haven't got Sicilian blood on both sides. Those are the rules."

I was hoping that would derail the conversation, but my father was set on his plan.

"Every man wants his son to have a better life than the one he had," he said gravely. "Maybe they could bend the rules for once."

"Hey, don't be so…officious with me."

My father looked at me like I was giving him a migraine. "Officious?"

"V-vin." Larry leaned over and grabbed my father's elbow in a show of old-man camaraderie. "May-maybe it's better like this. Look at my boy Nicky. If he could've stayed clean, like Anthony, maybe I wouldn't have to be here tonight trying to straighten this out with you."

My father grumbled. "And if Nicky woulda come in to talk about it himself, we could've had it out with him insteada you, Larry."

"You know about this?" Larry turned to me as a potential ally. "My Nicky had a little m-m-misunderstanding about the union p-p-pension fund."

"He was skimming an extra fifteen hundred a week," said my father. He stared at me. "Haven't you got something to tell Larry about that?"

"What?" I just looked at him.

"Don't you wanna say something to Larry?"

"No." I looked away. "What am I going to tell him?"

"That thing you said you were going to tell him."

My father's eyes were like two drill bits going through the side of my skull. I suddenly became aware of every breath being taken in the bar, the tick of the clock, and the catch in Tony Bennett's throat as he sang "Cold, Cold Heart" on the radio.

"I haven't got anything for Larry," I said.

My father was still staring. He punched me lightly in the shoulder.

"You sure about that?"

"Yeah, I'm sure."

I saw Larry's eyes shifting around nervously. If he'd

had any brains, he would've leaped up and run out of there.

I patted my pockets and stooped my shoulders as the blood began pounding in my ears. "I haven't got anything for him."

"Aghh." My father waved his hand in disgust and started to get up from the table. "I'm gonna go take a piss."

"Don't fall in," said Richie as Larry stood up to let Vin out.

My father walked around the circular chrome-topped bar and went through the brown door on the other side of the club marked "Mermen." Most of the tension went out of the room with him. The pounding in my ears subsided and I let the music from the radio wash over me. Tony Bennett was hitting all the high notes. Larry was going to be all right, I thought.

He sat back down and reached across the table to tap my hand.

"He's a real old hard-ass," he said softly. "B-but he loves you. D-don't ever forget that."

"I know, Larry. But he doesn't understand."

"Sure, but in his heart, he only w-wants what's best for you."

That disco ball was slowly turning on the ceiling and a thousand little stars of light chased each other around the room. They reminded me of the gulls outside.

I was about to tell Larry that this would be a good time to leave. But right then my father came out of the bathroom with a .357 Magnum in his hand, just the way I thought he would. He walked around the bar and raised it slowly, levering it at Larry from fifteen feet away. I got ready to hit the floor and cover my ears.

But then something unbelievable happened. Old Larry DiGregorio, who'd always had the reflexes of a Valium addict, whipped his hand inside his jacket and pulled out a snub-nosed .38. Before any of us could react, he fired off a round at my father and reality began to dissolve. The bang made Richie yelp like a schoolgirl finding a roach under her chair. My heart jumped up against my lungs. But my father only looked annoyed, like he just remembered he'd left his keys in the car. He fell to the floor in a heap as Tony Bennett finished his song. From somewhere far away, a foghorn sounded.

Larry turned to us slowly like a high school principal about to deliver a lecture. "You know, I want to believe neither of you boys had anything to do with this," he said in the steadiest voice I'd ever heard him use.

My breath froze. Richie farted so loudly it sounded like he was blowing his nose in his pants. Larry began to sit down. He didn't see my father rising up behind him like a movie creature back from the grave. With one hand, Vin grabbed the nearest bar stool and came rushing at him. And the next thing Larry knew, that bar stool was crashing down on his head.

All hell broke loose. The two of them hit the floor and started wrestling like a couple of old chimps under the banana tree. Spit was flying everywhere, chairs and tables were falling. They began rolling over each other back toward the bar, gasping for air. First my father was on top. Then Larry. A pair of bifocals fell out. Then a set of false teeth. Now a hearing aid. Something furry tumbled off Larry's head and I realized it was his toupee. It was like they were shaking parts of each other loose. Glasses tumbled off the bar and shattered next to their faces. An ice pick rolled off after them. My father grabbed it and tried to jab it in Larry's eye. Larry grabbed his hand and bit Vin's ear. It felt like someone had taken all the nerve endings at the back of my head and twisted them into a tourniquet.

My whole life's dilemma was squeezed into those

couple of seconds. Every fiber in my body was screaming Go, get out of there, drive a million miles away. But I knew I had to stay. Vin was more than the man who married my mother. He was my father, my protector, my sword and shield against the rest of the world.

"GIVITBACK! GIVITBACK GIVITBACK!" It was impossible to tell which of them was screaming.

I saw Richie sitting in the booth like a beached whale. My old man was on the floor making this horrible "ACK-ACK-ACK" strangling noise. He needed me. But they both had guns, which could go off any second. I forced myself to take a step forward, but then two sharp pops stopped me in my tracks ten feet away and I heard a *thwop* sound like a knife going into a pumpkin.

Peggy Lee sang "Is That All There Is?" on the radio.

Someone groaned. An ice cube cracked. In the revolving disco ball lights, I could see the outline of an arm going limp. There was another muffled *pop, pop* from the gun and then both of them got very still.

For a minute, I got scared that they both might be dead. That headache turned into a blinding whiteout pain right over my eyes. How could I explain what we were doing here? What would we do with their bodies? And what would I do without my father? Up until that moment, I hadn't realized I loved him almost as much as he loved me.

There was another groan and then slowly Vin began to disentangle his arms and legs from the pileup on the floor. He stood up and looked from me to Richie and then back to me again.

"Goddamn it," he said. "When I ask if you got something to tell him, you're supposed to jump up and strangle that cocksucker."

"I didn't bring the rope," I said numbly. I was still in shock about what had just happened.

"Ha?"

"I said, I forgot the rope. I guess it's still in the trunk."
That was a lie. I hadn't wanted anything to do with killing
Larry and my father knew it.

He cursed under his breath and started to wipe the
prints off his gun with his shirttail.

"You all right?" I asked.

"Yeah, he just nicked me." My father checked the
shoulder of his shirt where the bullet passed through. He
seemed more concerned about the rip in the material
than the scab forming on his skin.

I breathed a sigh of relief and went over to take a closer
look at Larry. He was lying very still with four bullet holes
in his chest and the ice pick through his kidney. His wig
was off, leaving his pale bare scalp exposed. He was covered with blood and half his blazer was stuck under his
back. I kept thinking he would've wanted it closed with
the brass buttons showing.

The stench was so overwhelming it was like a cloud
coming off him.

Looking back, I think I'd never felt so confused. I'd
known my father had killed people, but I'd never actually
seen it before. His violence sickened me. It didn't just
turn my stomach; it split my mind open. How could the
same man who walked me through the schoolyard do this
to another person?

But at the same time, I was secretly excited. There
was something incredibly powerful about watching him
just take a life. He and Larry had been locked in a mortal
straggle and now he was going to walk away and Larry
wasn't. It changed me—seeing that—but I didn't know
how much at that moment. Almost immediately, I went
back to being horrified and ashamed.

My father came over and nudged Larry with his foot.
"You were supposed to do this, you know, not me," he
told me in a raspy voice, pocketing the .38 that had been

lying at Larry's side. "We were waiting so long he would've left if I hadn't of shot him."

"He almost left anyhow," said Richie Amato with a smaller smirk.

"You shut up!" my father snarled at him. "You never got outa the fucking booth either."

He picked up Larry's beer, which had been sitting on the table the whole time, and finished it in one gulp. The ultimate macho fuck-you. Kill your enemies. Take their women. And if there are no women around, drink their beer.

What could I do? Call the police? This was my father. Besides, it was gradually beginning to dawn on me that by just standing here I was an accomplice to felony murder. I couldn't say anything to anybody without implicating myself.

"Ah, shit." My father started to wipe some bloody mess off his forearm with a cocktail napkin. His shirt was rank with sweat and his breathing sounded like rats running through a wind tunnel. "Well, now I got a problem."

He took another deep breath and heaved his shoulders. A single green vein pulsed above his left temple. His body was still radiating all the hate it took to rise up and kill Larry.

"What's up?"

He looked down at Larry and shook his head. "He wasn't supposed to get shot and stabbed like that. Teddy wanted him strangled and he wanted you to do it. It was part of the plan for having you take over the union envelope."

"So don't look at me," I said sharply. "I didn't want anything to do with this. I only came tonight because I thought there was a chance we might be able to work this out peacefully…"

But even as I was saying this I found I couldn't stop

staring at Larry's corpse. It was terrible what had happened, but somehow I found myself adjusting to the circumstances. Larry was dead. There wasn't a thing I could do for him.

"Well, lookit," said my old man, pulling the ice pick out of Larry's side. "Maybe there's something we can do."

"Like what?"

He bit his lower lip. "Maybe you could just throw a rope around his neck and say you did it and I gave you a hand toward the end."

"He's still got all them holes in him," said Richie, suddenly turning into a forensics expert. "They're gonna look at 'em and say that's what killed him, not any rope."

My father carefully surveyed Larry's face. "Well then we gotta figure out how we can get the tongue to come out and the eyes to bulge."

I straightened my tie and cleared my throat. It's amazing how quickly things can go back to seeming normal. The disco ball on the ceiling was still spinning, the music on the radio was still playing, the beers were still on ice behind the bar, waiting to be sold for three dollars a pop. The only thing different about the place was Larry lying there dead on the carpet.

"Look," I said, "forget about saying who did what to who. What are we going to do about him lying here?"

"Hey." My father shot me an irritated look. "I'm just trying to get you some credit with Teddy."

"Well forget it," I cut him off. "You tell a lie, it'll come back to haunt you every time."

This was the last thing I needed. I was already implicated in a murder. Now Vin wanted to put the weapon in my hand. I just wanted to get out of there, have a drink, and take some time to sort things out.

My father was glaring at me again. "You know, you fuckin' kids kill me," he said, turning from me to Richie.

"Will one of you go get a plastic mat so I can roll up this sonovabitch?"

Richie went springing off to a back room, all gung-ho since there wasn't any danger now. I was still looking at Larry. Just a couple of minutes ago, he'd been asking me how my business was doing.

"Officious," said my father, taking him by the ankles and starting to drag him away. "That the word you used before?"

"Yeah, Dad. Officious."

"You fuckin' kids," he said. "You kill me every time."

2

What was that bonehead's name?

Detective Pete "The Pigfucker" Farley watched the F.B.I. man duck under the yellow crime-scene tape and approach Larry DiGregorio's corpse. What was this fed's name? Something that rhymed with stain. Lane. Payne. Wayne, that was it. The F.B.I. man knelt down next to the body and began pawing through the pockets like a bear looking for honey.

Beautiful, thought Pigfucker. By the time he's done, he'll have his fingerprints on every useful piece of evidence.

The scene was beginning to take on the ambience of a nighttime baseball game. Dozens of people streamed over from the Golden Doubloon Casino across the street, trying to get a look at Larry lying in the dim, drafty alley behind an abandoned restaurant. Four heavyset bicycle cops in plastic helmets and blue shorts attempted to cordon off the area. A German shepherd barked from the back of a K-9 unit car by the curb and two guys from the medical examiner's office hung out nearby, leisurely smoking cigarettes.

From twenty feet outside the crime scene tape, Pigfucker watched Wayne the F.B.I. man carefully lift a key chain out of Larry's pants pocket with a pencil and then touch each key with his fingers. Brilliant that they sent people to Quantico to learn how to do that. No wonder most local cops and hoods called the feds "feebs."

Pigfucker, or P.F. as he was known, stood back, chewing a Tums and admiring the way the blue strobes lit up the crime scene and the light rain. At forty-three, he was already as creased and jaded as Chairman Mao just before he died. He wore a brown sports jacket with dark blotches on it, tan slacks, and a wan smile meant to convey he didn't care that people no longer thought highly of him. An unruly mop of black hair with gray frosting fell over his forehead and a thick mustache concealed the slight twitching of his mouth.

"What's the cause of death?" he asked when one of the medical examiner's guys walked by, carrying a transparent plastic bag.

"Four gunshots to the body and a stab wound through the kidney."

"I see, natural cause for a guinea." P.F. chuckled and tapped his foot in a gathering puddle of rain.

How many homicide scenes had he been at like this? Where the victim and perpetrator were clearly part of some great larger mechanism for controlling the ebb and flow of criminal enterprise. He told himself he didn't care anymore. All these organized crime cases were in the jurisdiction of feebs like Wayne anyway. Local cops like P.F. were only there to set the table and search the gutters for spent shells.

A young patrol sergeant named Ken Lacey brought over a potential witness: a stubby little black man wearing a torn Malcolm X T-shirt, with a black Nike Solo Flight on one foot and a low-top white Fila on the other. A beard as coarse as barnacles roughened the sides of his face and a tangerine-sized bump rose from the left side of his forehead.

"Do you know me?" P.F. looked him up and down.

"I don't even know myself no more."

"Didn't I used to chase you off this corner twenty years ago?" P.F. closed one eye and squinted through the other, like a jeweler examining a precious stone. "What's your name again?"

"Steven Ray Banks. And don't you wear it out."

"You found the body, right?"

"Motherfucker was sleeping in my house," Stevie Ray mumbled. "That's my Dumpster. I been in there every night the last three nights."

"I thought you were living under the Boardwalk. Didn't I see you coming out of there last year?"

Stevie Ray shook his head. "It got bad there, man. They got a lot of riffraff come into town. You know? People who aren't right in their heads. They see Merv Griffin on TV, they get themselves a bottle of pills and a one-way bus ticket to Atlantic City."

A white jitney bus across the street discharged a squad of doughy older women carrying pink change cups.

"Eh, you didn't happen to see who put him there, did you?" P.F. asked. "In the Dumpster, I mean."

Stevie Ray pushed his mouth up toward his nose. "You sound like all them other damn police officers. I told them, 'Motherfucker came in my house unannounced, just like all you motherfuckers do.' Why is that, man? Everywhere I go, I gotta be somewhere else. People always be telling me, move on, motherfucker, move on. Ain't I got a right to be somewhere?" He swung his leg like he was kicking an invisible ball across the street. "Got me living like a dog, without a home, man. And that is the sad truth."

"What can I tell you, my friend?" P.F. swallowed the rest of his Tums. "It's an imperfect world. Allow yourself to become nothing and you've got no place in it."

"Don't I know, don't I know."

Stevie Ray put his hands into his pockets and stared at the traffic whizzing by the open end of the alley. The TAKE A CHANCE sign for the Golden Doubloon casino blinked on and off as the F.B.I. man named Wayne got done looking through Larry DiGregorio's pockets. It was just a matter of time before he'd want to talk to this witness.

"You didn't know him by any chance, did you? The victim, I mean. Larry." P.F. felt the antacids warring in his belly.

"No, man, I don't have nothing to do with the Mafia." Stevie Ray wagged his head like a dashboard ornament. "I was in the casino business. I used to work right across the street here. At the Doubloon."

He stared off at the flashing TAKE A CHANCE sign across the street as if it were some distant constellation.

"Is that right?" said P.F.

"You're damn straight! I gave them people the five best years of my life. And what'd I get for it?" He moved his hands around like he was looking for the right thing to compare it to. "What I got was…squat. They left me with a dog food bowl that didn't have no food in it. It was all because of my damned shift manager, man. He say he caught me trying to steal chips out with my mouth. But that motherfucker wanted me to have sex with his sister and show it on public TV. So whenever I go over to someone's house, they've got me on the TV having sex with his sister. That's a damn shame. So now I have to live under the Boardwalk where they don't get public TV."

Half the time with guys like this, you couldn't tell if

they were really crazy or just faking to compensate for
life's disappointments. That's what the casinos did for
these people. They raised their expectations and let them
down brutally. A couple of years ago, you might've found
this Stevie Ray wearing a starched white shirt and gold
cuff links, dealing blackjack over at the Doubloon. Talking
about owning a house for the first time. But it never
lasted. The casinos never delivered on all the wealth they
promised. Eventually people like this Stevie would get
laid off and wind up out on the street again. Amidst forty-
eight blocks of drab poverty and gaudy desperation.

As they finally got done loading Larry's body into the
medical examiner's van, Pigfucker saw Wayne the F.B.I.
agent heading over his way.

"Say, man," said Stevie Ray. "Things have been a little
slow tonight. Why don't you let me hold five dollars for
you 'til tomorrow?"

"I'll tell you what," P.F. countered. "If you remember
anything about someone unusual hanging around your
Dumpster before they found the body, you got your five-
spot."

But it was too late. Wayne the F.B.I. man was already
standing between him and the witness. Sadowsky, that
was his last name. Wayne Sadowsky. The name flashed in
P.F.'s mind like a half-screwed-in light bulb. Big, pasty-
faced Southern kid with huge linebacker shoulders and a
brown perm that sat like a sick poodle on top of his head.
He moved poorly, though, like he'd once been badly
injured.

"Why don't you-all just back off now, Officer Farley?"
Sadowsky said, his accent rich with the kind of snide con-
descension young federal agents reserve for older local
cops. "This here is going to be a legitimate investigation."

Yes. Number 54, Wayne Sadowsky, out with a groin
pull.

"Wonderful," said P.F. "I've no need to engage in weenie-waggling with you anyway. You can have your grubby little case all to yourself."

He scratched his crotch with regal indifference and started to walk away.

"Hey," Stevie Ray called after him. "What about them five dollars? I wouldn't forget it, man."

"Ask your new friend with the federal government," said P.F., glancing back at Stevie Ray and then Sadowsky. "They're always ready to help out a man in need."

The agent took Stevie Ray's arm and pulled him away. The medical examiner's guys finally slammed the van doors on Larry DiGregorio. And the strip of casinos on Pacific Avenue kept shining like a golden chain extending into the night, dividing Atlantic City into a realm of light on one side of the street and darkness on the other.

3

After seeing what my father did to Larry, all I wanted to do was come home and have a quiet night with my family. But it was like trying to sit down to a normal meal after looking at the inside of somebody's stomach.

Almost as soon as I walked in the front door, with Larry's smell still on my hands, I got into a fight with my wife.

"I have a surprise for you," she said.

"Holy shit! What is it?"

"What do you mean, 'what is it'? It's a fucking couch. What does it look like to you?"

Twice I walked around this thing. It took me about two minutes each time. It was enormous. All done up in peach with these soft brocade pillows and a fringe hanging off the end that reminded me of the shawl my mother used to wear. It looked like the type of thing you'd lie down on before you died.

In fact, if Larry DiGregorio had any luck at all he would've been lying on a couch like this instead of the back-alley Dumpster where we'd left him.

"Where'd you get this thing from anyway?"

"From Spartz, two weeks ago," said my wife. "They just delivered it."

My face fell. "Why'd you go there?"

"What do you mean, why would I go there?" said my wife Carla, who was five months pregnant and had a voice that made the neighbors pull their windows down. "It's a fuckin' furniture store."

At the same time, both of us seemed to realize our two kids were in the other room, playing with the computer. Carla put her hand over her mouth, like she was ashamed of what she'd just said.

"I thought we were going to wait a while," I said, trying to lower the temperature a little. "Save some money, so we could afford one of those nice Scandinavian couches Dave D.'s gonna be getting in."

"I already went by Dave D.'s and he didn't have nothing I wanted," Carla whispered. "Everything he's got is made out of tan leather. It's like a fuckin' furniture store for fag bikers. I wanna wear leather, I'll go ride a motorcycle. I wanna sit on the couch with my baby, I don't sit on leather. Especially in the summer when it gets all sticky and I wanna wear shorts."

I looked at her stuffed into her mother's striped Capri pants and purple halter top, and wondered what had gone wrong with our lives.

I'd started going with Carla back in high school. I'd had a couple of other girlfriends before her, but neither was Italian, so my father and Teddy poisoned me against them. "You shouldn't have outsiders around the house!" Instead they asked me to take out Carla, who was Teddy's niece. Right away, we hit it off. There was a special connection between us. Psychosis I think is the word. She was the only girl in my grade who wore tattoos and motorcycle boots. The two of us were the class misfits. It was her and me against the world.

But then I went off to college and things changed. I started reading books and hanging out with a different crowd, people who were going into the kind of professions where you negotiated with a telephone instead of a crowbar. And Carla stayed home in Atlantic City and became more like her uncle's niece. Right then was when we should've broken up. But when I came back to town on Christmas vacation sophomore year, Carla took me for a walk on the Boardwalk and told me she was pregnant. And that was all she wrote. We were stuck together even though we didn't belong together anymore. It was nobody's fault.

"You shouldn't have gone to Spartz," I told her.

"Why not?"

"You should've waited. By summer, maybe one of those contracts would've come through for me, and we could've gone to Ikea and redone the whole living room."

"But I can't stand to wait," she said, putting her hands on her hips. "I'm already dead on my feet from carrying this baby around."

"It would've just been a couple of more months."

"That's what you always say. There's always a break just around the corner. But you know what your problem is, Anthony? You only talk to people you already know. It, it's…what's the word I want?"

"Like incest."

"It's retarded," she said. "You talk to the same people, you go to the same places, your life's in a rut. You're not going anywhere."

"Oh that's not true," I said, taking off my jacket and checking the sleeves to make sure none of Larry's blood got on them. "I'm always trying to get out. Don't you see me working morning, noon, and night trying to get out and make a name for myself?"

"You're only doing that to get away from me," she said, changing tack.

One minute I was hanging out with the same people all the time. The next I was trying to get away from her. I couldn't win with Carla. I guess we were just clawing at each other because we were unhappy and didn't know what else to do.

"You still should've waited," I said, kicking one of these little green Teenage Mutant Ninja Turtle dolls the kids left lying on the floor like claymore land mines. I'd finally saved enough to afford some toys and already they were out of date. "We could have had something modern in the house."

"Instead of what?" Carla was starting to raise her voice and her belly was beginning to shake.

"Instead of the kind of thing your Uncle Ted and Aunt Camille have."

It was a low blow but Carla took it better than I expected. She went over and stroked the end of the couch like it was a new cat she'd just let in. And what made that worse was that our walls already smelled from cats.

"Well maybe if you'd go work for my uncle full-time we could afford something nicer," she said softly.

"I'm not gonna do that," I muttered.

I was already in too deep with her uncle. When my father first gave me the sixty thousand dollars to go to college and start my business, he didn't tell me it came from Ted. Now the debt was hanging over my life like the Goodyear blimp.

"So how much is this going to cost us anyway?" I asked, giving the couch a little kick on the side.

"Just forty-five a month."

"Oh." I felt like I'd been kneed in the groin. "What're you telling me? What're you doing to me? I'm gonna have to make payments on a couch I don't want?"

"Maybe if you'd come with me just the once, we could've picked something out together," she said. I saw water forming in the corners of her eyes.

This was a couch we were talking about. The whole thing was crazy. We both knew we were broke because I wouldn't go work for her uncle full-time. So she went and bought a couch that we couldn't afford. In retrospect, I think this was what's called a cry for attention.

"You don't make no fuckin' time for me anymore," she said. "Oh, 'Go right ahead, Carla. Get whatever you want. Anything you want is fine. Just don't bother me.' "

"Yeah…but I didn't want…*this!*"

I was looking at this couch. In that moment, it became a symbol for everything that had gone wrong in my life. A fat, lumpy, lifeless hulk. It made me think of her uncle and my father and Larry lying there in the alley and us in this house that smelled like a cat even though we didn't have a cat and how I felt hemmed in by everything. If I'd had a gun right then, I would've shot that couch.

Meanwhile, my two kids playing with the computer in the other room were yelling at us to keep our voices down. *"Shut up, what's a matter witchooo?!!"*

I realized I hadn't been in to see them since I got home. So I gave Carla the time-out sign and stuck my head in. The two of them were sprawled out in front of the Macintosh, for which I was already paying a hundred fifty dollars a month on an installment plan. Rachel with her long black hair and her sallow face, looking as mournful as the Madonna at the age of seven. I could already tell she was going to grow up to be a worrier. Always concerned that everybody else is okay. Little Anthony, who was five, was more like me. A hustler, a fast-talker, constantly looking for an angle to beat the odds. His big drawback in life was that he was born deaf in one ear and hard of hearing in the other. But instead of giving up, he went along with all the special classes and hearing aids, and basically he was going to be fine, except for occasionally mispronouncing words.

They were playing a game called *Sim City* that allowed you to create an entire planet on the computer screen. With a keystroke, you could build a neighborhood or start a natural disaster.

"Daddy, Anthony's wrecking the economy again," Rachel complained.

I still don't know how I got lucky enough to have two kids who were so much smarter than me. "Come on," I said. "Enough of this bullshit. Let's play The Dirty Dozen."

"The Dirty Dozen" was just an excuse to wrestle the way I used to with Vin in the backyard. My kids forgot the computer and jumped on me. Rachel got me on the floor and started slapping my stomach. Anthony climbed onto my head and tried shoving one of those miniature Ninja Turtle dolls up my nose. Probably the same one he'd been keeping in the neighbor's cat's litter box.

"Sm-ELL Mich-EL-ange-LO!!" he yelled with that way he has of overenunciating. "Smell Michelangelo!!"

I think, looking back on it, that was the happiest I was ever going to be. Only I didn't know it at the time.

But then I heard my wife's voice calling.

"Anthony, come out here again. We were discussing something."

I hugged the kids and went back out, noticing a little rust-colored stain on the back of my left pant leg. I hoped it wasn't from Larry. Glancing back at little Anthony, I realized he had the same kind of Bell Tone hearing aid that fell out of Larry's ear.

"You don't like this couch—tough shit," Carla was saying with her arms folded over her chest. "Next time you come with me when I'm gonna get something for the house, instead of hanging out at the club."

"What do you think? I like being there? It's my business."

I thought of Larry lying there with his wig and his jacket unbuttoned.

"Oh yeah, what about all them girls you're bringing there? You think I don't know about that?"

"The live entertainment's all your uncle's idea. I just help count the money until we get some concrete work coming in. In case you hadn't noticed, there hasn't been a crane up in this town in a year."

And then there were all the bills to think about. In the next few years, there'd be more special schools for Anthony and probably psychiatrists for Rachel with the way she was going. Plus the fifty-five thousand dollars we owed on the mortgage and the sixty thousand I owed her uncle. I looked at the couch and the rust stain on my pants and I shuddered a little inside.

"Listen, Carla, I just gotta get out of here awhile, get some air."

"We are discussing something."

"I know, but I just have to get out."

It was all starting to get to me. The couch. The baby in her stomach. Larry in the Dumpster. I felt like the walls were closing in on me.

I looked around for the hundred-dollar khaki windbreaker I picked up from Macy's last year at the Hamilton Mall. I found it under little Anthony's toy helicopter with a yellow crayon mashed into the back.

"I'll be back in a little bit," I said, putting the jacket on over my suit pants.

Carla's eyes never left my face. "Anthony," she said in a high quavery voice. "I know you. And I know your mind hasn't been in this house for a long time."

"Carla, honey, that's not true. Everything's going to be fine. We can talk about it when I come back."

But the truth was that I'd been feeling trapped for years and now I was beginning to think there might be no way out.

I saw Carla looking down at the Disney World ashtray on the table like she had an idea about throwing it at me again. It already had two chips in it.

"Shut up, will you?!" I heard little Anthony yelling in the other room. "I can't hear myself think." He must've had the hearing aid turned up too loud.

"But where you going?" Carla asked. "I wanna talk to you."

"I'm going to see my father." I almost tore the zipper off my jacket as I was raising it.

"I thought you already saw your goddamn father to-night," she said. "What the fuck's the matter with you?"

"Well, I'm seeing him again. I'd rather be with him than take this kind of abuse from my own family."

Carla's cheeks were all red and her nose was swelling. "You better be going to see your father. Otherwise I'm gonna go over to Uncle Teddy's house, borrow his Ruger and you'll find something else waiting for you when you get home besides a fucking couch."

"Oh yeah? You're gonna shoot me when I come in the door? Very nice. Who's going to look after the kids when they take you away?"

"Anthony, don't go," she said, crying so hard it sounded like water rushing into a cove. "I feel like I don't know you no more."

For a second, I stopped by the door and looked at her. I was thinking about the way it used to be too. How we met on the Boardwalk one night in the summer after we'd both had fights with our parents. I remembered how we took off our clothes and went swimming in the shallow part of the ocean. Carla had long black hair then and it just kind of floated on top of the water. You could see the moonlight in the little ripples and once in a while one of Carla's breasts would break to the surface like the sea was offering up something good to the sky. We were playing a game. Seeing which of us had the nerve to go further out. But each time the tide pulled away, we'd hold hands so one of us wouldn't get taken off to drown alone in the middle of the ocean.

That was a long time ago, though.

"I'm sorry, Carla," I said. "Don't wait up for me."

It turned out I didn't go see my father again that night. Instead I went where I always go when I don't know what else to do. To the Boardwalk. It was a nice night. If I'd had my jogging clothes with me, I would've gone for a run. Instead I sat on a bench outside the Golden Doubloon Hotel and Casino, watching the lights go on and off on the TAKE A CHANCE sign over the entrance while the tide pulled the sand from the shore behind me.

Sometimes it seemed this was where I ended up whenever anything important happened. There are whole parts of my childhood that I don't remember, but I can still picture my real father Michael taking me for a long walk when I was seven. He was a tall, good-looking guy who always wore the best French shirts, Italian suits, and English loafers, even when he couldn't afford them. I'd hold his hand and think the Boardwalk would go forever if we could just keep walking. It was right around this spot that he pointed out a vacant lot and said that was where the two of us would build a castle one day.

About a year later he disappeared and it was Vin taking me for a walk down the Boardwalk. I can see myself pointing to that vacant lot again and asking what happened to Mike and the plans we'd made.

"I guess he made a mistake," Vin said.

The Boardwalk was empty in those days. A bunch of half-demolished hotels and broken storefronts. I remembered all the stories Mike told me about how this used to be the Queen of Resorts before I was born. The place where all the old robber barons, industrial leaders, and flappers from the 1920s used to come and sun themselves. This was where they had the first Miss America Pageant, the first movie theater, the first Easter Parade, the first bra-burning, the first Ferris wheel, and the first color postcard. And down at the end of the Boardwalk, there was the Steel Pier, where thousands of people would come to watch Sinatra himself sing with Tommy Dorsey's band while horses dove off the end of the pier.

All that was gone by the time my real father left. But there was always the chance that it would come back. "It's Atlantic City," I remember him saying. "Anything could happen here." And even in those ghost town years, I knew he was right. There was a special feeling about the place. Something about the way the sea met the sky as the salt air rustled the red-and-white-striped tents on the beach. Summer always seemed right around the corner.

And then it finally came. The state decided to allow casino gambling in A.C., and soon those castles my real father had been talking about began appearing all along the Boardwalk. Places with names like Bally's Grand, Caesar's, the Taj Mahal. Huge rectangles of chrome and glass that turned gold when the sun hit them just the right way.

Except by then, I had no way into them. Because I had Vin as a stepfather and Teddy as an in-law, I couldn't apply to work for any of the casinos. Any of the standard background checking would make it look like I was mobbed-up too.

So I was stuck on the porch of a rickety shack while these palaces went up literally in my backyard. And now, more than ever, I wanted to go into them. I had Larry's murder weighing on my mind and Carla, the kids, and the bills waiting for me at home. There had to be some other kind of life out there.

I looked up again at that sign blinking TAKE A CHANCE, TAKE A CHANCE over the entrance of the Doubloon. I just watched it awhile. I thought nobody was supposed to have flashing lights like that in Atlantic City. The local politicians used to say they didn't want anything too flashy or vulgar displayed. But here the Doubloon had this thing blinking so brightly you'd get the message if you were flying ten miles up in an airplane. I wondered how they got somebody to make an exception for them.

4

"The stones," said Vincent Russo. "I'm telling you, Ted. You can't believe the stones on this kid."

"Yeah?"

"He stands right up like a man, shoots Larry twice. I never lifted a finger. I was too scared, you know. Larry gets up, Anthony gives him two more for his health. Bang, bang. I had nothin' to do with it. My ass was sucking. You know what I'm saying?"

Teddy Marino, his boss, watched him suspiciously and said nothing.

The two of them were standing in a third-floor bathroom, where they were sure their conversation wouldn't be bugged. Noise filtered up from the social club on the first floor. The old lady down the hall turned her light off. Teddy, wearing a pinstripe suit without a tie, shifted uncomfortably in the doorway.

He was fat in the way of people who can't help themselves, rather than those who actually enjoy eating. His stomach stuck out over his belt like scaffolding and his jowls flowed over his collar like lava. Though he was turning sixty in a week, the pudgy boy who'd been tormented by his reform school mates in the shower was still close to the surface, biding his time, waiting for revenge.

"So I was thinking," said Vin, pulling on the hem of his green polo shirt. "Now might be a good time."

"A good time for what?"

"You know." Vin ran a hand through his shock of gray hair. "To think about inducting Anthony."

Teddy inhaled deeply and his jowls reddened slightly. "How many times I gotta tell you, Vin? It's a closed issue. Anthony hasn't the Sicilian blood on both sides so there's no way I can make him."

Vin started to say something, but Teddy was already waving a chubby hand in his face. "Look, this isn't my teaching," he said. "It's the way it's always been. You can't just pick and choose from tradition. It's either all or nothing. Like believing in God. You either buy into the whole program or go fuck yourself."

Vin bit his thumb and listened to the music pounding up from downstairs. Either "O Sole Mio" or Elvis Presley singing "It's Now or Never."

"There've been exceptions," he said.

Teddy watched him through two eye sockets that were like small ditches in his fleshy face. "Name one."

"Neil up in New York," said Vin. "He was gonna make his daughter. They had a date for the ceremony and everything."

Teddy stuck his hands in the pockets of his pinstripe jacket. "It's not the same thing. She was Sicilian. Like her father."

"They were still gonna bend the rules."

"Listen, Vin." Teddy tugged on his ear and drew back his lips. "Forget about him getting made. When is this kid of yours Anthony gonna stop being a cripple?"

Vin looked stricken. "Wha?"

"He's married to my favorite niece. Last month, I had to give her two hundred dollars to get a haircut and some shoes for the kids. Do I look like fuckin' Jerry Lewis running a charity?"

"No, Ted, but…"

"But nothing," Teddy huffed. "The kid's a cripple. I love him, but he's a cripple. I sent him to college and set him up in the concrete business. I haven't seen dollar one back from him. I wonder should I be so trusting. Now you want me to get him inducted. Well, it ain't that easy, Vin. If my own boy Charlie was still around, I'd have to go through channels…"

He stopped talking a moment and spit into the toilet.

"Is that what this is about?" asked Vin. "Because my boy's alive, and yours ain't?"

"That's got nothing to do with it."

"Because that ain't Anthony's fault. He didn't have nothing to do with what happened to Charlie."

Teddy started to frown, but before he could say anything, the door down the hall opened and the old lady came out. She was using a walker, and wild wisps of white hair flew from her pinkish scalp. Teddy moved out of the bathroom to make room for her, his stomach grazing the

door frame. Vin plodded out after him and they both
bowed their heads respectfully as the old lady went in to
use the can.

After a few minutes, a pale, oily-skinned ex-junkie
named Joey Snails came upstairs and handed Teddy a
thick envelope.

"It's the pickup from the roofer's union," said Joey, who
had crevices shaped like seahorses in his cheeks. "Richie
said I oughta get it this week, because you didn't want
Nicky D. doin' it no more."

Teddy opened the envelope a little and made a point
of touching each bill. "I hope it's all here," he said. "I'd
hate to hear that you skimmed some and put it in your
arm."

Joey Snails looked gravely offended. "It's all there."

Teddy pinched Joey's cheek hard enough to make the
seahorse disappear. "Go on, get outa here. If I find two
dollars missing, I'll kick your ass."

Teddy stuffed the envelope into his inside jacket pocket
and swallowed hard. Money had been tight the last few
years. The problem was the casinos. For all his time as a
boss in Atlantic City, Teddy had never been inside a count
room or placed a high-level executive in the industry.
There were too many state watchdogs around. For a while,
he'd had his share of crumbs spilling off the table—union
pension funds, carting and linen businesses—but when
the construction boom ended, there were fewer and fewer
crumbs to go around.

He waited until Joey was down the hall and out of ear-
shot before he turned back to Vin. "Remind me, I wanna
get somebody else to do that pickup," he muttered. "I
still don't trust that fuckin' hophead."

"I thought we were gonna give Anthony a shot at handling the envelope."

"See if you can find somebody else, I'm not sure I

trust that kid of yours either. He reminds me of his old man Mike." Teddy loosened his belt a notch and closed his jacket. "Anyway, I haven't got time to worry about it right now. I got Jackie and Sal coming down from New York to talk about something next week."

"What do they want?"

"I don't know. Something to do with the Commission. Some fuckin' thing where they want to make a ruling."

"Jackie. Ha?" Vin scratched his ass and looked impressed.

"Twenty-five years ago, guys from his crew would come into town and make me run to get their cigarettes." Teddy patted his abdomen like he was trying to calm an anxious child. "We come a long way. Now they treat us like equals."

"The way it should be," said Vin.

"I remember when the old man Ang from Philly used to come into town with Johnny Blowjob and they used to treat us like their shoeshine boys."

"Somebody shoulda put a bullet in his head long time before they did," said Vin.

The old lady flushed the toilet and came out, barely acknowledging the two men as she went back to her bedroom.

Teddy took out an unfiltered cigarette and stuck it in his mouth. "You know what the problem was with that old greaseball?" he asked Vin. "He was like a pay toilet. He wouldn't give a shit for nothing. He had dozens of young guys like you and me doing work for him, but never showed any gratitude. From '57 to '76 he wouldn't open the books and make anybody. Remember? We were prisoners." Teddy squinted through the smoke, still smarting from the memory. "He wouldn't move any of us up in the organization. Oh, he was an old hard-on."

Vin shrugged and sat against the rusty sink. "Well, now

you know how Anthony feels," he said to Teddy. "He's a
young guy, just like we were, and he don't have any way
to move up and make some money."

Teddy gave him a look that was meant to cut like a
buzz saw. "Don't give me any more grief about that, Vin.
I'm under enough pressure already."

He coughed three more times and spit something else
into the toilet. Before Vin could see what it was, Teddy
flushed it down.

"Will you at least think about it, Ted?" Vin pleaded.
"We been together a long time. It would mean a lot to
me. At least let him handle the envelope."

Teddy let the cigarette dangle out the side of his mouth,
Humphrey Bogart-style. His face was splotchy and there
was no luster in his slicked-back hair. "I'll think about it.
If you'll think about getting him off my welfare roll. It's
embarrassing having to support my own niece."

Vin looked like he would have fallen on his knees and
kissed Teddy's pinky ring if the floor hadn't been so damp.

"Thanks, Ted. I feel more a man after talking to you."

Teddy took the cigarette out of his mouth and looked
at it warily, as if it had done something to offend him.

"You're a good father, Vin," he said, putting a hand on
his old friend's shoulder. "That kid don't deserve you."

5

Over the next week, Larry DiGregorio's murder grew
like a fungus in my mind. I couldn't get rid of this image
of him lying there with his wig off and the ice pick in his
kidney. I kept thinking the police were going to come by
my house at any minute and take me away from my kids.

I loved Vin, but I had to get away from him and his crew. Their lifestyle was contaminating me.

And then I got my chance.

I had an appointment on a hot Monday morning with a guy I knew named John Barton. We were supposed to meet at the local P.A.L. and talk about some drywall work he wanted me to do on his garage.

He was a funny kind of guy, John B. He had a long angular face, coalblack skin, and tinted aviator glasses that made him look like some bad-ass pimp hustling girls on Pacific Avenue. But once you got to know him, you realized he was actually a very sweet, soft-spoken guy who painted boats for a living. He was so pathetically shy that he almost never looked you in the eye, and when he talked you had to lean in because he swallowed half his words.

Except when the subject was his older brother Elijah, former middleweight boxing champion of the world. When he talked about Elijah, John B. suddenly got the heart of a lion. Everything he said became clearer and more articulate. Even his posture changed, so he stood up an extra six inches and looked you straight in the eye.

I found him hanging out by the doorway, trying to feed a crumpled dollar into a vending machine. I traded him for a smoother bill and asked him how he was doing.

"Fine," he said in his regular mealy-mouthed voice. "Wanna meet my bro?"

"Say what?"

"I'm askin', do you-all wanna meet my brother?"

That was the other thing about John. Every time you saw him, he'd ask if you'd like to meet his brother. It was kind of sad. He just assumed that was the only reason anyone would want to talk to him.

"Sure. I'd like to meet your brother someday."

"He's here today, man," said John B., who wore a base-

ball cap with the name of a battleship his brother once
fought on.

I looked around the gym and saw a skinny black kid
jumping rope on the scabby red floor and an out-of-shape
cop doing situps on a crusty slant board. Finally, I noticed
a middle-aged man standing in the boxing ring near the
back, red-gloved hands on hips, trying to catch his breath.
I didn't recognize Elijah Barton at first. He was about
twenty pounds heavier than I remembered him and his
face was barely visible under his headgear. But here he
was, slowly beginning to move around the ring with a
strong-looking kid who had to be half his age.

By my calculations, Elijah had to be at least forty-three.
He hadn't been champion for nine years. I hadn't even
seen his last six fights. But as he ducked under one of the
younger kid's punches and swung his arms like a woods-
man about to chop down a tree, he didn't seem overly
frail.

"What's he doing here?" I moved closer to get a look.
"Trying to get in shape?"

"He gonna make a comeback." John followed me,
sounding protective. "He gonna move up to light heavyweight."

I watched as the younger kid moved forward and hit
Elijah with a sharp jab that he should've seen coming
when he woke up that morning.

"You sure he wants to do that?"

"He's just got to get hisself back to being the way he
was—you understand what I'm saying?" said John B.,
unfazed, as the words whistled through a space in his
teeth. "Been away a long time."

I noticed how little resemblance there was between
the brothers, even though John B. was just a couple of
years younger. Probably the benefit of not getting beat
up night after night.

"Well listen. What about this drywall work?"

"Wha?" he said, swallowing his words again now that the subject wasn't his brother anymore. "I don't remember what I said to you."

"Drywall. The job we were talking about. The one I was gonna bring in for twelve hundred for you?"

"Oh." His face went slack. "Well I been askin' around. And, uh, I talked to a man said he could bring it in for eight hundred dollars." He seemed embarrassed about getting a better price.

All right fuck you, I was going to say, but something stopped me. I was watching his brother. He was right up against the ropes, about ten feet away, when the younger fighter hit him with a solid left hook. Elijah's head snapped back. But by standing this close, I could see the blow wasn't as devastating as it might have been. Elijah had turned his chin just enough to take the force off the shot.

"He always take a punch like that?"

"Last five years," said John B., "he learned to take three for every one he throws. Kept his career alive."

Probably lost him some brain cells too. A right uppercut slammed into Elijah's jaw and he shook it off like a bad idea. He reminded me of my father shrugging it off after Larry shot him.

"So he must get paid pretty well to get beat up like that, right?"

"Ain't just the money," said John. "It's the pride."

Yeah, right, I thought. I'd heard about the kind of money fighters made off casino deals and pay-TV contracts. Before they locked Mike Tyson up, he was making twenty, thirty million dollars a bout.

"He feel like he has to come on and prove himself."

"So's he got any new bouts lined up?"

John B. rubbed his chin. "Well you know there's a spot

that opened up on that casino bill in the fall, but I dunno if we can git it."

I'd heard something about that. They were looking for somebody to fight Terrence Mulvehill, the current light heavyweight champ.

"Why can't your brother get the slot?"

John shook his head. "You know anything about boxing?"

Before I could answer, Elijah landed a strong right uppercut that caught his opponent on the chin and sent him staggering toward the corner.

"You got to give in order to get," John B. said. "You know what I'm saying? It takes money to make money. You got sanctioning fees, training expenses, you got to pay the lawyers and the sparring partners, and then you got to be down with the right promoters and managers and man, they are the worst. His old manager Frog Nelson ran off with half his money, man. We still suing that motherfucker." He put his hands in his pockets and his body sagged a little from the burden. "It's fifty thousand dollars just to get started on the way back."

"You can't borrow that kind of money? That doesn't make any sense. A guy like your brother, used to be champ, they're gonna get at least a million back on their investment."

Elijah Barton was chasing the younger guy across the ring, swatting him with his glove like a big old lion playing with his cub. In the meantime, John B. was watching me carefully, like something just occurred to him.

"Say Anthony," he said, more confidently. "Your family's got some money, don't they?"

"Oh no, John. You don't wanna get mixed up with them."

I could see what he was thinking. He was desperate to launch his brother on a comeback and he didn't care who his partners were. All he knew was he'd once been on top of the world with his brother and he liked the view from up there a hell of a lot better than he liked painting boats.

"Why can't I talk to your father or Teddy?"

"Because once they get their hooks into you they never let go. You think you can just borrow some money from them and return it, but it doesn't work that way. There's never an end to it. They always keep coming at you."

Besides, I thought, boxing was getting to be more of a legitimate business. The pillars of industry were promoting it: Time-Warner, Donald Trump, and my personal hero, Dan Bishop, who grew up on the streets of Atlantic City like me and ended up the most successful casino owner in Vegas. I knew there were still some rough characters around, but I remembered all the movie stars, magazine models, and CEOs sitting ringside at the last fight I'd seen on TV. That was what I wanted to be part of. Not watching two old men trying to bite each other's ears off on a filthy barroom floor.

"Well, maybe you know somewhere else we could get the money." John B. sucked the gold ring on his left hand.

I just stood there a moment, thinking and watching his brother in the ring. Elijah had this kid trapped in the corner again and was whaling the shit out of him. There were rights, lefts, hooks, uppercuts, open-glove slaps, closed fists, rattlesnake jabs that slithered past the kid's ear, and smashes that tore into his rib cage like flying Ninja stars. I never knew there were so many ways to hit somebody.

And I was thinking: This is what it's all about. You get put down and stomped on all your life; people try to obliterate and annihilate you. And then, just when it seems like you can't take it anymore, you find that you can take it. And you come back. You learn to take three shots for every one you give. And when you see an opening, you lunge for it.

If I'd been born a rich man's son, I might have gone to law school. If I'd grown up among honest working people, I might have wound up being a cop or running a grocery store. But I grew up with gangsters and boxing was the only legal way I knew of to make a million dollars without real qualifications. Money I could use to pay off Teddy once and for all. But it was more than that; it was a way out of one world and into another.

Elijah Barton once got three million dollars to fight a man. So when the opportunity came up to be part of his comeback, I lunged at it.

"You know, John," I said. "There might just be another way to raise that money."

Later on that day, we stopped by his brother's house on Maine Avenue. We found Elijah stretched out on a couch in his living room, wearing a pressed yellow shirt and navy trousers. His wife was in the kitchen, cooking and listening to a religious program.

"So you're the young fella who's gonna help me get my name back," Elijah said, getting up slowly to shake my hand.

"We'll see. I hope so."

His face was wider than it used to be. Not just puffy, but expanded sideways, like in a carnival mirror.

He began to bend back his arms and limber up his shoulders, like he was about to step into the ring again.

"You know, a lot of these young boys who get in the ring now, they got a lot of spunk, but ain't none of them know how to go the distance," he said in a voice as light as pillow feathers.

I noticed that he hardly ever blinked. I guess that reflex didn't work as well anymore since he'd been hit in the head so many times.

"Can you go the distance?" he said, starting to throw a right hook at my head.

I ducked and then realized he'd just been faking. "Yeah, I can go the distance."

"Then how you gonna raise the money?" Elijah asked.

"Don't you worry about that. I'm very motivated."

A grin broke up Elijah's face and he weaved and bobbed and popped me on the shoulder with a quick left. It only hurt a little.

"That's real good," he said. "It's important for a man to be motivated. I remember I had a motivation for every fight I ever had. My first fight was for a diamond ring. My second fight was for a car. By my twelfth fight, I was buying my family a house."

"So what would this fight be for?" I asked, wondering what I was getting myself into.

"To get back everything I had before," Elijah said solemnly.

John B. broke in, basking in the glow of his brother's celebrity. "When my brother was champ, there wasn't nobody who didn't know who he was. We could go to Zambia or New Zealand and brothers would come out the kitchen, saying, 'Elijah, Elijah, we love you.' "

A cloud passed over Elijah's face. "But the last time at the airport, that girl behind the counter couldn't spell my name right," he murmured.

"So that's why you want to fight again? To get your name back?"

"That, and the money." Elijah put up his guard and rocked from side to side. His wife's religious program in the kitchen seemed to get a little louder. "Like I say, I'm in it to go the distance. Some of these young boys, who fight now, they just wanna kick butt. I've kicked enough butt. Now I want security."

"All right," I said, playing devil's advocate to make sure this deal was going to be worth all the effort I'd have to put into it. "But what about all those people who are going to say you're too old to fight and you're just risking more brain damage?"

He threw a big brown fist in my face and for a second my whole world was his knuckles. Then as fast as it came it was gone. The punch stopped short of my nose by less than a quarter inch. If it had connected, I would've spent two months in a hospital easy.

"Does that look like brain damage?" He danced away.

"So you're not afraid of getting knocked out?"

"Hell no." He threw a quick combination at the lamp in the corner. "Though it must be something. Having the night close up on you like that." He stopped dancing and punching for a second. "They say it's hard for a man to live with himself after he gets stopped. I heard tell of one man was lying on the dressing room table after he got knocked out and started to see visions of baby Jesus fighting and boxing with the angels. Imagine that. Baby Jesus, gettin' in the ring. Man got so scared he ran out naked on the street."

"Why'd he do that?" I asked, feeling a peculiar chill on the back of my neck.

"I guess he must've lost faith," Elijah said gravely, staring at the ceiling like he'd just seen a ghost flying by up there. "Man spends his whole life fighting, telling himself he's the baddest man alive. He gets knocked out, he can't be that way no more."

He grew still and quiet. No matter how you came at it, this man was forty-three and had been in a lot of fights. There was even scar tissue on the back of his thick, rolled-up neck. But that was part of the beauty of Elijah. In a way, he was just an ordinary middle-aged man trying to chase down his lost youth. Like millions of other paunchy middle-aged men across the country. A fair percentage of whom might be inclined to watch pay-per-view fights on cable TV. I could even imagine a slogan: "If there's hope for Elijah Barton, there's hope for the rest of us."

"So have we got a deal?" I said. "I get twenty percent as your manager for covering your training expenses and sanctioning fees up front."

"Twenty percent." Elijah shook my hand. His grip was surprisingly loose and delicate, like an old lady's.

I started to leave. "Sounds like a helluva thing," I said. "Getting knocked out."

"I wouldn't know." Elijah sat back down on the couch and took two pills. "It's never happened to me."

It was only later that I learned that he'd been stopped cold before the third round in two of his last three fights.

6

Just after ten that night, Pigfucker walked into a bar called the Irish Pub, put a fifty-dollar bill on the counter and began drinking whiskey until a halo of colored lights appeared around the bartender's head.

"Keep pouring," he warned when he saw the kid hesitate after the seventh drink. "Keep pouring, or I'll take out my gun and shoot you right here."

The bar was a little sanctuary of nostalgia. Its dark-paneled walls were covered with pictures of scenes from yesteryear: Lillian Russell in petticoats, Cagney in *The Fighting 69th,* the 1921 Miss America contestants, and Harry Greb, middleweight champion of 1923. Yellow stained-glass light fixtures gave everything a soft autumnal glow. But when P.F. saw his own face in the mirror behind the counter, it was stark and ghostly. With long sad eyes and no halo of colored lights going around it.

"Hey," he asked the bartender. "Where's my goddamn halo?"

A trio of cops came in and sat down at the table five feet behind his stool. Even in his drunken haze, he recognized one of them, Earl Mack, a black patrol sergeant he'd argued with frequently in the last few years. The other two he didn't know. One looked exactly like a baby, with light, thin hair and wide, innocent eyes. The third was tall and swarthy, with black curly hair. Pigfucker couldn't tell if he was Italian or Puerto Rican.

"You know," said P.F., turning halfway on his stool to face Earl and the others. "I feel sorry for you."

"And why's that?" Earl Mack's eyes barely left the list of mixed drinks on his brown placemat.

"Because you are condemned to clean up after federal gang bangs like this DiGregorio homicide, while I enter the vibrant and exciting world of casino management."

"Is that so?" Earl bit down on his lips.

"It is," said P.F. with a sage nod, the whiskey making him boisterous and arrogant.

He saw Earl and his tablemates smirking and thought: To hell with them, the lowly beasts. Let them think he was kidding. His ego was rising as free and lofty as an untethered parade float on Thanksgiving Day.

"In eight months I'll have twenty years on the job," he said. "And I've already spoken to my good friend, Father Bobby D'Errico, vice president in charge of operations at the Doubloon hotel-casino, about his hiring me as head of security." He leaned over and winked at Earl. "Maybe I could even take on one of you boys as a square badge. You know, as an act of charity."

"Really?" Earl flashed a very small smile and gave the waitress his drink order.

P.F. saw the halo of colored lights turning counter-clockwise around Earl's head.

"Do you all know Mr. Pigfucker?" Earl asked his table-mates above the din of the Clancy Brothers singing "The Unicorn" on the jukebox.

The baby and the Puerto Rican shrugged.

"Detective Peter Farley," he said, leaning off his stool to shake their hands. "Pigfucker, number one."

"You're all aware why he's called the Pigfucker, right?" Earl steepled his fingers.

"It's from the old Republican political campaigns," explained P.F., glad of the chance to hold forth. "You call your opponent a Pigfucker and then sit back and wait for him to deny it. Same thing that we do at the station house. Throw the perp in the cell and ask him when he started beating his wife. Presumption of guilt. It's the corner-stone of our legal system."

Earl sniffed. "Too bad old P.F. here ain't done a lick of work in about twelve years. He's been relying on uni-formed officers to find his witnesses and boost his clear-ance rate since I came in the department."

P.F. saluted him dismissively. Sour-graping from the small people. Typical. Soon all of this would be behind him anyway. He'd have his own office at the Doubloon with a long-legged secretary and a view of the ocean. He'd walk the casino floor, shaking hands with the high rollers and granting favors to the cocktail waitresses.

"Say, P.F., what was the name of that case?" Earl taunted him.

"Which one?"

"You know. The one you couldn't clear from 'bout twenty years ago. Paulie Raymond was the detective on it."

"I don't know what you're talking about."

"Bullshit you don't. You kept that file on your desk until about five years ago. It was that Irish guy that was mixed up with Teddy and the Mafia. Mike something."

"Michael Dillon," P.F. said quietly.

He stared down at his drink as if calculating the different kinds of sorrow it could cause.

"That's it!" Earl snapped his fingers and turned back to his tablemates. "Good-lookin' hustler, they probably buried him out in the Pinelands somewhere. P.F. used to get all misty-eyed because he left a little kid behind and his widow was too crazy to look after him. He even kept the kid's picture in his drawer."

"Hey, Earl." P.F. looked up. "Smoke my joint, all right?"

Earl raised his right hand up to his mouth like a poker sharp figuring how to play a bank-breaking hand. "You know what they say, right? They say you and Paulie couldn't clear that case because you-all were on Teddy's payroll."

"Bullshit, all bullshit," P.F. muttered, finishing his drink and signaling for the bartender to bring him another. "What do you know about Teddy anyway?"

"I know all about Ted," Earl said expansively, putting his hands on top of the table. "I grew up in the Virginia Avenue Court projects and when they started dealing reefer and heroin in the courtyard, we all knew it came from Ted. But what blew my mind was coming out of there and finding some of my brother police officers were on his payroll too."

P.F. gave them his back and tried to think of something to say, but the words wouldn't come. Instead he was left staring at the mirror behind the bar. His face looked somehow strange but familiar. The tired eyes, the down-turned mouth, the crooked nose bending away like it was ashamed to be seen with the other features. No question about it, he was starting to look like his father. In fact, it couldn't have been more than twenty-seven years ago, he'd walked into a bar like this one and found his father drinking the same brand of scotch, with a hooker named Sally Jessy Mayfield on his lap, while he was supposed to be on duty. Captain Andy, who used to be his hero. It turned out he'd been drinking, whoring, taking protection money from the old man who ran the rackets from Philadelphia.

P.F. stopped talking to his father after that day he'd found him in the bar. But in the time he'd been on the job since then, what did he have to show that he was any better? At least his father had the whore on his lap. All P.F. had was three divorces, a son and a daughter who wouldn't speak to him, a largely undistinguished service record, and the Mike Dillon file stuck away somewhere in his dusty locker.

"Some cases weren't meant to be solved," he said so softly that no one else could hear him.

"What'd you say, P.F.?" Earl sat forward, with his elbows on his knees. The two other cops were grinning.

"I said no one gives a shit about that anymore," P.F. said, propping himself up. "It's past. Prologue. History. I don't need to muck around in it anymore. I've got this job with the Doubloon."

A slow easy smile rolled across Earl's face. "Well if that's true about you and the security job, how come I heard the chief assigned Ray Youngblood to work the security detail at the fight next fall?"

P.F. flinched like he'd been slapped across the face. "What are you talking about?" he said. "I have final say about who gets on that detail. I worked it out with Bobby. It was part of the transition for when I retired. They wouldn't just give all that overtime to a black guy like Ray without asking."

He saw a muscle tense in Earl's cheek and knew he'd

said too much. "Promises were made," he protested. "The deal was set."

"Then the deal is off," Earl noted with grim satisfaction. "Part of the new order coming down. Community policing, minority recruitment. It ain't enough just to be Irish anymore. Your time is over. It used to be you folks ran the department, made your little arrangements, and had your pick of the litter. But now it's someone else's turn."

"And I'm telling you that is fucking ridiculous!" P.F. staggered to his feet and pointed a finger at Earl. "It's absurd. My word still means something in this town."

"Have it your way," said Earl, raising his drink cheerily. "I just can't help noticing you got a fifty-dollar bill on that bar counter and in the old days, all your drinks would have been on the house."

P.F. glanced back at the bar and the crumpled-up fifty-spot seemed to cast an unnatural glow on the counter. Maybe his influence was declining. The shame and embarrassment burned in the pit of his stomach and sent a fog up to his brain. He suddenly had an urge to get out of there and pass out in peace. He started to leave.

"Hey, P.F." Earl caught him by the arm. "Next time you're coming by, let me know. I'll buy you a round."

7

Over the next few days, I began to see new vistas and opportunities opening up before me. Soon I'd be negotiating major endorsement deals and worldwide satellite hookups with men twice my age at mahogany conference tables.

One of the great things about boxing is that it's easier

to get a manager's license than it is to get hired by a casino. There's not as much checking into your background. For once my family connections wouldn't hold me back.

I even managed to forget about Larry lying there with the ice pick in his side. Or at least I did until I had to go to Teddy's sixtieth birthday party on Wednesday night. I showed up at the restaurant called Andolini's, just off Arctic Avenue, at about quarter past eight.

A dozen of the guys from the crew were in the back room talking over their latest scam. What they had on the table I can only describe as a pigsty. Pieces of salami hanging off plates. Slices of provolone and cigarette butts in the ashtrays. Lumps of red peppers on the checkered tablecloth. And presiding over it all, Teddy, the king hog in his cheap Sears suit.

I sat next to my father, two seats down from Teddy. My old man was busy explaining some new idea to all of them.

"This guy Murray Weisbrod works at the savings and loan up the parkway," he said. "He got in deep with Danny Klein. Owes him about three K. Now he's working for us. He'll vouch for any of our people. So all we gotta do is send a guy over to the casino, have him play awhile and then ask for a nine-thousand-dollar marker. They check our guy out with Murray, he'll say the player is okay, and the casino will give our guy nine thousand in credit to buy chips. So then our guy cashes his chips and splits the money with the rest of us."

"And who we gonna get as a player?" asked Teddy, spitting out two olive pits and laying them alongside the provolone in the ashtray.

"I was thinking about my boy Anthony here," said my father, putting a dry hairy hand on the back of my neck. "He hasn't been in to play that much. I can't think of a single reason they wouldn't want to lend him the money. It's not like he has a record already or anything."

His breath smelled from scampi and wine. The waitress brought in a few more platters covered with veal chops in mustard sauce, osso buco, garlic bread, anchovies, eggplant parmigiana, and strips of marinated steak.

"How do you eat that shit?" I said as she set the plates down.

"What're you talking? 'How do I eat it?' " Teddy sucked his teeth and hooked his arm protectively around his plate. "It's food. What's the matter with you?"

"It's not food, it's a hospital bed." I started picking the red candle wax off the Chianti bottle in the middle of the table. "My arteries are clogged just looking at it."

"So order something you want. It's a free country."

"You got any plain fish?" I asked the waitress, a pale chunky girl with dark curly hair. She shook her head.

"What'd I do, Teddy?" said my father, wringing my neck and pinching my cheek. "I raised a fuckin' yuppie."

"I'm just trying to watch my cholesterol," I said as the rest of them laughed along with him.

It didn't matter, though. All those guys were slobs anyway. Faces as rough and scaly as tortoiseshells. They all wore polyester polo shirts with horizontal stripes and ropes of gold chains around their necks. Not a suit among them, besides Teddy's. A bunch of no-account jerk-offs who couldn't tell a quartz watch from one with a Swiss movement or understand why Jerry Vale wasn't as good a singer as Frank Sinatra.

I noticed Richie Amato trying to stuff a three-inch-high hero into his mouth at the other end of the table. He was sitting next to a guy called Tommy Sick, who was always smiling and saying things like "That's sick" or "I'm sick!"

"The youth," said Teddy, running three sausage-like

fingers through his oily dyed-black hair. "They're always going around like they got some kind of stopwatch jammed up their ass. They don't know how to stop and enjoy the finer things."

Truthfully, Teddy's life was about as interesting as scrap metal. Sitting around all day sipping espresso with Vin at a social club with torn-up green vinyl chairs and Italian flags on the wall. Maybe once a week, they'd hear about a hijacked truck full of toothpaste and drive for an hour to get someplace where the other guys wouldn't show up. And by then it'd be dark and time to think about dinner.

"I got my own schedule, Ted," I said diplomatically.

"I'm telling you you oughta learn to go with the flow." Teddy speared a piece of prosciutto off my father's plate. "Listen to your old man when he has a good idea. I seen you rolling your eyes just now when he was talking about you getting a marker off the casino."

"Yeah, that's all right, but I've got my days planned out already."

I wasn't going to mention anything about my talk with John B. I already had Teddy hanging over my shoulder looking to grab half of whatever I made.

"Look at it," said my father, reaching into my pocket. "He's got a little black book he carries around with him."

I pushed his hand away from my Filofax as the rest of them started to crack up again. As the laughter started to die out after a couple of seconds, I heard a round of sniffling from the other end of the table. Maybe some of these guys still had their cocaine habits after all.

"Listen," I said, fixing my cuffs and smoothing back my hair. "If I got a clean record, why would I wanna blow it for a nine-thousand-dollar marker?"

"The high roller," said my father, grabbing my arm and punching it playfully.

I ignored him and went back to scratching the wax off the Chianti bottle. "All I'm saying is I don't need the pressure. I got better things to do with my life."

Teddy stopped chewing and just looked at me. It suddenly got very quiet. I could hear the busboy stacking dishes in the kitchen.

"What's that supposed to mean?" Teddy touched a spot just below his stomach.

No one was talking. Even the mural of Caesar on the wall looked tense.

"Nothing," I said.

These were guys who'd just as soon blow the back of your head off as change a television channel. And since I'd seen what happened to Larry, I had a good idea of what that might feel like.

"No, go ahead," Teddy said in a cold voice. "You were saying you're better than us."

"No, I wasn't saying I was better, Ted. I was just saying I got other plans."

Teddy sucked his teeth again and tugged his earlobe, the way Humphrey Bogart would. In his mind he was a dead ringer for Bogey, even though he weighed three hundred pounds.

"I give you all this money and get you started in your own business, and you're making 'other plans'?" he said.

I saw my father almost doubling over in his chair from discomfort. When he'd originally loaned me the money to go to college and start my own business, I had no idea how it would change my life. Now I had no way to pay it back. I'd tried everything. A couple of years before, I'd had a legit job managing some buildings on Atlantic Avenue. So Teddy muscled in on them, went partners with the owners, and burned them down for the insurance money. A few months later, I was running boat tours around the island Atlantic City is set on. What happened?

Teddy got interested and all the boats sank. The same thing would happen with Elijah and the boxing match if I wasn't careful.

"I'll get it all back to you with interest," I told Teddy. "Just be patient."

"And what am I supposed to do in the meantime?" His eyes tightened. "Watch my favorite niece and her children starve because you can't provide for them?"

"Hey, Teddy, I'm doing my best. I just haven't gotten the right break yet."

It was like trying to put out a fire with gasoline.

"The right break?!" His lip curled. "My own son, rest his soul, should've got the same breaks as you."

His son Charlie hanged himself when we were in school together. He'd been a friend of mine. Skinny intense kid, who always listened to the rock group Kiss. Instead of saying "hello," he'd say, "Love Gun!" I used to smoke pot with him under the Boardwalk. He couldn't stand being part of his father's life either. Every day he'd get teased by other kids at school: "Okay, Mr. Mafia's son, let's see how tough you really are." And every day they'd kick the shit out of him. He didn't have someone like Vin to protect him around the schoolyard. So he'd run home and have Ted ride him for being a weakling. As long as Charlie lived, his father's enemies would be his enemies. He killed himself at the beginning of eleventh grade.

I took his suicide as an object lesson of what would happen to me if I didn't get out one day. And judging from the look Teddy was giving me, I should've already been buried on the mainland.

"Charlie had problems," I said, maybe a little too off-handedly. "He was, you know, like clinically depressed."

Teddy looked at me like I'd just tried to bite his nose off. "Clin-ically de-pressed? What's that supposed to mean?"

"I'm just saying he had problems. He hanged himself."

Teddy began stroking that spot below his stomach faster. "So what're you saying, it's my fault he's dead?"

"No, Ted, I'm just saying he was depressed. You know, he was always talking about 'Love Gun.' "

I heard Richie trying to say the word "clinical" in the background while Tommy Sick giggled and muttered, "That's sick."

"You little motherfucker, I'll give you something to be depressed about." Teddy stood up abruptly and reached into his pants.

You would've thought we were in the middle of a rodeo with the way all the other guys jumped up, trying to calm him down: "Whooa Ted! Down Ted! Chill Teddy!"

But Teddy was like the bull about to charge. "This little prick's saying it's my fault Charlie's dead!"

He pushed them all away, snorting hard through his nose and staring me down with those beady red eyes. This was the way things started with them. You'd say you didn't like the color of their car and wind up locked in the trunk.

My father reached up and put a hand on Teddy's shoulder. "Hey, Ted, take it easy. Anthony didn't mean nothing."

But then Ted turned that same dead-eyed glare on my father. "You just watch it, Vin. You could die too."

I started thinking maybe I'd try talking Vin into retiring to Florida if I managed to get out of this place alive.

"Hey, Ted," my father repeated. "Sit down. We're not done eating."

"...trying to blame me for putting a rope around my boy's neck," mumbled Teddy, his lips turning white.

"Teddy?" My father cleared his throat. "Why don't you just back off a little? Ha? Anthony did right by you the other night, didn't he?"

Teddy grunted.

Casino Moon   67

"So maybe you oughta cut him a break. Right?"

I didn't know what he meant at the time, but it stopped Teddy in his tracks. He dropped the fork and slowly sat down. The other guys at the table lowered their eyes and exhaled in relief.

"Remember," said my father, still keeping a hand on Ted's shoulder. "Anthony's had a lot of frustrations too. Like we talked about the other night. Maybe he thinks he's owed something."

I still didn't know what he was talking about, but Teddy's mood was cooling by the minute. He took an enormous slab of meat off my father's plate, and comforted himself by chewing on it. As his face began to soften, I knew I'd probably live through dessert.

"Yeah, I guess," said Teddy grudgingly.

"You wanna tell him something about that?" said my father, holding Teddy's gaze the way a lover would. "What we talked about?"

Teddy wiped his mouth and looked over at me. "Thank you, Anthony," he said, like a little kid who'd just been scolded for his bad manners.

I was going to ask for what, but my father cut me off.

"What about the other thing?" he prodded Teddy. "The thing you were going to see about."

Teddy just looked at him, not prepared to give any more ground. "I can't do it, Vin. I'm sorry."

I realized there was a whole level of the conversation I was missing. Some of the old-timers at the other end of the table were getting it, though. They were whispering to each other and pointing at me.

"Look, Anthony," said Teddy, his mood shifting for about the third time in five minutes. "I know you been under a lot of pressure. We all been under a lot of pressure. I hear from your father that things haven't been going exactly the way you might've planned with getting made and all. But I just want you to understand we appreciate everything you already done for us."

I must have given him a blank look. I hadn't done anything for Teddy lately. But he coughed and went on.

"Larry and his son were becoming pains in the ass to all of us," he said. "Thanks for helping us send a message."

All of a sudden, everything was clear. When I saw my father folding and unfolding the napkin on his lap, I knew he'd told Teddy that I'd whacked Larry. And here was Teddy saying it out loud in front of a dozen potential witnesses. My mouth went dry.

I saw my father and Richie exchange a look down the length of the table and understood instantly they'd made a deal not to talk about what really happened.

"Now normally," Teddy said, smearing some butter on his garlic bread, "that would be enough to get you made. But tradition is tradition. If you ain't got the blood of Sicilians running through you, I can't make you."

My father's mouth twisted. "Hey, Teddy, we can bend the rules a little. Can't we? It's not etched in stone."

"I'm sorry, Vin," Teddy said. "I already considered it. I know it's hard and I know it's unfair. But somebody's gotta uphold the old ways."

That was maybe the biggest joke of all. Teddy upholding the old ways. The only reason he ever got to be a boss was because he happened to be living in exile in Atlantic City when the referendum on casino gambling passed. And by then, he'd been out of the Mafia mainstream for so long he actually had to call somebody up and ask them how to perform the induction ceremony.

"So again, Anthony, I must apologize," he said. "I can't change what's come before. It's tradition that makes us stronger. If we lose that, we lose everything."

Actually what made Teddy strong was being willing to

stab his friends in the back when they had something he wanted. My father passed a palm over his plate, signaling to me that he'd work things out later.

"It's all right, Teddy," I said. "I understand."

"So that's why you should do the right thing and listen to your father," he said, taking half my father's veal off his plate. "You may never get the button, but you can make a few dollars doing this casino thing he was talking about. Be smart is all I'm telling you. Take your breaks where they come. The rest is up to you."

"Yeah, I'll think about that, Teddy."

He reached over my father and pinched my cheek so hard I almost yelped. "You know what I figured out?" he asked in a fake-affectionate voice. "I figured we've been too lenient with you and it hasn't been doing you any favors. We been spoiling you. So maybe it'd be better if we put you on a schedule. Say if you don't pay me the full sixty you owe in six months, you come work for me full-time."

Which meant I'd have all the risks and none of the protection of a made guy. My butt cheeks slammed tight as a cell door. Made guys looked out for each other. But unmade guys, like I would be, had all the exposure. They wound up in prison or dead by the side of a service road with twenty-dollar bills stuffed in their ass. Not me. Now I had twice as much pressure to pull this boxing business off in six months.

I stood up and asked to be excused.

"Here's looking at you, kid," Teddy said, cramming the veal into one side of his mouth.

I bowed to the other guys at the table and asked my father if I could talk to him a minute out by where the cars were parked.

It was a cool night and all the stars were out. I could see Ursa Minor hanging over the red-brick housing project across the street. My car was parked by the curb right in front of the restaurant's door. In the old days you could just leave it there, because even in a bad neighborhood like this, people understood the meaning of respect. Especially for guys who ate at Andolini's. But now any little hood from the projects thought he could just slash your tires with impunity. So the owner had a guy sitting out front in a lawn chair, making sure nothing happened.

"So you told him I pushed a button on Larry," I said. "That's terrific. I'm just overflowing with gratitude."

"I didn't say nothing about it. I just told him you were man enough to do the right thing."

"Why'd you go and do that?"

"I wanted him to show you some respect. Or at least set it up so you could handle the envelope."

"And now I got six months to pay him off. Very nice."

Across the street, I could hear the sound of children's laughter echoing through the housing project. But all I saw were clotheslines full of sheets and shabby shirts strung up between the little red buildings. It was kind of eerie, like hearing the ghost of a good time.

I thought of the dead-eyed look I'd seen Teddy give my father inside.

"Hey, Dad," I said suddenly. "What happened to Mike?"

I don't know why I thought to ask about my real father right then. The question just popped out of me. Maybe because I'd been thinking lately about how my life could've been different if he'd stayed alive.

Vin looked like I'd just dropped a safe on his head. "Why the fuck you asking about that now? We been over it a million times."

And the answer I got from him was always the same. "I don't know." "He must've made a mistake." "It's better not to think about it." But I wondered. Especially after seeing that look on Teddy tonight. I wondered if somebody gave my real father a look like that before he disappeared.

"Why you gotta bring that up again?" asked Vin. "Ain't I been a good father to you?"

"Yeah, of course, but that's not the point…"

"Haven't I always provided for you? Given you everything you ever wanted?"

I could see he was hurt that I'd even thought to question that. He had been a good father, in spite of his obvious shortcomings. Vin wasn't cut out to be a family man. He was put on this earth to scam and squeeze, to muscle and murder. If he'd run a car dealership, he would've had me working out on the lot. But the mob was the only world he knew, and borrowing money from Teddy was the only way he could think of to help. So I cut him a lot of slack. Maybe too much, as it turned out.

Above the jagged rooflines across the street, I could see light green laser beams shooting out of one of the casinos on the Boardwalk and crisscrossing the sky like marionette strings.

"I don't know what happened to Mike," he sighed. "It could be he had a problem with the old man in Philly. Maybe one day you'll find out and tell me. He was my best friend in the world besides Teddy."

For the first time, it occurred to me that he might be lying to protect someone.

"Listen," he said, putting an arm around my shoulder. "I'm sorry if you were upset about what happened in there. Teddy and me, we've been getting all stressed lately."

"Yeah, well, you shouldn't have told him that I was the one who whacked Larry."

"I know, I know." He ran the comb through his wild hair again, but it had no effect. "I'm just trying to get you the button, that's all."

"But I don't want that," I said vehemently. "I want you to go back in there and straighten it out. Tell him what really happened."

"Yeah, yeah." But I could see he was thinking about something else. His hair was still standing up higher than usual.

"I'm serious," I said. "Don't help me with the button anymore. I'll help myself."

"One day you'll appreciate what I done for you," he told me wistfully.

"Yeah, right." I gave him a hug just to let him know everything was okay between us. "So next year on my birthday, don't get me anything, all right? The kind of presents you give, I'll end up doing eight-to-twenty-five in a state prison."

8

"When I first come out here, there was nothing," Teddy was saying the next day. "We had to build it up. The Boardwalk was so empty, you could've fired a cannonball and not hit anybody."

"Yeah, I heard that," said Jackie, the new mob boss visiting from New York.

"It was right after the Democratic Convention in '64," Teddy went on. "When all the press said Atlantic City was a shithole. 'The glory days are over.' You know. Because people weren't coming down to the shore anymore. But I tell you, it only really got bad after the stories in the media. Right? Correct me, Vin. Anytime anything goes wrong you'll either find a lawyer or a newsman behind it."

They were sitting in Teddy's backyard at the Florida Avenue house. A gentle breeze rustled the rose garden by the twelve-foot-high brick wall. Teddy and Vin were sitting on one side of a brown picnic table under a large white umbrella. Jackie "J.J." Pugnitore and his underboss

Sal Matera were on the other side. A platter full of cold
cuts sat between them. Jackie still had not touched any
food. He was forty-nine years old and wore a beige linen
suit with a bright red shirt and a black handkerchief in his
breast pocket. His nostrils were as wide and dark as his
eyes. He'd first made his name as a street fighter in the
Bronx, beating up blacks for being in the wrong neighborhood. He would've been disturbed to know that his
ancestors in Sicily were referred to as "those Africans" by
their neighbors on the Italian mainland.

His underboss Sal had slicked-back hair and a closed-
off face. His designer polo shirt was a size too small, to
emphasize the roundness of his pectorals and the broad-
ness of his shoulders.

"Eat something," Vin urged the guests.

"In a minute." Jackie touched his heart.

"Anyway that's what Vin and I inherited when we came
out here," Teddy continued, enjoying the sunny day and
the attention of his visitors. "A pile of shit. We had to lay
the foundations. Us and a guy named Mike Dillon."

Vin flinched a little when Teddy said the name.

"In fact," Teddy went on, "I got sent out here as punishment by the old man in Philadelphia. Vin and I beat up
a shine liquor salesman who wouldn't give up his parking
space on Rosemount Avenue."

"There was a Mercury behind it we wanted to steal,"
Vin explained, rolling up the sleeve of his blue-and-white
running suit so he wouldn't get oil stains on it.

"It wasn't our fault the guy dropped dead four days
later in the hospital." Teddy took two slices of salami off
the platter and put them in his mouth. "Poor Vin got
charged with manslaughter and did a five-year stretch in
Graterford for the both of us."

Teddy laid a heavy, appreciative hand on Vin's shoulder.
"He never once opened his mouth either," he said. "He

did his time like a man. Not like these rat kids, running around now. Can't wait to find a federal agent to snitch to."

Jackie seemed interested in something Teddy said before, though. "You were in Graterford, Vin?" he asked, one eyebrow arching up toward his perfectly coiffed gray-black hair.

"Five years." Vin took two slices of rye bread and made Teddy a sandwich.

"You know Billy Nose while you were in there?" Jackie asked.

They were all quiet. Billy Nose had been boss of the biggest crew in New York. Jackie had had him killed two months before in a power struggle.

"Yeah." Vin put mayo on the sandwich. "I think he was doing a stretch for driving somebody else's Rambler on the Turnpike with thirty G's in the back."

Jackie gave his underboss a sidelong glance and then turned back to Vin. "And how'd he do his time?"

"How'd he do his time?" Vin handed over the sandwich. "The worst I ever seen."

"Really?" Jackie seemed pleased.

"I'm telling you." Vin scratched his nuts. "He was always running to me whenever he had a problem. Always crying, always. He said, 'Vin, when I'm with you, I'm so comfortable, it's like I'm sucking on my own mother's tit.' "

Both of Jackie's eyebrows shot up. "He said that? Those were his words?" His mouth twisted in disgust.

"You show me someone who can prove he didn't, I'll let you fuck me in the ass," Vin said.

Everyone smiled. Teddy's wife, Camille, came out of the house with a tray full of glasses. She moved slowly, as though permanently stunned, and wore a dark pair of Ray-Ban shades. She put the tray down with trembling, bony hands and returned to the house without looking at any of the men.

"Thank you, Mrs. Marino," Jackie called after her.

Teddy poured each of the four of them a glass of Remy Martin and proposed a toast. "Here's lookin' at you, Jackie," he said. "No one deserved to be boss more."

They raised their glasses and clinked them together. Teddy and Vin downed about half their drinks. Jackie and Sal barely sipped theirs.

"Tell you the truth, I'm glad Billy Nose is dead." Vin turned sideways and looked out toward the rose garden.

"I heard he was an old scumbag," Teddy added, biting into his sandwich.

Jackie ran his fingers along his lapels and looked philosophical. "You know what the trouble was?" he said. "He was an old man. No offense, Teddy."

Teddy lifted and dropped his shoulders. No offense taken. He was only about eleven years older than Jackie himself.

"I mean, he thought like an old man," Jackie elaborated. His underboss Sal nodded. "He was afraid to make changes. He wouldn't move anybody up. He was jealous of the young guys like me."

Teddy wiped his hands on a paper napkin and looked over at Vin. "We were just saying, our old man in Philadelphia was the same way," he said. "All them old greaseballs are like that. They see a young guy like you, Jackie, and it reminds them they're gonna die one day."

"Right," said Jackie as Sal Matera leaned back and grabbed his own crotch. "Billy Nose just stopped making people. I'm serious. After Apalachin, he didn't induct one soldier. Not one. Until the eighties. You had a whole generation of guys backed up, because they couldn't go anywhere. It's frustrating, you know."

"Yeah," said Vin, seeing an opportunity and jumping in. "We got a young guy just like that ourselves. Very capable. My own boy, in fact. We're trying to move him up…"

Teddy cut him off with an angry glance.

Mrs. Marino came out of the house again with another tray full of glasses and a tall green bottle of Pellegrino water. She poured two glasses for Jackie and Sal and they smiled appreciatively. She returned to the house and could be seen weeping through the kitchen curtains.

"Ted," said Jackie, raising the water glass. "I just want you to know we went through proper channels before Billy got whacked. We talked to everyone on the Commission before it happened. I know you weren't able to make it down to the last meeting, but I just wanted you to know we did the right thing."

"Jackie, on my son's grave, it never entered my mind."

They all stopped talking a moment and looked out at the garden. Since Atlantic City was set on a barrier island, it was difficult to plant anything more than a rose garden out here. Another salt breeze riffled the plain short blades of grass. Smoke from a barbecue rose from the other side of the brick wall. Teddy sniffed, looked down at his glass of Remy Martin, and finished the rest of it.

Jackie watched him carefully. "I wasn't sure if anybody mentioned it to you, Ted, but there was something else on the agenda the last time the Commission met."

"What's that?"

"We were talking about some of the unions down here and it was decided that Ralphie Sasso over at the hotel workers' should now belong to us."

Jackie sat back with a hand on each of his lapels, waiting to be challenged.

"What're you talking about?" Teddy's face began to

burn. "That's been our union for twenty years. You can't just come in and claim it!"

Jackie folded his arms across his chest and Sal Matera sat up a little straighter.

"I'm sorry, Ted, but that's the way the Commission wanted it," Jackie explained.

Teddy's mouth was hanging open. Vin was tearing furiously at his shock of gray hair.

"Look, Ted," said Jackie, crossing his legs. "We're all getting squeezed now with these federal cases and the economy the way it is. We're gonna have to learn to share."

Vin shook his head. "I just saw Ralphie the other day. He didn't say a thing to me."

Teddy was furious. "This is unbelievable, Jackie. You think you can come in here and put my balls in your pocket?"

"Hey," Jackie interrupted him. "It wouldn't hurt so bad if you hadn't given up the narcotics to the niggers or if you'd gotten a little further with the casinos."

"What're you saying?"

"I'm saying," Jackie raised his voice, "that everyone knows you've never placed an executive at one of these places."

"You try doing it with all these cameras and state troopers around," Teddy protested. "It's off-limits. You can't get in there. It can't be done. They got regulations up the ying-yang. No one's ever had an *amica nostra* on the payroll."

"And for twenty years, you've been feeding off the crumbs from the unions." Jackie put a hand flat on the picnic table and stared him down. "And now it's time for you to share it with the rest of us."

Teddy started to stand up. "This is bullshit, Jackie!" he

shouted. "It's absolutely indecent. You're trying to cut my fucking balls off!"

Jackie looked over at Sal, who reached down toward his sock as though he had a gun holstered there.

Vin put his arm across Teddy's wide chest, trying to calm him down.

"Listen, Ted," said Jackie, standing up and buttoning his jacket. "You got a problem with this, take it up with the Commission. Otherwise, that's the way it's gonna be. It's decided."

Teddy sat down, still sputtering angrily, but afraid to do anything about it. Vin put an arm around his shoulders. Jackie checked his Rolex and then signaled for Sal to stand up and leave with him.

"It's not right, Jackie, not right." Teddy wouldn't look at him. He stared down at the picnic table as his stubby fingers grappled with each other on his lap. "You come down here, eat our food, and then you stab us in the back."

"Hey," said Jackie, pointing to the platter, which was still piled high with cold cuts. "We hardly ate anything."

The two guests left abruptly, without saying goodbye. Teddy sat quietly stroking his middle for a few minutes while Vin tried to comfort him. More smoke came from the barbecue on the other side of the brick wall. Mrs. Marino peered out once from behind the kitchen curtains and went back to crying about her dead son.

Teddy stuck a finger into the platter of cold cuts and poked at them awhile.

"All this food I just bought," he said to Vin. "It's all gonna turn to shit."

9

It was time to start raising money if I was going to get serious about the fight game. Fifty thousand dollars was what John B. said we needed. But I couldn't have Teddy know I was going after that kind of money, or he'd want it all for himself.

That night I had to drop by Rafferty's, to look at invoices. And since the place was usually crawling with wiseguys and union officials, I figured it might be a good time to renew old contacts and see about getting a little work for my contracting business.

I spotted Paulie Raymond, a guy who I knew had union connections, sitting with his brother Albert the hunchback at a round table. I went over to join them.

They looked like they were having the time of their lives. It was the first night we had Foxy Boxing and Hot Oil Wrestling at the club. Since topless dancing wasn't allowed at bars in Atlantic City, Teddy decided to have the girls fight instead. Paulie had a ringside seat. He was all red, like a lobster, and every time you saw him he was wearing another piece of jewelry. This night, he had on a gold bracelet with his name spelled out in diamonds. Even though he was over sixty, the skin was tight around his jaw and lizardlike down his neck, as if he'd just had plastic surgery. It didn't matter though; he still looked like an old fag you'd see hanging around the bus station late at night. It was hard to believe he'd been a detective with the Atlantic City Police Department for more than thirty years.

But Paulie was one of those cops who act more like

wiseguys than wiseguys. The badge was just a license to steal. He was into everything: money laundering, ripping off drug dealers, securities frauds, insurance swindles. And on the side, he'd also gotten himself into a position where he was a go-between for Teddy's crew and one of the local construction unions, where his uncles and cousins were all members. You had to treat him with respect because he had access to half the major building contracts in town.

"You're lookin' good, Paulie."

"Yeah?" he said, watching the girls fight in the makeshift ring we'd set up.

A greased blonde in a string bikini was throwing a body block on this busty redhead in a green one-piece bathing suit.

"I told that fuckin' doctor to do something about my hands," Paulie said.

"He's got hands like an old woman," said his brother Albert the hunchback. Albert was a quiet guy who liked to listen to classical music and go out with seventeen-year-old girls.

Paulie held up his hands. The knuckles were raw and the backs were well-mapped with blue and green veins.

He was wearing a fresh coat of clear nail polish and I thought of my mother lying there in the casket with her hands folded, after the last pill overdose. The memory made me gag and I had to stop myself from throwing up right there at ringside with the girls tossing each other around.

"It's amazing what they can do with hands now," Albert was saying. "They can give you another guy's prints even. I swear, they had that when I was young, I wouldn't have never had no record."

"Larry felt bad about his hands too," Paulie said, putting down his champagne glass.

"Who's this?" I waved for the waitress to bring me a ginger ale.

"Larry DiGregorio, he had a carting business over in Brigantine," said Paulie, looking right at me. "He was always looking at his hands and saying 'How come I never hauled a piece of garbage in my life and I always look like I got dirt under my fingernails?' "

He shrugged and turned all the way back toward the girls in the ring. The redhead was biting the blonde's arm now, even as the blonde had her in a headlock. Their bodies shined and rubbed together. I wondered if Paulie was watching them so intently just to prove he wasn't a fag.

The waitress brought over my ginger ale. I thanked her and gave her a five-dollar tip.

"You know they found Larry in a Dumpster the other night," said Paulie, without turning back to the table.

"Is that right?" I kept a poker face even as I stared at the spot by the bar where Vin stabbed him.

"Yeah. His son Nicky's all hot about it. Says he's gonna cut the heart out of the guy that did it."

I just rubbed my fingers together and didn't say anything.

In the ring, both girls were down on the canvas, wrestling. If you weren't watching carefully, you'd think they were fooling around like kids in a sandbox. But as close as I was, I could see they were really grimacing and grabbing each other by the hair.

The blonde sank her teeth into the other girl's arm. She was familiar, I decided. Thin nose and eyes just a bit too far apart. She looked a little like Shelly Francis, the girl I went with just before I met my wife. I started rooting for her for old time's sake.

Paulie stuck his fat red claw with the gold rings into the popcorn bowl on the table. "So what's your business with me?" he said. "I know you didn't come over to inquire about my health plan."

I acted insulted that he wanted to get to the point so quickly. "I was just interested. I heard Teddy wasn't happy about Lenny Romano getting that job fixing the parking lot over at City Hall."

He stuffed the popcorn into his mouth and just stared at me as he crunched it. I wasn't sure if he knew what had happened with that contract. Normally the way it worked was that Teddy would have Paulie or one of his other contacts at the union threaten to throw a strike if one of Teddy's phony construction firms didn't get hired by a builder.

But in this case, that didn't happen. I'd tried to get the contract legitimately. I went before the City Council with estimates for price, labor, and material, showing I could bring the job in for under three million dollars. But instead they awarded the contract to cross-eyed old Lenny Romano, whose lawyer Burt Ryan was also representing half the council members in their corruption trials. So I got screwed for playing it straight. If I'd gone through Teddy, he could've exerted pressure and gotten me the job. But I didn't want to be any further in his debt, so I'd never asked him to get involved. I was gambling Paulie wouldn't know that, though, so I could bully him into helping me get another job.

"So how 'bout it?" I said.

But Paulie saw through me immediately. He started huffing and puffing, like a bellows blowing into a fireplace. "Teddy didn't have nothing to do with the City Hall parking lot. That was Burt Ryan's contract."

"That's what I'm saying." I stirred my drink. "It's one of the first construction sites to open up in about a year and it doesn't go to one of Teddy's people. That's why he's upset about it."

Paulie looked down his remodeled nose at me. "Well if Teddy's got a problem, why doesn't he come talk to me himself?"

I guess maybe he'd retained a few cop instincts. But I was still determined to try to bluff him out. I figured that if I acted like I had Teddy's support, Paulie might go back to his people at the union and find me some work.

"Teddy doesn't need to talk to you himself," I said. "He knows he can rely on me. I'm married to his niece."

"Oh, that's bullshit!" said Paulie, spraying me with spit on the *b* sound. "What're you trying to do, start trouble or something?"

"No." I met his eyes. "I'm just saying what Teddy wants."

Teddy had been dominating my whole life. I thought I should get something out of the association.

In the ring, the redhead threw the blonde against the ropes and got ready to kick her in her midsection. Paulie watched them a minute and then gave me his full attention.

"Let me tell you something, Anthony. Teddy ain't such a big man anymore. In fact, as far as this union's concerned, he's out and Burt Ryan's in. It's a lawyer's game now. So I wouldn't go throwing around Teddy's name like it meant something."

"I'm not throwing his name around." I frowned. "You know, you shouldn't be so disrespectful, Paulie. My family goes back a long ways with you."

"Listen, you little fuck," he shot back. "I know all about you. I know how you got this act where you come on like you're Mr. Nice Guy trying to make a buck and then you turn around and screw your partners into the ground."

"I don't know what the hell you're talking about."

"Oh yeah?" He gripped his champagne glass like he was about to crack it. "What about them cigarettes?"

"What cigarettes? I don't smoke cigarettes."

"This fuckin' guy." Paulie leaned back to include his

brother in our conversation. "He gets three thousand dollars off our cousin Bimmy and says he's got a line on a truck full of untaxed cigarettes off an Indian reservation. Then he takes the money and leaves Bimmy waiting for the cigarettes."

He was talking about a scheme Teddy and my father got me involved in years ago, back when I was in high school. They had me go to an albino grocery store owner named Bimmy and tell him I could get him the cigarettes for forty cents a pack. Then they took his money and gave him nothing in return for it. And now I was getting the blame.

"Look, Paulie," I said. "That was a long time ago. I don't do that type of thing anymore. And besides, I didn't even know that guy was related to you."

"You're another fuckin' con artist just like your old man," said Paulie. I could smell the champagne excretions on his breath. "You're both grown out of the same dirt even if you don't smell the same. You'd fuck your grandmother if you could get a contract out of it. The only difference is you don't have enough balls to squeeze a trigger when you have to."

In the ring, I saw the blonde pick herself up off the canvas and give the redhead a stiff elbow to the jaw. I knew that if she was in my position, she wouldn't take this type of abuse from Paulie.

All of a sudden I got a very cold feeling inside. "What do you know about my father?" I asked Paulie.

He opened his mouth, but no words came out.

"Hey." I stuck a finger in his face and kept it there awhile. "Don't you ever talk about my father."

It was one of those moments when I was so mad that all the sound in the room cut off and all I could hear was the pounding in my head.

Whatever look I was giving, it sobered Paulie up. He
turned pale and started fooling with his bracelet.

"You shouldn't talk about things you don't know about,"
I said.

The blond girl in the ring was getting kicked in the
stomach again, but it didn't slow her down. It just made
her mad. There was something special about her, I decided. She wasn't beautiful exactly. She had a little meat on
her hips and some kind of weird scar down by her navel.
When she tossed her hair, you could see the roots were
dark. But you couldn't take your eyes off her. It was the
way she moved. She put her whole body into everything
she did. When her hip went by you, it was like a force of
nature passing through. In a funny way, she reminded me
of Vin and Elijah. She was the kind of person who never
quit. And in a flash, it came to me that I should've married someone like her instead of my wife.

Paulie moved his chair back and tried to give me a
smile like we were really still friends after all.

In the meantime, the bell was sounding that the fight
was over. The referee was holding up the redhead's arm.
The blond girl was looking over at them with a mixture of
disgust and determination. Like she'd known the fight
was rigged all along, but she'd given it her best anyway.
She was someone just like me. Who'd been put down all
her life and had to struggle just to stay on par.

Seeing her fight had inspired me to stand up to Paulie,
who was hunkered down at the table like some mean old
toad protecting his stool. I knew he wasn't going to help
me get any contracts, but I wasn't ready to take any more
shit from him either.

"Just watch yourself, Paulie," I said, standing up and
giving him a pretty good knock on the shoulder. "Your
cousin got what he deserved. No one gets taken who

wasn't greedy in the first place. If he's got a problem he should talk to me himself. Otherwise I don't wanna hear it. I've got no respect for people who can't take care of themselves."

10

Her stomach still hurt where that other girl had been kicking her all night long.

As she looked in the dressing room mirror, she saw parts of her face were bruised too. That bitch. Who told her to throw anybody around like that for sixty dollars a night? You made more getting your ass pinched serving drinks at the casino. At least there the black-and-blue marks didn't show.

There were two knocks on the dressing room door. "The sign says do not disturb," she called out. "The bathroom is downstairs."

She wriggled out of her bathing suit and put two sticks of gum in her mouth. Pain shot through her jaw as soon as she started chewing and she had to spit it out right away. The whole time she was married she never caught a beating like this. But then that was all mental torture, after he closed up inside. Long stony silences over dinner and mornings shooting up in the bathroom. She still remembered waiting for him in bed and staring out the window at a gray sky where the seagulls looked like eraser marks.

It was awful to abuse yourself like that. Not that she'd mind a drink herself, her jaw aching like it was. But everyone was on her to watch her weight these days. It was bad enough she had the cesarean scar showing when she wore a bikini. She told the shift manager, just let me wear the one-piece. But he said, no, fuck it, wear the bikini, the customers are too drunk to notice the scar. But watch the cellulite, he told her. A customer wants to see cottage cheese thighs, he can go home and look in the mirror. Maybe she could get herself one of those Richard Simmons exercise videos and a can of Ultra Slim-Fast.

What did they all want from her anyway? She was the only girl over thirty on her shift and as far as she knew the only one with a kid. So for all that, she didn't look too bad, did she?

There was the knock at the door again. A little more urgent this time. Probably some drunk trying to use the bathroom.

"Sir, are you hard of hearing?" she called out. "The john is downstairs."

She pulled on her blouse and jeans and began brushing her hair up while looking in the mirror. She was starting to hate these little in-between moments. They gave her too much time to think about how things were going.

On good nights, a secret dream of moving out west and finding a new career kept her alive. On bad nights, she'd pretend her life was happening to someone else.

Tonight, she wished she'd brought her Walkman. That way she could listen to her own music and block out everything else: the crap they were playing on the speakers outside, the things men would say in the parking lot. Who needed the aggravation? Sometimes she wished she had a Walkman on all the time. That way she could take care of Kimmy, her mother and the two jobs without any distractions.

She finished teasing her hair, put on her sneakers, and went out to the bar, looking for some ice to put on her cheekbone before it started to swell up.

The place was almost empty now. A blue etherish light reflected off the smoked mirrors and an old Hall and

Oates song played over the loudspeakers. The drunk who'd been pounding on her door was stumbling out into the parking lot, probably looking for a good Hyundai to piss on.

The guy totaling up receipts behind the bar was the cute one she'd noticed before. With the dark brown eyes and the longish hair he could've pulled back into a ponytail. Anthony, she'd heard someone call him.

"How about some ice, Anthony?" she said, hearing her mother's arch, almost formal sound in her voice. "I'm turning into a cyclops."

"Yeah, you might want to put a slab of meat on that." He smiled and gave her a glass full of cubes. "Or how about a drink? You look like you had a rough night up there."

"Don't tempt me. I've got to get up with my kid in the morning."

He tapped a couple more buttons on the register and put down his receipts. "You got a kid?"

"Yes. Is there something wrong with that?"

"I don't know." He shrugged and she decided he must be eight years younger than her. Probably the nephew of one of the goons who ran this place. "It's just surprising, that's all. You don't expect somebody who does what you do to have kids."

"Well I could say the same about you," she said with a crooked smile. "I thought everybody who worked behind the counter here had something to do with the mob. But you don't look like any gangster to me."

He winced, just a bit.

"So what are you anyway? The hired help or part of the Corleone family?" She glanced back at the booth where Teddy usually sat.

"Just trying to pay some bills."

"I hear that."

She took out her wallet and showed him a picture of Kimmy smiling that guileless toothless four-year-old smile that made her feel teary-eyed and fiercely protective at the same time.

"She's beautiful," he said. "I've got two of my own. I'd kill for them."

"All I have to do is wrestle other women." She crossed her legs and showed him the bruise down by her ankle. "Every time I get one of these, I tell myself I'm paying for braces."

"You sound like someone else I know." He leaned over the bar to look down, seeming to take in the smell of her. "Another fighter."

She decided he was sweet, even if he was the nephew of a Mafioso. Too bad about the wedding ring he was wearing, though.

"That's the life of the single parent," she said, letting her hair fall back. "Everything's do or die. Half my pay-check goes for insurance. They ought to have a Purple Heart for mothers."

"So maybe I can help you out one of these days."

"And how are you going to do that?" She lit a Merit, en-joying the attention without taking it too seriously.

A gruff-looking older man with unruly gray hair was watching them from the other end of the bar.

"Well, you know." Anthony glanced at him once and looked back at her. "Something could come up," he said in a quiet voice you'd use to tell your best friend your deepest secret.

"Like what?"

He looked from side to side again and then peeked under the counter, like he was expecting to find a surveil-lance mike among the dirty glasses. "Remember Elijah Barton, the old middleweight champion?"

"Yeah, maybe." Was this a boxer he was talking about?

"Well I could be getting a chance to co-manage him in a title fight this fall. At one of the casinos."

"Oh. Huh."

"Maybe I could get you a little work on the side, you know. Something a little more kinda dignified."

He suddenly stopped talking, as if he was worried about offending her. She decided she really did have a little crush on him. Even if he was full of those silly dreams people talked about after-hours. She'd once dated a bartender who thought he was going to be the next Engelbert Humperdinck. He ended up stacking records in a jukebox.

"So why are you so anxious to help me out?" she said, humoring him. "You don't even know my name."

"It's Rosemary. Right?"

"Rosemary Giordano." She gave him her hand. The warmth from his palm went right up her arm and into her heart.

"Well, Rosemary," he said, letting go of her hand and sitting back on a stool behind the bar. "You seem like the kind of person who's had a couple of bad breaks in life."

"Whatever. I guess so." She checked her watch. Half past twelve. Her mother would be asleep by now. Too late to pick up the kid. Rosemary would have to sleep over there herself, with the noisy old fan in the window and the neighbors arguing next door.

"I've had a couple of bad breaks too," Anthony was saying. "So I figure us bad-break people ought to stick together."

"It's a deal." She stood up, making sure her handbag was closed. "As soon as you get your fight together, I'll be there to sing the national anthem with bells on."

"Now you're laughing, but you'll see. This is going to work out with the fight. I'm going to end up helping you."

"And what did I do to deserve such luck?"

"I don't know," he said, suddenly turning serious. "There

was something about the way you fought tonight. With so much heart."

She looked hard at him again to see if he was kidding, but couldn't catch a glimmer of a smile.

It was time to go. The song on the sound system had changed to a hit from a few years back. "Every time you go away, you take a piece of me with you," it went. She didn't want it to mean anything, but it made her think of the good times when she was married, before the eraser-mark skies and the syringes in the sink.

"The way you fought," Anthony repeated. He touched his chest with his fist as if to say he was out of words. "I'll never forget it."

II

"Camille, get me another piece of that carrot cake, will you?"

Teddy sat at the kitchen table with a forest green composition book balanced on his lap. His wife brought him some more dessert and tiptoed away like a terrorist leaving a car bomb.

"Next time bring me a slice with more icing on it."

He ate half the piece in less than a minute and then turned to the page marked "Income." He picked up a pen and began to write in a slow, childlike scrawl. L.S. (for loan-sharking)—$1257 for the week. Policy—$941. More than $1250 from Ralphie Sasso at the hotel workers' union, but with Jackie from New York claiming Ralphie was his now, there wouldn't be any more where that came from.

Teddy turned and looked at the telephone on the wall. "Come on, ring, you motherfucker, ring already."

It was after twelve and the people from the Commission still hadn't called back. He couldn't believe they'd just taken away half his power without asking him. Snatching Ralphie and the union from him. He felt like he was walking around with his arms cut off.

"They wanna play games, we'll play games," he muttered in a grinding, vindictive voice. "This will not stand."

"Is this about those gentlemen who came from New York this afternoon?" his wife asked.

"Yeah, Camille. They're real gentlemen. You're a real shrewd judge of character."

"That was lovely hair the younger one had."

Teddy just glared at her.

He had a momentary urge to take a leak, but decided to let it pass. He was getting up three, four times a night lately, but the stream was just a trickle. He told himself it was nothing worth talking to a doctor about.

He turned to the page marked "Disbursements" and took another bite out of the carrot cake. There were fewer names here than there used to be. Only two dozen men were left in his crew. And since he tried to have his bookkeeper Buddy Milito whacked for cheating him, Teddy had been forced to keep the records himself, painstakingly transcribing each figure from the crumpled-up slips crew members gave him into the composition book.

He paused and finished the piece of cake on his plate, noticing he'd given his niece Carla three thousand dollars in the last six months.

"Camille," he said. "Get me another piece of cake. And bring me some grappa while you're at it."

"You sure you haven't had enough?" she asked meekly.

He stared at her until she backed up into the kitchen like a dog afraid of being hit with a rolled-up newspaper.

The truth was he never got enough. Not since his days in the reform schools and foster homes. Food seemed to fill some deep gnawing need inside him. On the long winter nights, after he was first exiled to Atlantic City, he took solace gorging himself on cheese-steak hoagies the way other men stuck needles in their arms. And when things turned around and he became a boss, he indulged himself at the best Italian restaurants in town.

Still it wasn't enough. He went back to writing on the disbursements page as his twenty-three-year-old retarded daughter Kathy knocked over something upstairs.

"There she goes again." He grimaced. "What's the matter with her?"

His wife brought him the grappa and another piece of cake, with her head bowed. "She's been having spells, kind of. She keeps asking for Charlie."

Teddy looked up at her and felt something tear in his chest. "Why's she doing that? She fuckin' knows he's dead."

"I dunno." His wife began to cry again. "I guess she still misses him."

Teddy took a sip of grappa and went back to writing. "Well go look in on her. Make sure she isn't breaking any of them German car radios we left in her room."

He shook his head as his wife floated out of the kitchen in a haze of barbiturates. If she wasn't out of her mind on pills these days, she was crying herself blind with grief. The memory of Charlie was the only thing that mattered to her anymore.

When Teddy thought back on the boy, it was in isolated moments of not knowing what to say. To Charlie on the floor, watching TV. Charlie spending too much time alone in his room. Charlie coming home late with a split lip and bloodshot eyes.

Teddy once controlled half the unions and most of the drug trade in town, but he could never find the nerve to ask his only son if he was shooting dope. Thinking it over now, he didn't blame himself for the boy's suicide, but he wasn't sure who else to hold responsible. So he settled for raging at the rest of the world a little bit every day.

Mosquitoes flew into the zapper on the porch and fried themselves. Nighttime traffic rumbled by. And the phone remained silent. The Commission people had abandoned him.

He turned back to the income page and looked in the shoebox under the table, thinking mere must be more money somewhere. Maybe some slips were misplaced. He couldn't believe they were getting squeezed this tight. He turned back to the disbursements page and saw he'd given his lawyer Burt Ryan seven thousand dollars in the last two months without Burt making a single court appearance. With the racketeering indictment due any day, that number was sure to double or triple.

That yawning void opened inside him again. He quickly finished the grappa and stuffed down the rest of his carrot cake, feeling the satisfied ache in his gut. He shut the book, thinking he could handle only so much suffering in one night.

He walked through his wife's bedroom, taking off his shirt and pants, and went into his smaller green bedroom on the north side of the house. He lay down on the sofa bed and watched the leaves outside form shaking shadows on his ceiling. He hoped sleep would come quickly, before the hunger returned again.

12

I didn't want to waste time learning the ropes, so I asked John B. to introduce me to the top people in boxing right away. On a cool blue Friday afternoon, he brought me over to a press conference at the Golden Doubloon Casino at the Boardwalk.

The first guy we met in the Admiral's Ballroom was an executive named Sam Wolkowitz. I'd seen him on cable TV being interviewed before the fights. He was a senior vice president at the corporate outfit that helped sponsor these events. His company was part of a vast global communications network that included $75 million movies, several huge record divisions, four or five publishing companies, and the most massive interactive computer system in the world. In other words, the kind of contact I'd been trying to make all my life.

"Nice to meet you." I grabbed his hand and shook it.

He just looked at me with twinkling blue eyes. He wore a beautifully tailored brown Hugo Boss suit, a custom-made white shirt with a light red stripe and French cuffs, and a hand-painted tie Liberace would've strangled for. His hair was cut short and neat and his ears stuck out like a Toyota with both doors open. After a couple of seconds, I realized he was still looking at me, expecting me to say something, but my mind had gone blank.

"You, ah, you look much better than you do on TV," I said finally.

His eyes narrowed and the left corner of his mouth turned up. He must have thought I was coming on to him. I started to flush with embarrassment.

Fortunately, John B. interrupted. "My man, Mr. Sam," he said, pushing the brim back on the cowboy hat he was wearing that day. "I got a proposition to discuss with you."

Since the subject was his brother, the champ, John was in his confident mode. The other corner of Sam Wolkowitz's mouth came up, but it still looked like he was sneering.

"A proposition?" he said. "I hope this isn't another one

of those complicated arrangements that you suggested
we try in Anaheim last year."

"Oh no, not like that!" John B. said with a laugh so
hearty it made his eyes bulge and his knees bend.

For all I knew, John B. had suggested they try going to
bed with the same hooker in Disneyland. I smiled like I'd
been along for the ride.

"No, this is serious." John straightened up. "You know,
my brother and I been talking about this opening you got
coming up with the fight this fall."

"Hmm," said Sam. His face was like a blank computer
screen.

"You know, he's been training awful hard, my brother."
John B. dipped his head in admiration. "And when he
was at his best, there wasn't another like Elijah. He had
people come up to him, every airport, every city, just to
tell him he was the greatest inspiration to their lives. So
we was wondering if like you might be interested in, like
him, you know, fighting on that bill, seeing as you had the
other man dropping out."

John B. finally noticed that Sam wasn't jumping up and
down with enthusiasm. "Well John," he said in a pointy
nasal voice, "as I am sure you are aware, that was not just
a regular bout we had to cancel. It was a world-class title
fight. It doesn't make sense from a business standpoint to
substitute a fighter like your brother."

"Oh," said John B., squaring off into a boxing stance
that didn't look right on him. "I know what you're worried
about. You're worried about all that booll-shit they say
about brain damage. But it ain't true. You want the CAT
scan? You want a doctor's report? We can get that to you."

"You're missing the point." Wolkowitz held up two fingers like goalposts. "Strictly speaking, the decision to give
Elijah the fight is not ours to make."

"Well then who are we supposed to talk to?" I asked.

Sam Wolkowitz gave me a look that was supposed to cut me dead. Lips pressed together, eyes turned slightly away. It was a look that must've sent people crawling out of the executive suites on their hands and knees. But I'd seen my father stick an ice pick into somebody.

"Excuse me," Sam said. "But who are you?"

"Oh, this here is my business partner." John looped an arm around my shoulders. "Anthony's just helping us out with our organization."

"I'm just looking out for everybody's best interest."

Sam checked me out like a butcher inspecting a bad piece of meat. "John," he said, without taking his eyes off me, "I thought surely you'd understand we can't put a champion in the ring with a fighter who's no longer ranked in the top ten. We couldn't sell a noncompetitive fight like that. Our markets wouldn't take it."

"So how do we get our guy ranked?" I asked.

Sam's mouth turned into a thin line of disapproval. "Well, John," he said. "As I'm sure you know, that decision would be up to the World Boxing Federation."

"And who do we talk to there?"

Wolkowitz raised one eyebrow and looked from me to John B., as if asking, "Is this guy for real?" A couple of minutes ago he'd thought I was some gay flirt.

"The head of the WBF is Mr. Pedro Hoyas Ospina." Wolkowitz examined his buffed nails. "A great advocate and a very dear personal friend. I often go down to visit him at the headquarters in Panama. The common view— and I'm not saying I agree or disagree—is that he controls the ranking system. I believe he'll be appearing on the panel today."

Wolkowitz nodded toward the stage at the front of the ballroom, where various fighters and casino executives were taking seats on a long wooden dais with a blue-and-gold Doubloon banner hanging off the front.

"So you're saying that if we get to this Ospina, we got a shot at the fight?" I asked Wolkowitz.

"I'm not saying anything. I'm just putting things in context. You have to respect the integrity of the process."

Oh go fuck yourself, I thought. I smiled as he shook John B.'s hand and gave me a sidelong glance.

"Good luck to you, John," he said. "And be careful about the kind of company you keep."

He drifted away like smoke off a cheap cigar and the press conference began. Pedro Hoyas Ospina of the WBF got up to make a speech. A little fireplug of a man with skin like a bad fruit and a tan leisure suit. He looked like someone Teddy might have had parking his car a few years ago. He began talking about how much he loved boxing and how he'd sacrificed everything in his life for the sport. He grew up in a little town near Caracas, he said, where a boy had to learn how to fight or dress up like a chicken for a month and let other children pluck him.

"I made myself," he said with a choked-up, heavy accent. "That little chicken grew up to be a man…A man… Oh God!"

Then he started crying big honking sobs and burying his face in his handkerchief. Other people looked down and shook their heads, like they'd all shared the pain of dressing up like a chicken.

"*Jesucristo*, I love America," Pedro Hoyas Ospina said between honks.

I felt a tap on my shoulder and turned around, expecting John B. to tell me something. Instead there was a tall, pale man wearing chinos and a white silk shirt with a paisley ascot underneath it.

"I understand you wish to speak with the commissioner," he said, bowing slightly to John B. and then me.

Soft hands, light Spanish accent, skin as smooth as a

leather briefcase at an airport duty-free shop. Obviously not a street guy like Ospina. I wondered if he was the appointments secretary or something.

"Yeah," said John B. "My brother, he's looking to get the title belt put back around his middle, where it belong."

"Ah, yes, your brother Elijah," said the man in the paisley ascot. "We've often passed pleasant afternoons playing golf on the courses of South Florida. Many humorous hours have gone by, looking for his balls in the woods."

He smiled at us, but something about him made my gut squirm. He said his name was Eddie Suarez. I couldn't figure out how he knew what we wanted. I'd seen Sam Wolkowitz go up to the panel on the stage and sit down next to Pedro Hoyas Ospina without giving any signal.

"So your brother is intent on making a comeback," said Eddie Suarez, standing with his back against a long marble pillar as Ospina went into the tenth minute of his speech.

"We want to see him get ranked," I jumped in. "We understand it's the only way he can get the fight."

Suarez solemnly touched his lips with his fingertips. "You know, my friends, the commissioner is very concerned about the youth of today. Many more temptations are available to them. The drugs, the credit cards, the pornographic videos…"

"They have it too easy!" said John B.

"The commissioner feels it is important for the youth to have an outlet for their…energies," Suarez continued. "A place to go. You understand. So that is why the commissioner wishes to build a gymnasium in Panama City."

"What do you want us to do about it?" I asked.

Suarez's eyes got a little wider and a little darker, as if they were trying to fill the gaps in what he was saying. "A contribution is needed. Certainly you are both familiar with the high cost of construction, even in a country as poor as ours."

"Yeah, so for how much?" I asked.

"In the neighborhood of ten thousand dollars," he said.

I whistled loud enough to turn several heads nearby.

"So this is a bribe?"

His smile said you wouldn't want to see his frown. "I have no authority," he told us. "I'm merely a friend to all parties. A builder of bridges."

Fair enough. I guess a lot of bridge builders get paid off too. Except we were already fifty thousand dollars in the hole for the normal expenses.

I swallowed hard and tried to look unconcerned. If we didn't pay this guy off, we couldn't get Elijah rated in the WBF top ten, and therefore, the TV guy Wolkowitz wouldn't talk to us. In my father's trade this was what was known as a shakedown. Except these guys had custom-made suits and corporate offices. I should've turned on my heel and left right then. They were exactly the same as Teddy's crew. It made me think of that kid's game, Chutes and Ladders. You start off at the bottom and end up at the bottom with hardly any time in between.

But it was still my one chance at getting out. Sure, boxing was a dirty business, but it was a way into the legitimate world, where I belonged. I couldn't go back and work for Teddy in six months. So instead of Chutes and Ladders, I told myself it was an obstacle course, with a great reward waiting for me at the end.

I asked Suarez for his card and said we'd get back to him.

"Do not make the mistake of waiting too long, my friends," he warned us. "This fight is scheduled for ten weeks from today. It is possible another light heavyweight may be chosen from the ranks."

"It wouldn't be the same as having Elijah up there," John B. told him in a panicky voice.

I tried to play it cool. "We'll come to terms when we come to terms," I said. "We're not desperate, you know."

13

P.F. wasn't sure if it was the hangover or the clams that were nauseating him as he stood in front of the grocery on Florida Avenue, talking to Teddy and his two soldiers, Joey Snails and Richie Amato.

"So I've been asking myself," said P.F. with a hand over his stomach. "Who would wanna do a thing like that to poor Larry DiGregorio? Senseless."

The heat was like a gorilla suit. Teddy, sitting on a milk crate, pried open a clam, sucked out its insides, and threw the shell into a white plastic bucket at his feet.

"That's three times I been asked the same question," he told P.F. "First I had the feebs. Then the state troopers and now I got you. The man was a friend of mine. Ask anybody. I never wanted to see him chopped up like that."

On their milk crates nearby, Richie and Joey Snails exchanged bad-boy smiles and talked about the movie *Dances With Wolves.* The baking sun turned the sidewalks salt white and conjured a murky stench from the bucket at Teddy's feet.

P.F. felt the gorge rising in his throat. "Well the word is you were having some kind of problem with Larry's son Nicky…"

"Ah, bullshit." Teddy struggled for a few seconds with a clam that wouldn't open and then tossed it into the bucket at his feet. "You know the only reason you come around asking questions like that is because I have a last name that ends in a vowel. It's discrimination, that's what it is. Being Irish and a drunk like you are I would've expected better from you."

P.F. gave up a smile he'd meant to keep to himself. On his crate, Joey Snails put his fingers up to his head like horns and told Richie "de-tonka" was Indian for buffalo.

"God forbid a robin should fall out of a tree, I'd get blamed for it," Teddy went on. "Why don't you do something about real crime? I heard there was a shooting down in the Inlet last night. I don't see you working on that."

"I had no idea you were so concerned about the violence in our minority community. You ought to think about organizing a volunteer patrol."

"There's crime going on everywhere, you wanna look for it. Look across the street there."

Teddy pointed to a small Vietnamese restaurant with a yellow-and-red sign out front. "Every night I see twelve guys coming and going out the back of that place," he said. "So don't tell me they haven't got a card game going back there or an illegal shipping operation."

Three young Asian men dressed in black and wearing sunglasses got into a white Lexus and drove away laughing.

"Sure that's not just jealousy?" asked P.F.

He'd heard Teddy was getting squeezed these days. Something about Jackie from New York coming into town.

"Poor fuckin' buffalo," said Joey Snails. "They hadda go whack most of 'em. But there are still a few left. I saw some the other day when I was driving up the Turnpike…"

"Get the fuck outa here," said Richie, admiring the new biceps and traps the steroids had given him. "There ain't no buffalo in Jersey. They're all in upstate New York. That's why they named a town after them…"

Teddy coughed uncomfortably and dropped another clam in the bucket. "You know," he said, looking up at

P.F. "I hope you didn't come by here looking for a payoff again, like you used to with your old partner."

The memory and the gorge in P.F.'s throat seemed to rise simultaneously. Twenty years ago. Coming by with Paulie Raymond, to collect televisions and carpets as bribes.

"No," P.F. said, trying to keep himself bottled up. "That was Paulie's game. I was just along for the ride."

"Good thing too," Teddy grumbled. " 'Cause there ain't any more where all that came from. A man oughta work for a living anyway."

"I had occasion to think of those days recently." P.F. cleared his throat. "Michael Dillon. He was a friend of yours too. I wonder whatever happened to him."

Teddy took part of a clam into his mouth and spit the rest of it into his bucket. "I don't know. Maybe a building fell on him. He wasn't too cautious, you know. Mike."

P.F. remembered. The smiling tan face. The shoes that he couldn't afford. And the payoff Paulie took to stop investigating his murder. Thinking about it was like picking at an old scab.

"I wouldn't go around asking too many questions about that," Teddy warned him with hard, slitted eyelids. "It might reflect badly on you, if you know what I mean."

Joey leaned over and asked Richie if he thought a buffalo would make a good coat.

P.F. put up a hand like he was trying to slow traffic. "I just came by to see what you knew about Larry," he said. "I remembered he was a friend of yours and thought you might have something to add to the investigation."

"And I already told you. I don't know nothing about nothing." Teddy went back to concentrating on his clams.

"Beautiful," said P.F. "No wonder you go around confused all the time."

14

Vin had finally arranged for me to pick up the weekly
envelope from the roofers' union, but I wanted nothing
to do with that. I was determined to raise the boxing
money legitimately. What I found out, though, is when
you try doing things in a legitimate way, people can get
hurt too.

A week after I'd seen Elijah Barton at his house, I was
home having dinner with my wife Carla. The kids were in
the next room, watching some piece of mayhem on the
VCR. He-Ra the Slaughterer or She-Man the Magnificent,
one of those superhero cartoons about people getting their
skulls crushed. I was eating the Spaghetti-Os that Carla
had heated up—little ringlets of death—and thinking
about how I'd improve my diet once I started to make
some real money.

Then out of the blue, Carla looked up and said, "I got
a call from Mr. Schwarzberg at the bank today."

We'd barely spoken since that blowup we'd had about
the couch. I just sat there, stupefied.

"Yeah, what'd he want?"

"He said you were talking to him this morning about
us getting a second mortgage." She opened her right hand
like a fan. She'd painted all five nails fire engine red.

The house we lived in wasn't what you'd call spacious
in the best of times. But now I felt the off-white ceiling
getting a little lower.

"Schwarzberg called you about the mortgage?"

"Yeah," she said. "You didn't say nothin' to me about
that."

She took out an emery board and began filing her fingernails with it. I felt sick. Not just because chipped bits of fingernail might go flying in the red sauce, but because it was the type of thing her mother might do. Marie the cow. Teddy's sister. Filing her nails over a steaming plate of linguini while her husband Jack droned on about scamming auto insurance companies.

"Well, we haven't been saying much of anything to each other lately," I said.

Even though we'd been fighting, I hadn't quite lost all the feeling I had for Carla. Maybe because we'd been through so much together. She turned sideways in her chair and rested her hand on where the baby's spine would be.

"And what kind of second mortgage you think we're gonna get?" she asked as if she was just curious.

"I don't know. I thought we could maybe renegotiate a home equity mortgage. See how it goes. What'd we start off with? A house worth fifty-five thousand dollars? I figure it's worth almost twice that now."

Her face got all knotted up and for a second I thought the baby must've kicked her in the kidneys. Something about having this third kid had really put the years on Carla. All of a sudden she was starting to look like her mother, heavy under the chin and sad around the eyes.

"What're you, crazy?" she said. "You think this house is worth more now than when we bought it? You take a look outside lately?"

Our house was a blue two-story with a red triangular roof and a brown porch in what used to be a beautiful neighborhood. Years ago, it was all Italian, maybe a couple of Jews, and not a single piece of trash on the street. People used to be able to leave their doors unlocked at night. Now vandals regularly broke into the abandoned houses on the block to steal the plumbing fixtures and sell the parts for scrap. Some of the other houses were falling apart because the old Jews who used to live there moved down beach to Margate and rented their places to four or five Asian or Puerto Rican families at a time. When you walked by, you'd see the broken windows and the children scrawling graffiti on the walls.

"You never know. Things could turn around."

Carla dropped her fork and her cheeks started to get all red and puffed again. "Anthony," she said, "the man told me you wanted a loan of thirty-five thousand dollars." I was hoping she wouldn't find out about that. The guy at the bank said he'd call back, but I'd been counting on picking up the phone myself.

"Listen, if you didn't spend money like we were at a county auction, I wouldn't have to do this. It's only 'cause we don't save like we should. That's why I need the money right away."

She deflected the lie like a champion turning away a weak left jab. "What're you telling me? You're in so deep to a bookmaker you gotta borrow thirty-five thousand dollars?"

Her nostrils were flaring, like they always did when we were arguing. I decided I wasn't going to knuckle under, though.

"Never mind what I need it for," I said. "You wouldn't understand anyway."

"Anthony, they're gonna charge like eight and a half percent interest!" She leaned forward, pressing the baby in her stomach against the table. "You'll be dead before you finish paying off the interest. We've barely made a dent in the fifty-five we owed them in the first place."

I suddenly had this vision of us sitting in this same kitchen fifty years in the future, all old, worn-out and toothless, with the kettle on and the ceiling falling in on us. Her in her mother's housecoat, her flabby arms hanging out like dead flounders. Me in the same cheap moth-eaten suit. Talking about the good old days that weren't actually that good.

"You just don't understand the way things could be," I said, raising my voice. "You were the one saying I was stuck in the rut. Now I'm trying to get us out of it and you're slapping me down."

She put a hand on her forehead. "What're you saying?"

"I'm saying I need this money to start up a new business."

"What new business?"

I wasn't going to tell her about the boxing and let her call me crazy or stupid. It was too early and I needed to work some things out. So instead I shifted the subject. "I can't go on the way I was," I said. "Construction is dead in this town."

"But if there ain't no more construction, how can our house be worth more?" she asked, half rising in her seat to make the point. "Don't you get it? If you're saying Atlantic City is dead, our house can't be worth any more than we paid for it. We haven't got the assets. What're you gonna tell the bank appraiser when he comes to our house?"

It occurred to me that we'd been talking about one thing when we were trying to say something else completely. We weren't fighting about the mortgage. We were fighting about trying to stay alive inside. Rosemary was actually a few years older than my wife, but in some way, I was drawn to her because she was still fighting and hadn't given up yet. But when I looked at Carla in her old tank top and her mother's bouffant, I thought of a soldier raising the white flag. She was already starting to sink back down into herself.

"What about that casino guy, Donald Trump?" I said, thrusting a finger into the air like I was trying to win over a stadium full of doubters. "Or Dan Bishop."

"Oh, don't bring up Dan Bishop again."

"Why not? He started off just like me, running numbers in the Inlet, and now he owns one of the biggest casinos in Vegas. Just last year he got the banks to loan him twenty million when he didn't have the assets to cover it. It's the exact same situation. He had to get people to make the leap and believe in him."

"Yeah, but Anthony, he had a name. His name was worth something."

"And one day my name will be worth something," I blurted out.

We were both quiet a minute. I started jiggling my knee and pulling at the edge of the lace tablecloth. It wasn't real lace, but some vinyl substitute she'd picked up at Caldor.

I caught a whiff of that cat smell that's always haunted our house. The lady who used to own the place had one of her cats get run over by a car. The one that was left behind was so distraught he went around spraying the floors for a year. The smell permeated the wood, and there was no way to get it out. So now we had to live with the memory of a heartbroken cat for the rest of our lives.

"Anthony," my wife said slowly. "What do you think would happen if you defaulted on this loan?"

"I'm not going to default."

"But if you did," she said a little louder. "We'd lose this house."

"I just told you. There wouldn't be any default." Hell, if this thing worked out with the fight I'd clear five times what I owed them at least and finally be able to pay Teddy off.

"Anthony," she said, using my own name to beat me over the head. "If we lose this house, where are we gonna live?"

"We're not going to lose the house."

"Where would your children live?"

"They'd live better than they ever did."

It was like I was having to defend a dream against the daylight.

"We'd end up on welfare, like the coloreds your father's always complaining about."

"I would never let that happen," I said, dropping my napkin and starting to stand up. "I would never allow that."

"Yes, you would." Her lips began to tremble.

"What kind of man do you think I am? What're you doing married to me in the first place?"

"You'd sacrifice all of us for some idea you had."

"And you want to keep me down. Because you're afraid I'll leave you behind if I start to get anywhere in my life."

I saw her eyes get wide and then start to recede back into her head. It was like watching somebody get stabbed.

"I don't know, Anthony," she said in a voice like a little ship heading off into the fog. "Sometimes I feel like I don't know you no more."

That night I went to sleep on the couch. Carla was in the next room snoring. I couldn't get comfortable. There were crickets outside and little Anthony kept calling me to get him a drink of water. Every time I got back to the couch, it seemed like it had gotten a little shorter and narrower. Finally I drifted off at about a quarter to one.

I don't know how much later it was that I heard something stir. I looked up to see Carla staring down at me. It was still dark outside, except for the street light, and the leaves on the sycamore by the window cast a shadow over her face. With the light like that, she looked young again, the way she did when we went on those midnight swims.

"Anthony," she said. Her voice felt soft and downy in my ear. "I don't see why we gotta fight like this."

"I don't see why either," I mumbled.

"This ain't the way it was supposed to be," she said. "It was supposed to be me and you against everybody, like we was the last gang in town."

I started to wipe the crust of sleep off my eyes. She had her nightgown open. Her breast was floating just above my head. And for a second I forgot all of our problems. That breast was as young and perfect as the moon above the Boardwalk. I didn't even mind the cross lying next to it. A little more of that feeling I used to have for her came back. I began to think about how it would be if we patched up our lives again.

I guess even after what I'd done and said about leaving her behind, she still wanted to be with me. I reached up to touch her breast, just to let her know I still cared, but then her eyes caught the street light coming through the drapes and my fingers froze. Those eyes reminded me of the type of motel rooms where guys go alone to blow their brains out. I didn't want to go there with her. I knew right then that if I stayed with Carla, I'd never get out of this place.

"Hey," I murmured. "Maybe another time. Maybe we can talk in the morning."

I turned away, so I wouldn't have to see her looking disappointed. She must've stood there another minute or two watching me, because that's how long it was before I heard her trudging back to the bedroom.

I opened my eyes one more time and saw the bright red casino sign way beyond the boarded-up house across the street, burning the words TAKE A CHANCE against the dark sky.

I didn't hear from Carla the rest of the night. And of all the awful things I've done since then, turning her away like that may be one of the three or four I regret the most.

15

"Law and order, Vin," Teddy Marino was saying. "We gotta have it. Gotta have it."

"I absolutely agree," said Vincent Russo.

"It's like taking care of a car or your body. Once you let one thing go, the whole package is in trouble. You got problems with your ignition, eventually it's going to get in your engine. Something goes wrong with your stomach, it'll end up in your heart. Right? This is how things break down."

"Of course," said Vin. "A hundred percent."

"Here," said Teddy. "Take part of this thing. I don't wanna eat it all myself. I'm turning into a fat pig."

He handed Vin half his twelve-inch-long salami and Swiss sub sandwich with lettuce, tomatoes, and peppers.

They were sitting in a booth at the White House sub shop on the corner of Arctic and Mississippi Avenues. The tourists at the next table all wore Baltimore Orioles baseball caps. Celebrities like Jerry Lewis and Susan Sarandon smiled down from photos on the walls. The line of people waiting for sandwiches went out the front door. Others sat hunched over their food at the counter, like auto workers on an assembly line.

"Where are we going?" said Teddy, taking a bite out of the half sandwich he'd kept. "By my count we got problems at three of the unions now."

He ticked them off with his fingers. "We got that punk from New York trying to horn in on Ralph Sasso and the hotel workers. Number two, I got Paulie Raymond not returning my calls at the construction union. I told you,

you can never trust a cop no matter how much jewelry he wears. And number three, I hear from the roofers' that your boy still hasn't come by to pick up the envelope."

"He hasn't?" Vin put down his half of the sandwich.

"This is how we break down." Teddy reached across and took the sandwich back. "We let things get out of control. That's why we have to bring back law and order. Just the other night, we had a card game robbed at the Ocean Club. Would that have happened last year?"

Vin stared at him vacantly.

"I don't know either," Teddy said. "But if I find out that fucking kid Nicky had anything to do with it, I'll strangle him with my bare hands. I tell you, Vin, we should've whacked that kid and his father at the same time."

Vin stared down at his empty plate a moment and scratched at his wild tangle of gray hair.

"Jeez, Ted," he said, tearing paper from the edge of the plate and putting it in his mouth. "I didn't know that about Anthony not picking up the envelope. I'm gonna have to have a talk with the kid about it."

"Never mind," said Ted, finishing the first half of his sandwich. "I gave the job to Richie. He's gonna handle it from now on. Your boy doesn't want it, he don't have to have it."

Vin tried to hide his disappointment as he tore another strip off his plate and began chewing it.

"None of these new kids we have is any good," said Teddy. "They're all junkies and bums. They don't understand this thing of ours. We've gotta install discipline in our soldiers again. Especially with this indictment coming up, we don't want anybody else turning rat on us. This is gonna be a Cosa Nostra 'til the day I die. Be it an hour from now or a hundred years from now. We're gonna have unity and harmony even if it kills us."

But Vin wasn't listening. He was staring at the back of

someone's head over by the cash register, some twenty feet away. The head was covered with thick black hair. A small gold earring winked from one earlobe. But without even seeing the face, Vin knew it was someone familiar. The feeling burned across the room, like someone had lit a fuse on the floor. Then the head turned and Vin saw Larry DiGregorio's chinless face. He felt his head get light as his heart went still. Larry, back from the dead. It took a moment to register that it was actually his son Nicky. They were identical, except Nicky had long dark hair flowing over his collar and more natural color in his face.

He rose off the stool and walked right over to the booth where Vin and Teddy were sitting.

"Happy Father's Day, you fat piece of shit." He slid into the booth and faced Teddy.

Teddy's face got tight and shiny. "Is it, is it, ah, Father's Day?"

Nicky gave Jerry Lewis's picture a surly look. "No, asshole, that was two weeks ago, but that ain't the point. Every Father's Day, Larry took me here for a sub. It was our tradition with each other. This is the first year I wasn't with him."

"Hey, Nicky, we're all sorry about what happened." Vin, who was sitting beside him, put a furry hand over the sapphire ring on Nicky's left pinky.

"Yeah," said Teddy, putting down his sandwich slowly. "Larry was a good man. You get the flowers I sent over for the funeral?"

Nicky stared across the table at him. "I know you did it, Ted."

"Did what?"

"I know you had Larry killed."

Both Vin and Teddy reached for napkins out of the steel dispenser at the same time.

"Oh now Nick, you don't have call to go around saying things like that," said Vin, wiping his mouth. "Larry was a friend of ours. We wouldn't let nothing happen to him."

"Oh yeah?" Nick's head slowly rotated to the side, like a department store security camera picking up a shoplifter. "Maybe you were the one that did it, Vin. It's your style, ain't it. Putting an ice pick in him, like an animal."

Vin took his eyes away, as though the conversation no longer interested him. "You don't have any evidence to say that, Nick. You oughta watch it. You could get sued by somebody."

"That right? I don't have any evidence?" Nicky leaned over and put his broad face down by Vin's. Even sitting down, he towered over the older man. "Then how come when I went by the union the other day, they told me it was your son Anthony who was going to pick up the envelope from now on?"

"Hey, I don't have to take this." Teddy started to rise.

"Just hold the fuck on." Nicky leaned back and dropped his hands under the table. "Right now I'm holding a Glock machine pistol on both of you. So which one of you bastards wants to get his balls blown off first?"

All the blood drained from Teddy's face. Vin went on chewing his plate.

"Whooa, Nicky." Teddy's features began to smear. "We don't know anything about this. If you got a problem with Anthony, why don't you take it up with him?"

Vin squinted over at him for clarification. "We're not saying Anthony had anything to do with what happened to your father," he said quickly, pulling on his fingers.

"Well, that's not for us to say, Vin," Teddy interrupted. "If it's a problem between the young kids, it's not for us to settle it."

Nick DiGregorio hit the table with his free hand and the napkin dispenser rattled.

"I don't care who, what, or where," he said. "But some-one's gonna fuckin' pay."

"Hey, come on, don't be like that," said Vin, urging Teddy with his eyes to help him calm the young man. "We're all friends here, Nick."

"Fuck friends."

Nick DiGregorio grabbed the cup of soda out of Teddy's hand and poured it out on his lap. Then he stood up quickly, tucked the gun back in his waistband, and left the place, like a storm cloud heading out to sea.

"Aw, look what he did here!" Teddy tried to stand in his seat but the table got in the way.

Vin gave him a hard look. "Why'd you have to do that?"

"Do what?"

"Tell him my Anthony whacked his father."

"Well he did, didn't he?"

Vin scratched his head. "Yeah, but you didn't have to tell him that."

"Why not?" Teddy shivered. "If Anthony pulled the trigger on his old man, why shouldn't he have to deal with the consequences?"

"Because he's not expecting to get that kinda call from Nicky. We're leavin' him out there by himself."

Teddy gingerly moved out of the booth. "Hey, Vin, it's his problem now. He should take care of Nicky the way he took care of his father. If he got rid of the tree he can get rid of the branch."

Vin shook his head and examined the greasy skim on the tabletop. "It's not right. We're leaving him exposed."

Teddy wasn't listening. He was too busy plucking at the dampened front of his pants. "Aw, I can't believe this," he said, looking for something he could use to wipe himself. "Total lack of respect. It demeans all of us."

Vin threw a couple of balled-up napkins at him. "Clean it up yourself."

16

As we pulled out of Rafferty's parking lot, the red I-Roc behind me flashed its high-beams in my rearview mirror. I should've recognized it as a danger signal.

"How's the fight?" Rosemary asked as she settled in on the passenger side and fixed her seat belt.

"Which one? My whole life's a fight."

"You know." She crossed her legs under the glove compartment. "The one you were telling me about."

"Oh."

It'd been so long since Carla was interested in what I was doing that the question caught me off guard.

I ignored the way the I-Roc followed us out of the parking lot. "I was just over at the Doubloon the other day, talking to some people."

I mentioned the name of Sam Wolkowitz's company and Rosemary nodded as if she was impressed. After the last fight I'd had with Carla, it was a relief not having to explain everything.

"You know I was making fun of you the other night," she said. "But then I thought—when was the last time you ran into anybody with any goals around here? My ex-husband Bingo, he was a degenerate gambler—actually he was just a degenerate, he'd show up at the party already wearing the lampshade. Anyway, he'd gamble on anything. He would bet on the sun coming up in the west if he could get the right odds. He never understood how you have to work toward something."

Listening to her was like hearing someone speak my language for the first time. I turned the corner onto Atlantic Avenue and a casino billboard practically screamed from on top of one of the buildings: DREAMS COME TRUE AT OUR SLOTS. The I-Roc was still on our tail.

"You mind if I turn on the radio?" Rosemary asked.

I flipped on an oldies station for her. I was in the mood for one of those old doo-wop songs from the fifties, with the singer's voice rising out of his throat and climbing to the top of the night to light my way. Instead, I got a forlorn lady with an orchestra. I started to change the station.

"Leave that," said Rosemary. "It's Billie Holiday."

I'd heard the name before, but I'd never really paid attention. Billie Holiday didn't sound happy. We pulled up at a red light. All she had left was a bare ruined choir of a voice that made me think of empty bottles and old roses. Every time she'd reach for a high note, her voice would start to crack and she'd move away from it the way a girl would move down the bar from a guy who'd broken her heart too often.

Still you could tell she'd once been a great singer, same as you could tell Atlantic City was once a great town. There were little hints everywhere if you knew where to look. Over on the corner of Missouri Avenue, a sign said this was where the 500 Club used to be. Where Dean Martin met Jerry Lewis, where Frank Sinatra, the Chairman of the Board himself, would drop by unannounced and riff the night away with Sammy Davis Jr. or the Pete Miller Orchestra or whoever else was around. Now there was just a parking lot. Back a few blocks, there were vacant, rubble-strewn lots where grand old hotels like the Traymore and the Shellburn once stood.

Up closer to Texas Avenue, where I lived, Jack Cashard's Steakhouse was a cinder with a name on it, and the dance hall next door hadn't survived the fire either. In the old days, when all the celebrities and businesspeople came down here, a kid could make forty, fifty dollars a night just parking Cadillacs and Lincoln Town Cars around back. Now all you had was Pick-a-Flick video across the street and dozens of pawn shops with neon WE BUY GOLD signs out front.

"You've changed," Billie Holiday sang in that broken bell of a voice she had. "That sparkle in your eyes is gone/ Your smile is just a careless yawn/You're breaking my heart/You've changed."

"You know what I think sometimes?" I said as the traffic light turned green and the blue-and-red neon from the Doubloon down the block flashed over my windshield. "I think the casinos might have been the worst thing that ever happened to Atlantic City."

"How's that?" Rosemary asked. "The place was a dump for years before they came in."

"I know, and then they came in and everyone thought the streets would be paved with gold. But look at this place. Me and my family could never even get a contract to replace the toilet paper dispensers at the casinos."

Rosemary closed one eye and put a bobby pin in her hair. "You know, Anthony, I don't understand something. You've got all these balls in the air. First you say you don't have anything to do with the people who run the club. Then you say something about getting in the fight game. Now you're telling me you couldn't get a contract from the casinos." She touched my wrist and in a half-ironic voice she asked: "Are you trying to tell me you're in the Mafia or something?"

In the rearview mirror, I saw the silhouette in the I-Roc combing his hair. "Why do you say a thing like that?"

Billie Holiday was still singing on the radio: "You're not the angel I once knew/No need to tell me that we're through/It's over now/You've changed."

I looked up and saw there was a half-moon hanging over Bally's Grand. It was what I used to call a casino moon, because the yellow casino sign was so bright, the moon looked cheap and unimpressive by comparison. That was Atlantic City. You couldn't trust anything about it.

"There's no such thing," I said.

"What?"

"No such thing as the Mafia." That was what my father taught me to say whenever outsiders asked you about the Family.

"Yeah? So what do you and your father do for a living?"

"We're businessmen trying to get a little something for ourselves. Just like these people running the casinos."

She laughed as we went by the Italian Dimension clothing store and neared Our Lady Star of the Sea, the old yellow church my mother dragged me to once before she died. I was feeling all these emotions I didn't know what to do with, so I just kept them inside.

There were stragglers out on the sidewalk in front of the 7-Eleven. Hookers and low-level drug dealers mixing it up in the glare of the red-and-white sign. They weren't human really. They were more like shadows of what other people wanted at midnight. You put a light on them and they'd disappear.

"Look at these women, will you?" I tried to change the subject. "Any one of them would give you a blow job for ten dollars."

"Twenty-five dollars," Rosemary told me with absolute assurance.

I started to ask how she knew, but then the street light changed and I had to hit the brake.

"I was wondering if I could buy you a drink somewhere."

The I-Roc had pulled in so close behind me it was almost nudging my rear fender. After a few seconds, the traffic light turned green.

"Yes, I suppose that would be all right," she said. "But

I can't make too late a night of it. I've got my mother still watching my daughter."

We headed south toward Ventnor. I tried to think of some out-of-the-way place where they at least washed the glasses, but it'd been so long since I'd been out with anybody besides Carla that I had no idea which bars were still standing.

I saw a familiar old crumpling tenement on North Carolina Avenue, facing a funeral parlor with silver tinsel around its front sign. "I think Dan Bishop grew up there," I said. "Before he went out to Vegas."

"Dan Bishop." Rosemary got a faraway look, like she was trying to place the name.

I showed her the magazine clipping I carried around:

The secret to Bishop's success is his bold conception of the Horn Hotel and Casino as a kind of adult Disneyland. He eschews the traditional stark single light over each table that reminded players of Jimmy Durante saying, "Goodnight Mrs. Calabash, wherever you are." Instead, he splashes the walls with pastels, electric blues, and vibrant yellows and dresses his cocktail waitresses in skimpy satin wench outfits. Players are greeted in the lobby by a three-dimensional hologram of Blackbeard urging them to blow their life savings at poker. The elevators sing the winner's theme whether gamblers are going upstairs to bed or coming down to play. And once an hour, a full-sized replica of a pirate ship explodes in the middle of the casino floor with thirty barely clad dancers doing the boogaloo on the poop deck, at a cost of $50,000 a day.

"What we're offering is the total entertainment experience," says Bishop, 49, a gruffly charming man with the air of an East Coast gangster mixed with the civility of a Mediterranean maitre d'. "We're not trying

*to remind people of what their lives are like at home.
What we're about is testing the limits, scraping the
sky."*

"He was a local kid like me," I explained to Rosemary.
"Now look at him."

That article was my talisman. Whenever I looked at it,
I felt like I had a shot in life.

"You know what his secret is? He understands no one
wants to be a square. Everyone likes to take a chance and
gamble once in a while. That's why you get lines around
lottery places and casinos in the middle of the desert.
Gambling's the way of the future. That's why I'm in
boxing."

But Rosemary glanced at the picture of Dan Bishop
standing by a swimming pool wearing a tuxedo with a ruffled shirt underneath and said he looked like a pastry with
hair on it. I took the article back from her.

"You know, you shouldn't make fun of other people's
dreams."

We were almost at the edge of Atlantic City when we
hit one last stoplight at the Memorial Circle. The statue
of old Captain O'Donnell had his back only half turned to
my side of the car, as if he didn't trust me entirely.

Rosemary put her head on my shoulder and ran her
fingers through my hair. "Hey, Anthony. Look at me."

I turned my head. Rosemary was giving me this deep
soulful look with her bruised lips and her full dark eyes. I
felt something rise in my pants and knew my life and
wedding vows would never be the same.

"I am almost thirty-eight years old," she said in that very
proper way she had when she was trying to make a point.
"You don't have to tell me any stories about Vegas and
light shows. I don't make judgments. I have two jobs, a
daughter at home and my mother waiting up to chew out

my ass. I've been divorced, I've had two abortions, plus the one I lost, and I must have danced on top of every bar from here to Admiral Wilson Boulevard in Camden. Now I am aware you are not taking me to the Waldorf-Astoria. Things are what they are. So if you or your family have done some things maybe you aren't proud of, I really don't care. I haven't met anyone who's lived the perfect life yet."

"Well it's not too late to start trying," I said.

I was going to kiss her right there, but then I looked up and saw that red I-Roc pulling up beside us. At the wheel, with his long dark hair and nonexistent chin, was Nicky DiGregorio. He'd been following us since the club. My breath caught in my throat and stayed there.

"Oh my God," said Rosemary. "Look at that guy, Anthony. I can't believe how ugly he is. He doesn't have any chin."

The light was still red and traffic flowed freely through the intersection in front of us. It was too dangerous to just step on the gas. Instead, I tried to sink under the dashboard, pretending to look for something. But then I heard the I-Roc's door open. I looked up and saw Nicky standing next to my window, glaring down at me.

"That's right, you cocksucker," he said. "Crawl down on the floor where you belong."

I started to roll up my window, but he reached inside the car and grabbed my hand. "That's very rude, Nicky," I told him. "Didn't your father teach you any manners?"

Some gritted teeth appeared in his mouth. I thought he was about to start crying. But instead he smacked the door frame with his fists. Everything shook, including the kids' roller skates in the back.

"I oughta blow your fuckin' head off right here and now." He put his face right up to mine so I could smell the Sambuca he'd been drinking. "But that would be too easy. So you know what I'm gonna do now, Anthony? I'm gonna wait, and I'm gonna hurt you the way you hurt me. All right?" He stuck a long fingernail in my face. "Because I'm not just gonna hurt you. I'm gonna hurt your whole family."

He flicked the fingernail and took some skin off the end of my nose. My hands flew up toward the stinging sensation.

"Excuse me, ma'am." Nick leaned in to get a better look at Rosemary. "I didn't mean to interrupt a pleasant evening."

He went back to his car as the light finally turned green. I stepped on the gas and got out of there as fast as I could.

"Jesus," said Rosemary. "What was that all about?"

"Bad tile job," I told her. "He thinks I charged him too much."

17

"He always out this late?" asked Teddy.

His niece Carla filed her nails nervously and leaned against the refrigerator. "I think he's been working onna couple of business things," she said, "and they been taking up a lot of his time."

"Well he better come back soon. I got a job for him."

Vin sat at the kitchen table, making percolating sounds, like a belligerent coffeepot. Teddy looked at the clock on the stove. It was past ten-thirty and Anthony still hadn't shown up, so they could warn him about Nick DiGregorio. Carla, who was almost six months pregnant, tapped her foot and pulled the belt on her yellow bathrobe. Pieces of tinfoil were twisted into her hair as part of her color treatment.

Even with her swollen stomach, she looked like a little girl to Teddy. Could it be eighteen years had gone by since she was wearing pigtails and playing on the jungle gym in the backyard with his Charlie? Now Charlie was buried in Brigantine and she was married to this kid Anthony, who found a different way to get on Teddy's nerves every day.

"I hope you're not covering up for him or anything." Teddy sniffed the vague cat odor in the walls.

"I'm not." Carla shook her head and the tinfoil rustled like Christmas tinsel.

"Because if I ever find out he's not doing right by you, that'll be the end of him." He cut the air with the flat of his hand.

Vin began cracking his knuckles again. The kids were in the other room, still watching television. Some sexy show where the lawyers were all good-looking and worried about ethics.

"Look." Carla hugged herself. "Everything's fine. It's not any of anybody's business."

"How can you tell me it's not any of my business?" Teddy dropped his hands to his sides. His thighs still felt sticky from the soda Nick poured on him. "You're my favorite niece. I love you like I loved my own children."

"That's real nice, Uncle Ted." Carla raised her chin, like she was ready for a fight.

"Nobody's trying to butt in," said Vin, playing peacekeeper again. "We just came over here to tell you to be careful."

"Why?" Carla dropped a protective hand over the baby in her stomach. "What's going to happen?"

"Nothing." Teddy perused the kitchen cabinets. He looked over at his niece. "Say, you got anything for dessert?"

"I think there's still some Jell-O left in the refrigerator," said Carla, her mouth scrunched up and her eyes shifting. All this scrutiny made her uncomfortable.

"How 'bout a little grappa to wash it down?"

"Hey, Uncle Ted," she said, bumping against the refrigerator. "Is Aunt Camille starving you or something? I thought you were trying to lose weight."

Teddy waved for her to move out of the way so he could look in the refrigerator for himself.

Just lately, the hunger had been worse. When he tried to fill it, there was a pain. For some reason, he couldn't eat enough anymore and he wasn't sure why.

He fixed himself a bowl of strawberry Jell-O and sat down at the kitchen table across from Vin. His chubby right arm curled around the bowl protectively, a habit he'd learned in the reform school mess hall, where other boys made a sport out of stealing his lunch.

Carla put her nail file down and brushed a stray piece of foil off her shoulder. "Why do I have to be careful?"

"You should always be careful," said Vin, lighting a cigarette and putting his feet up on the kitchen table. "It's a dangerous world out there."

Teddy stopped eating for a moment and reached inside his jacket. He took out the .38 caliber revolver that Larry DiGregorio had fired at Vin and set it down on the kitchen table. "There," he said. "If anybody tries to give you a problem, you show 'em that."

Carla's mouth formed a perfect O of horror. "What the fuck are youse two doing?!" she cried out. "I got children in this house! I don't want any guns around here!"

Teddy frowned and went back to eating. "Carla," he said, letting the Jell-O gush along the gutters inside his cheeks. "I don't got any son to succeed me and my own daughter's feebleminded. I know you're only the girl in the family, but it's up to you to look after yourself sometimes. I'm sorry it has to be that way, but maybe if you'd married a real man of respect, things could be different."

Carla was still looking at the gun like it was a poisonous snake on her kitchen table. "Get rid of that fuckin' thing! I don't want little Anthony playing with it!"

Ted looked over at Vin, who took the gun and hid it in the red flour can on Carla's counter. Carla watched him, trying to decide whether she should protest any further.

"Maybe I'll send Richie over," Teddy said to Vin, who was taking a long drag on his cigarette. "He can sit here in the kitchen and make sure nothing happens."

"Oh no," said Carla, forgetting the gun and wagging her head furiously. "I am not having Richie Amato in my house."

"Why?"

"Don't you remember?" She put her hands on her hips. "I used to go with Richie. You wouldn't treat a dog the way he treated me. Whatever bad you can say about Anthony, at least he ain't Richie."

She looked over at Vin, who was sitting down and putting his feet back up on the kitchen table. "Hey, get your damn feet down and stop smoking in here. Don't you know I'm pregnant?"

Vin took his feet off the table and grabbed an empty beer can out of the garbage, so he could put his cigarette out in it.

Teddy was looking up at the little peels of paint that looked like fish gills on the ceiling over his head. "You know you could use a paint job in here," he said. "You sure that Anthony's providing for you?"

"He provides," said Carla, going to get a glass of water.

"You don't sound too sure."

"What do you want me to do, Uncle Ted?" She whirled around to glare at him and the tinfoil in her hair made a soft *tsshh* sound. "Walk out on him? With two kids and another on the way?" Her pale hands and red fingernails flew up in dismay. "What choice do I have? I can't just pack up and leave. Either I make my marriage work or the roof caves in. So don't go talking subversive to me, Uncle Ted."

"Where do you get a word like that?"

"I heard it from Anthony," she said, without embarrassment. "So don't try turning me against him. I got too many responsibilities depending on him."

"I still say he's a bum," Teddy muttered under his breath.

"And I say you don't know him," Carla lashed back, her face turning red. "Anthony was the only boy who'd talk to me in high school and we pledged our love. We may be having our problems now, but we'll work them out. And if we can't, I'll be the one to take care of it."

She glanced over at the flour can where Vin had left the gun. Teddy stood up and started to put his arms around her, but there was too much flesh between them.

"Carla, you're a very special girl," he said. "Any man who doesn't appreciate you, doesn't deserve to be around himself."

18

I forgot about finding a bar and took Rosemary back to the Family's stash house in Marvin Gardens. The apartment was empty that night, though you never knew when somebody was going to come by to drop off some money or pick up a gun. The white shag carpet fired off little static shocks as I walked in.

Rosemary took a look around the place and saw the bar next to the kitchen, the wall with the mirrors on it, and the black leather couch from Dave D.'s that folded out into a bed. The lamps all had identical bulb-shaped bodies and shades thick as plaster. The door to the other room was opened just enough so you could see some of the swag stored in there. My father had just gotten in a shipment of Iranian pistachio nuts and Nigerian hand soap from someone he knew in New York. I hoped Rosemary wouldn't ask me about any of it. She was probably already thinking it'd been years since a woman had a say in how the place looked.

"Let's go for a walk on the Boardwalk," she said abruptly.

It was a beautiful night, with a soft breeze coming off the ocean and amusement park lights blazing from the other end of the Boardwalk, but I hardly noticed it. I was too busy thinking about all the things that had happened since my father killed Larry. Now I had Nicky coming after me and my family. I figured that he wouldn't do anything right away. It would be better to wait and torture me. But I knew I had to get my wife and kids out of the house soon to protect them.

"Hey," said Rosemary. "Are you a made guy?"

"I don't know what you're talking about."

"Yeah, right."

We walked along quietly for a couple of minutes as a light from a Coast Guard ship cut through the fog on the water.

"You know, I always thought you had to be Sicilian to be a made guy," she said. "You don't look like any Sicilian to me."

"How come you know so much about it?"

"I read books. Just because I dance doesn't mean I can't read."

"My father now," I told her, "he's Sicilian."

"What do you mean, 'my father now'?" She stopped walking. "Isn't he your real father?"

"You know, it's very rude asking questions like that.

Something could happen if you ask too many questions."

"Oh, I am so scared." She opened her eyes wide.

"I mean, how would you like it if I started asking questions like that?"

"Go ahead." She opened her arms and the wind riffled through the light hair in her armpits. "Ask away. I've got nothing to hide."

"All right," I said, seeing that she was trying to provoke me anyway. "How did you know a blow job cost twenty-five dollars when we were talking about it before?"

"Because I used to be a hooker," she told me matter-of-factly.

I just looked out at the ocean. A tide was sweeping over the beach like a strong white arm.

"Whooaa," I said.

"Are you surprised?"

"Well, shit."

"It was just for a little while." She joined me at the steel railing. "And I do not have AIDS, if that's what you're thinking. I've been tested."

"Yeah, but how'd you end up doing a thing like that in the first place? I mean, you don't seem like a skeezer."

She sighed and brushed back her dyed-blond hair. "You know, you fall into these things a little bit at a time. I think a lot of it had to do with my second kid."

Now I was really confused. She'd only shown me the picture of one little girl. "Who was your second kid?"

"The one that didn't make it." Her lower lip came up like a gate protecting the rest of her face. "She was born too soon. I always used to blame my husband, Bingo, because he was a heroin addict, but I wasn't really taking care of myself in those days either. We were going to call her Melissa. Anyway, we were waiting in the hospital four days after she was born to see if she'd make it. She was a preemie and she had some terrible blood infection, you know."

She sniffed. "I used to go to N.I.C.U. and look at her under the bilirubin lights with all those tubes running in and out of her." She paused. "She was so little and helpless in that little glass box. It was hard to believe she was real. And I remember this sign up on the wall: BABIES ARE GOD'S WAY OF EXPRESSING HIS OPINION THAT THE WORLD SHOULD GO ON. So I made a deal with God. That if he let her live, I'd make my life over and be good all the time."

Her jaw got tight. "And then he let her die," she said quietly.

It was scary watching her talk about it, because she didn't do anything dramatic like start to cry or put her face in her hands. She just stood there, with her body getting more and more tense, from trying to keep it all inside. It was like watching someone tear themselves apart without moving a muscle.

"So after that, I said fuck it." She gripped the steel railing. "I couldn't kill myself or let my life go all to hell, because I already had Kimmy to look after. So I just decided I'd do whatever I had to to get by and be there for her, but I just wouldn't feel anything about it. And after that, you'll put up with anything. I mean, if you can stand having a junkie for a husband, it's not that far to turning tricks to support his habit and feed your kid."

"I guess it isn't if you don't give a shit about anything," I told her.

She forced herself to smile. "You know what's funny? I used to have a whole other idea about how my life would turn out. I had all these aspirations. I thought I could be an actress or a teacher. Something where I'd get to perform. For a while, I even thought about becoming a hand and foot model, so I could be in one of those J.C. Penney catalogs."

She had very nice hands. I hadn't really noticed her feet.

"So do you do that anymore?" I asked. "Turning tricks, I mean."

"No." She frowned. "But don't think there aren't still people asking. The night after you stopped by, I had a guy offer me five hundred dollars to sleep with him."

"No shit," I said. "Who was he? A lawyer?"

"Uh-uh." She bent her left knee and her high heel dangled off the end of her foot. "He was a fighter. I figured you might know him. His name was Terrence something."

"Terrence Mulvehill!" My heart jumped like a fish on a line. "That's the guy. That's the champ. I'm trying to set it up so my guy Elijah will fight him."

"Whatever." Rosemary pursed her lips. "He was very nice about it when I said I wouldn't sleep with him. And he tipped me a hundred and fifty bucks because I danced for him."

"He gave one-fifty just to watch you dance?!" It was the first thing she'd said that I didn't believe.

"Some people consider it an art form."

When I started to laugh, she scowled. "Do not go judging me, Mr. Mafia. I see you're here with me and you've still got a wedding band on."

I stuck my left hand in my pocket. For all the fighting we'd done lately, I still wanted to do right by Carla and the kids. But our marriage was killing me. If things stayed the same, I'd not only never leave Atlantic City, I'd probably end up going to jail because of something her uncle got me involved in.

In the meantime, Rosemary was patting my hand on the Boardwalk railing. "I'm sorry. I didn't mean to snap at you. Like I said before, none of us have lived a perfect life."

That was what I liked about Rosemary. She'd been places. She wasn't going to just dry up and waste the rest of her life in some obscure corner.

"Hey, I don't even mind that you're in the Mafia," she said. "I could probably use the muscle sometime, being a single mother and all…"

"I already told you I'm not in the mob." Though it was a hard argument to make after she'd seen the talk I'd had with Nicky.

"All right, have it your way," she said with that crooked smile. "I wouldn't mind it if you weren't in the Mafia either. I think a lot of those guys are faggots anyway. The way they're always kissing each other and worrying about their hair and nails."

I looked down at her hand resting next to mine on the Boardwalk railing. It was a gorgeous hand, as smooth and white as marble. I could see why someone might use it in a catalog. I decided that if she didn't move it in a couple of seconds, I'd stay.

"So are you a faggot?" she asked.

"What do you think?"

She looked at the top of my head. "I don't know," she said, keeping her hand where it was. "You got pretty nice hair."

I took her by the shoulders and mashed my mouth into hers. When she started to resist, I used the weight of my body to push her up against the Boardwalk railing.

Then all of a sudden she wasn't resisting anymore. I felt her grabbing hold of me. It'd been years since Carla held me like that. I'd gotten used to her just lying there, barely tolerating the things I tried to do. But Rosemary was different. She put her tongue right in my mouth, like she knew just what she wanted. Other guys in the Family said they didn't like it when women got too aggressive, but here I was with maybe the biggest hard-on of my life and we were only just getting started.

The thing had a mind of its own. She reached down to touch it and I heard her moan a little. It felt as though I was holding a club between my legs. I wasn't sure how I was going to go waddling down the Boardwalk with the front of my pants sticking out when it came time to go back to the car.

"Still scared?" she murmured.

"No, but I guess you are, you keep asking."

Her eyes lit up and she did something that truly surprised me. She spit on her hand and reached under her skirt, so I could see she wasn't wearing any underwear.

She touched herself as nonchalantly as a garage mechanic changing a tire. That should've sent me running home, but it didn't. Blood was pumping straight from my heart to my cock.

Before I knew it, she had my zipper down and her skirt up. "Don't worry, baby," she whispered in a feverish voice. "I can't get pregnant no more."

She was crazy, I realized, as crazy as my father or any of the other hit men I'd known. But before I could say anything about it, she had my cock in her hand and she was guiding it quickly and easily into her. More easily than it ever went into Carla in eight years of marriage. This was different. My cock seemed to go right into the deepest part of Rosemary right away. She felt incredibly hot inside. Not just warm, but blazing like she had a boiler going. It made me think of the oath made members of the Family take: "May I burn like the saints in the fires of hell should I ever betray my friends."

She turned me around and straddled me, so she faced the ocean and her legs hooked through the middle railing. Then she started grinding down on me. If anybody who knew Teddy or my wife saw me doing this on the Boardwalk I'd be a dead man, for sure. But the thought of death just made me fuck harder.

A seagull's cry merged with Rosemary's voice, asking me to give her more. If I wasn't careful I was going to come too soon, so I tried thinking about other things.

Coffee grounds in a white garbage bag. Ice hockey. My wife's couch in the living room. Nose hair. The way Nicky looked at me. My son's Ninja Turtles. Smell Michelangelo.

Rosemary licked my ear and I picked her up and turned her the other way, so now I was the one facing the ocean. Thick foamy waves pounded into the shore. I looked down the Boardwalk to where the amusement pier was still going strong. I could see the green-and-yellow neon of the Ferris wheel and the switchbacks forming bold patterns against the stark black sky.

It wasn't doing any good. Rosemary's pussy kept getting hotter and wetter. Her voice was crying out like she was starting to come. The seagulls screeched back at her. She dug her nails through the back of my pants and into the cheeks of my ass as she drew me on and on. I felt the juice creeping up toward the tip of my cock like mercury rising in a thermometer.

"Please," said Rosemary. "Please don't stop."

I exploded inside of her. The first shot was like a cannon blast, but the second was just as strong. The third didn't have quite as much force, but the payload was just as big. And so it went with Rosemary holding on for dear life, until I was just spent and hollow.

Over her shoulder, I watched the waves roll away from the shore, carrying the sand and empty Budweiser cans out to the sea and the rest of the world.

Then I closed my eyes and my wife Carla's face came to me, with her sad eyes and her full disappointed lips. And when I thought about her I felt an overwhelming sadness that made me want to fall to my knees and cry.

Not just because I'd let her down or betrayed her, but because after all this time and all these years, I finally knew what I'd been missing.

19

Most people don't know it, but being around concrete can be a very sensual experience. Watching it pour slowly down the chute. Sloshing around in it in your rubber boots. Feeling it settle. Hearing the whine of the trucks. Most mob guys only get involved in construction so they can show a legitimate source for their income, but I actually liked the work itself. There was just something satisfying about beginning a job and seeing it through to the end.

It also took my mind off all the trouble I had brewing. After the threat from Nicky, I'd had to move Carla and the kids over to her mother's house until I figured out how to protect them. Then there was Rosemary. My thoughts kept coming back to her body like it was the melody of a song. I didn't want to be the kind of bum who ran out on his wife, but I knew I belonged with somebody else. And on top of all that, I still hadn't raised the money to get Elijah into the fight game.

For the moment, though, I was in some lady's yard, installing steps from her driveway to her front door. I had my truck and four Puerto Ricans mixing cement, sand and water on the sidewalk with their shovels. Everything was going just fine until Vin came up behind me and scared me half to death.

"What the fuck?" I said, jumping back a little. "How the hell did you find me?"

"Richie had the address on a bill at the office. You know, you oughta get a beeper. Give us a way to find you."

"Yeah, that's all I need. First job I get in a month,

you're out here, bothering me. The lady inside sees you, she's gonna think she's paying for an extra man."

In fact, she already looked like she was having a fit. Tall redhead in a New Jersey Giants jersey. She'd been standing at the screen door watching us all morning, as if we weren't trustworthy.

I went back to stirring the soapy-looking concrete in my wheelbarrow as my father stood there looking over my shoulder.

"You sure you got enough sand in there?" he said. "You know that's the most important thing."

"Ah, what do you know about it? Sand isn't the most important thing. It's the aggregate. You got to have the right mixture of big rocks and little rocks. That's what you don't understand. It's having the right balance that makes it work. Just like the casino business."

"Wha?"

"It's like a casino," I said, taking off my bandana and wiping my brow with it. "If you read that article I showed you about Dan Bishop, you'd understand. You don't make all your money off your high rollers or your slot players. What you need is a mix of the high, low, and middle."

My father glanced over his shoulder at the lady of the house, still watching us from the screen door thirty yards away.

"Women," he said. "I think they're all getting too much power."

"Just don't blow this job for me."

"Let me tell you something." He spat on the grass. "You went with Teddy full-time you wouldn't have to work like this in the first place."

I noticed he had a brown paper bag in his hands and he was balling it up nervously.

I tipped the wheelbarrow a little and wiped my palms on the sides of my jeans. "How many times do I have to explain this to you? I don't want anything to do with the crew."

He wasn't listening. He was staring at the screen door. He gripped the brown paper bag with all his might and thrust it into my hands.

"Here, take this fuckin' thing already," he said.

The unmistakable weight of a gun went right from my hand to the pit of my stomach.

"What's this?"

"It's for Larry's son Nicholas," he told me.

I started feeling a little dizzy.

"I've got nothing to do with him." I twisted the top of the bag into a paper swirl and looked for a place to drop it. "Why're you giving me this?"

"He thinks you did his father," my old man explained, running his fingers through his shock of gray hair and taking a half-done cigar out of his pocket.

I rested my butt against the side of the wheelbarrow and tried not to slide in. Something behind my eyes was starting to swell. "Why's he think a thing like that?"

"I dunno." My father lit the half cigar. A couple of embers fell and clung to his polo shirt. "People get ideas. Teddy wants you to go with Richie, take care of it."

I looked up at the overcast sky and the fading sun as though there was someone up there I could appeal to. "But this was your deal all the way. I'm not even part of the Family."

My father looked somber. "Teddy wants to see you do some work."

"So what? If Teddy wanted me to chew glass, would I have to do that too?"

All my life I'd been trying to get away from that fat fuck, and here he was coming after me again.

"Why can't you just see the man is an asshole?" I asked my father. "He's dragging both of us down into the mud."

"He is not an asshole! If it wasn't for him I'd still be boosting cars off the street in South Philly."

"And what're you doing now?" I almost shouted. "You say that like your life is so wonderful now! Don't you see it? This whole way of life doesn't mean anything anymore. It's for the museums and history books!"

"It means nothing, ha?!"

My father suddenly grabbed me by the scruff of the neck and pulled my head down. "Come here, you little motherfucker," he said, ripping his shirt open with his free hand. "Look at these, look at these."

Through the thickets of gray matted hair on his chest, I could see at least three bullet scars, not counting the nick on his shoulder from Larry, and countless stab wounds. I looked up at the knobs and ridges on his face.

"Does this mean nothing?" he demanded. "Is this for the history books? I took ten bullets and lived. I been stabbed by more cocksuckers than you ever shook hands with. I did five years in Graterford. And you're trying to tell me it don't mean anything?"

"That's not what I said."

"I've lived and I'll die to keep this way of life."

He stood back from me and banged his hands together, grabbing air and expelling it hard like an old steam engine.

"I never asked much from you," he said. "I never expected your love. And if you don't wanna follow my footsteps in the *borgata,* I guess that's all right too. I'll have to learn to live with that." He paused and took another deep breath. "All I ask of you is that you be a man among men."

A man among men. He might as well have struck a gong between my ears. Yes, that was what I wanted. To be a man among men. My father was like an old ape beating his chest and bellowing at the sky. He had this brutal churning force going inside of him and he was trying to pass it on to me. And the truth was that deep down I wanted it too.

The lady of the house was still gaping at us from the screen door. My father's shirt was open and my jeans were falling down. We straightened out quickly and both started laughing like it was some big joke. She must've thought we were both crazy.

My father buttoned his shirt and got a long brown Ace comb out of the back pocket of his chinos. "Now Nicky has gone around making threats against the family," he said quietly, trying again to tame his hair. "Your family. As a man, you know what you have to do."

"And what happens if I say no?"

"I dunno." He gave up and put the comb away. "A guy loses his nerve, anything could happen."

"It's not right," I said halfheartedly.

But it was a foregone conclusion. Something had to be done about Nicky. We couldn't go to the police and ask for protection. Because then we'd have to talk about what happened to Nicky's father.

I picked up one side of the wheelbarrow and looked at it. The mixture was beginning to harden and if I didn't pour the rest of it quickly, the whole load wouldn't be of any use.

"It wouldn't be the worst thing in the world for you, do some work," my father said, looking at the unfinished steps. "You could get outa doing this awhile."

"I told you, I like doing this." I started picking pieces of dried concrete off my arms and shoulders.

"Well, you ain't any good at it." My father stepped on one of the forms I was using for the steps. "It's all uneven here. Besides, you gotta reinforce it. We're on an island here. Otherwise, a year from now, this will all be cracking and they'll have to rip it out. You should've asked somebody what you were doing first."

I put down the paper bag and picked up the trowel. We both stopped talking and just stared at the steps awhile.

I wondered if it was too late for me to get into demolition work.

20

Teddy and Richie Amato were sitting in a car parked outside a discount department store on Atlantic Avenue. A homeless man with long nappy hair and no shirt lingered on a fire hydrant nearby.

"All right," said Teddy. "You got everything?"

"I got everything." Richie looked at himself in the rearview mirror, admiring the way the Anadrol and horse steroids pumped up his shoulders and made his neck swell like a tree trunk.

"Well, if you don't, speak now. You don't get any points for not asking."

"I got everything. I told you."

Teddy struggled out of his seat belt and took a pack of Camels from his coat pocket. "Remember. Bang, bang. Get in, get out. You see Larry's kid Nicky, you fuckin' shoot him. No hanging around looking at the scenery."

Richie frowned and his brow looked like a girder coming down on his eyes. "What do you think? I never done this before?"

"If you'd ever done it before, you wouldn't still be trying to make your bones."

Teddy stuck the cigarette in his mouth and lit it. He looked like an enormous time bomb waiting to go off. The homeless man got up off the fire hydrant and went into the department store.

"You know, it may take a couple of weeks for me and

Anthony to track him down," Richie warned him. "I know Nicky's been running around a lot."

"Just don't draw it out longer than you have to. Remember how long it took with them horses. What're you using anyway?"

"I got a .45," said Richie. "Anthony's gonna have the .25 his father gave him."

Teddy blew out enough smoke to fill the car.

Richie put his thumb and forefinger up to his nose and caught a drop of blood coming off the tip. It was all these steroids he'd been taking. They'd given him a body he'd only dreamed about as a boy. A fifty-three-inch chest, nineteen-inch arms. But when he saw the side of his neck in the rearview mirror, it was a boiling stew of veins and sinews. Maybe he ought to try tapering off on the 'roids. That story on TV the other day said they could shrink your balls to the size of peanuts. He hoped it wasn't too late.

"Don't be an asshole and leave them guns lying around afterwards." Teddy coughed twice into his fist.

"I know."

"And listen," said Teddy. "If this other kid gives you a hard time, don't be afraid to whack him too."

"What?" Richie looked stunned. He fingered his wide, heavy jaw as if he'd just been slugged. "We're talking about Anthony. You're kidding, right?"

Teddy looked at him a long time. The homeless man came out of the department store, holding a Barbie doll and kissing it.

"Yeah," he said. "I'm kidding."

"What were you saying? You wanted me to whack Anthony, instead of Nicky."

"It was a joke, you moron."

"Don't call me a moron." Richie turned his neck like he had a kink in it.

"Well, don't act like one."

21

On July 4th, Richie Amato and I were sitting in a borrowed car on a side street near the Inlet. I think it was a red 1991 Reliant. Richie was in the driver's seat running his mouth.

"Let me tell you something. I got a lot of respect for Joey Snails but he's a no-good motherfucker."

"Why's that?" I looked over the dashboard at the street in front of us.

At any moment Nick DiGregorio's car would come rolling along, and then one of us would have to get out and shoot him. And with the way my stomach was turning itself inside out, I hoped it wouldn't be me.

"I'll tell you what Joey's problem is," Richie said, shifting in his seat and jangling the chains on his runway-sized chest. "He's a dumb shit, that's what he is. The other night we're supposed to do a job, right? So what does he do? He shows up shit-faced and instead of bringing a gun like he's supposed to, he's got a crowbar, a radio, and a coat hanger…"

"A coat hanger?" I had trouble focusing. My mind was on what we were about to do.

"Yeah, he thinks he's gonna go in through the side and puncture the intestines," Richie said. "I know it's fuckin' stupid, but I figured with the crowbar is okay. I mean, we're only supposed to be breaking legs here. We're not animals, are we? Anyway, fuckin' Joey Snails. As we're coming into the stall, he trips over a fuckin' bale of hay or something…"

I came back into the conversation. "Wait a second. As you were going into the stall?"

"Yeah, that's what I said."

"Wait." I gave him the time-out sign. "You went into a stall to whack somebody?"

"That was the contract."

"What were you doing? Putting a hit on a horse?"

"Yeah," said Richie. "You didn't know about this? Ted worked out a deal with someone he knows at an insurance agent. We do this racehorse and he's supposed to split the money. Except fuckin' Joey Snails let the horse out of the barn. He got this idea in his head he's gonna get this horse Snowflake to stand in a tub of water while he throws a radio in. Make it look like a heart attack. Instead he lets it out and we have to go chasing it in the middle of the fuckin' night. With a crowbar, a coat hanger, and a radio. I tell you the guy's an idiot."

You should know, I thought, adjusting the rearview mirror. Look at him sitting there. Fuckin' Richie Amato. Poster child for anabolic steroids. Who once made a bartender who owed him money blow him in front of a room full of people and then got mad when somebody called him a faggot afterwards. Fuckin' Richie. With his monobrow and his $250 Italian loafers and the light slacks he paid a hundred dollars for and still couldn't fit into. Richie's idea of a good time was carrying around Ted's coat for him on a summer afternoon and then hanging out in a bar with him all night, laughing at Teddy's jokes and checking his own hair in the mirror.

What a life. Everything you did, you gave half to Teddy. And if you were a dope like Richie, half the money you got to keep you wasted on clothes, gambling, or broads. God forbid you should get pinched driving around drunk or something stupid like that, because then the Big Guy would make you pay for your own lawyer.

But here was Richie smiling away at himself in the mirror. Like his life was just so terrific. He wasn't even a made guy yet, but anything Teddy told him to do he'd do. Go ahead. Shoot somebody in broad daylight. Do it cowboy style. Make some fuckin' noise. That's what the Big Guy wanted. Hell, if I'd left it up to Richie we'd be doing this hit in the lobby of the Taj Mahal instead of a quiet side street near the Inlet.

In a way it didn't matter. I was just counting on Richie to pull the actual trigger. I didn't want to be responsible myself.

"I hope this fuckin' guy shows up soon," Richie was saying. "I got a date later tonight with this broad in Ventnor and I wanna be in the mood for some serious helmet when I get there…Jeez, I hope nothing happened to this Nick."

"Yeah, I have to do something too."

I was supposed to pick up Rosemary after work at the club.

"Oh yeah?" Richie looked at me. "She anybody I oughta know?"

I froze for a second, wondering what he knew. Richie and I had always been competitive. Ever since Carla broke up with him and started dating me. It only made it worse that he knew I hadn't really killed Larry DiGregorio like my father had said.

"I'm not seeing any girl," I lied. "I'm talking to Danny Klein about borrowing some money."

Richie suddenly put his arm out for me to stop talking.

Behind us, I heard twigs and old cans crunching and crinkling under an auto's wheels and the sound of an engine dying. A slamming car door took a chunk out of the night.

Up in the rearview mirror, there was Nick DiGregorio getting out the driver's side of the car. Twenty-seven years old and as chinless as Larry.

One of those laser-beam headaches started to sear the

back of my eyes. I wanted to put the key back into the ignition and drive away from there as fast as I could. I'd been putting this moment off all my life, it seemed. But here it was, like a math test where you didn't know any of the answers.

I watched in the mirror as Nick crossed in front of his I-Roc and went over to the passenger's side. Someone else was getting out and Nick was holding the door solicitously like an animal trainer trying to coax a chimp out of a red wagon. Finally she emerged. Just under five feet tall, just over eighty years old. But built like a little buffalo in her flowered sundress.

"Ah shit," I said. "That's his goddamn grandmother. Now what are we gonna do?"

"We're gonna finish the fuckin' job." Richie checked his gun and opened his door. "We been following this bastard all fuckin' week. I'm not gonna waste another night on him."

With that, he was out of the car, running toward Nick and his grandmother. I had no choice but to follow. I took a second to close the car door behind me and then broke into a trot. The air was warm and felt good in my lungs.

Richie was already closing in on Nick and his grandmother. Trees rustled and garbage cans rattled. When Nick saw Richie raise his gun, he began to run the other way across the street, leaving his grandmother rooted to the spot on Rhode Island Avenue.

She reached up as Richie went by and grabbed him by the throat. He sank down to one knee and yelped in agony. And as I caught up to them, I saw her long red nails digging into the back of Richie's neck.

"Ah lemme go you old bitch!" Richie shrieked, trying to swat her off his back. He looked up at me with tears in his eyes. "Go get that piece of shit! And watch out if he has a gun!"

Thirty yards away, Nick was disappearing between two drab wood-framed houses across the street. I went after him.

The moon was like a bare lightbulb throwing light around the sky.

I followed Nick's path and heard two dogs start barking. There was a Cyclone fence and beyond it the weeds were swaying. I hesitated for a couple of seconds and then started climbing it. About halfway up, my pants got caught on a loose wire and the left pocket started to rip. A brand-new pair of linen pants. I must've paid seventy-five dollars for them. It was one thing when an imbecile like Richie got all worked up about his clothes, but these were really nice pants.

I jumped down the other side of the fence where the dogs' barking was much louder. The ground was soft and muddy and my Bally shoes sank down an inch or two. I lifted my eyes to curse the heavens, but then I heard the bushes shaking about ten yards away and I remembered what Richie said about Nick's having a gun.

I ducked down and kept moving forward. The area was more swamp than woods. Weeds stretched a foot or two higher than my head. The air was heavy and fetid; sweat soaked my shirt collar and mosquitoes probed my ears. Roots like giant arteries swelled out of the ground and almost tripped me.

For some reason, I started thinking about being a kid and going out for a night with Vin. I remembered being in the car with him and driving out to the Pine Barrens. I could picture the top of the dashboard and the car headlights flashing by when he left me by myself for a few minutes to do something. I couldn't have been more than eight years old. I remember being afraid and starting to cry because I thought he'd never come back for me and I'd die by myself in the woods. And when he came back, wiping the dirt off his hands, it was as if my life had begun again. Afterwards, he took me for a walk on the Boardwalk and bought me a milkshake, while the moon was shining on the water and Sinatra was singing on the jukebox.

A burst of red, white, and blue firecrackers over my head brought me back to the present. It was a fireworks display sponsored by one of the casinos.

I pulled out the .25 Vin had given me and walked on carefully. I went where the weeds were stirring and followed a mossy path about a quarter mile out toward some lights. I found myself coming out on New Hampshire Avenue, facing the ocean and a rotting section of the Boardwalk. On the street directly in front of me were rows of two-and three-story houses with lousy paint jobs and lopsided roofs.

Black people lived here. When I looked up, I saw some of their houses had yellow rights pouring out the windows as if the families inside were having dinner. For a moment, I felt a stab of envy. I should've been home with my family. But then I'd have Nicky lurking around outside, waiting to get us.

I saw him suddenly darting out from between two of the houses and heading for the Boardwalk. The chinless bastard was limping a little, but he managed to keep up a brisk pace when he heard my footsteps coming after him down the empty street.

Just as I seemed to be gaining on him, Nick ran under the Boardwalk. I hesitated for a split second and then followed him under.

It was dark under the Boardwalk. As soon as I heard rats scurrying, I knew he hadn't gone far. A smell hit me that was a cross between fresh seaweed and a fart that had lingered in the air about three hundred years. Little bits of light seeped through the slats overhead and a weak flashlight shone against a wall about a hundred yards away.

Within a few seconds, my eyes began to trace the outline of sleeping bags and lanterns. I'd always heard people lived under here. There were boxes of cereal, pots and pans, and even a small television. And crouching behind one of the wooden beams was Nick DiGregorio.

"Anthony I'm begging you," he said in a shaky voice. "We've known each other since kindergarten."

That was certainly true, though I didn't remember much about Nick except he was one of the boys who teased me the day after the cops came and said my real father, Mike, probably wasn't coming back.

I took my gun and aimed it. The ocean tossed and roared and tossed some more. God's indigestion.

I still didn't know if I had the nerve to go through with this. But I wasn't sure if Nicky had a gun either.

In the distance, I heard faint pops and explosions from the fireworks display.

"Come on, Anthony, let's be men about this," he said in a slightly stronger voice. "I know you had nothing to do with what happened to my father. I wasn't gonna let nothing happen to you."

He had come out from behind the beam. Even in the dim light, I could see his eyes were the same color as the oysters you found in the sand. I could even hear what was going on in Nick's stomach from ten yards away. A noisy question mark of gas swallowed itself backwards up his intestine.

"Anthony," he said, once more using my name as a form of supplication. "I swear on my grandmother's life I wasn't gonna do nothin' to you or anybody else in your family."

But Nick's grandmother was with Richie, and swearing on her life didn't mean much. We both realized it at the same time. I thought of this little prayer I used to recite sometimes when I was young before I went to bed. Please Dear Lord, make it so I am not myself living this life.

Make it go quick and fast, so it's like I am a million miles away watching it.

Nick reached into his jacket like he was about to pull out a gun. The .25 in my hand choked and spit fire at him.

The noise was lost in the last burst of fireworks overhead.

When I came out there was no one around. All I saw was a solitary seagull circling and screaming over the Boardwalk and a cloud drifting across the moon.

22

Phenomenal. There wasn't another smell in the world like it, Pigfucker thought. Death had its own odor. Not just the rotting, stinking corpse, but death itself. You could smell it coming up the block or going through a toll plaza. His third wife, Baby Jane the ball and chain, thought it was just the adrenaline rush of seeing dead bodies and knowing there was work to be done. But it was more than that. It was a real smell out there in the world. A smell that told you one thing was over and another was just beginning.

What was beginning tonight was the investigation into who killed Nick DiGregorio. But P.F. didn't have much to do with that. He just stood in the weeds by the edge of the Boardwalk, watching state troopers and federal agents once again trample over any usable leads. The M.E.'s wagon was getting ready to take Nicky to the same place they'd taken his father a month before. And that German shepherd was still barking away in the back of the K-9 car.

A dozen or so black people from the neighborhood stood on the street corner, watching supervisors shout orders at each other. Beautiful. If P.F. had been working the case himself, he would've waded in among the spectators with a black uniformed officer and come up with three decent witnesses in five minutes. But once you had this many suits involved, nothing got done.

He watched a third assistant from the M.E.'s office come over to help hoist Nick's body into the red Dodge van with the blacked-out windows. Ridiculous. He felt a burning sensation in his stomach and swallowed another Tums, remembering the first time he'd laid eyes on Nicky D. It had to be almost twenty years ago. He was a rookie officer then and Nick was a little kid with a John Travolta disco haircut, running to get coffee for Teddy. He couldn't have been more than seven years old. A little kid wrestling on the floor with Teddy's son Charlie.

The M.E.'s guys slammed the van doors on Nicky and went around the front to drive him away. P.F. hummed an old half-remembered country song.

A heavy hand fell on his shoulder and a familiar voice sounded in his ear. "Hey, buddy!"

He turned and found himself facing Wayne Sadowsky, the F.B.I. man. The pasty-faced ex-jock with the slight limp and the Southern accent.

"I was talkin' to a friend of yours the other day."

P.F. winced involuntarily. The idea of this bonehead conversing with an actual friend was like having him touch the food on your plate.

"What friend of mine would've said anything to you?"

Sadowsky looked up at the sky. His nose was mashed in like he'd had a youthful habit of chasing parked cars. "A Mr. Robert D'Errico," he said finally. "Over at the Doubloon Casino. He said they were thinkin' about hiring you as head of their security department."

P.F. felt a pair of pliers grip his intestines, but tried not to react too much. "Wonderful," he said. "And how is it he ended up talking to you?"

"He'd just been calling around to check out your ref-

Casino Moon   151

erences and ended up on my telephone line. Seems he'd
been hearing some old story about an investigation you
conducted a few years back with another friend of yours,
a Detective Raymond. Seems you got called up before a
grand jury because of it. At least that's what Father
D'Errico heard over at the Doubloon."

P.F. felt the pliers' grip tightening and turning in his
stomach. "So what'd you tell him?"

"I told him I'd surely look into it," Sadowsky drawled
with a smile. "I believe that was part of a state probe into
local police corruption."

The pliers began to tug P.F.'s guts downward and he felt
an uncomfortable widening in his bowels, remembering.
It happened a little bit at a time. First, Paulie Raymond
the detective brought him by to meet Teddy. Then it was
free drinks at Teddy's social club. And meals on the arm
at Andolini's. Soon Teddy was giving them color TVs and
carpets to take home. "Sure, whatever you need, kid." It
was inevitable there'd be a phone call to ask for a favor in
return. And it came in the middle of the Michael Dillon investigation. Paulie just stopped asking the right questions
and P.F. didn't have the nerve to pursue it on his own.

He'd never quite forgiven himself. Pete Farley, former
altar boy and all-state hockey defenseman. He still remembered every question he'd been asked before the
grand jury. It was only having a good lawyer like Burt
Ryan that saved his shield back then. A breeze came in off
the ocean but it wasn't the kind of wind that cooled you
off. It just blew your shirt against your skin and reminded
you how much you'd been sweating.

"So what can I do for you?" he asked Sadowsky coolly.

"Well I'll tell you, partner," said the agent with exagger-
ated folksiness. "We could sure use a hand with this case
we have right here."

He looked off after the M.E.'s van following a squad car

racing down New Hampshire Avenue, with lights blazing and sirens going.

"What do you have so far?" he asked Sadowsky. "I thought Nick's grandma saw the whole thing."

"That poor sweet lady's in the hospital with a stroke—she won't be IDing anybody any time soon." Sadowsky grimaced. "You know the expression, *to gowno warte?*"

"No." But it sounded hilarious with a Southern accent.

"It's Polish, means we got jack shit. We're gettin' our asses kicked, and that is the sad and sorry truth of it. Why, we still don't know who killed ol' Larry."

He thrust out his lower lip, and for a moment P.F. almost felt sorry for him. A big Polish kid from the South in a white-bread outfit like the F.B.I. It couldn't be easy. But then he recalled the way Sadowsky had been squeezing his balls a minute before and his sympathy went away.

"So what am I supposed to do about it?"

"I was thinking maybe since you obviously knew some of the gentlemen in Teddy Marino's crew, you could maybe ask around for us a little."

The venom splashed in the pit of P.F.'s stomach. "Why the fuck should I do anything for you?!"

Sadowsky broadened his grin and his accent. "Well, shit, I was thinking about your Mr. D'Errico and those questions he was asking. Your cooperation would certainly cast them in a different light. I'm not saying anybody would outright lie for you, but the truth has a way of being shaded."

This feeb might have a future in New Jersey politics, P.F. thought.

"Well, if I admit I know people in Teddy's crew, aren't I opening myself up for more questions?" he countered.

"It's strictly off the record," said Sadowsky, hands in his pockets like he was carrying the most valuable lint in the state. "You scratch mine, I'll scratch yours. No one else needs to know about it."

P.F. watched a few more of the black people on the corner drifting back to their houses when the Mormon-looking F.B.I agents tried to question them. He hated to do anything to help the feebs. It violated something in his bones. On the other hand, he wanted this job at the Doubloon as badly as he'd wanted to lose his virginity. And these old questions about his past with Paulie could hang him up.

"I'll see what I can do," he said, hoping that would be enough.

"Well, Father D'Errico should be calling back in a few days, so I'd try to do better than that," Sadowsky pressed him. "Remember, I've got supervisors too and they're squeezing me for answers."

"Shit rolls downhill," P.F. muttered.

"Even faster when it rains."

Only after he said this did P.F. notice it had begun to drizzle again. Something about the death of a DiGregorio brought on the rains. The street took on a sleek shine and the rest of the people went back into their houses. Sadowsky put his collar up and lit a cigarette. He probably likes this, thought P.F. Standing in the rain, smoking a cigarette while they haul a body off to the morgue. Maybe it makes him feel like he's on some old *Dragnet* episode. It figured Sadowsky didn't have a wedding ring on. Men who'd been single all their lives could afford to hold on to their romantic delusions about themselves.

"I'll get back to you soon as I can," he told the agent.

"That sounds just fine." Sadowsky patted his shoulder. "And by the way, if things work out with you getting the job at the casino, do you think you could get me seats for the title bout this fall? I always do enjoy a good fight."

23

The world came back to me in pieces. First there was the ache in my ears. Then the throb in my right ankle. The brown metallic taste in my mouth. And the hangover that felt like a broken tooth in my brain.

I propped myself up on one elbow and looked over at Rosemary, just waking up on the pillow next to me.

Her body gave off a sweet, heavy female odor and her face was smooth and unspoiled by makeup.

"Jesus," she said, her eyelids fluttering. "What got into you last night?"

"Why? What's the matter?"

She rolled over and winced like an injured athlete hobbling in off the field. "We did it from all points on the compass and a few I hadn't been to before."

I sat up straight and the hangover poked at the top of my skull, like it was trying to break through the bone. "So how was I?"

She got up and drew the bedsheet around her breasts. "You were a little out of control."

I felt a raw soreness in my right hand and looked down at it. There was a light red welt in the palm. Slowly I started to remember. This hand gripped the gun that killed Nick DiGregorio.

The rest of the night began to reassemble itself in my mind. Nicky's eyes opening wide. The heat coming off the barrel of the gun. Going back to the car with Richie. Getting a drink. Finding one drink wasn't enough; it took almost a pint of Chivas to calm down. That powerful feeling. That feeling of being powerful. To give or take a life. I'd felt like my dick was twelve inches long and I could fuck the earth with it. I flashed on taking Rosemary home from the club and balling her in every room of my house. My wife and kids weren't home.

I still wasn't sure if I'd acted like that because I wanted to lose myself and forget what I'd done. Or if I'd been maybe a little turned on by it. Just considering that possibility made me feel disgusted with myself all over again.

"You want a cup of coffee?" Rosemary was staring at me.

"Yeah, yeah, sure. The instant's on the kitchen counter."

She left the room, trailing the bedsheet behind her.

I stood naked and shivering with the sunlight coming through the blinds and my mother's eyes watching me from the black-and-white picture on the chest of drawers. Jesus stared down, exasperated, from the cross above the bed.

I wondered how long it would be before I was punished for what I'd done.

In the kitchen, I heard Rosemary putting the morning news on television and the clatter of pots and pans. I pulled on my boxers and went in to see what all the commotion was about.

"What have you got in that flour can?" she asked, pointing to the red canister on the counter. "Something weighs a ton in there. I was trying to move it and get at the coffeepot."

"Just don't move anything around too much." I watched the TV weather girl with glazed eyes. "My wife and kids will be coming back here soon."

"Where are they now, anyway?"

"I've had her over at her mother's awhile."

"Something smells like a cat in here," she murmured.

The light coming through the window above the kitchen

sink shifted, stripping shadows off the far wall. And all of a sudden, I was reminded why I had to kill Nicky. It was so my wife and children could come home and be safe.

Maybe I wasn't so bad after all. But then the phone rang. My heart gave two dull thumps and stopped. I was sure it was some relative of Nicky's promising to come get me.

But it turned out to be a friend of my daughter Rachel, looking for a play date.

"She's not here right now," I said, out of breath from sprinting across the room to pick it up. "Can I take a message?"

"Okay," said a little voice that could've belonged to a boy or a girl. But then he or she hung up.

I just stood there for a second, feeling the cold sweat on my neck and looking at Rosemary's long brown legs. How could I have brought her back here? What was the matter with me? She put one foot on top of the other and made a bow with her knees as she sipped her coffee and watched the news. She had beautiful thin ankles, not the swollen kind Carla had. This was who I should've married. But then I saw what she was watching on TV. There was a black-and-white mug shot of Nicky DiGregorio on the screen. Trying to look tough without a chin. The announcer was saying he'd been found dead under the Boardwalk last night.

"Did I tell you about this dream I had?" I said suddenly, just to distract Rosemary.

She turned and looked at me blankly.

"It was about my mother." I found myself in a panic, trying to come up with something. "She always used to have these weird dreams. Like she'd dream of teeth and say that meant something bad was going to happen. Or after my real father disappeared, she'd dream about him crying. And then she'd say, 'I don't know what your father wants from me. He doesn't have a grave for me to put flowers on.' "

"So what was your dream?" Rosemary tapped her bare foot on the scuffed linoleum floor.

"Oh. I don't know. I guess my mother was crying to me this time." I was just making it up. "What do you think it means?"

Rosemary looked down. "I think you need your floors swabbed more often."

We went back to the bedroom to get dressed so I could drive her home. I didn't know if she'd seen Nicky's picture on the TV. And if she had, I wasn't sure she'd remember he was the same guy who'd yelled at me that night we were in the car. I stuffed my muddy clothes into the back of the bathroom hamper. There was still sand in my socks from chasing Nick under the Boardwalk. I was so nervous putting on a new shirt that I could barely get the buttons through the holes.

"You had better watch it with that drinking," Rosemary said. "I don't think you're cut out for it."

Downstairs, I had trouble starting the car. The engine bucked and whined three times before it finally turned over. And then once we got into traffic, I heard a strange rattling in the glove compartment. It occurred to me that I might have stashed the gun there in a drunken stupor.

Rosemary took a cigarette out of her pocketbook and rolled down the passenger side window. "So why'd you kill him?"

Her voice was so calm I wasn't sure I'd heard her correctly at first. "Why'd I kill who?"

"That guy on television. The one they found under the Boardwalk."

"What makes you think I had anything to do with that?" I gripped the steering wheel and saw my knuckles turn white.

She lit her cigarette and blew smoke out the window. We were stuck behind a line of cars trying to make a left onto Atlantic Avenue.

"Do I look stupid?" she asked. "Because if I do, go ahead and tell me what you've been telling me. I saw you come into the club last night, roaring drunk, with your clothes all muddy. And I saw the way you acted when we got home. So do not tell me any more lies. Was this some kind of Mafia hit?"

"I'm not in the mob," I said dully.

"I know you're in the mob, like I know my daughter is having her breakfast now."

I checked the dashboard clock and saw it was ten after nine. I wondered what my own kids were doing.

"Well you're under a misapprehension."

"I know what a misapprehension is, Anthony," she said in the arch formal voice she used when she was mad. "And this is not one of them."

I was quiet for a few minutes as we finally inched into the left lane going north on Atlantic Avenue. One car after another was passing me on the right. But there wasn't enough room to switch over and join them.

"Listen," I said finally. "You asked me a question before, about whether I was in with the mob. And I told you the truth, that I wasn't."

Her lips rubbed together, like sticks about to start a campfire. "So how come that guy wound up dead after you had an argument with him?"

A spasm in my neck drew my head back. I put on my right hand signal trying to switch lanes again, but there still wasn't enough room. I was stuck. The signal made a tick-tock sound on the dashboard, like an old clock running down.

"All right," I said. "I'm going to tell you something and it's not something I ever talked about with anybody else."

I stopped and took a deep breath. "Some of the people in my family, they're, you know, they're in with the mob." My teeth were chattering just from talking about it. "And sometimes, they get into certain situations like, like the kind with this Nicky. The guy you saw on television. But that's not me. I'm not a killer."

I realized I was saying it as much for my benefit as for hers. Rosemary stared at the side of my head.

"You see, that's why I've been struggling so hard to get away from that life. There's more to me than that."

"I don't know if I should believe you," she said quietly.

"Then believe what you want," I snapped. "It's the truth. I know who I am."

She took a long drag on her cigarette and began to laugh softly to herself.

"What's so funny?"

"You know, when I was growing up I used to watch the Miss America Pageant with my mother and carry around the broomstick like it was a scepter. Really. I used to pretend that I was Miss New Jersey. I'd perform all the different parts for my mother in the living room. The talent competition. Miss Congeniality. The swimsuit bit. It was just me and her, pretending."

"I still don't get it. Why's that so amusing?"

"Because now I'm driving around with a married man whose father is one of the heads of the Mafia."

"He's not one of the heads." I pumped my foot up and down on the brake. "He's just an old guy who should retire to Florida. Besides, I already told you I'm trying to get beyond all that. I'm this close"—I showed her with my fingers—"to being able to raise all the money for this boxing thing."

Actually I wasn't any closer at all. That was the second weight pressing down on me today. I still owed fifty thousand dollars for training expenses and sanctioning fees, plus the ten thousand the shakedown artists at the boxing federation wanted.

Rosemary folded her arms and crossed her legs. "Well, if you're so anxious to get away from the mob, why are you going into a sleazy business like boxing?"

"Let me tell you something." I finally saw an opening between two cars on the right and slipped into it, following the flow of traffic downtown. "I can't afford to be a snob about where I came from or how I'm getting out of it." The wind ran through my hair. "And frankly, Rosemary, neither can you."

24

The station wagon pulled up in front of a brownish red-brick housing project on Virginia Avenue. Rosemary climbed out and kissed Anthony once on the lips.

"Call me," she said.

She walked across the sidewalk and in through the steel gate entrance. The project was four square buildings arranged around a vast open courtyard. Drag dealers lingered in doorways along the inner periphery, hidden from the street and passing police cars. When cops did bother stopping by, tenants rained garbage and beer cans down on them.

As Rosemary took out her keys and headed for her building on the north side, she passed a young black man by the sprinkler wearing a gray Georgetown T-shirt and a beeper on the waistband of his jeans.

"All right, I like them titties!" he called out.

She flipped him the finger and prayed for the day she could move out of this hellhole with her daughter. She entered her building, leaving the awful wavering heat of the afternoon outside. The elevator was broken again and she began to climb up through the steep, graffiti-smeared stairwell.

It was all a matter of what you were willing to accept, she reminded herself. If you could turn tricks for your junkie husband and wrestle other women to support your daughter, what was the big deal about going for a ride with a mob guy's son? After all, it wasn't like Anthony was really a killer. Hadn't he just got through telling her that? He was too gentle and solicitous to hurt anybody. The wild-man act last night was a fluke, she told herself. He was probably upset after hearing that someone else in his family had bumped off that chinless man.

It wasn't that she was one of these women who always made excuses for her man. She was just trying to get ahead and find a safe haven. She could do worse than to hitch her star to Anthony's wagon, she reasoned. So what if he was already married and would never be serious about her? She was getting something out of it too. If he did make this boxing promotion come off, maybe there'd be a little money in it for her. Perhaps she could go back to school and get a teacher's degree. Even if it was just to be a phys ed instructor, at least she could make a living with her clothes on. What was a little sacrifice and discomfort? It was all a matter of what you could endure to change your life.

Anyway, she was in control. That's what she reminded herself. Now all she had to do was ignore that flashing signal warning her that she'd always been attracted to men who were no good.

She paused on the second-floor landing to massage her sore back and listen to the sound of children laughing down the hall. Through the grimy stairwell window, she could see the gleaming casino towers rising above the low-slung tenements and shacks.

Someday all this would be a memory. And she'd be living out west with Kimmy. Somewhere like Seattle. She'd never been there, hadn't even seen that many pictures of it, but she liked the sound. Seattle. It sounded like "settle." She could picture herself in a quaint ranch-style house with Kimmy. With a Chrysler in the driveway and sprinklers and a wading pool in the backyard. And clean-scrubbed kindergarten classmates for Kimmy. Their mothers would invite Rosemary to after-school teas in bright solariums, where they'd sit and laugh and commiserate about the suffering the men in their lives put them through.

And with time, she might even forget being here in A.C. A woman's blue espadrille was lying sideways near the third-floor landing. A couple of steps up, there was a torn pair of panties and brownish-red splatter on the wall.

Rosemary continued on to the fifth floor and took off the red shoes Anthony had given her the week before. They were not quite the right size. Her feet were cut and swollen. No one would ever use them in a J.C. Penney catalog now.

She pulled open the steel door and walked down the long, narrow hallway to her apartment. Anthony. He was a funny mix. He could go from smooth to coarse in the time it took to strike a match. Last night had been an eye-opener. He'd started off drunk, but sweet and nice, the way he usually was. Sometimes he reminded her of a little boy who'd wandered off and gotten lost in the park. He haunted her. But then they went to bed and all of a sudden he caught fire. Not in a good way, either. There was something desperate and relentless about how he'd been making love. He could learn a thing or two from Terry, that fighter she'd slept with a month back. One of these days she'd have to sit Anthony down and tell him about that. She hoped he wouldn't be too hurt.

She put her key in the door and went into the apartment, feeling sweat mat down the front of her shirt. The TV was on in the living room. She peered around the corner and saw Kimmy sprawled out in front of the set with her butt in the air like a little hill. With the whitish drapes drawn, everything in the apartment looked old and broken. On the TV screen, a blond talk-show host was interviewing a panel of women who said they'd been sexually molested by ghosts. Four years old and she was watching this. Rosemary's mother sat at the kitchen table in the background, wearing her formal white blouse with the high collar and her stiff dark skirt. She was sewing a shirt for Kimmy and looking stern, though she had contrived this scene herself to demonstrate Rosemary's lack of fitness as a mother.

Not that she had any ideas or any alternatives to Rosemary working the two jobs, at the club and at the diner out on Route 30.

"You are late," her mother sighed.

Rosemary recognized the world-weary tone and the slowly raised eyebrows. Her mother glorying in her suffering again. Rosemary was starting to do it herself these days.

"So I'm late. So what else is new?"

Her whole life she'd either been too early or too late. When she'd developed tits two years too soon at Catholic school, the nuns acted as if puberty was God's swift and terrible judgment; she was destined to be a whore. After graduation, she'd traveled out to San Francisco ten years too late for the Summer of Love and hung around just long enough to miss most of the good entry-level jobs at the casinos back in Atlantic City.

"Your father, rest his soul, would take a belt to you if he saw how you were running around," Rosemary's mother said.

"Then I'm glad he's not here."

His timing was less than wonderful also. He'd come down from Brooklyn and worked like a dog for twenty years to open his own dress shop on Pacific Avenue. Two months later, Caesar's opened a shop in its hotel lobby across the street and wiped him out. He died two and a half years later, a month after his insurance ran out.

"There's no food in the house," her mother scolded her. "Your daughter is starving."

"I left a twenty for you in the petty-cash drawer." Rosemary stopped and rubbed her thigh, noticing there was a little bit less of it than there used to be. Maybe the Slim-Fast was helping. "You could've just taken Kimmy to the market around the corner."

"You know how I hate to leave the house in the morning."

Or the afternoon, or the evening, Rosemary thought. It was another one of those arguments. The kind that always started because there wasn't enough money. To buy new shoes for Kimmy. Or an air conditioner. Or more to the point, a hair appointment for her mother. Her mother was used to the finer things. She still saw herself as part of some distant pre-Castro Cuban aristocracy, entitled to rights and privileges not granted to the common people. She refused to recognize that all of them had slipped down life's greasy pole and there was no easy way up.

"Ma, I cannot do everything," Rosemary began to complain.

But before she could go any further, Kimmy ran up from behind her and threw a bear hug around her knees. Rosemary looked down and saw the little brown eyes shining and pleading with her not to leave again. She was turning into a clingy child, afraid to go to sleep with the lights off. And it was getting harder and harder to leave her at home with her mother. Rosemary had been having nightmares about the other baby lately. Melissa—a little, fragile, feminine name. Not strong enough to survive in this world. The name Kimmy sounded more compact, more robust.

"I waited all morning for you," Kimmy said in a practiced heartbreaker's voice. "You told me you would take me to see Lucy the elephant today."

Lucy was a rotting sixty-five-foot-tall plastic replica just to the south of the casinos. Who knew what a little girl saw in it? Maybe the elephant made her feel secure. Which was probably more than Rosemary did for her sometimes.

"I know I told you, sweetheart. But I have to go to work."

"But you promised."

Rosemary heard her mother clucking her tongue in disapproval. This was what she wanted. For Rosemary to see her own inadequacies in the cold light of day.

"I heard you didn't have breakfast yet," Rosemary said brightly, trying to change the subject.

Kimmy stuck out her lip and rubbed her stomach. "I'm hungry," she said, forgetting about the elephant.

Sometimes distraction was two-thirds of parenthood, Rosemary thought. "Maybe we can make two eggs in a special way. With the onions and peppers we have in the refrigerator."

Rosemary saw her mother flinch and knew she had not even noticed the egg carton on the side door. As a daughter of the aristocracy, her mother considered the task of actually cooking something to be beneath her. Cooking was for servants. No wonder they were always hungry.

"Come on," said Rosemary, hoisting her daughter onto a chair by the counter. "You can help me break the eggs."

"Yeeeaaa!" Kimmy threw her head back and gave Rosemary another of those helpless little gap-toothed smiles that made it seem worthwhile going on with the day.

As Rosemary turned to get the eggs from the refrigerator, she happened to glance out the window and see Anthony's station wagon still idling outside. He looked lost in thought behind the wheel, but from this high up it was hard to tell. Something had definitely been bothering him all morning. Strange boy.

When he finally pulled away, a blue Toyota was following him. She hoped he wasn't in any real trouble. She was just starting to really like him.

25

Teddy and Vin went for a walk around the block with Richie Amato that afternoon.

"You done good," said Teddy, keeping to the outside part of the sidewalk.

"Yeah, yeah," Richie mumbled, drawing his collar up over the scratches and gouges left by Nick's grandmother.

It was turning into an ash-gray day with threatening clouds overhead. Salt-corroded cars lined both sides of the street.

"Today might be a day you'll remember as maybe the greatest day of your life," said Teddy, swinging his right foot over the curb. "Because today, we can talk about bringing you officially into this thing of ours, that's been going for hundreds of years. You earned your button last night and I'm proud of you."

He squeezed one of Richie's shoulders. It was as hard as a coconut shell and as big as a football. But his face couldn't handle a smile.

"So tell me," said Teddy, "what was his last words?"

"I don't know."

"Whaddya mean, you don't know? You pushed the button on him, didn't you?"

Richie didn't dare look him in the eye. "Well if you wanna get like specific, Anthony did that part. I was tied up with the old bitch."

Vin began to cackle. "What'd I tell you, Ted? What'd I tell you? The kid's got stones."

A white Atlantic City Police Department car rolled by slowly and Teddy hushed both of them into silence. He stared after the car and wouldn't allow the others to speak until it was out of sight.

"You mean you let that mutt pull the trigger?" He glared at Richie.

"Either he was gonna do it or it wouldn't get done."

"Hey, Ted, you wanted Anthony to do a piece of work," Vin interrupted. "Why you getting upset about it?"

"I just want to make sure he'll keep his mouth shut." Teddy softened his tone. "We gotta be extra, extra, extra cautious from now on. There's gonna be surveillance all the time now. They do that whenever they got two in a row dead, like this Larry and Nicky, and nobody locked up for it."

"He'll keep his mouth shut," Vin assured him.

Teddy eyed the unmarked blue Chrysler across the street and turned his residual wrath on Richie. "Anthony get rid of the gun he used?"

"Yeah, I think so."

"Think so isn't good enough," said Teddy. "It's the little details that can fuck you up…Where'd you put the clothes from the last time?"

"Clothes?" Richie looked at Vin, like he needed an interpreter.

"Larry's clothes, you moron," Teddy said emphatically. "You got rid of them. Right? I don't want anybody finding any fucking carpet fibers from the club."

"Hey, what'd I tell you about calling me a moron, Ted?"

"You said you didn't like it. So I hope you're not still driving around with them clothes. There's a lot of guys got picked up for driving with an expired license and ended up doing time for murder."

"Well, my license ain't expired," said Richie as they turned the corner and came up on the Baltimore Grill, an elegant old restaurant with a red-and-white sign out front.

"Fine," said Teddy, patting his abdomen nervously, "then we ain't got nothing to worry about."

26

Patrolman Wendell Long never wanted to be part of a modern urban police department. In his mind's eye, he saw himself as a Clint Eastwood-style state trooper, with mirrored shades, knee-high boots, and a spotless uniform, riding up and down the curving highways of Southern California on his motorcycle. He imagined profiling typical offenders, pulling over young male blacks driving expensive European sports cars. He yearned to use a command voice and tell people to assume the position against their vehicles, so he could search and humiliate them. While others talked about how horrible the Rodney King videotape was, he secretly burned with envy for the LAPD.

Yet every day, he found himself touring the drab province of Atlantic City, looking for some hint of excitement and adventure. On this bleak Tuesday afternoon, he had to settle for pulling over the bull-necked, shaggy-haired

Italian-American male driving a navy Impala with a broken taillight down Indiana Avenue.

"What was I? Speeding?" said the Italian-American, who had a monobrow and the body of a steroid addict.

Patrolman Long was prepared to write a routine traffic summons. But when he asked for a driver's license and registration, the Italian-American first hesitated and then handed over two conflicting pieces of identification.

"Ah shit," said Richie Amato, making his second mistake of the day so far. "Gimme those papers back. I gave you the wrong ones."

"Would you get out of the car, please, sir?" asked Patrolman Long.

Stupidly, Richie tried to shove the unregistered .45 semiautomatic further under his seat. He only succeeded in giving the cop probable cause to search the car. Patrolman Long found not only the gun, but the trunkful of bloody clothes in back.

"All right," said Richie, trying to sound flip even as he swallowed hard and began sweating. "What would it take to make you forget what you just found?"

"Go ahead," said Patrolman Long, smiling and finally getting to use a phrase he'd only uttered in dreams. "Make my day."

Richie was brought down to the dungeon-like police holding facility, under the old Masonic Temple on Ventnor Avenue. Flies buzzed past dank stone walls, and the exposed pipes knocked overhead. He was put in a cell and handcuffed to a bench, facing a white alcoholic wifebeater and a ragged black man in a Malcolm X T-shirt. After a few minutes, the black man took out his penis and began to urinate on Richie's brand-new Tony Lama snakeskin boots.

"Hey! Hey!" Richie strained at his handcuffs and cried out to the guards at the nearby officers' station. "This guy's pissing on me!"

The black man finished soaking Richie's pant cuffs and put his penis away. "Not anymore I ain't."

The guards laughed and several hours passed while Richie waited for the paperwork to be filled out so he could call his lawyer. The trouble ahead of him seemed endless, sickening. The cops were sure to find the two outstanding warrants he had for armed robberies, and soon they would realize the bloody clothes in the back of his car belonged to Larry DiGregorio.

If by some chance he did manage to get out, Teddy would have him killed for sheer sloppiness.

A new pair of guards came on duty and for the next two hours they steadily ignored his requests to go to the bathroom. He felt his urinary tract backing up and his liver catching fire from the steroids. If it wasn't for the pain, he wouldn't even know where his liver was. At four o'clock, the black prisoner's penis appeared in his fly again, like the bird coming out of a cuckoo clock, and began to spray Richie's pants, as though part of a normal routine.

"Oh God!" Richie shouted. "Please help me!"

P.F. walked by a few minutes later.

"Detective," Richie called out to him. "Can you get me out of here? I need to call my lawyer."

"Not my case." P.F. shrugged and started to stroll away.

He'd almost forgotten the conversation he'd had with Sadowsky the F.B.I. agent. Fat chance he was going to implicate himself by volunteering information about Teddy. But here was Richie, begging him to stop and talk. "Wait a sec, wait, wait."

P.F. paused and half turned toward him.

"How long are they gonna keep me waiting?"

"I don't know," P.F. said out of the side of his mouth. "What are you in for?"

When Richie didn't respond, P.F. went by the officers' station to check the arrest report. The details about the gun and the bloody clothes brought an immediate smile to his face.

"Beautiful," he said, coming back to face Richie through the bars. "You must be very proud of yourself."

"I gotta talk to my lawyer," Richie insisted. "I didn't do nothin'."

"Well now, see, you're in a situation," said P.F.

"Whaddyamean?"

"You're a known O.C. associate with outstanding warrants, and you're driving around with that shit in your car. Brilliant. It must take you an hour and a half to watch *60 Minutes*."

"Fuck you," said Richie. "Get me my lawyer."

"And my lawyer too!" said the black prisoner, whom P.F. recognized as Stevie Ray Banks.

P.F. put his hands in his pockets and started to walk away again. "I'm sure they'll give you a call as soon as they get done with all the paperwork."

Stevie Ray took out his penis again.

"Love to Ted," P.F. said.

"Come on, come on!" said Richie, jiggling slightly. "Help me out here."

" 'Help me out, help me out.' That's the problem with our culture now. We live in a society of victims. Everyone feels aggrieved. 'Help me out, help me out.' Unbelievable. Like they expect something for nothing. My day, you had to work for a living."

"You gotta get me out of here."

His pathetic tone interested P.F., and he took a couple of steps back toward the cell. "Well, now, let's go back to the old merit system. What do you have that's worth bartering for? You didn't happen to be around the Boardwalk the other night, did you?"

"I never go to the Boardwalk. That's just for tourists."

"Ah well, that's too bad, isn't it. The way I figure it, you'll do a nickel and a dime at least in prison for what they found in the back of your car."

"No way, no day." Richie shook his head.

"Sentencing guidelines, Richie. They're a bitch. They're talking about bringing back the death penalty in some of these cases too. Seems a shame to waste your youth." His eyes flicked down to Richie's neck. "What happened? You cut yourself shaving?"

Richie nervously fingered the scabs and gouge marks on his throat. "I don't know anything about any Boardwalk."

"Oh, then you can't tell this friend of mine what happened to Nicky D."

Richie looked down at his damp boots and wrinkled his nose. "I don't know any Nicky."

"Then that's the biggest shame of them all," said P.F. "I know a guy over at the F.B.I. that might have been able to help you out. But since you don't know anything, there's no point. Right?"

Richie stiffened. "I'd have to talk to my lawyer first."

"Absolutely not," P.F. said. "We either talk about cooperating now or forget the whole thing. You call your lawyer and take your chances with Teddy back out on the street. And I bet he'd have some kind of wild hair up his ass with you getting locked up the way you did."

He felt good saying it. This was how it was before. When he was actually doing police work, instead of just coasting on bad memories. Call 'im a Pigfucker and wait for him to deny it.

"I'm not scared," claimed Richie.

"A fine thing too. A man can do a lot without fear in his life."

The other two prisoners eyed Richie hungrily, like cavemen watching a water buffalo. He rubbed his wrist where the handcuff had been digging into it.

"I wouldn't talk about everything, you know," he murmured to P.F. "And I want them to drop all these fuckin' charges with the car. I don't want anybody to know I been arrested again."

"That is none of my affair," said P.F. "I'm merely passing the message."

A half hour later P.F. was down the hall, calling Sadowsky's beeper number. The witness might or might not cooperate, he said when he got the callback. It was too early to tell. But he hoped Sadowsky would keep his word about talking him up to the casino people.

"You got it, old buddy," said the agent.

P.F. knew he was lying. But there was something exhilarating about getting involved again. He had to fight the urge to go tearing down the hall, bellowing about his prowess as a detective. The guards on duty would think he was some old fool. But there was no denying it. He was making a comeback. Porcine coitus was about to take place.

"Anything else I can do for you in the meantime, old buddy?" asked Sadowsky, sounding pleasingly anxious.

"Just lay off my job at the casino," said P.F., trying to tamp down his enthusiasm. "I want at least one thing I'm sure of."

27

I brought Carla and the kids home that night, but I was so nervous that every time the phone rang, I thought the police were going to come through the line, and arrest me in my kitchen for killing Nicky. So I had my heart in my hand when I picked up the receiver the next morning.

It turned out to be Elijah Barton's brother John B.

"I was talkin' to the man," he said, in the usual half-swallowed voice he used when the subject wasn't his brother the champion.

"Who?"

With John, "the man" could have meant Jesus Christ or the head of the World Boxing Federation.

"Mr. Suarez," he explained. "He say we better come up with that money soon or somebody else gonna have the chance to fight for the title."

I remembered the leathery skin and the paisley ascot. Suarez was the guy we'd met at the Doubloon conference a month back. The one who'd asked for the "contribution" in exchange for getting Elijah ranked in the top ten. Scumbag. Without that ranking, we had no shot at talking to Sam Wolkowitz the corporate guy and making our deal to fight on television. I saw my brave new world of spacious boardrooms and designer suits washing away with the nine o'clock tide.

"Tell that greaseball to go fuck himself." I picked up a bread knife from the kitchen counter.

For a second, I was taken aback. It was Vin's voice coming out of my mouth. I wondered if I'd become more like him by virtue of killing somebody. But I told myself it was just the pressure. I put down the bread knife and tried to sound more reasonable. "Exactly who does Mr. Suarez think is going to fight their guy, if not Elijah?"

"They been talkin' about Meldrick Norman," John B. mumbled. "He's ranked number four among the light heavyweights."

"But he's a nobody! He's a tomato can! He doesn't have a fifth the name recognition that Elijah has. How could they give him the shot instead of us?"

"It's that kind of business." John B.'s voice cracked

mournfully on the line. "You got to give in order to get."

I hung up on him and started pacing around. My whole world was falling in on me. My marriage was dead. I had a murder on my conscience. And my one chance to pull out of the tailspin and finally pay off that fat bastard Teddy was fading like the fog off the ocean. My mouth was dry. I opened the refrigerator to get something to drink, but all the orange juice was gone. I'd heard Carla go out the door a half hour before, saying she was going shopping. But I needed something now. There was a can of Budweiser on the door. Sensuous water beads slid down its side just like they do on a beer commercial.

Without even thinking, I opened it and took a swig. The clock above the sink said it was about nine-thirty in the morning. I'd never had a drink this early in the day before. Drinking when the sun was up was for cretins like Joey Snails, I thought. But the beer felt good going down my throat and cooling my belly. By the time I'd finished it, a kind of peace had settled over me for the first time since I'd killed Nicky. I wondered if this was why people became alcoholics. I closed my eyes and relaxed awhile, listening to the hum of the air conditioner in the living room. A 5400 BTU Carrier my father took off the back of a truck in Mays Landing. Maybe one day I'd be able to buy the family a new one with my own money.

I started to hear a high-pitched squeal. Sort of a piercing sound that went right through your eardrum and into your teeth. At first I thought it was the air conditioner. But then I realized the sound was coming from the back bedroom. Maybe someone had broken in through one of the windows. An F.B.I. man or a friend of Nicky's. I tried to remember if I had that gun in the house, the one I'd used on Nicky. But it was still locked away in the glove compartment of my car, waiting to be tossed off the Brigantine Bridge. My only weapon was the empty Budweiser can in my hand. I crushed it and got ready to grind it into someone's face.

But when I stepped into the bedroom doorway, all I saw was my son, Anthony Jr., sitting in front of the goddamn computer. Carla must have left him here, figuring I could look after him while she took Rachel shopping. The squealing sound was coming from Anthony's hearing aid. He had it turned up too loud again, and it was feeding back like a heavy metal guitar player's amplifier.

He looked up at me with those big brown eyes. "Dad-dee, I DEE-stroyed the world," he said. "Now I'm sad."

He was using that game, *Sim City*. The one where you play God, creating the economy, the environment, and everything else between heaven and earth. Except without his older sister around to control things, little Anthony usually got too excited and would let a rainstorm wash civilization away.

"I'm hun-GRY," he said with that overemphasis he had because of his hearing problem.

"Come into the kitchen, I'll get you some breakfast."

He padded in with me, holding my hand. It was a good feeling, being able to have my family home because Nicky was out of the way. But between the fight and Rosemary, I'd been so preoccupied lately, I'd barely noticed Anthony. So now I felt guilty for being a bad father.

"What do you want to eat?" I threw away my can and lifted him up to the cupboard. "Count Chocula or Trix?"

"The COUNT!"

"All right, the Count." I pushed aside the Trix box with the white rabbit on it. "Forget the rabbit."

"Screw the rab-BIT!"

I just looked at him for a second, realizing he must've heard talk like that from my wife or me. I decided it would be better not to say anything.

I put him down and mussed his hair. I had a feeling he actually wasn't that hungry; he probably just wanted to be with me. I put some milk in a bowl and gave him a spoon.

"Pour your own poison." I sat him down at the breakfast table and handed him the cereal box.

He filled the bowl to the brim with little brown balls and smiled at me gratefully. "Sugar puh-lease?"

"That's good," I said. "You say please and thanks. You get farther in this world being polite than you do being rude."

I saw him put his tablespoon in the sugar bowl and swing the heap unsteadily toward his cereal. His tongue was sticking out a little because he was concentrating so hard. He really was my son, I thought. Not just the way he looked like me, but the way he was so determined.

"D-ad," he said. "Why you sleep in a di-fferent room from Mommy now?"

"She snores too much."

He ate a couple of spoonfuls of his cereal and thought about it.

"There was some-THING else I wanted to ask you." He tilted his head a little to the side, like he was trying to figure out the right way to get the next question out. "Why are all Ninja Tur-TLES green?"

I reached over with a napkin and dabbed his mouth where the milk was leaking out. "I don't know," I said. "Don't ask too many questions. It might not be good for you."

The phone rang again but there was no one on the other end. I hung it up quickly, feeling a cold finger on the back of my neck. Anthony Jr. put a little more sugar on his cereal and ate a couple more spoonfuls, without taking his eyes off me.

"You know, I shouldn't have said that before," I told

him. "Ask me anything you want. It's good to be curious."

"O-KAY." He chomped loudly on his cereal. "Then why, why, why do we have to have egg-onomics?"

"You mean economics?"

He nodded slowly, giving me that wide-eyed expectant look. He was so smart sometimes. The only thing holding him back was that hearing problem. I wondered if there was some renegade gene in Teddy's family. Between his daughter Kathy being retarded and his son Charlie committing suicide, I thought there might be something wrong that Carla, as his niece, passed on to our Anthony.

My little boy carefully put his spoon down on the table and leaned forward so he could hear exactly what I was going to tell him. I loved him so much that it killed me to think he was going to have a hard time later in life. I knew we were going to have to send him to some kind of special school. And that would cost money. Money that I didn't have now. I had to keep going with this boxing business. I didn't want my Anthony to grow up thinking his old man was a failure, who couldn't provide for him.

"Economics is just a way of keeping score of who's up and who's down," I told him. "It changes all the time."

"Oh."

He watched his cereal and didn't say anything for a long time. I was sure he was going to ask me whether I was up or down. But instead he picked up his spoon and began eating again.

After three mouthfuls he stopped and looked me right in the eye. "Da-DDD, I just thought of something."

I knew he was about to give me a live report right from the bottom of his heart. There was no faking with this kid. He could devastate you with an innocent question or a frown. Maybe he was about to ask me if I was going to leave his mother. I got ready for him to let me have it with both barrels.

"What?" I asked.

He took a deep breath. "Maybe all Nin-ja Tur-TLES are green because they all want to be the same."

"Yeah, maybe," I said, feeling a bubble of relief rising in my stomach. "Probably makes life easier that way."

28

"Can I ask you-all something, Rich?" asked the tall F.B.I. agent named Wayne Sadowsky. "You a homosexual?"

"No, I'm, you know, I'm not like that." Richie Amato looked puzzled and hurt. "Why you say that?"

"Because we've been meeting in this here hotel room and jerking each other off for three weeks now. Right? That's what homosexuals do, ain't it?"

"I don't know," said Richie, kneading the thick pink bedspread with his fingers and sticking out his lower lip.

They were on the third floor of a Howard Johnson's motel in Absecon. Since getting arrested, Richie had been laying off the steroids and his body was beginning to steadily deflate like a great balloon losing air. He must have pissed away twelve pounds in the last week and a half. Folds of skin were hanging off his arms in places and there were touches of gray in his hair.

"Well, the way I see it, a real man wouldn't do what you're doing," said the agent. "A real man would make an agreement and stick to it. He wouldn't agree to cooperate and then try jerkin' another man off."

"I'm not jerking you off."

"Well you sure ain't telling me nothin' I don't already know," Sadowsky said sharply.

He leaned on a pillow at the foot of the bed and his pant cuff lifted, revealing a pale hairy calf and an elastic garter holding up his sock. The two large men were only about a yard apart but they were barely looking at each other. Something about the intimacy and silence of the room was embarrassing to Richie.

"You know," Sadowsky said. "It's just gonna get to the point where we'll say, 'Hey, man, this ol' dog won't hunt. This man said he would cooperate and now he ain't giving us anything. So forget the deal. Let's just go charge him and see what happens.' Is that what you want?"

"No." Richie crossed his legs and hung his head like a sullen teenager.

"You know the lab result came back and said that was Larry's blood on the clothes in the back of your car," Sadowsky reminded him.

Richie said nothing and hugged himself, rocking slightly back and forth on the bed.

"Let me tell you, Rich, I am not without compassion," said Sadowsky. "I understand how tough it can be for a bright young fella such as yourself. You-all grow up around wiseguys like Teddy and Vin all your life, and all you want to be is a made guy. I want to tell you, I know what it's like to have to give up on a dream. I wanted to be an all-state linebacker when I was growing up and then I got polio. They thought they'd wiped it out but somehow I done went and got it anyway. And I used to dream every night about gettin' on out of that wheelchair and kickin' the shit out of some skinny-ass quarterback in the end zone. Joe Montana. I'd sit on his face. Who-haa!"

He clapped his hands and grinned as he made the sound of impact. Richie almost jumped in surprise. But then the smile began to melt from Sadowsky's face. "Yeah," said the agent. "That was my dream. But when I woke up in the morning and saw I was still a gimp, it broke my heart all over again. So don't think I don't understand. I know what it's like to feel like you don't have any power to control what's going to happen."

Richie slowly raised his head and looked at him. "Well, if you know what I'm going through, why don't you just let me go?"

Sadowsky laughed and laughed. "Come on, Richard. Let's get serious," he said, slapping his knee. "Tell me what you-all know about who whacked Larry and his son Nicky."

29

In the two years I had at Temple University, I learned that everything comes in stages. There's death, with rage, denial, acceptance, and all that. Then there's wisdom, with satori and nirvana. But now I was finding there were different stages to desperation. Like hysteria, numbness, and oh-God-I-can't-believe-I-have-to-deal-with-this-asshole.

The asshole in this case was a loan shark named Danny Klein. A cruddy little guy in a blue running suit and glasses, who always smelled like the bottom of a birdcage. I'd arranged to meet him in a lounge just off the Golden Doubloon's casino floor.

He was reading a copy of the *Wall Street Journal* when I walked in, and he barely bothered lowering it as I sat down across the table from him.

"Y'know, they tell me there was a war going on a while back," he said. "Something about oil in the Middle East. The fuck do I care? I'm already fighting the war in here."

"What war is that, Danny?"

"The war for survival." He folded the paper in half and put it on the table. "I'm a degenerate compulsive gambler with a severe bipolar personality disorder and a drinking problem and here I'm lending money to people in the middle of a recession. So don't talk to me about war. I know war."

I noticed there was a white strip of adhesive tape holding together the center nosepiece of his broken glasses. He looked like a demented college professor who'd been thrown down the stairs a couple of times too many.

"What can I do you for?" he asked with a sniff and poke at the adhesive tape.

"I'm looking to borrow some money."

I didn't know any other way to begin. I'd stayed away from people like Danny Klein for most of my life. With the money I already owed Teddy, I had no business with loan sharks. But I was at that third stage of desperation.

"How much?" he asked.

"Sixty large."

He whistled and I could see his eyes swimming behind his glasses. "What're you gonna do with it? Run off and start a circus?"

"Never mind what I need it for. You'll get it back with your interest."

Danny's eyes narrowed. "See, I have a problem with anxiety management, and it gets worse when I hear 'don't worry about it, Danny. I'll get it back to you.' I already have a very strict regimen of pills I'm taking. Prozac, Valium, Lithium." He began taking out little orange prescription bottles and lining them up on the round table. "I'm trying to balance them out with my alcohol intake. And now you sit down and announce you want sixty thousand from me and won't tell me what it's for. Does that seem fair?"

"I'm sorry, Danny. I didn't mean to upset you."

But I wasn't going to tell him about the boxing promotion either. A lot of Danny's money came from people like Teddy and my father, and I didn't want Danny telling them what I needed it for. It was bad enough having to sink to these depths. But I didn't see any other way.

Danny rattled a highball glass with ice cubes in it and asked the waitress for a drink called Sex on the Beach. I just had a beer to settle my nerves. Another bad habit I was falling into.

"Anthony, let me tell you a little story," said Danny, suddenly sitting upright. "Did you know I used to be a millionaire?"

"No, I didn't."

"I used to be one of the top bookmakers in Philadelphia," he said, taking a pill at random from one of the bottles and gulping it down with the drink the waitress brought him. "Every Saturday, I had forty phones ringing with schmucks trying to bet on college football. It was like a disco, everybody mumbling, 'I gotta get down, gotta get down.' I hadda start working with another bookie, just so I could lay off some of the action. Ever see a job opening for a bookmaker? No. Because it's a great goddamn business, that's what it is."

"Look Danny," I started to say. "All that's very interesting, but I promise you'll get your points..."

He chopped me off with his hand. "Listen, shmendrick, I'm trying to teach you something." He paused, making sure he had my full attention. "I used to get into these manic phases where I would come down here to Atlantic City and gamble my brains out. I'd play blackjack, roulette, and baccarat, screw fifteen hookers, and then get so drunk I wouldn't remember any of it."

"I'm not borrowing money to gamble, Danny." I smiled.

"Wipe that goddamned smile off your face," he hissed. For a little guy Danny could be fierce. "I'm trying to tell you how I lost every cent I had and had to go borrow money from your father Vin and Teddy. Do you know what happened when I couldn't pay it off?"

The question hung in the air between us for a second, and I became aware of the bells ringing and change spilling on the casino floor.

"Your father held me down on the floor by the arms," said Danny, "and Larry DiGregorio spread my legs. And then Teddy came up and stomped up on my balls."

I felt my scrotum shrivel.

"Yeah, you don't know the half of it," Danny said bitterly. "I was in the hospital a month. They hadda amputate one of my balls because it got gangrenous." He leaned across the table and blew that parakeet breath of his right in my face. "So I wouldn't expect much in the way of mercy if I were you, Anthony. Not if you're thinking about missing a payment. Like I said, it's a war in here. And in a war people get hurt. Just ask Larry."

I started to stand up. "So are you going to lend me the money or what?"

"Yeah, I'll probably spot you some, seeing as you got a house and a cement truck as collateral," Danny said, scratching the back of his head furiously, like he had fleas. "But it's a large sum you're asking for. I wouldn't just go to one source to get it, like Teddy. I'm learning to diversify. Like in banking. It's an interesting parallel. The emphasis on paying off interest before the principal. I'll discuss it with you sometime."

"Well don't go telling Teddy or any of the others that I'm looking to borrow all this money."

If Teddy found out, he'd flatten my head the way he flattened Danny Klein's ball.

Danny smiled enigmatically. "I know the value of discretion, provided you hold up your end of the bargain."

"I will."

"That's good. Because I'd hate to tell Ted what you're up to." His smile faded.

I understood the consequences. I raised my glass for a

toast and he clinked it with one of his orange pill bottles.

"By the way," he said. "I knew your real father."

"Mike?"

"He was one of my best customers. Never bet with his head when he could bet over it."

"What do you mean?" I gripped the arm of the bamboo chair.

"I mean, he took a lot of chances," Danny explained. "He was always overextending himself. Driving a car he couldn't afford. Living in a house that was too big. Wearing clothes that put him in debt. Mind you, he was never late in paying me. That's the only *reason* I'd consider lending you the money."

I felt like Danny was fooling around with the cords to my heart. "So he was a good guy?"

"He was all right." Danny shrugged. At that moment, he looked like he could've been born shrugging. Like he came out and said, I'm here, Mom, now what am I supposed to do?

"You have any idea what happened to Mike?" I asked.

"Should I know?" Danny shrugged once more. "He was in the war and he got hurt. That happens sometimes when you take too many chances."

30

Mrs. Camille Marino was having another one of those dreams—the kind in which she was a Miss America contestant and her late son, Charlie, was the pageant host. She was about to kiss his cheek and accept the crown, when a voice from above asked where her husband was.

She opened her eyes slowly and saw a tall, square-headed F.B.I. agent kneeling at her bedside with a gun in his hand. He put a finger up to his mustache and indicated that he wanted her to be quiet. At least six other agents were standing by the open bedroom window with their guns drawn. Curtains flapped in the breeze.

"Just tell us where to find your husband, Mrs. Marino, and no one in your family will get hurt," said the agent beside her bed.

Camille tried to speak, but no sound left her throat. A scream was stuck in her chest. At this ungodly hour, she didn't know if she was more traumatized by the agents breaking into her house or losing Charlie again in the dream.

"Come on, Sadowsky, we got him!" called a voice from the other room.

All the agents went rushing into Teddy's adjoining bedroom. Camille struggled to her feet, found her pink robe and fuzzy slippers, and went in after them. Teddy was down on his knees at the foot of his sofa bed with his hands behind his head. He wore only a striped nightshirt, exposing his big white butt.

"What are you waiting for?" he snarled at Camille. "Call Burt Ryan."

She saw by the digital clock at his bedside that it was a quarter to six in the morning.

Kathy walked into the bedroom hanging on the arm of a muscular agent, like a lovesick teenager. She had no idea who these men were or what they were doing here, but she was lapping up the attention.

It was all too much for Camille. She sat down on the carpet and put her face in her hands. She heard the agents forcing Teddy into some street clothes as they slapped the handcuffs on him and read him his rights. From what she could understand, they were charging him with some kind of racketeering and tax evasion. She tried to shut out their voices. As far as she was concerned, her husband was in the linen business.

They yanked Teddy to his feet and started to haul him away. She went to the window and looked out. Birds were chirping. At least two dozen reporters and cameramen were gathered on the sidewalk. The TV vans were from as far away as Philadelphia. She turned her head and saw Teddy coming down the front steps. His hands were cuffed behind his back and he was surrounded by eight F.B.I. agents.

Kathy was already standing out by the model of the jockey on the porch, hopping up and down excitedly, like she was seeing her first Easter Parade.

The agents brought Teddy over to an unmarked blue Ford parked by the curb. The swarm of reporters followed as if drawn by magnetic force.

One of the agents put a hand on top of Teddy's head while another opened the car door. The reporters were murmuring as Teddy looked up and saw Camille watching him from the window.

His face looked dark and haggard. For the first time in years, she felt something for him. But it was only pity.

They forced his head down and shoved him into the car, slamming the door after him. Another agent ran around the front and got into the driver's seat. The cameramen and reporters closed in around the car windows, but Camille could see from the look on Teddy's face inside he had nothing to say. The car started suddenly and drove away. A couple of reporters made a halfhearted effort to run after it. Most dispersed to their cars and were gone within two minutes. But Kathy was still jumping up and down on the porch, waving and shouting, "Goodbye, Daddy, goodbye."

With nothing better to do, Camille wandered back into

her bedroom and found her sleep mask. The Valium bottle was still open by her bed. She considered taking one. Or two. Or three. Or why not twelve? But then who would take care of Kathy?

No. Relief wouldn't come so easily. She was stranded in this life, at least for a while.

She put the sleep mask back on and lay down again. And once more went looking for Charlie in her dreams.

31

With the sixty thousand dollars I borrowed from Danny Klein—at three percent interest, due every two weeks—I was finally able to pay for Elijah Barton's training expenses and sanctioning fees. Eddie Suarez from the boxing federation took his ten thousand with about as much grace as a parking attendant accepting a two-dollar tip. I swore at him under my breath, but we were on the road. And with Teddy getting arrested, I didn't have to worry about his interference for a few days.

The first thing John B. did was arrange a public workout at the Doubloon, to drum up press and show everyone Elijah was still in good shape.

But when Elijah walked into the Admiral's Ballroom that mid-August afternoon, I noticed his face looked a little more bloated and bovine than before.

"What's the matter with him?" I asked John B. as his brother slowly climbed through the velvet ropes of the ring they'd set up. "Has he been mainlining Häagen-Dazs or something?"

John tried to play it off. "No, no, man. That just the way he look when he's in training. He's already been sparring awhile. That's why his face get all puffed up."

Elijah began to walk in a circle within the ring, like a shaman priest trying to summon the spirit. He wore a long red robe with his name and the words "...Once and Future Champion" in white on the back. A red Everlast head guard covered most of his face like a mask. He shuffled a little as he walked, like a drunken sailor trying to cross the deck on a rainy night. I wondered if I'd made a mistake in borrowing all that money from Danny K.

But it was too late to back out. The sparring partners and trainers had already been paid off and now gamblers from downstairs were streaming in to take seats in the folding chairs around the makeshift ring.

"You sure he's not punch-drunk?" I asked John B. quietly.

"He just playin' possum."

The first of the young sparring partners climbed into the ring and the bell rang. Elijah shucked off his robe and started bouncing around. Rolls of fat jiggled at his sides. I found myself worrying he wouldn't make his weight for the fight.

"Sure he's not eating too much?" I asked John B., who sat next to me in the first row.

"It's all protein. Brain food. It go right to his head."

Elijah suddenly lunged forward and swatted his sparring partner with a quick right hand. He seemed more alert now that the bell had rung. The sparring partner danced away from him and bobbed his head from side to side. I noticed this kid was built the same as Terry Mulvehill, the current light heavyweight champ, who we'd be fighting in the fall. Same big head, wide shoulders, and narrow hips. I wondered if Elijah had the strength and stamina to keep up with someone half his age.

"Is he going to be able to defend himself come October?" I asked John.

"Look at his legs," John said proudly.

I looked at Elijah's legs. They were like tree trunks. The most powerfully developed part of his body by far. You could break a chainsaw on them.

"Legs like that, he won't never go down. They'll keep him standing all night." John elbowed me.

"Great," I mumbled. "It's just the rest of him that'll get destroyed."

But I had to admit Elijah was more than holding his own in the ring. He threw a fast jab and a cross combination and then backpedaled in a half-circle. The sparring partner staggered for a moment and had to steady himself against the ropes. It was like a scene from a Bruce Lee movie where the old Kung Fu master teaches his young charge some new tricks. Elijah took a run at the kid and clapped him with a right on the ear as he soared past him. The crowd, which had grown to about one hundred fifty people, laughed and began to applaud.

I started to relax and enjoy my surroundings. The glass chandeliers, the red damask curtains, the gold embroidered wainscoting along the walls. This was where I belonged. Not under some grubby Boardwalk, firing a gun. I fell into a daydream of what it would be like to run a place like this. Men in gray suits running up to ask my opinion about things I didn't really care about. People at the slot machines taking a break to shake my hand.

But then a side door opened and snapped me out of my reverie. In walked the reigning champ Terry Mulvehill with his father Terrence Sr., who was also his trainer, and a stocky bald white man wearing an expensive suit. Even sitting fifteen yards away, you could feel the heat coming off this Terry. He wore a bright red T-shirt that was straining at the seams, like the manufacturer had never intended for it to be filled with muscles this big. Dreadlocks fell over eyes that didn't move or widen. His whole presence was like a fist, with all the parts drawn together and clenched for the purpose of annihilating another man. I went back to being nervous about Elijah fighting him.

The white man at his side had a shaved head that gleamed like the tip of a missile. I made him for about fifty years old, but he was bursting with good health. He had the bull neck and rounded torso of a weight lifter and the bearing of a Roman senator. He wore the same double-breasted brown Armani suit that I'd coveted months before in *GQ* magazine. It grabbed him across the chest and seemed to declare, What a man this is!

"Who's that?" I whispered to John B.

"That Frank Diamond," he murmured. "He's the pro-moter for the fight."

"Why haven't we met him yet?"

"Oh, he'll go along with the other people we been dealing with…" But when John swallowed the rest of what he was saying, I knew we had trouble.

The bell rang, signaling the end of the round. Elijah went over to his corner and stood there breathing heavily. Terrence Mulvehill walked across the room to look up at him.

"Old man can't catch his breath," he said loudly.

Elijah ignored him and just stared straight ahead with his gloves resting on the top rope.

"I say old man fight like a old woman!" Terrence taunted him again, even louder this time.

There were scattered giggles in the crowd and then a long silence. Terrence put his hands on his hips and waited for Elijah to respond. You could hear the squeaking sound of people shifting uncomfortably in their seats. I looked over at John B., who had his head bowed. Finally Elijah spit out his mouthpiece and looked down at Terrence at ringside.

"Next time I appreciate if you call me by my proper name," he said slowly and deliberately.

"Kiss my black ass, motherfucker!" Terrence turned back to the spot near the side door where he'd been watching with Frank Diamond the promoter.

The bell rang and Elijah stuck his mouthpiece back in. I realized I was rooting for him in the way I rooted for Vin to get off the barroom floor after he was shot. Elijah walked right to the center of the ring, dropped his hands to his sides, and stood stock-still in front of his sparring partner. It was a defiant gesture, meant more for Terrence Mulvehill than his immediate opponent. Terrence smirked to show he wasn't impressed.

"C'mon, champ!" John B. shouted. "It's your show, E.! It's your show!"

Elijah threw a head fake, offering his chin, but his sparring partner didn't take advantage of the way he dropped his guard. So Elijah did the head fake again, almost as if he were teaching the kid a lesson. When he did it a third time, the kid hit him squarely on the jaw.

Elijah's mouthpiece flew out and he fell backwards into the ropes. The crowd gasped as the mouthpiece landed like a bloody grenade on the canvas. He turned halfway toward us, and through his headgear I could see his eyes rolling back in his head. If he wasn't actually knocked out, he was on his way to oblivion. My future was struggling on the ropes beside him.

"He all right, everything gonna be all right," John B. mumbled uselessly as he jumped to go help his brother.

"Old man oughta stay in the old man home," Terrence announced as he turned to leave with his promoter.

32

"Can I explain, Ted?" said the attorney named Burt Ryan. "A majority of these lawyers and judges are known as erudite, professorial, ah, 'egghead' types. They will not accept words in a brief to the effect, 'Go fuck yourself!' "

"So don't do our work then," said Teddy, leaning forward in the leather armchair. "Don't do my fuckin' work."

"No, I'll put it in." Burt took a shot of asthma spray. "That's not the problem. But the court won't accept it."

That was what was wrong with these fucking pansies, Teddy fumed. Why couldn't he have one of those sharp New Yorker lawyers like Gerry Shargel or Bruce Cutler? Someone who'd stand up and do battle with a judge. These soft-spoken types like Burt made him nervous. With their Scandinavian office furniture and their brusque young secretaries staring into computer screens.

And then there was Burt's manner. A weedy small man in a gray suit with constantly blinking eyes, he wasn't effeminate exactly, but something about his fey voice and precise little hand gestures made Teddy's anxiety level rise steadily like the line on a fever chart.

"Anyway," said Teddy. "Where the fuck were you the other day? They had me in lockup twelve hours before you bailed me out."

"I had other appointments." Burt twirled his index finger in a small arc.

"My ass. You were wearing goddamn jodhpurs, for fuck sake. What were you doing, playing polo?"

They were sitting in Burt's spacious office in Pleasantville, just a few miles outside Atlantic City. Sunlight

streamed in through the window and reflected off the top
of Burt's balding head, causing Teddy to squint when he
looked back at him.

"What I was doing is immaterial," said Burt, drawing
a line through the air. "What we need to focus on is the
case the prosecution is preparing. So far you've only been
charged with racketeering. But my sources at the U.S.
Attorney's office tell me there's a strong possibility they
might bring a superseding murder indictment."

Before Teddy could respond, Burt Ryan's phone purred
and his secretary told him he had Dave Kurtzman the casino owner on line one. Burt put up his hand to indicate
the call would take less than a minute.

"Yeah, yeah," he told the phone in a high, wheezy voice.
"No, that's not in your contract…No…No, Dave…Dave,
no…That's not an option…I'll get the doctor and tell
them to back down."

Teddy simmered in his seat, like a sorority girl waiting
for a date to show up. He felt that tender ache down in
his balls again. He was still getting up in the middle of
the night and finding he couldn't piss.

When Burt finally hung up the phone, he grimaced.
"Superseding murder indictment? Based on what?"

"Based on the two DiGregorio homicides." Burt took
another quick hit off his asthma spray. "Or so I'm told.
Do you have any idea what witnesses might be talking to
them about that?"

"No!" Teddy's cheeks leaped up toward his eyes. "That's
what I pay you to find out. I'm giving you three hundred
fifty dollars an hour."

The phone purred again and this time the secretary gave
the name of a prominent real estate developer. "Francis, I
thought I wasn't going to hear from you today…" Teddy
went back to stewing and reading the two neat piles of
documents parked at the edge of Burt's desk. His eyes

stopped on a request for proposal from Lenny Romano's firm, concerning repairs on the City Hall parking lot. The tender feeling in his groin returned.

He flashed an angry look, but Burt ignored him until he got off the phone.

"I didn't know about this contract," Teddy said sternly, as Burt placed the receiver back in its cradle. "Why didn't anybody tell me?"

Burt leaned forward and calmly took the document from Teddy. "I thought this had your approval," he said, looking it over. "Lenny's company is with you, isn't it? Are you going to tell me you don't know what's going on with your own companies?"

Teddy drummed his fingers on the leather armrests and blushed. "I know what's going on. I just didn't know you were handling the contract."

Burt seemed just ever so slightly annoyed. "Well, the other day I was over at the Doubloon casino, talking to my old college friend, Sam Wolkowitz, who's in the cable television industry. And he told me your friend Vin's son Anthony might be involved in managing a fighter named Barton, who might be on TV. But was I asked to be the lawyer representing the contract? No. Because that's done at your discretion, Ted. And I know everything he does must meet with your approval. So who am I to get upset?"

Teddy felt like he'd been picked up and thrown across the room. Lenny Romano getting the City Hall contract, Vin's son getting involved with the fights. And no one giving him a percentage. He didn't want to tell Burt he wasn't aware of these things, but he wasn't sure how to keep from screaming either. His insides squeezed together tightly, alerting him that he'd soon have to go pass blood into the toilet again. How could he control his crew if he couldn't control his own body?

He was having a bad moment. All the details of his life

that he'd carefully arranged like items in the composition book were scattering like autumn leaves. And suddenly the leaves were in his abdomen and his head, swirling around, chasing away certainties. If Vin's son wasn't giving him a percentage, who was? And if no one was giving him a percentage, what made him a boss? And if he wasn't a boss, what was he? He felt dizzy and sick, like he was about to vomit dry leaves on Burt's expensive Oriental rug.

The phone rang once more and Burt picked it up directly. "Oh hi, Bunny…No, no. That's all right." He giggled. "You will? Oh sto-o-op!" Burt's voice took a languid upper turn that made Teddy picture him wearing Hawaiian shirts and reading magazines about interior design.

"That's entirely up to you," said Burt, his hands performing a delicate arabesque through the air as he watched Teddy fidget from the corner of his eye. "You can get back to me anytime you want."

He hung up the phone and turned back to Teddy as if he hadn't missed a beat of their conversation.

"Jesus," said Teddy in a woozy daze. "I remember when Dixie Dalton was my lawyer, he hardly had any other clients. He'd never take a call when I was in his office."

"Well, you just can't afford to have me on retainer like that," Burt explained with a hand over his heart. "You're not my only client. Speaking of which, you're aware, are you not, that you already have an outstanding bill of twenty-seven thousand dollars you owe this office?"

"Madonna!" Teddy almost cried. "I had to put my fuckin' house up to make the two hundred fifty thousand dollars' bail. And now I got you squeezing me? Shit, Burt. Have a heart. It's fuckin' highway robbery."

"Coming from you, Ted, that's a compliment," said Burt, picking up the phone again.

33

It was two days after Elijah had got his clock cleaned at the public workout. I was driving little Anthony to his special hearing class when I heard that rattling sound again and realized the gun I'd used to kill Nicky was still in the glove compartment. I didn't know why I was taking so long to get rid of it. Maybe I wanted to get caught. We hit a bump in the road and I heard the gun slide toward the front of the compartment. Anthony Jr. looked down like he was thinking about opening it.

Just to distract him, I put on the radio. The first thing we heard after the weather was a sports report saying Meldrick Norman would be getting the title shot against Terrence Mulvehill in October, not Elijah. I almost drove off the road. I couldn't believe it. Here I was putting my balls on the line—literally, if you believed Danny Klein—and they were running a train over them.

For a few seconds, I don't know what I said or did. All I know is when I looked up, my little Anthony was cowering in the backseat. He looked like he'd seen one of those scary green monsters from his nightmares take the wheel.

"Hey, Anthony, take it easy." I reached back to pat his knee. "Daddy was just fooling."

But he shied away from my touch.

I dropped him off at the hearing school and drove right over to John B.'s house. He was crazed too, running around in his underwear with the cellular phone in his hand. He had no idea why his brother was out and Meldrick was in. Just the other day, the doctors had cleared Elijah to keep fighting, even after what had happened at the workout. For a second, I considered whether John might've just pocketed all the money without paying off the right people. But then he mentioned Elijah's name and got that reverent look in his eyes again, and I knew he'd never do anything to hurt his big brother. His only role in life was to be the loyal younger sibling, forever carrying Elijah's robe.

So we headed over to the Doubloon to try to find out what went wrong.

We found Frank Diamond the promoter standing in the lobby, talking to a bunch of reporters by the elevators. His shaved head looked newly waxed and buffed and his custom-made gabardine suit fit even more snugly around his barrel chest and broad shoulders.

"What's up?" John B. asked crisply.

"What's up?" Diamond turned to share a smile with the reporters like John was the butt of some joke he'd been telling. "Balloons are up. The sky is up. I'm up. If you had my stock portfolio, you would be too."

They all laughed. John B. gave him a stone face. For the first time I saw a resemblance between him and his brother.

"Say, my man. We got business to discuss."

"My man. My man." Frank Diamond did a Stepin Fetchit-y imitation of the way John talked. "Hey, John, it's thirty years since Martin Luther King, how come you're still talking like a Pullman train porter? Didn't you go to high school or anything?"

If I were John, I might have smacked him. But John just kept giving him that slow-burning look.

"We had a deal," he said to Diamond. "I already worked this out with the boxing federation and the cable TV people."

The reporters leaned in a little closer. Until a second ago, they'd been just casually bullshitting with Frank. Now they were getting ready to reach for their notebooks.

"Would you gentlemen excuse me a moment?" he asked the press.

They groaned a little and he took us into the 20,000 Leagues Under The Sea coffee shop just by the entrance. We sat at a table in the corner.

"We had a deal as of yesterday," said John B. "So why I gotta hear about Meldrick Norman today on the radio?"

"Yesterday I was lying, today I'm telling the truth," Frank Diamond explained carefully.

"But we had a handshake."

Frank Diamond sighed and asked the waitress to bring him a coffee with some Sweet'N Low. He rubbed the top of his bald head. Maybe he missed his hair.

"Listen, John," he said with the kind of measured impatience you'd have talking to a senile grandparent. "I am going to make it very simple for you. Your brother isn't worth as much to me as Meldrick Norman."

He sat back and fixed the silk polka-dotted handkerchief in his breast pocket. He might as well have been licking our blood off a butcher knife.

"I don't understand," I said. "We've already paid the sanctioning fees and made our arrangements with the boxing federation people. Why do you get final say to knock it all down?"

"Because I am the promoter." Frank flicked his hand through the air haughtily. "You've been dealing with the stage managers. I own the actors. Right now I have the champion, Terry Mulvehill, under contract. Anyone who fights him has to give me options on their next six fights. Now, Meldrick Norman is twenty-eight years old and relatively drug-free, as far as I know. So if he happens to knock my guy out, I've still got the champion another two or three years. Understand? Meldrick Norman becomes my fighter."

I nodded. It was a daisy-chain operation. My father and Teddy would've been impressed. No matter who won, Frank remained the promoter, entitling him to revenues from the TV rights and ticket sales.

He poured half a packet of Sweet'N Low into his coffee and then folded the rest of the packet in half and left it next to his cup. Fish designs swam around the dark blue border of his saucer. To me they looked like sharks.

"Now, I like your brother, but he is an old over-the-hill warhorse," he told John. "And if by some chance he managed to throw a lucky punch and knock my guy out, what would I be left with? An old man ready to retire."

"But we had a handshake with the boxing federation," John B. insisted.

"Not worth the paper it isn't written on," Frank said, stirring in the powder with the end of his spoon.

He rubbed the top of his head again. And smiled.

I felt my heart sinking. I'd borrowed sixty thousand dollars from Danny Klein and most of it was already spent on fees and expenses. I had no way to pay it back. Which meant Danny would be sure to tell my father and Teddy. I felt my balls retracting into some cavity within my body.

Frank sat back and sipped his coffee. His eyes scanned the rest of the green-and-red coffee shop, like he was searching for someone else to fleece. The late-afternoon crowd was starting to thin out. I wondered if the casino deliberately made the food unpalatable here so people would spend less time eating and more time gambling.

I put up the best argument I could make, spur-of-the-moment. "Don't you think you're being kind of short-sighted? I mean, Elijah Barton's a name with worldwide recognition. No one's heard of Meldrick Norman."

Frank Diamond wrinkled his brow. "Excuse me, but who are you anyway?"

"This is my partner, Mr. Russo." John B. lowered his

eyes and swallowed his words again. In his mind, he was already flat on his back painting boats again.

Frank Diamond gave him a long look, like John B. had just let his Rottweiler shit on his putting green.

"Well, Mr. Russo, let me explain something to you," he said. "Elijah Barton couldn't draw flies to a dump."

I started to interrupt, but he held up his hand.

"I'm not running a nostalgia business," he said, thrusting out a jaw so big you could have boiled coffee in it. "I am an attorney and a fight promoter. I have a fiduciary responsibility to go out there and try to make the best deal. As it stands, we're barely going to sell out the seats in the arena, but that's okay. The casino will make its money back at the tables. I am not, however, going to associate my good name with a third-rate production."

It was a little bit like talking to Teddy. Except instead of eating the pancakes off my plate, he was just tasting them and spitting them back in my face.

Frank ran his hand over his smooth scalp once more. He didn't miss his hair. He was jerking off his head because putting us down felt so good.

"People all over the world love my brother!" John B. protested.

"He couldn't draw flies," Frank Diamond repeated slowly with a level stare. "The sooner you understand that, the better off we'll all be. Especially your brother. It doesn't do a man his age any good getting himself hurt in the ring. We all saw what happened at the workout the other day."

My head was spinning. I couldn't imagine what Teddy would do to me when he found out I'd borrowed another sixty thousand on top of the amount I owed him. Stomping on my balls wouldn't satisfy him. He'd probably want to pour battery acid on them.

I wanted to fall on my knees and beg Frank Diamond

for mercy. But Vin had taught me there were limits to what a real man would do. And a real man would never debase himself in front of another.

So I reached over to grab Frank's wrist. "Promises were made to us."

Frank swatted my hand away. "You know, you people are too much. You live in this dreamworld where somehow everything's going to come true and work out if you wish hard enough."

I was about to jab a finger in his face and warn him not to talk to us like that, but instead I knocked over my water glass and broke it.

Frank Diamond flapped his hands dismissively, like he'd had enough of this tomfoolery. "Maybe it's too much sun or too much saltwater taffy. The rest of the business world's not like Atlantic City. One day you have to wake up and face the reality that what you've got isn't worth anything to anybody else."

"You oughta watch it," I said, as my lap got soaked and my future sailed over the cliff like a junked car. "One day you might just need the people you're stepping on."

"When I need something I call room service," Frank Diamond said as he got up to leave. "Otherwise, I don't want to be disturbed."

34

Teddy sat on an examination table. Dr. Josephson, a thin, wiry-haired urologist, adjusted his glasses and looked at his chart.

"I see you've already had a checkup, so this is just another step in the process," he said. "I notice Dr. Lawrence examined you. We went to med school together." He smiled.

Another bloodsucking parasite, Teddy thought. Doctors and lawyers. Burt Ryan estimated his legal bills would be well into six figures by the end of the year. And who knew how much this clown was going to charge? They were already down to under thirty-seven thousand dollars in the coffers.

"I'm going to give you a prostate exam," said the doctor. "You've had one of these before, haven't you?"

Teddy shook his head nervously. He'd avoided going to the doctor for years, as much out of superstition as frugality. If they didn't find anything wrong, there wouldn't be anything wrong. But since that little breakdown the other day in Burt Ryan's office, he'd realized he couldn't put off the visit any longer.

The doctor took a deep breath and slipped on a rubber glove. "Please lower your pants and lie on your side."

Teddy inched away from him. "What're you gonna do?"

"It's a routine digital exam."

"You're gonna put a finger in my ass?"

The doctor opened a jar of Vaseline. "I can assure you there's nothing unusual about it."

Teddy couldn't believe his ears. He'd once had a man beaten unconscious with a crowbar for making fun of his weight, and now he had to let this creep stick a finger up his butt. It was like being back in reform school. The things the other boys would do to him in the showers. Uncle Benoit in his first foster home. A little bit of that clammy, weak feeling spread down to his knees. For years, the extra weight had been like a layer of insulation, protecting him from the pain and humiliation. But here was someone trying to get inside him again.

He closed his eyes and bit the interior wall of his mouth. What was this world coming to?

35

The sky had never seemed so low and the Atlantic Ocean had never looked so cold. I was standing next to Rosemary on the Boardwalk, watching the parade before the Miss America Pageant.

"This is it," I said. "My life is over. They're going to cut my heart out and throw it in the ocean."

"Can't you get your money back?"

"It's already spent."

With Frank Diamond kicking us out of the fight, I now owed Teddy over a hundred thousand dollars and had no way to pay it back.

"Maybe you could sue the promoter," Rosemary said. "Breach of contract."

"By the time the lawyers got through, my corpse would be rotting."

Miss Virginia rode by in a red convertible, kicking a leg out of her blue satin gown, so the crowd could see the whole of her thigh. Rosemary's daughter Kimmy ran up and down in front of the spectator seats on the other side of the Boardwalk. I half wished the police would ride up and arrest me for killing Nicky, to spare me the agony of what would happen next.

"You know, Terry Mulvehill came by the club again the other night," Rosemary said.

I found myself wincing. "Yeah? What'd he want?"

"The usual. Go back to his hotel, screw our brains out, get high on cocaine."

Just the words made my stomach hurt. "So what'd you tell him?"

"I told him I didn't want to do that. I'm with you."

The back of my neck was burning. "You know, I ought to tell those boxing commission people he gets high. They'd probably take the title away from him."

"So why don't you?" She looked through her handbag for her daughter's sunblock.

"Who'd believe me?"

A dozen men dressed as turkeys walked by strumming "You're a Grand Old Flag" on banjos.

"It just makes me so mad." Rosemary rubbed her hands together and pulled on her fingers. "Maybe if I went up there and got high with him, they'd believe me," she said casually, as if she was talking about renting a car. "They have those tests to prove it, you know."

I just looked at her. "I couldn't ask you to do that. That'd be like making you a whore again."

She took a deep breath and put on a pair of sunglasses. "Look, there's something I have to tell you."

"What?"

"I want to have everything straight between us." She peered around, looking for her daughter, and then turned back to me. "That ship has already sailed. I've been with him before."

She might as well have cracked me across the face with a baseball bat.

"When was this? Why didn't you tell me?"

"I didn't want you to get the wrong idea." She tried waving Kimmy over, but the little girl was having too much fun dancing up and down in front of the grandstand. "It was a long time ago. Before I met you. Back when I was turning tricks."

"So you'd go back up there now?"

The corners of her mouth turned down as she began to think about it seriously. "I don't know...I was just talking before...I really just wanted to get it off my chest about

Terry and me, because we're starting to get close..."

"You know, it's not a bad idea," I interrupted.

Now she was frowning. She hadn't really thought I'd take her up on her offer, but she didn't understand how truly desperate I was. I'd been lied to, betrayed, and hustled by everyone I knew, including her, it seemed. I was in a corner and I needed to get out.

Miss Iowa drove by in a red Ford, followed by a man dressed as a frankfurter.

"I know somewhere I could score some coke," I said.

Her sunglasses hid her eyes, but her hands were still torturing each other. "Oh, I don't know, Anthony," she said in a squeamish voice. "The more I think about it, the more it doesn't seem right. We're talking about blackmail here."

"No, we're talking about people who broke an agreement with me three weeks before a fight and put my neck on the chopping block. Literally."

"So you want me to sleep with him again?"

The old guy wearing a Budweiser hat in the deck chair next to us looked up, realizing this was getting to be a pretty unusual conversation.

"Keep your voice down. I'm not saying you have to sleep with him. I'm just saying you could drop by and see what he's up to. That doesn't require you going to bed with him, does it?"

She rolled her eyes, as if to say, "Oh Anthony, how could you be so naive?" But I wasn't being naive. I knew what I was asking. I was just trying to sugarcoat it.

With each thing I'd done in the last few weeks, I was taking another step away from the person I wanted to be. It was as if by breaking faith with Carla, I'd broken through my own skin. Killing Nicky, borrowing money from Danny Klein, and pimping my girlfriend were the secondary infections. Now I was sick and I didn't know how to get better.

"You know what it would require," she said with her mouth drawn tight. "Is that what you're about, Anthony?"

"What?"

"Being a shakedown artist. Like your father. You want me to go by there and get him to do some blow with me, so you can blackmail him with a drug test and get your fighter back in the ring. It stinks, Anthony. And you know what really stinks about it? You always say you're not going to be like the people in your family, and here you are, pulling the exact same kind of scam."

"I didn't make the world the way it is," I said. "I take it the way I find it. All I want is for them to keep to their agreement to fight Elijah. This is the only way I know to make them do it. If my father had been a used car salesman, maybe I'd know how to sell cars."

"And that is bullshit!" Rosemary said vehemently, kicking the railing. "You are responsible for everything you say and do in this life. You can try to make all the excuses in the world, but the truth is no one else can make you live in the gutter if you don't want to."

"Well, maybe that's where I belong."

She clamped her mouth shut and steam seemed to rise from the top of her head. Miss Nevada drove by in a Cadillac, coyly flashing a giant set of playing cards.

"At least think about it," I said.

36

Rosemary stood at the boardwalk railing, watching Anthony play with her daughter in the wash and drain of the surf.

She felt nothing.

The Miss America Parade had been over for an hour

or so, but there was still a beautiful day going on, probably the last one like it for the summer. With the sun
casting a bright, clarifying light on everything below.

But Rosemary didn't care about that either.

Anthony picked up Kimmy and held her over his head
so their faces were just a foot apart. She laughed like a little homicidal maniac and Anthony kissed her on the nose.

How could he be so good with her kid one minute and
ask her to do this terrible thing the next? What kind of
man was he? After all the time they'd spent together, she
still couldn't quite get a handle on him.

And then there was the matter of that guy Nicky who'd
turned up dead under the Boardwalk. But she'd made a
definite decision not to think about that anymore and she
had to stick to it.

One of those old wicker rolling chairs went by behind
her and a voice with an Irish accent asked if she wanted a
ride. She didn't bother answering.

Anthony had Kimmy by the ankles and was swinging
her around like she was a propeller. She screamed with
glee. This would be a day she'd remember for years, especially if they bought her some saltwater taffy later. Her
own father never took her out and played with her like
this. Just looking at Anthony, you'd think he'd be the perfect stepfather.

Rosemary felt as though she was watching the whole
scene from somewhere very far away. It was the same way
she felt sometimes when she used to dance on top of bars.
Like her body wasn't really her body. It was just a thing she
could rent out for other people to look at awhile.

Maybe she could do this thing she was talking about
with Anthony.

Someone with a bullhorn nearby was announcing that
tickets were still available for the Miss America finals at
the Convention Center tonight. Miss America. They took

these girls from all over the country, they made them up like dolls, and they brought them here. To hold their contest and lengthen the summer season. They brought them from Nebraska, Iowa, Wisconsin, and a million other places she'd probably never go as long as she lived. Girls who were young like she used to be. Who didn't make all the wrong decisions. Who didn't drop out. Who didn't marry junkies. Who didn't end up supporting their husbands' habits in the backseats of Hondas. Who didn't live in housing projects. Who didn't have a kid to look after by themselves. They trained, they smiled, they gave speeches about how they wanted to help others less fortunate. They performed in the talent competitions, they gave interviews, and they modeled elegant evening wear. And in the end, they used their bodies to get what they wanted. That was the deal they made with themselves.

So who were they or anybody else to sit in judgment on her?

Anthony caught Kimmy in his arms and hugged her as the little waves lapped around his thin white ankles.

Rosemary came down the Boardwalk steps and walked across the beach toward them. She took off her shoes and hard cracked shells in the sand cut into the soles of her feet. Kimmy was looking over Anthony's shoulder, waving and smiling with the gap in her teeth showing.

"Hi, Mommy!"

Maybe in the end she wouldn't remember any of this. Maybe it was just another day of being four and seeing the boats on the water. And the other children with pails and shovels building dribble castles in the sand. And in a little while, she'd have front teeth and forget everything that happened this afternoon. Maybe by then they'd be in Seattle with the sprinklers and the wading pool in the backyard.

So what did it matter what you did at any given moment

or any given hour in your life? Just as long as you got by and went on to the next thing.

Anthony turned to face Rosemary, with Kimmy still hanging over his shoulder, looking the other way.

"So what do you think?"

"I don't know, Anthony. The whole thing gives me a very bad feeling. But if I go ahead and do it, I want half of whatever you end up making from the fight."

It was just another deal she was making with herself. To get something, you had to give up something. The only question was, how did you live with yourself afterwards?

"Good." Anthony smiled. "I'm glad you came to a decision right away. Life's too short."

"Yes, that's true," said Rosemary. "And I'm not too thrilled about it either."

37

Teddy sat in Dr. Josephson's office after the exam, staring at the edge of the brown oak desk. He felt vaguely ashamed about what the doctor had done to him.

"Mr. Marino, are you a man who can handle bad news?"

"That's my trade," said Teddy.

"Then let me be straight with you. I did find a nodule during the examination. And I think we need to proceed with the tests to determine whether you have prostate cancer."

The words barely registered with Teddy. They were just pebbles falling in a deep well. He stared directly at the doctor, waiting for correction or clarification.

"I see no reason to wait," said the doctor. "So I'd like to schedule you for a PSA, an ultrasound, and—if it's necessary—a biopsy within the next week or so."

Teddy blinked. "What's a PSA?"

The doctor leaned back in his leather chair and shrugged. "It's a blood test."

"And what about that biopsy?"

"Well, hopefully it won't be needed. It's just to determine whether you have a malignancy."

Teddy stiffened, feeling the words come closer and closer to his heart. The pebbles in the well turned into huge boulders, hurtling down. "And how do you do it?"

"Do you really want to know at this stage?"

"I'm telling you, be straight with me!" Teddy demanded, anxiety finally beginning to get the better of him.

"We usually go in through the rectum with an eighteen- to twenty-four-inch needle," the doctor said reluctantly.

Teddy's eyes began to water and the floor began to swim under his feet. His head felt light and he started to list heavily sideways, tipping over his chair.

He hit the floor before the doctor could say he hoped surgery wouldn't be necessary.

38

Rosemary came out of the bathroom wearing a black rayon teddy.

"I'm sorry I took so long," she said, "but I'm feeling kind of shy."

Terrence Mulvehill was still lying on the bed waiting for her. He was a powerfully built young man, standing five foot ten, weighing 170 pounds. Muscles wrapped around his arms like steel cables and stretched across his chest like dark armor. He turned his body and casually threw back the sheet, as though he was used to having his physique studied. Thick dreadlocks fell over his eyes.

"Listen, like, I really wanna fuck you. You know?"

"I know, but I'm all nervous."

"Can I tell you something?" he said in a high, delicate voice. "I ain't been out in about a month. I stopped trying to fuck anybody. Now when I go out to a club I gotta have three bodyguards around me all the time to keep the women away. Because you never know when someone's gonna like sleep with you and then say it was rape. Right? There's a lot of bitches and hoes out there."

"Yeah, that's for sure." Rosemary sat on a pink chair in the corner of the room and looked a little pale.

"Like the other night, right, I went out to this club in New York. The Palladium. Right? I'm dancing with this girl and she's beautiful, you know. The ass was like right on time and she had the kinda titties you see in them magazines. Right? So just when I'm about to ask her to come home with me so I can make it with her, my body-guard Amal comes up and says, 'Yo, Terry, that's a guy.' I'm like, 'Get the fuck outa here.' And he says, 'No, man, that's Jack Pearson. I went to school with him at De Witt Clinton.'"

"No shit," said Rosemary.

"No shit."

Terrence sat up and the covers fell back from his erection. "So then like I see this other girl and I look at her a long time to make sure it's a girl. Right?" He rested the side of his face on his hand. "She's four foot eleven and she got tiny little hands, so now I'm sure this is like a female. So Amal goes up and he starts talking to her, man. And I'm just like hanging back, waiting for him to bring her over. I'm dancing to Bobby Brown and just hanging."

He closed his eyes and twitched his shoulders, savoring the memory of the beat.

"But then I look up and Amal's got his arm around this girl. So I'm like, 'Yo, Amal. What's up with this shit? What am I payin' you for, man? I ain't payin' you to hang around flirting with girls.' I was disgusted. I was really disgusted, man. I walked right out and went to my car. My brand-new Porsche, right. And some like homeless guy is scratching his name on the side with a rusty key."

"Oh no." Rosemary started to laugh.

He went on, "I'm like, 'What the fuck are you doing, man?' " he asked in appalled falsetto. "And he's like, 'This is Terry Mulvehill's car.' I'm like 'Fuck, I am Terry Mulvehill. Stop writing on my damn car.' "

He shook his head, mortified. "Damn," he said. "I don't never have fun no more. It's got so I don't trust no one. I'd rather be by myself."

He touched his erection again and became very still. To Rosemary, he seemed like a confused child trapped inside a warrior's body.

"That's all right," Terrence said, rolling over on his side. "I don't mind being alone. I just close the curtains and stay in bed all day. Only time I get out is to train."

Rosemary crossed her legs and lit a cigarette. The tinfoil packet of cocaine was on the ivory-colored bureau next to her. "I read that once," she said. "I read how when you're an athlete you're not supposed to sleep with anybody the night before."

"Man, that's bullshit," Terrence told her, putting both hands behind his head and doing half a sit-up. The muscles in his stomach bulged like oranges packed tightly into a crate. "When I was married last year, I fucked before every fight I had and I knocked every one of them suckers out. That don't have nothing to do with it. It's just they all bitches, man. Every one of them. Even my mother. They just after the money. My mother didn't even call me 'til I got the title. My father brought me up and taught me how to fight. He taught me everything I know about women. And I love and respect the man for it.

Otherwise them bitches would have all my money by now."

"You always have to watch yourself," said Rosemary.

In the mirror across the room, she saw herself swinging one leg over the other with the cigarette burning down in her hand. His erection never wavered, she noticed. Men were all the same. You'd have to strap a stick of dynamite to it to truly get their attention.

"That's why when you called, I say 'come on up.' " He smiled eagerly, "You ain't gonna charge me, right?"

"Nope, this one's a free ride," she said in a tired voice.

"Yeah, yeah, see. And I know you like being with me just to be with me. Right? Like you like me 'cause you a natural freak. Right? You don't want nothing from me. You just like to fuck me."

He was so sincere, so anxious to be liked, it was almost painful to listen. She caught sight of herself in the mirror again, guiltily tapping out her cigarette in the ashtray.

"See, that's why I let you up, when you called before," said Terrence. "Because I know I can trust you. And we just gonna hang and have a good time. Right?"

She forced herself to smile. "We're gonna do the do, Terry."

"Yeah, yeah. 'Cause otherwise I think I'd just rather sit by myself in the dark."

He looked down at his penis sorrowfully as though it were a wounded pet.

"That's kind of depressing."

"Yeah, it do get lonely sometimes," Terrence said. "I get to feeling so bad, I think I never find no one wants to be with me. Like sometimes I think I'd rather be dead. Just the other night, you know, I was standing right out on that balcony over there, thinking what it'd be like if I threw myself off."

He stared at the window ten feet across the room, as if

he was still considering jumping. Then he lowered his eyes and balled up part of the bedsheet in his fist. His left knee came up protectively in front of his groin.

"But then you called," he said. "And things got much more better."

He smiled and his gold incisors flashed at her. "Anybody ever tell you, you got like beautiful eyes?"

"Gee, I, uh, yeah, I guess so."

"Well like don't tell anybody I said that to you, 'cause they might like think I'm gettin' soft. I'm supposed to be the Monster, you know."

She forced another smile as she picked up the tinfoil packet from the bureau top. "I like you too, Terry."

"So can we like do it now?"

"I don't know," she said. "I'm still kinda nervous. You sure you won't get high with me first?"

39

"You believe this?" said Teddy.

He sat on a bed in the Atlantic City Medical Center a few days later, wearing a large white hospital gown with blue polka dots on it. An IV needle was stuck in his right arm and a catheter tube ran under the covers into the head of his penis. He regarded both of them miserably.

"Prostate cancer," he said.

"I thought it was your stomach," said Vin, sitting by the bedside.

"They still don't know what's the matter there. I got that cough too. Every fucking thing is breaking down at once. That's why they wanted to operate right away."

Teddy held his mouth shut, as if he wasn't sure what to do with all the bile he'd accumulated inside. An elderly man's voice groaned behind the beige canvas curtain that divided the room. Vin turned on the radio on Ted's night table to drown out any potential wiretaps.

"Vin, I got one question for you," Teddy said with a loud racking cough. "Where are we going?"

"I know."

"I'm serious." Teddy coughed again and looked at the radio playing "Greensleeves." "A couple of days after I got pinched, I had a sit-down with my lawyer Burt Ryan. He tells me about this contract for fixing the City Hall parking lot. Turns out Lenny Romano got it. You know, Nat the bookmaker's son, from over Margate. 'Why's that?' I ask. 'Oh,' says Burt. 'I thought he had your permission.' Like I'm an asshole and I don't know what's going on. He says he thought Lenny was a 'friend of ours.' *Minchia!* Where are we going here? What am I gonna do, act like I don't know what's going on in my own *borgata?*"

"Of course," Vin assured him, running the Ace comb once through his hair.

"Plus, I got Danny Klein borrowing thirty large from me and not telling me who it's for. You see, Vin, it's no good. We can't have that. We can't have a circus. All these little factions are running around trying to conquer the market under our flag. It all comes down to the same thing. Where are we going? I mean, not for nothing, but your own son Anthony…You know I don't like Anthony. I love him. And he loves me. I know that. Every time he sees me, he says, 'Teddy, I only got one love, you.' "

"Right," said Vin, though he didn't look too sure.

"So why do I have to hear from Burt that Anthony's getting involved with some fight at the Doubloon this fall?"

"I don't know nothing about that!" Vin looked stricken. "Burt musta got his facts wrong. Anthony wouldn't get involved with anything serious without clearing it with us."

"Vin, I given that kid every chance in the world. I bankrolled his entire life. If I find out he's been making money without putting anything in the elbow…"

Vin jumped up. "It's not true! Anthony's pledged the first dollar he makes to you. But the kid's broke. You seen how he's living."

"Vin, look at me."

"I'm looking."

"No, Vin. Look at me."

Vin met his eyes.

"Is this what our marriage is about?" Ted glared at him.

"No, Ted…"

"Is this what it is? Lying, deceiving each other? Over money?"

"No, Ted…"

"Then why don't you level with me?" The strain put a crease between Teddy's eyes. "If Anthony's doing a fight at the casino, there's gotta be at least a million coming out of it. And I'm entitled to at least half of that. Am I right?"

"Of course, Ted. But Anthony wouldn't lie to us about that."

"Yeah, why not?"

"He's my son, Ted."

"He's not your son. You couldn't have a son. Remember? Low sperm count, the doctor said. Not enough firepower." Teddy jerked his catheter tube to emphasize the point and swore when he hurt himself.

A nurse came in, looked at his chart, and left.

"Let me ask you something," said Teddy. "Who are you loyal to? Me or Anthony?"

Vin shook his head. "Teddy, why you wanna hurt me like this? You're my *rappresentante*. You know my love is only for you."

"Then prove it," Teddy demanded, putting his wide

white fingers over Vin's stony knuckles. "Get me that
fuckin' payout. Between these fuckin' doctors and
lawyers, I'm already a hundred G's in the hole."

Another nurse came in, saw the two men holding
hands, and smiled. She changed the bag of fluid feeding
into Teddy's IV tube and left.

"Ted," Vin began in an earnest voice. "I'm gonna get to
the bottom of this. I'll go over there and talk to Anthony
right now. I'm sure it's all a misunderstanding."

"It better be." Teddy frowned at his catheter again.
"I'm getting tired of waiting for him to do what's right."

40

The sun was just barely making it above the horizon when
I put my key in the front door of my house. The sky was
as gray as smoke, with streaks of salmon shot through it.

A few hours before, I'd stopped by Frank Diamond's
room and explained the situation about his fighter using
drugs again. He wasn't happy, of course, but we both
agreed it was in everyone's best interest not to call for a
public drug test. Instead, we made a deal to reinstate
Elijah as the challenger in the title fight.

I watched a heron rising from a hedge on my front
lawn. I was going to make it after all. I'd managed to get
back into the fight game and now I stood to make enough
money to pay off both Danny Klein and Teddy. I wasn't
going to end up by the side of a road with my vital parts
missing. I was going to be able to provide for my family.
So why did I still feel so ashamed?

The heron flew over the roof of my house. I wondered
if I could still be a good father to my kids after I'd killed a
man and used a woman for blackmail. It was a tough sell

any way you looked at it. But at the moment, all I wanted to do was see them and hold them. Maybe that would bring me back to the way I was. I tried not to make too much noise as I let myself in.

The living room was dark except for the glowing end of a cigarette. Probably Carla, waiting up for me. Ready to give me hell because I'd left bedsheets on the sofa or, worse, because she'd heard stories about Rosemary and me. I braced for the storm.

But then the cigarette moved. It came toward me and dropped abruptly. I heard a dull muffled sound and felt a blunt massive pain suddenly spreading up my leg. I grabbed my knee and fell to the floor as the overhead light went on.

My father was standing over me, putting a cigarette out on the rug with his foot. In his left hand, he had a golf club.

"Where you been?" he said.

All I could do was moan and think about throwing up.

"I asked you something. Where you been all night?"

The golf club shook in his hand, like it was about to get used again.

"At the casino. I was just at the Doubloon Casino. That's all."

Vin went into the kitchen, brought back an ice tray, and threw it at me. "There, put a couple on your knee. Two days you'll be good as new."

I looked around, surprised Carla and the kids hadn't come out with all the noise. But both bedrooms were still quiet and dark.

"Where's the rest of them?"

"I told them take the night off, 'cause I wanted to talk to you. They're at the EconoLodge near the video arcade, so the kids can play in the morning."

I propped myself up against one of the old purple stuffed chairs and rolled up my pant leg. My father had hit me just below the knee, but the pain was a steady pulse I could feel all the way up to the back of my neck.

"So what're you doing?" he said.

"Nothing."

He touched the edge of my shoe with the head of the club. "Don't tell me you're not doing anything. Now why don't we try and talk honest with each other like a father and son are supposed to, so I don't have to kick the living shit out of you."

"All right."

"So what're you doing? You getting into the fight game?"

"What? Who told you that?"

"I heard it whispered in the fucking trees," he said. "What's your angle?"

I shrugged like I didn't know what he was talking about and tried to hold those ice cubes on my knee.

"Come on, I know you. You gotta have an angle on this. You shaking somebody down at the casino?"

I watched the golf club warily. "No, it's not like that."

My father's face was impossible to read. The hard cast of his nose and mouth always made him look like he was in a bad mood. The only thing that told me he was feeling worse now was the position of the golf club just over my kneecap.

"It's no big deal," I said. "John B. asked me to give him a hand looking after his brother. There's no money in it yet. So I'm just following through. That's what you said, right? Always follow through when somebody tells you something."

I saw my father's grip on the golf club tighten. "Nah, there's gotta be more to it than that. I didn't raise you for nothing. You've gotta have an angle on a guy."

"It's nothing."

I didn't want to outright lie to my father. But if I told

him anything, it would get right back to Teddy and he'd sink the whole ship.

"So how much are they gonna give you?" my father said grimly.

"It's complicated. It's not like walking into a candy store with a gun in your hand. It's business. You're dealing with major corporations and Wall Street lawyers. It takes a certain…finesse."

My father looked at me in a dreamy kind of way before he raised his arms and swung the golf club as hard as he could at my right foot.

My shoe absorbed most of the punishment, but the shock waves traveled up my leg and into my crotch.

"What did I tell you?" he shouted. "What'd I ever teach you? Anything you make goes right into the elbow! You understand, you stupid piece of shit! Teddy gets fifty per-cent of everything you do. That's the way it is."

"But Dad…"

"Don't 'but Dad' me. You'll get the both of us put in a fuckin' lime pit. Where'd you get the balls to do that?" my father said, his face turning red from outrage. "There's guys been in this town twice as long as you've been alive and never seen a dime off the casinos."

"That's not my fault."

My father gnawed on one of his knuckles. "You still owe Teddy sixty. You know, sometimes I wonder why I took you in after your real father died. I could've just left you in a state home, you know."

The pain pulsed through my body again, and for a mo-ment this idea flashed through my mind that maybe both Vin and Teddy had something to do with what happened to Mike. But it was more than I could contend with. I loved Vin. In the back of my mind, I'd been thinking I could use some of my fight revenues to help him retire

down to Florida. The thought that he was in a way responsible for Mike's disappearance would've melted the
glue that held my brain together. So I just forgot about it.
For a while.

"Look, Dad," I said. "We've talked about these casinos
a long time, haven't we? It's the modern era. We both
know Teddy's way of doing things is over. You just don't
walk up to somebody and put a gun in their face to get
their money."

"But those were the days," Vin said wistfully.

"Well, that time is gone. Now you have corporate heads
instead of *caporegimes*. It pays to be legitimate."

"We're a Cosa Nostra." My father leaned on his golf
club like it was a cane. "If you'd follow along and do the
right thing by your padrone, you might get somewhere,
and not just be another *coojine* on the street, like me."

"So that's what I'm trying to do. I'm trying to take a
step up in the world. I mean we've been stuck outside the
doors of these casinos since they opened up in '78. And
now that I got a foot in there, you wanna break it off.
I don't understand it, Dad. You work for this man your
whole life and what've you got to show for it? You might
as well have been working for General Motors all the
gratitude it got you."

Vin was still giving me that dubious look. "You should've
come to me. We could've worked it out."

"We still could. How's Teddy going to know unless
somebody tells him? What I'm doing with the fight at the
casino is my business. Nobody else from the Family is
involved. Why do I owe him anything?"

He stared off into space a moment, like he was trying to
figure out a magic trick. The golf club had moved a couple
of inches away from my leg.

I looked at him and tried to bend my leg. What I was
feeling was all tangled and jumbled-up. On the one hand,

Vin had just given me a pretty good beating. On the other hand, I couldn't accept that he was a threat to me. My life just didn't make sense that way. Vin was my protector. I had a blind spot about his flaws. So I worked it around in my mind this way: everything bad he'd done was because of Teddy. Teddy was the reason he'd gone to jail for killing the guy over the parking space. Teddy was the one who'd controlled him all the years since then. And Teddy was the reason he'd just hit me with the golf club. Teddy was the one we both needed to get away from.

"Listen," I said, "don't worry about any of that. The less you know, the less chance there is of Teddy hearing about it."

He started to argue again, but I put my hand up. "Right here and now, I'm making you a guarantee that you're gonna see at least a hundred thousand dollars in the next few weeks. That's a hundred thousand you won't have to share with Teddy. Come on. Live a little for once in your life. Be independent."

"I don't wanna be independent, I wanna be loyal to my *borgata*," he flared, but there was less fire in it this time.

"Then let me be independent," I said. "I never pledged myself to Teddy. Don't I deserve a chance to live?"

My father rumbled like an old garbage truck, but couldn't think of anything to say.

"Hey, listen," I tried to cheer him. "I'll make sure you have the best seats at the fight."

Vin was still looking down at the golf club, like he was trying to decide if he wanted to use it again. Some kind of emotion passed across his face. A more complicated expression than I was used to seeing on him. But it was gone before I could read it.

"One other thing," he said, putting the golf club down. "I want you to stay away from that girl you been running around with."

"Who?"

"What do you mean 'who?' I know who. The blonde down at the club people been seeing you with. Teddy finds out you've been stepping out on his niece, he'll cut your dick off and stuff it in your mouth."

I dropped my eyes, feeling abashed. "I think she's kind of done with me anyway."

"Good," said my father. "You shouldn't have people talking about you like that. This is a decent family."

41

The old man's hair was a joke, Rosemary found herself thinking the next night. It stood straight up, like he'd stuck his finger in a light socket. But his face was a warning to take him seriously. Clenched jaw, missing teeth, a nose that had been broken at least a half dozen times. His eyes looked like they'd seen hellacious things. His hands looked like they'd done worse.

"I hear you been seeing my boy," he said, leaning on her dressing table.

They were standing in her dressing room a few minutes before show time. When he'd first walked in and introduced himself, she was suspicious about how little he looked like Anthony. But then she remembered this wasn't his real father.

"So what business is this of yours?" she asked.

"His business is my business. That's the way it is in our family."

He began picking up mascara and lipstick cases off her table, and looking at each of them. He seemed like the kind of person who thrived on knocking things down and putting them in his pocket.

"We had an arrangement." Rosemary hitched up the strap of her orange bikini top. "I don't see why that should concern anyone else."

"He's married, that's why." The old man dropped one of her lipsticks into a garbage can. "He's married with two kids and another on the way. That's why it's my concern."

"I understand that. But we still had an arrangement."

"Your arrangement is off. Pack your bags. You're outa here."

With one sweep of his arm, he knocked the rest of her lipsticks and mascaras to the concrete floor. And then he looked up with eyes the color of hot coffee, almost daring her to make something of it.

Rosemary stared at him. She'd once read a newspaper story about a woman chopped up and left in an oil drum, and wondered what kind of man would do such a thing. Now she knew. What surprised her was that she wasn't more scared. But then again, maybe somewhere between losing a child and getting into the back of Honda Preludes with strange men, she'd lost her fear of the worst that could happen.

"Does Anthony know you're talking to me about this?"

"Anthony's like his mother," the old man said in a voice as dead as stone. "He flies off the handle sometimes and he needs someone to bring him back."

"Is that a yes or a no?"

He showed her a half-smile and a few more broken teeth. "What're you, tough? You like to talk back?" He took a step toward her and raised his arm, like he was getting ready to backhand her across the room.

"I just want what we agreed to." She pulled out some of the bikini that was sneaking up her butt again. She wished she had something more substantial back there for protection. "A deal's a deal."

"Pack your fucking bags and don't ever let me see your

face again," he said. "You can pick up your last paycheck in the parking lot."

She raised her chin, like she was giving him a free shot at it. "It better have every dime I'm owed, or I'll make a stink about that too."

He laughed and it sounded like a truck stopping. "Tough broad, huh? If I'd a been twenty years younger I might've gone for you myself."

She didn't smile. "Mister, that is the scariest thing you've said so far."

42

Ever wonder what you must smell like to other people?

I knew what my kids smelled like. I could tell them in the dark. When Rachel threw up, she smelled like an old man disgracing himself in a bar. The farts out of little Anthony would drive the rats off a garbage scow. But when you stuck your nose in their hair, they smelled as fresh and sweet as the woods after a hard rain. You can learn a lot about a person from the way they smell. A guy can lower or raise his voice, put on a hairpiece, change his clothes, but no matter how much perfume or cologne he puts on, his true odor always comes through. The honest sweating-through-the-underwear funky smells.

So as I was sitting there in Frank Diamond's $5,000-a-night hotel suite, I naturally started worrying about how bad I smelled. Because with the way Frank was looking at me, I must've stunk like a pile of old gym socks.

"You know, I helped build this place," he said, rubbing the top of his shaved head. "It's true. I was one of the original lawyers who helped structure the financing. Everyone thinks it was the mob and Teamster pension funds that

built the casinos, like in Vegas, it wasn't. It was the junk
bond market. But I'd imagine all that's a little too sophisti-
cated for you."

I hadn't really had a chance to check out the room before. It was one of those high-roller suites named after a
famous pirate like Jean Lafitte or Freddie the Casserole.
There was a gold Jacuzzi over by the window, a Louis XIV
cabinet with a huge color TV rising out of it, separate en-
trances for servants and children, and a bar stocked with
150-year-old bottles of wine.

Still, five thousand a night seemed a little steep. The
colors weren't as vivid as I thought they would be and
the furniture didn't look that comfortable. But it must
be worth it, I figured, just to know that the guy downstairs only had 75-year-old wine. No question, this was
the place to be if you didn't want to be anywhere else.

"So that was a cute play you did with Terry and that
girl of yours," said Frank, who was wearing a maroon polo
shirt, white pants, and white slip-ons without socks.

I was surprised he wasn't more angry with me, but I
played it cool. "I don't know about any play. It was just
nature taking its course."

And that was all I had to say about it. I stared at him. He
looked disappointed, and after a minute he changed the
subject.

"So what about your entry fee?"

"Entry fee?" I wasn't sure if I'd heard him right. "I'm not
giving you anything. We're co-promoters now."

He chuckled to himself. "I believe you mean you're the
co-manager of one of the fighters."

"Okay, all right."

"Well as the manager of the challenger you'll be expected to put up some of the money for the sanctioning
fees and the other expenses…"

"Fuck you," I said. I couldn't have been more indignant

if he'd walked right over and stuck a hand in my pocket. "I already paid the sanctioning fees. Are you going to try robbing me too?"

He turned his back to me for a second, and very casually opened a tall black cabinet and took a cassette out of an expensive-looking Japanese tape deck. He'd been recording our whole conversation.

"You mind turning that off?" I asked, trying to remember if I'd said anything incriminating.

He hit a switch, fading the little red lights.

"Listen." I started to sit down on a rich blue sofa with black swirls. "I expect to do some serious negotiating. Now, I'd appreciate it if you made me a real offer. It's less than two weeks until the fight…"

"Don't sit on that," he said suddenly.

"Why not?"

"They just Scotchgarded all the furniture in the room. You can't sit on anything for an hour. We have to use these."

He pointed to two big brown beanbag chairs shaped like boxing gloves, side by side in the corner.

"Gifts from a potential sponsor," he explained, sitting in one of the giant gloves and trying to get comfortable.

I sat down in the glove next to him and felt my ass sink deep into its pocket. "I don't imagine this is very good for your back."

"I was thinking of giving you something in the neighborhood of three hundred thousand dollars for your fighter and options on his next three fights."

"Are you kidding?"

He frowned like a wine steward who'd been handed back a bottle with a screw-on top. "No, I am not kidding. Most managers would pay me to get a shot at the title."

"I guess if you don't ask you don't get." I squirmed in the glove. "All you're forgetting is there's a girl who could knock the whole fight off the rails."

I peered across the room, trying to make sure he'd turned off the tape recorder.

Frank Diamond changed the position of his eyebrows so he could play the role of the aggrieved businessman. "My offer is still three hundred thousand."

Obviously the key to this game was staying cool. I perched on the edge of the glove and crossed my legs. "I thought the casino and the TV people were putting up twenty million dollars for this fight."

"That's an exaggeration," he said, his bald head touching the top of the glove. "And now that we're using Elijah instead of Meldrick, the figure is closer to ten million."

I didn't say anything for a minute. You had to hand it to the man. He lied with the greatest of ease. It wasn't that he expected you to believe any of it. It was just that he knew he could wear you down by holding back the truth. I could learn more in an hour with this guy than I could in ten years with Teddy.

"Look." I tried a new tack. "I don't care about having my name on the poster or any of that bullshit. I know about printing costs. I can wait until the next fight."

Frank glanced down at the glass of vodka by his side. If my head had been small enough, he would have tried drowning me in it.

"I'm man enough to admit what I don't know," I said, heaving myself out of the beanbag chair. "All I want right now is five million dollars and a chance to hang around and learn the ropes."

"Oh, that's all." Frank smiled. "And where's that money supposed to come from?"

"Your fighter's getting most of the ten million, right?"

"That's deceptive," Frank said. "There's a lot of money going in and out. It gets very complicated. Terrence's manager gets a third of what he makes."

"His manager? I didn't even know he had a manager. I

knew he had a trainer and a promoter, but what's his manager's name?"

"William Diamond," Frank said absently.

"Who's that, your brother?"

"My son," he replied with muted pride. "Who else is supposed to manage him? A stranger?"

"But where is he? I haven't seen him around here."

"It's not necessary. He'd be redundant. Between his trainer and me, we've got everything covered. My son is not that interested in the business anyway, I'm sorry to say. He is a musician," he said calmly, balling up his fists and pounding the sides of his beanbag chair with them.

"I'm glad he's only taking a third then."

"It's all that's permitted under state law."

"That still leaves two-thirds." I went over to the bar to make myself a drink. "Maybe we could take some out of your end."

Frank Diamond laughed for a long time.

"All right, forget about it," I said, looking for some ice but not finding a bucket. "That still leaves the fighter, and he's got at least five coming by my count. Why can't you give me two million out of his share?"

"Actually it comes to a little bit less than that." He took a Kleenex out of a gold dispenser and blew his nose. "Because Terrence has got an entourage and all kinds of other expenses. I mean, just his training camp in upstate New York costs him more than a thousand dollars a day."

"Let me guess. It's on your property."

"What am I supposed to do? Loan it to him? It's not a charity operation, you know."

"And it's legal for you to do that?" I found the ice tray in the freezer, but it was empty.

"Why not? I'm feeding them, paying property taxes…"

"You're already taking a third. I thought that's all you were allowed."

Frank Diamond leaned back against the thumb of his glove, finally finding a position that allowed him to look powerful and debonair.

"Nothing done by me or any other members of my family is illegal," he said forthrightly. "Is it unusual? Maybe. But a lot of things are unusual in boxing."

"Jeez, this is some business." I finally figured out how to get some ice from the slot in the wall. "Let me ask you something. How'd you get this kid Terrence to go with you as his promoter when you make deals like that?"

"He had no choice." He sat back and put his hands behind his head, so I could see what good triceps he had for a middle-aged guy. "I had the champion before him and in order to get a shot at the title, Terrence had to give me options on his next six fights. Otherwise I'd never let him get in the ring with my guy."

"How do you get away with that?" I asked, not without admiration.

"Whether you succeed or fail in this business depends on one thing: strength of character." He took a pipe off a table near his chair and stuck it in his mouth. "Remember that. All other qualities come and go. Character endures."

Character endures. The business where you could say things like that and make money like this was the one I wanted to be in. Growing up around wiseguys was the best preparation I could have had for the fight game. The only difference was one thing was legal and the other wasn't.

"So after taxes and all that, you're talking about one, maybe one and a half million left over for Terrence," Frank said, lighting the pipe. "So I can't cut you a million out of that. It wouldn't be right."

I noticed there was no smoke coming from his pipe. He didn't even have tobacco. He was probably one of those older men who'd been advised to give up smoking, but retained the affectation with the pipe.

"'Tell you what," he said quickly, putting down the pipe and picking up a calculator. "Let's work something out." He punched in a few numbers. "We can start off with a more compact unit."

I was trying to figure out the amount I'd need to pay off Danny Klein and Teddy while leaving myself enough to start a new business and send my father to Florida. Frank Diamond handed me the calculator. The readout said "325,000."

I just looked at him. I was trying to figure out how many people my father and Teddy had shot or beat up for showing this little respect.

"What're you doing?" I asked.

"How do you mean?"

"I ask you for five million, you're showing me three twenty-five. Why would you insult me like that?"

"It's not an insult, it's reality," Frank said, standing up to show me he was about three inches taller than I was. "I'm having to put up my own money for this fight."

I was sure this was a lie.

"Look," I said, "if this girl starts talking, there isn't going to be any fight. Because your guy is going to test positive for drugs. Because I know he's got a record and if she says what he did, he's gonna get tested. All right? And that's gonna cost you a helluva lot more than three twenty-five if he can't go and fight."

Frank was still unmoved. "Pay-per-view television receipts," he said, taking the calculator back from me. "That's what you're waiting for. That's when you start seeing real money, when those subscriptions come in. Up until then it's chump change really."

He was talking about cable TV receipts while I was trying to stay alive. Still, my respect for this man grew and deepened with each lie he told. Dan Bishop was a face in a magazine. Frank was real. He was the mentor figure I'd been waiting for all my life.

"What about the gate?" I asked. "They've been selling tickets for weeks now. You gotta be seeing some of the box office receipts already."

Frank Diamond held up his hand in the scout's-honor salute. "The market's soft. So far sales have been slow."

I finally got done calculating what I'd need to get by. If Elijah got $1.5 million, I'd be entitled to twenty percent as his co-manager, or three hundred thousand. About a hundred twenty thousand would go toward covering my debts to Teddy and Danny Klein. The rest would easily cover my wife and kids' expenses, my father's Florida trip, and my new business. I might even have enough left over to make another dent in the mortgage.

"Enough," I said in a steady voice. "I want a million five. And half of it up front. That's non-negotiable."

Frank looked at me for a long time. He seemed to be taking my measure. Maybe he had the sense I'd recently killed a man. They say that can hang over you like an aura.

"I'll have to get back to you," he said finally. "The most anybody gets up front is a third. And I usually don't give that. You only get the rest after the fight if you've fulfilled all the conditions of the contract."

I sat back on the couch, feeling kind of warm inside. I'd held my own with him, at least for a few seconds.

His face turned dark. "That means I don't want to see any stories in the newspapers or get any calls from lawyers about this girl of yours. You're sure she'll keep her mouth shut?"

I realized I'd barely spoken to Rosemary since the day we set Terrence up. I decided to stop by the club and see how she was doing. I looked at my watch and saw it was almost ten-thirty. She'd just be starting her act now.

"She'll be fine," I told Frank.

"Good thing, too. There's been enough surprises around here already."

43

Rosemary was still furious at ten-thirty when she came out to do her last show at the club.

The cycle was complete. Every man she'd ever known had let her down. Her father had died, leaving her and her mother broken and mired in poverty. Her husband, Bingo, decided he loved heroin more than he loved her and had probably passed on the weakened immunities that killed their second daughter. And here Anthony had broken his promise to provide for her after she'd helped set up Terrence. Sending his father back to menace her. These deals you made with yourself. They were never worthwhile.

Just to make matters worse, the club had added a special feature tonight, inviting male members of the audience to join her and the other Foxy Boxer in the ring. A drunken insurance salesman who called himself Ben stumbled between the ropes, wearing a pair of green-and-pink-plaid pants, a navy blazer, and a bright yellow necktie with naked mermaids on it. Rosemary forced herself to smile.

What was it about men? Did their brains release a secret enzyme that rendered them unreliable once they reached a certain age? The bell rang and the match began. She had to tell Ben to wait in her corner. He was just the manager, there to give her a rubdown between rounds. But he followed her out to the middle of the ring anyway, reaching around to squeeze her tits. She gave him a playful shove back into the corner and got down to the humiliating business of wrestling another woman. Miriam the busty redhead was making a big show of scratching and biting tonight. Rosemary had to keep throwing her into the ropes just to get away from her.

As the bell rang to end the round and she returned to her corner, Rosemary happened to glance up and see Anthony waving to her from the club's entrance. The lousy prick. He didn't even have the nerve to fire her himself. She'd been treated with more class in the backs of Hondas. She resisted the urge to give him the finger and instead turned her attention to Ben the insurance salesman, her "manager." This jerk had already stripped off his jacket and shirt, leaving his tie hanging listlessly between his sagging hairy pectorals. He reached for her again and she could smell the Jaegermeister he'd spilled on his chest. When she put up a friendly hand and asked him to slow down, he tried to pull off her bikini top.

The men in the audience began to stomp and shout, "GO FOR IT!" She had to slap Ben's face to get him to stop.

"Don't make me do that again." She smiled.

But after the next round, old Ben was coming at her again, trying to throw her down and get on top of her. The men in the audience were on their feet, cheering louder, their voices like storm troopers' boots on a tarmac, "FUCKHERNOW! FUCKHERNOW! FUCKHERNOW!"

They were all the same. All trying to strip her of whatever pride and dignity she had left. It was enough. Something inside her snapped. She grabbed Ben's flabby arm, and using his sluggish weight against him, she performed an old-fashioned judo flip, pulling him over her shoulder so that he landed on the canvas with a loud *thwacck!!* He lay there for a few seconds with his eyes glazing over, like an immense useless baby.

"OH C'MON, BEN!" someone shouted from the audience. "HOSE THE BITCH!"

Rosemary flashed her best little-girl smile and then

dropped onto Ben, straddling his marshmallow stomach with her strong tawny legs. Miriam the redhead handed her a can of shaving cream and Rosemary began squirting it onto Ben's chest and face. He tried to squirm away but she pressed down on him with her full weight and used her legs to pin his arms to his sides.

She quickly moved up to his face and began to smother him, thrusting her pudendum down on his mouth and nose so he couldn't breathe. He tried to throw her off, but he was too drunk to do more than struggle like a spider under a paperweight. Now the men in the audience did not cheer so loudly.

Smiling more ferociously by the moment, she turned around and went to work, ass to his face, as she opened the top button of his plaid slacks and squirted shaving cream down the front of his underwear. The momentum had shifted in the last few seconds, and the other men in the audience were now laughing and urging her to abuse Ben in any way she saw fit.

She looked up to make sure Anthony was still watching from the entrance before she fired another shot of shaving cream down the front of Ben's pants. More laughter. But then she stunned them all into near-silence by reaching in after the shaving cream and pulling out Ben's flaccid penis. Oh yeah. Tits are great. Pussy's better. But let no woman expose the shrunken totem pole to ridicule.

She began yanking on it. One yank for Bingo, who'd put her out on the street. One yank for Anthony, who'd promised her the moon and left her in the gutter. And one yank for his vicious old man, coming by to kick her in the head when all she needed was a job. Yank this. Ben began to groan like he was in great pain.

The other men in the club groaned along with him and soon someone at one of the front tables said what they were

watching was rape. Damn straight, thought Rosemary.
Ben's penis grew taut and his body began to convulse.

"Lose the bitch, Ben!" they were shouting. "Kick her
off."

But it was too late. Ben's left knee began to tremble and
his face closed in on itself. He was coming in public. As
his body gave one final jerk, Rosemary leaped to her feet
and pranced around the ring, flicking drops of foam at the
men in the front seats.

"Here he is," she sang with her brightest smile yet. "Mr.
Premature Ejaculator…Here he is, your ideal…"

Ben rolled onto his side and covered his face with both
hands.

Her fists raised triumphantly, Rosemary climbed from
the ring and saw Anthony still standing at the back of the
club, his mouth hanging open a little. She walked right up
and kissed him hard on the lips. Not a lover's kiss. More the
kind of kiss one mob guy would give another before killing
him. She grabbed his hair and pulled his head back.

"Terry was ten times better than you," she whispered.

She spun away and went out the side door into her
dressing room, her cheeks bouncing in her bikini bottom.

Anthony slowly smoothed his hair and then smelled his
palm, as if trying to figure out what she'd left up there.

44

"What the hell was that all about?"

It was ten minutes after Rosemary did her little perfor-
mance at the club. I was in her dressing room, still trying
to decide what she'd rubbed into my hair.

"What do you think it was about?" she said, throwing a

red high-heeled shoe at me. "You have your father come
back here and threaten me? And fire me from a job I need
to feed my child? Is that how you keep your promises?"

The shoe had sailed past my ear and broken against the
far wall, the heel separating from the sole. I picked up
the pieces and tried to put together what had happened
in my mind. My father must have come back here and
tried to scare her off, thinking Teddy would find out I was
cheating on Carla. Now I had my work cut out for me. I
had to convince Rosemary that everything was still the
same between us.

"Look, I don't know anything about what my father
said."

"How can I ever believe you again?" She untied her
bikini top. "First you say you care about me. Then you use
me like a common whore. And then you break your word."

"You make it sound like that's never happened before,"
I blurted out.

"But I expected better from you!" she screamed.

And what made it hurt was that I did too.

She picked up a quart bottle of Evian water and threw
it at my head. It bounced off my shoulder and splashed
on the Gianni Versace shirt I was wearing.

"Hey, come on!"

"Anthony," she said. "I didn't think it was possible, but
you broke my heart again tonight."

Her bikini top fell off. Her breasts looked like they
were about to open fire on me from across the room.

"Rosemary, I'm sorry. This was all a mistake. My father
doesn't know about the understanding we have."

"Anthony, do not insult my intelligence," she said in
that arch way of hers. "All I want is for you to keep to the
terms of our agreement." I started to say something, but
she cut me off. "I don't want to hear any more about affection or see your stiff prick. I just want half the cash

you're making from this fight. Because you couldn't have done it without me."

She pulled off the bottom of her bathing suit and stood there, naked and intimidating. This is what they called a tough broad. If she'd been a man, she would've had a crew ten times the size of Teddy's. The water she'd thrown at me was soaking my skin and raising goose bumps on my chest.

"Listen," I said nervously. "I was just over at Frank Diamond's suite at the Doubloon nailing down the schedule of the payments. Everything's just about set."

Though now I had to figure out how to cut her off a slice of the money I'd have left after I'd paid off Danny Klein and Teddy.

"I can even get you a job at the fight, to put you on the payroll," I explained. "It's a lock. It's guaranteed."

"Well, that's one thing you've got right, Anthony. Since I've got insurance." She came toward me like a panther stalking her prey.

"What're you talking about?"

"I know about you and that guy Nicky they found under the Boardwalk."

I felt pressure building up behind my eyes as my skin turned cold. "I told you I wasn't responsible for that."

"I heard." She stood five feet in front of me and looked right through my eyes down into the pit of my stomach. "You said it was your family. I'm sure that would be enough to interest the police, or the F.B.I., or whoever's investigating that case."

"I wouldn't talk about that if I was you." I clicked my heel on the concrete floor. "Something could happen."

"Fuck you," she said. "Don't pull that with me. Your father already did it. And he's way better at it than you are."

She picked up her panties and began to put them on. Here I'd been worried she'd talk and ruin the deal I had with Frank Diamond. And in the meantime, she was thinking about putting me in prison for life on this homicide. I began to have what I think is called an olfactory hallucination—when you smell something that isn't there. Except it wasn't Nick under the Boardwalk that I smelled. It was that terrible cat odor in my house.

"Is this any way for two people who care about each other to talk?" I asked.

"It's the way people who don't trust each other talk." She slowly started to pull on her bra. Somehow she didn't seem as threatening with her clothes on.

"Come on. Let's go for a ride. We can get a drink somewhere."

"Forget about it, I brought my own car." She fished her keys out of her handbag and rattled them at me. "From now on, you and I are not friends and we're not lovers. We're just business partners. And the only word you have to remember is 'half.' As in 'half' the revenue. "

She put on the rest of her clothes without talking or even looking my way. I was still shivering from the water she'd thrown on me. I knew I should just go and cut my losses, but there was one question that'd been bothering me the whole time we were talking.

"That thing you said before?" I asked her. "About how Terrence was a better lay than me? You said that just to hurt me, right? You didn't mean it, did you?"

"Oh yes I did."

45

I woke up at about ten one morning the week before the fight to the sound of my kids playing on the jungle gym I'd built them in the backyard. It was the nicest thing I'd heard in months.

I went out onto the back porch to have a look at them. Carla was lying in a deck chair beside the jungle gym, with her belly swollen and a wet towel over her face, not wanting to deal with the world. And I was sorry all over again that I'd abandoned them in the name of getting ahead. All I ever should have wanted was an ordinary life.

But before I could get the screen door open to go out and play with my kids, a voice from the kitchen stopped me.

"Where do you think you're going, you little cock-sucker?"

I turned and saw Teddy sitting at my kitchen table. I must have walked right by him in my daze. He looked terrible, like he'd dropped about twenty pounds in two weeks. His skin had a pale cast and for some reason, his eyes reminded me of an old lady's. But the most unusual thing about him that morning was that he wasn't with my father.

"Siddown a minute, will you?"

I sat. "How's it going, Ted? I haven't seen you in a while."

"All right, enough of that bullshit," he said, cutting through the social amenities. "I want to have a serious talk with you. Because of the great affection between your father and me, I sometimes feel I can't speak my mind in front of him. Particularly when it comes to you."

"Speak your mind."

I was wearing just a pair of white boxer shorts and I suddenly sensed he was staring at my legs. I crossed them and moved my chair away from the table a little.

"As you must know, our *borgata* has been under a lot of pressure lately because of these fuckin' homicides and federal investigations. Especially on account of this fuckin' Nicky gettin' whacked."

"I know what you mean." Ever since I'd killed Nicky, I'd felt as if there was a cage around my heart.

"Anyway." He coughed and frowned. "When they put pressure on an organization like ours, people sometimes don't do the right thing, and they turn on each other. So I have three things I want to tell you."

"Shoot," I said. And immediately realized that was exactly the wrong word to use.

"Number one," he said, raising an index finger that was as fat as a thumb. "If I ever find out you or anybody else is talking to the feds or the local bulls, I will sever your motherfucking head. Is that clear to you?"

"Yes sir."

"Number two." I'd never seen Teddy go so long without eating. "If I ever find out you've been running around on my beloved niece with another woman, I will sever your fucking head."

"Okay. That's fine."

"And number three." He stopped talking for a second and his lips quivered. I wondered how sick he was. "Number three is this," he said. "I heard a rumor that you were managing a fighter and getting a big casino contract. But at the hospital the other day, your father told me that wasn't true."

"Yeah, right, it's not true," I lied with a poker face.

"Well, I just wanted to come over here and emphasize it for myself. That if I ever learn you been making money off another business, like a trucking concern or boxing promotion, and not paying back the money you owe me, I will sever your motherfucking head. Now what do you think of that?"

"It sounds like you're kind of anxious to sever my head, Teddy."

He didn't crack a smile. "You know, your real father, Mike, he liked to make a joke outa everything too. And look what happened to him."

His words put a chill inside my heart, and I knew for the first time with absolute certainty that Teddy was the one who'd killed my real father. I just stared at him for a long time, wondering if I could kill him without destroying all the legitimate things I'd tried to do in my life.

"Remember," he said, starting to stand up. "You got ninety more days to pay me the money you owe me. Or else you come work for me full-time."

"I remember."

"Give my love to Carla and the kids. I never get to see enough of them these days."

46

P.F. waited until Teddy was about to sit down on the crate outside the grocery store on Florida Avenue before he honked the horn and called him over.

"What do you want?" Teddy lumbered over to the driver's side window. "I thought I said I had nothing to say to you."

"People who need people are the luckiest people in the world," P.F. sang.

"Yeah, you're starting to look like Barbra Streisand too."

Actually, it was Teddy who was starting to look like a woman. An old woman, to be precise. With round feminine haunches and a big butt replacing the sandbag he used to have on his stomach. P.F. wondered if he'd been taking estrogen hormones. Maybe the rumors about Teddy's operation the other week were true.

"I heard you stopped by to see Mike Dillon's boy the other day," P.F. said laconically. "Funny."

"Not as funny as the police having the biggest meat-eater in the department following me." Teddy squinted. "How's that television I gave you? Zenith, right? Is it still working?"

P.F. smiled as if the dig didn't hurt. "I'm not here on police business. I'm just checking out something for a friend."

"Bullshit. You don't have any friends. Whores have customers. And that's all you are, a whore."

"Thanks, Ted. I love you too."

P.F. caught sight of his own eyes crinkling in the side mirror. The crow's feet had lifted a little since he'd cut back on his drinking. Instead of the long march around his eyes, the birds were just doing a light foxtrot.

"All right," he told Teddy. "I'm not working for a friend. I'm here for a higher authority."

Actually, he was there on behalf of the Golden Doubloon Hotel and Casino. Father Bobby D'Errico, the former Franciscan priest who'd just been named the casino's new vice president for operations, had asked him to find out why there'd been a last-minute switch, with Elijah Barton replacing Meldrick Norman in the title fight. "Consider it your audition for the job as head of security," Bobby had said. It seemed the casino's new corporate management was somewhat concerned that Barton's manager was a front for the mob. Though why that mattered to them

P.F. couldn't say. Half of these corporate outfits acted like mobsters themselves.

"I wanted to talk to you about the boxing thing," he told Teddy.

"What boxing thing?"

"The story about Michael Dillon's boy managing one of the guys in the fight next week."

As frail and discolored as he looked, Teddy scrambled around and got in on the passenger side of P.F.'s cruiser.

"What do you know about this?" he said with grumpy aggression, like he was talking to an aging errand boy.

P.F. looked around and tightened his belt, as if he was in no great hurry to begin. "What I know is you've got your boy Anthony in there, representing you as manager of one of the fighters. But the thing is, he hasn't applied for the proper licenses or tax exemptions from the state athletic commission…"

Whether any of this was true or not, P.F. had no idea. It was just part of a strategy for finding how much Teddy was involved. He figured if he squeezed Teddy a little, there'd be an indignant phone call from Burt Ryan or some other lawyer within forty-eight hours demanding to review the boxing contracts and procedures, thus confirming the connection between Teddy and the fighter.

But instead of playing it cool with a Bogartesque tug of the ear, Teddy surprised him by rising to the bait immediately. "How much is he making from this fucking fight anyway?"

He leaned across the seat and P.F. caught a whiff of something like dead fish.

"I don't know what Anthony's take is, but the overall purse for the fight is something like ten million."

Teddy began snorting through his nose like some beast about to come charging out of the swamp on *Wild Kingdom*.

"I'll kill him," he muttered. "I'll fucking kill him."

P.F. tilted his head on one side. "Are you making a threat in front of an Atlantic City police officer?"

"Only one who used to come by my stash house with Paulie Raymond," said Teddy, coming to his senses. "You're as big a thief as your old man. Try putting that on your wiretap and playing it back in court."

"Are you saying you don't have anything to do with this kid managing the fighter?"

"What? Me? No. Fuck." Teddy stared at the scratches on the windshield, as if they could explain his confusion.

"Then where would this Anthony get the kind of money to get started in the fight game?"

"I don't know." Phlegm rumbled in Teddy's chest. "But if you meet the man handing out the cash, give him my name too."

Just then, Richie Amato pulled up alongside of them, in the navy Impala. Teddy got out of P.F.'s car and went over to clap Richie on the ear with the flat of his hand.

"What's the matter with you? You were supposed to be here five minutes ago. Don't you keep none of your appointments these days?"

Richie winced resentfully. "I had to get my other taillight fixed. Remember how you warned me?"

Teddy shook his head and looked back at P.F. in exhausted dismay. "What can I tell you? You can't trust anyone under thirty now."

47

"How's this thing working?" said Vin, sitting down in a chair beside Teddy and his hemodialysis machine.

Lying on his couch, Teddy stared up at the ceiling, with

bored eyes and a grinding mouth. "It's all right, unless it goes too slow or too fast. That's when I start getting tired."

The four-and-a-half-foot-tall machine hummed along quietly like a BMW. Since the prostate operation last month, Teddy had been having trouble with his kidneys and now he had a needle stuck in each of his lardy purplish yellow thighs. Long clear tubes siphoned the juices out of his body and into the machine for cleansing.

"It must be hard," Vin said sympathetically.

Teddy grunted. "Fuck it, I ain't worried. Every day of my life I've had some kinda cancer trying to eat me. You know what I'm saying? I don't mean I had cancer cancer, but there was always something trying to nibble away. You know what I say? Fuck you, you cocksucker! You'll never get me. You know why? I got too much life force."

"That's right."

The effort of speaking left Teddy temporarily drained. His face went blank as he closed his eyes. After a moment, he clenched himself up inside, ready for another outburst.

"You try to put me down I'll kick you over, fuck you right in the ass," he said, struggling to clear his throat. It sounded like he was cooking a goulash in his chest. "That's the way it is. You don't like it, I'll fuck you in the ass too. Because I'm a survivor."

"Absolutely."

"So that's why I got so pissed when I realized you'd lied to me about your boy Anthony getting in the fight game."

"What?!!" Vin reacted like his old friend had just put jumper cables on his eyelids.

"I heard it with my own ears." Teddy said calmly. "Some fuckin' cop has to tell me about it yesterday. Pigeater, whatever the fuck they call him. Paulie Raymond's old partner. Says your Anthony's managing a guy who's gonna fight for ten million dollars. Then I turn on the TV to watch the weigh-in on SportsChannel, I think I see Anthony standing over in the corner."

Vin's eyes went back like the pictures of lemons on a slot machine. He stood up quickly and turned on the television in the corner, to drown out any wiretaps.

"You sure it was him?" he asked, returning to Teddy's side.

"No respect." Teddy sat up and sighed. "This fuckin' kid don't even give me the illusion of respect. It's right on TV. Practically counting the money in my face. I thought I asked you to see about our end of it. And now I have to hear about this from a cop."

"But Ted..."

"Not even the illusion. He puts it right in my face. Conquering the market under my fucking flag. The only reason Anthony's getting in there with the casino people is 'cause he's saying he's with me. That's the only reason. He's in there talking like he's an *amica nostra*. And not a penny of tribute to us. And you know what hurts me about this, Vin? You know what really hurts? The fact that you lied to me about it."

Vin sputtered and pointed to his mouth, as if putting Teddy on notice that something worthwhile was about to come out. "I didn't know nothin' about this," he finally managed to say. "What's a, what's a word you use? I was misinformed."

"I wanna believe that," Teddy said slowly, putting his head down on the pillow and trying to get back into the rhythm of the dialysis machine. "I wanna believe we mean more to each other than lies. But I already told you, Vin, I'm gonna have to get a piece of that. Didn't I?"

"Yeah, sure."

"So where's my piece? All I'm hearing is lies. Anthony's gotta be clearing a mil for this fight. What're they gonna say about this in Philadelphia? In New York? On the

Commission? The son of one of my own is giving me the finger."

Vin put his hand over his heart. "Jeez, Ted, I, I don't know. The kid must nota told me the truth."

Teddy's eyes stared straight up again. "That's why he's gotta go," he said.

"But Ted…"

"He's dying of ambition, your boy. See, I know he thinks I'm dying, because everyone's talking about it, but he's wrong. See, I still got the life force going inside me. But him, he's the one that's dying. You got no respect, it's like a malignancy. It eats away inside you, a little bit at a time. You gotta cut it out or it's gonna kill the whole body. You understand what I'm saying, Vin? Sometimes you gotta sacrifice a vital organ to save the rest."

"Teddy, what're you telling me? Now I gotta whack my own kid?"

Six more angry coughs racked Teddy and then a kind of serenity settled over him.

"Come on, Ted, you don't mean that," Vin beseeched him with clasped hands. "Lemme try and straighten him out. He's a little confused, is all."

A volcanic tremor came from somewhere deep inside Teddy. "What're you, turning into a frail on me, Vin?"

Vin pushed himself up against the back of his chair. "Nah, I'm just saying, you give him an opportunity to stretch his wings and he'll prove his loyalty," he said with his voice cracking. "It's like a little bird leaving his nest and coming back with twice as many twigs."

"What's the matter with you? Don't you understand I want this fuckin' kid clipped in the ass?"

"Let me talk to him one more time. I'm sure he didn't mean any harm."

Teddy just looked at him.

"Look at all the things I done in my life," Vin went on.

"Sometimes I look back and I think raising that boy was the only one that meant anything. After his mother died, it was just him and me. I brought him up like he was my own."

Teddy kept glaring. There was a slightly jaundiced, yellowish tinge in his eyes.

Vin was almost off the couch and on his knees. "On my life, Ted. I'll work this out. From now on, it's my responsibility."

"That's what I'm telling you!" Teddy flared like old embers in a fireplace coming back to life. "It's your responsibility to whack him."

"But if I whack him, how are we ever gonna see any money out of this? See what I'm saying, Ted? Leave it to me. If I don't turn Anthony around and make him work for you, you can give me all the blame. I'll take whatever I got coming."

Teddy touched his ear and the crease along his brow began to soften. With great effort, he leaned forward and slapped Vin's knee with a pudgy, liver-spotted hand.

"All right," he said with another cough. "You talk to him. Tell him I want sixty-five percent of whatever he's making. And don't take no for an answer. No more lies. That's the end of it."

"He'll do the right thing."

"Good, because otherwise he's gonna get this." Teddy made the sign of a gun with his hand.

The dialysis machine began to make a sputtering noise. Teddy slapped it a couple of times, but it didn't help. Nothing was going through the tubes. Finally he turned a dial on the machine and some of the fluid began to flush through again.

"Life force, Vin, it's a remarkable thing." Teddy tried to roll onto his side without pulling one of the needles out of his thighs. "There's days I think I'm gonna live forever."

He coughed five times in a row. Vin leaned over and touched his hand. "You are, Ted. You are."

"Yeah." The machine seemed to shake. "But now I gotta go for my radiation three, four times a week and take this fuckin' female hormone."

"You're still more a man than anyone I know." Vin gripped his hand and kissed it.

Teddy looked up at the saline solution in the clear plastic bag over his head. "You know, Vin, the only part I'm sorry about is I don't have a son of my own to pass things on to no more."

"No one could blame you for that," Vin assured him.

Teddy fell into another one of his long brooding silences, as his eyes followed the path of one single bubble in the clear tube, trying to make its way from his thigh to the humming machine.

48

The day before the fight, my father asked me to meet him out on the Boardwalk at six o'clock in the morning. A chill wind strafed in from the Atlantic and a lazy sun was just beginning to climb out of the water. The sky was the color of a bruise.

"You remember when you were a kid and I used to take you for walks along here?" he began.

"Yeah, sure."

How could I forget the way he took me by the hand after my real father died?

"You remember the stories I'd tell about the way Atlantic City used to be?" He handed me a cup of coffee.

"I'm not sure."

The stories Vin told had a different flavor from the ones

I heard from Mike. My real father liked to talk about the old hotel palaces, and Sinatra, and the diving horse on the Steel Pier. With Vin, it was another world.

"You know, they made history here once," he said. "The old-timers. Capone, Luciano, Lansky, Siegel, Dutch Schultz, Maxie Hoff from Philadelphia. They all came into town one weekend in 1929 and decided to get rid of all the Mustache Petes from the old country who'd been running things. They wanted to make it more of an American business and not just a bunch of animals killing each other. They were supposed to be staying right down there at the Breakers."

He waved his hand at the row of casinos and cut-rate hotels down toward the south end of the Boardwalk.

"I told you that story, right?" He took a sip from his coffee and smiled when it seemed to burn his tongue. "How they tried to check in all at once under assumed names, but the guy at the desk got wise and tried to throw them out? Lansky had to intervene just to keep them from shooting the place up. Instead they packed up their violin cases and moved on down to the Traymore."

Steam rose off his coffee and evaporated in the salty air. Now that he'd brought it up, I realized he had told me the story about a million times before. But I had a feeling he was trying to make a different point this time.

"It's all gone now," he said, putting his coffee down on a green bench. "Back then, there was..." He put his hands together, trying to think of a word.

"Cohesion?"

"Cooperation. They knew how to work together. They even helped each other move their bags to the other hotel when the Breakers wouldn't take them in. And they had the greatest sit-down in the history of man. Divided up the whole country. That was the way they did it back then.

They worked for a common goal. It all goes back to the old country. I ever tell you how they started this thing of ours?"

Yeah, yeah, yeah. Some French soldier raped a Sicilian girl on the day of her wedding and her mother cried *"Mia figlia, mia figlia"* and that night all the peasants sneaked out and killed the French soldiers. That story's engraved on my cranium too. I still wasn't sure what he was driving at.

"But that was the old country," my father said with a sigh, briefly working over his hair again with the Ace comb. "Here, it's different. It's every man for himself. Like the way you live."

Before I could defend myself, he put up a hand to cut me off.

"I'm not blaming anybody," he said. "If I was starting off now, maybe I'd be the same as you. But that wasn't the way I was brought up. I was brought up the old way, to think of the good of the whole *borgata* when I did something. Maybe if I was brought up your way, I could've learned to be more independent…"

I brought him up short. "So what's the problem, Dad?"

He just looked out at the whitecaps rolling in and crashing on the beach. "Teddy found out that you still got a piece of this fight. And he wants to know when he's getting his cut."

"Tell him he's got a long wait."

"He ain't gonna wanna hear that."

"Then fuck him! What's he going to do about it?"

Without a word, my father pulled up his shirttail and showed me the nine-millimeter tucked in his waistband. That knot tightened at the back of my skull.

"What are you saying? He was going to have you shoot me if I didn't come across?"

The sun was rising higher, but my father still looked cold. The Boardwalk was empty at this hour, except for a couple of old bums rolled up in sleeping bags on the green wooden benches by the bathhouse.

"Look, I'm in a tough spot," my father said, dropping the shirttail over his gun and looking embarrassed. "All my life I been a loyal soldier to Teddy. We came up in reform school together. I known him a helluva lot longer than I know you. Just throw him seventy, seventy-five thousand on top of what you already owe him. Show him some respect. You'll make a sick man happy."

"No!" I told him. "This was my deal all the way. I raised all the revenue, I took all the risks. Why should he be able to come in at the last minute and take a cut?"

"Because the man is dying. He feels like everything in his life's been taken away from him. First he lost his son. Then Jackie from New York stole the unions. Now his health is going." Vin gestured at the darkened casinos that sat like still white elephants along the Boardwalk. "Twenty years ago, he could walk around and feel like he owned this town. But then all these casino corporations and lawyers pushed him out. You don't know what's been taken from him…"

"What's been taken from him?!" I exploded. "What's been taken from him?!! What about what he took from me? He took my fucking childhood!! He took my fucking father from me!!"

Vin looked crestfallen. "I been a good father to you."

But I wasn't going to be put off any longer. This had been a long time coming, like rain after a humid spell. "I'm not talking about that," I ripped into him. "I'm talking about Mike. The man whose blood runs in my veins. I want to know what happened to him."

"Why, wha, I told you none of us know." Vin couldn't look me in the eye.

"All right, that's enough," I told him harshly. "That's enough of the lies. Now I want to know the truth. I waited all my life. I already know Teddy killed Mike. Now I wanna know why and I want to know what you had to do with it."

The tide flowed in and rolled out the way it had for five million years, but the breath my father exhaled sounded even older than that. A sandpiper ran along the shore with a clam in its mouth.

"Come on." I stared at him. "You owe it to me."

He ignored me for a few seconds and tried to light a cigarette. He flicked his lighter three times without producing a flame and then threw it across the beach. He stared after it for a long time before he spoke again.

"Well," he said finally. "I guess you gotta be told sometime."

I realized I was shaking, the way I did before I killed Nicky. "Tell the story."

"Mike, yeah, Mike," he mumbled, like he was trying to find the right place to begin. "He was a lifeguard, from over Margate. Good-lookin', smooth talker. He looked like that guy on television. What was his name? Edd 'Kookie' Byrnes."

77 Sunset Strip. I remembered the song Mike used to sing.

"Yeah, Mike did the whole California bit with the blond girl and the red Corvette convertible. But what he really wanted to be was like Hugh Hefner and Howard Hughes rolled into one. A millionaire and a playboy. He was a dreamer, you know. Except he didn't know how to do any of the things that got those guys where they were. He didn't have any fuckin' money. So that's why he had to hook up with a couple of mugs like Teddy and me. He needed the muscle. And we needed somebody presentable-like like him to go in and talk to people in banks and such, because me and Teddy, we'd get thrown out before we got through the fuckin' lobby."

So that was Mike. I wondered if I would've gotten along with him as an adult.

"Anyway," said Vin, looking down at the gray Boardwalk railing. "The three of us got involved in a real estate deal. We bought this hot dog place on the Boardwalk called Manny's on the Boardwalk. I used to go in there once a week and slam the guy's hand in the cash register. Eventually, they decided to just give us the deed instead of paying the protection money. So then about six months later, this hotshot lawyer from New York has a sit-down with us and wants to buy the property for a hundred twenty-five thousand dollars. Mike says fuck you, because he's a dreamer."

"What do you mean?" I strained to remember Mike's face, but all I could picture at the moment was the back of his head and the shine on his shoes.

"You know," said Vin. "He wanted to build one of these golden palace hotels like they used to have in the old days in Atlantic City. So he was holding out for more money. Which made Teddy nuts. He never liked Mike. Was always jealous, because Mike was so handsome and Teddy, he was kinda on the weighty side. And the two of them had a disagreement. Botta beep, botta bing, who remembers all the details? Mike wound up dead."

"No botta beep. I want the real story. Tell me exactly what happened. Did Teddy get somebody to stick an ice pick in him?" I was in a rage. I wanted to tear the truth out of Vin.

He was already holding his sides like he was in pain. "Ah, shit. It was nothing. We were sitting around the living room, having some drinks, discussing things, and Mike went to the kitchen to get Teddy some pretzels. And when he came back in, Ted took a gun from behind one of the sofa cushions and shot him once."

"Where?"

Vin's mouth opened in disbelief. "What, do you gotta know everything?"

"Where did he shoot him?" I said louder.

"In the face. All right? Teddy shot him in the face. He never liked the way Mike looked. It was over in two seconds."

A brief wind shifted the sands and another wave crashed on the beach, breaking into a million fragments. But something inside me had turned to stone. "Then what happened?"

"Please," Vin said in a quiet voice. "Don't do this to me. I'm your father. I love you…"

"Screw you. I want the rest."

He threw his arms around himself. "It was all Teddy's idea," he said. "He had me pick you up in the car and the two of us drove out to bury Mike in the Pinelands. Teddy figured no one would stop a car with a little kid in front. Afterwards, I bought you a hot dog on the Boardwalk. I always thought you remembered it. That's why I couldn't understand that you'd keep asking me."

I should've remembered it. I tried to bring it all back and picture it. But all I could see before me was the sea, the beach, and Vin, a trembling old man. The real memory was locked away behind some door I couldn't open. Maybe it was better that way.

"So what happened to the real estate deal?" I asked, just to finish the story and lay it to rest.

Vin shook his head. "I guess Mike was right," he sighed. "We wound up selling the property for a hundred twenty-five thousand dollars. And then the lawyers we sold it to went and tore down the hot dog stand and built the Doubloon Casino. We could've all been millionaires."

I just stood there for a second, watching the Doubloon's red TAKE A CHANCE sign thirty yards away blink on and off in the early-morning light. When the sun hit the casinos at this angle, they really did look like palaces and castles. Especially before all the losers, hustlers, scavengers, high rollers, hookers, sidewinders, and people who've just never caught on to how the world works came streaming out onto the beach.

All this time, it had been so obvious. But I didn't want to see it. Now that I knew it all, I didn't so much feel angry as half dead inside.

"I don't think I can be around you anymore," I told Vin.

A gust of wind blew through the tower of his hair, leaving it lopsided. "I understand," he said.

"Tell Teddy whatever you want about the fight. I don't see how I owe him anything else now."

I started moving away, toward a broken part of the Boardwalk.

"What about you?" Vin tried to keep up with me. "What're you gonna do."

"Never mind about me."

I still hadn't worked out whether I was going to try to stay or get out of town after the fight. Either way, I wanted to make sure I'd have enough money to give my wife and kids.

"Anthony, gimme a hug."

I turned to look at Vin. This murderous old man, who'd destroyed the life I could've had. I'd never noticed how hairy he was before. He had hair in his ears, hair in his nose, hair curling off the back of his neck. Larry DiGregorio must have felt his hairy fingers pressing down on his windpipe. Somehow I couldn't find it in my heart to hate him. I just knew I had to get away from him.

He held out his arms to me.

"I'm not going to do that." I stiffened.

Vin bowed his head, accepting that was the way it was going to be. "All right," he said. "The only thing is, just make sure you get Teddy the sixty you already owe him. Otherwise, even I can't protect you."

"Don't worry. He'll get it."

The wind whistled down the beach like a long train sigh and the tide crested along the nearest jetty. I looked down and saw the Boardwalk was littered with thousands of pieces of clamshells that had been dropped there by seagulls and crushed underfoot by tourists.

"Hey, Anthony." Vin suddenly grabbed my arm and turned me to face him one last time. "I'm sorry."

"About what?" Where could he begin?

"I dunno." He let go of me and started to walk away with his hands in his pockets. "I guess everybody oughta be sorry about something."

49

On the afternoon of the fight, Rosemary stopped by the club called Rafferty's to pick up a few clothes and the spare set of keys she'd left in her dressing room. She found a hugely pregnant young woman sitting in her chair, with a black vinyl handbag on her lap.

"You're older than I thought you'd be," said the young woman, thrusting a hand deep into the bag.

Rosemary had the unmistakable feeling there was a gun inside. "Excuse me?"

"I said I thought you'd be younger. I'm Carla. It's my husband you're stealing and my children whose mouths you're taking food out of, you slut."

The outline of what looked like a barrel poked against the side of the bag.

"I'm afraid you are making a mistake," Rosemary said, looking back at the door and wondering who'd let this crazy person in.

"No, you're the one making a mistake," Carla informed

her. "You think you can just walk away with my Anthony and not have to deal with the consequences? How old are you anyway?"

"I'm thirty-eight." Rosemary suddenly wished she hadn't worn the tight ribbed tank top and the short denim skirt that showed off her tan legs.

"Well, you've kept your figure very nice for a woman your age." Carla swallowed hard and closed her eyes for a second. The baby was obviously kicking her. "You got a glass of water back here? My throat is killing me."

Rosemary brought her a full cup from the water cooler in the corner. "How many months are you?"

"Eight." Carla took the water and smiled gratefully. "I thought this was when it was gonna get easier. With my first two, I got all this energy toward the end."

"This is what happens when you don't eat right and don't drink enough fluids." Rosemary backed away from her. "The baby just takes what it needs. In my eighth month, I wasn't getting enough calcium, so my daughter just took it from me. Sucked it right out of my bones. I thought my teeth were going to fall out."

"You have kids?" Carla gave her a queasy look, but the outline of the gun was no longer visible against the bag.

"One and one that I lost." Rosemary felt her bare knees knocking together.

"Well, at least Anthony went for a woman with some miles on her, and not some bimbo like I thought he would."

Rosemary sensed this woman was not dangerous or even very angry. Just sad. But you had to be careful with guns and jealousy.

"I told you before. I am not having an affair with your husband."

"Then how come the guy behind the bar told me you were his girlfriend?"

Rosemary froze, but just for a second. "It's because I

wouldn't give him a blow job. You know how guys are. If you don't come across, they'll say anything about you."

Carla narrowed her eyes. "I sure hope you're telling the truth, because if it isn't me coming after you, you'll have the rest of my family to deal with."

Rosemary thought of Anthony's stepfather threatening her in this same spot a few weeks back, but didn't say anything. These people were truly insane. She wondered how she'd allowed herself to get involved with them. After the fight tonight, she was going to take her money and her daughter and get the hell out of town before another of these crazy Russos popped up and tried to shoot her.

"Listen, I am sorry if your husband is having an affair," she continued to lie out of self-preservation. "But it really has nothing to do with me. I've sworn off married men. Once you get mixed up with them, you spend your whole life waiting for miracles that'll never happen."

"That's me," Carla said, taking the words more seriously than Rosemary meant them. "I'm always waiting for miracles out of Anthony."

"Well, you can't live your life like that," Rosemary said. She was just riffing now. Trying to move things along, so this pregnant girl would leave soon. Poor girl. In spite of the loaded handbag, Rosemary felt sorry for her. This Carla literally looked like she was dying for a little encouragement. She must've grown up around beasts like that Vin.

"You have to take charge of your life," Rosemary counseled her. "Nobody else is going to rescue you."

"Yeah, I guess that's right," said Carla, struggling to her feet. "You know what I think? You got too much on the ball to be messing around with my Anthony. Now tell me if they got a bathroom back here. I've gotta pee like a racehorse."

50

Seven hours before the fight, I was standing on my porch, watching my son spin some kind of disc on the concrete driveway.

"What's that you got there?" I said, hoping it wasn't one of my old Springsteen records.

He brought over a miniature roulette wheel, the type you can buy at a novelty store.

"Where'd you get this from?"

"Un-CLE TED brought it over."

I gave it a good look. The number six slot was bigger than the others. Only another five-year-old could believe the game wasn't fixed.

"So what are you supposed to do with this?"

Anthony Jr. took a deep breath. "Un-CLE Ted said I should bring IT to school and bet num-BER six."

"He wants you to run a crooked game in kindergarten?"

I got down on one knee and gave it a spin. Sure enough, the ball nestled in number six.

"I hope he didn't ask for a percentage."

"He say I can keep anything LESS than five dol-LARS," he said with earnest concentration.

"Is this what's going to happen to you if I go away?" I took the wheel from him and tried to fit it in my pocket. "You're going to grow up to be a little knucklehead?"

He looked alarmed. "Are you going somewhere?"

I didn't meet his eye. "Look, forget the roulette. Go get me a baseball, will you? I wanna show you a few things about throwing it."

He went tearing back into the house, eager for the

chance to do anything with his daddy. But what kind of father was I, anyway? All the time I'd been sick—blackmailing, hustling to put the fight together, killing Nicky, turning myself into a monster—I told myself it was all for the kids, so I could provide for them. But what was this legacy I was leaving for them? I'd already turned into a thug like Vin and now I was thinking about disappearing from their lives like Mike.

Maybe it would be better if I just went away, I thought. I remembered how Teddy's son, Charlie, used to get high and turn paranoid about his father's karma catching up with him. "He's done a lot of bad shit," he'd say, "and it's all gonna come back." At the time, I didn't know what he was talking about. But now I found myself worrying about what kind of damage I'd already done to my kids.

I almost didn't notice that dark-haired detective with the basset-hound eyes moseying across my front lawn.

"Afternoon, junior," he said in a husky voice. "Must be a big day for you."

He looked me up and down. I was wearing my good blue suit with the trim waist and the peaked lapels.

"Do I know you?"

He flashed a badge and showed me some I.D. Detective Peter Farley, Atlantic City Police Department.

"What can I do for you?" I felt my back teeth floating. Had somebody given me up for killing Nicky?

"Actually I'm not here on police business," said Detective Farley, pulling out a roll of Tums and offering me one. "Some of our mutual friends at the Doubloon Casino had some questions they wanted me to ask. Seems they're a little concerned about the sudden change on the bill. They don't understand why Meldrick Norman is out and Elijah Barton is back in."

"These things happen all the time in boxing." An answer Frank Diamond would've been proud of.

"I know, but the casino people are a little worried that everything might not be—how shall I put this?—kosher."

"Why's that? I wonder."

"Well, Vinny Russo's your stepfather, isn't he?" He sounded almost apologetic about asking.

"We're estranged." I folded my arms across my chest.

Little Anthony came charging out of the house, clutching a rubber softball. When he saw me talking to the cop, though, he stopped to watch us from the porch, about twenty feet away.

"If everyone had their family background held against them, half this town would be out of work," I said, nervously clicking my heel on the driveway. "I am and always have been a legitimate businessman. And if you want to get technical, Detective, my real father was a man named Michael Dillon. He was legitimate too."

"I know," said this Farley. "I knew him."

For a second, he looked like he wanted to tell me something about Mike. He'd half grimaced when I mentioned Mike's name, as if it gave him some kind of pang. But then my son started tossing the softball against the porch railing and demanding to know when we could play catch.

"So cut to the chase," I said to the detective. "Do you have any reason to believe I'm anything less than legitimate?"

If I was in trouble, I figured I wanted to know about it right away and get myself a good lawyer.

"No, no reason." Farley shrugged.

"Then I don't see any point in us continuing this conversation, do you?"

He hesitated, drawing back one corner of his mouth, as though he'd just realized he had a toothache. "No, I guess not." He turned as if he was getting ready to walk away. "Just one thing, though," he said. "You know, there are some people who might be less than thrilled about your success in the fight game."

Clearly he was talking about Teddy. Now it was my turn to shrug. "Thanks for the heads-up."

"Anytime." He gave me one more thorough look before he backed down the drive. "I think Mike would've been pleased with the way you turned out. Anybody ever tell you you look like him?"

"No one who counts."

He smiled and I went to play catch with my son.

51

The prosecutor in a previous case had entered an AK-47 assault rifle into evidence in Judge Leonard Scibetta's federal courtroom in Philadelphia, so when Teddy and his lawyer Burt Ryan walked in for a status conference to set a trial date, the judge was still looking down the sights and aiming the gun at the jury box.

"Judge, I was hoping we could move this along quickly," said Burt, wheezing and ducking as the judge swung the barrel around and pointed the gun at a clerk. "It's no secret my client is not in the best of health, and I think it's in everyone's interest to have a speedy trial."

Teddy coughed into his fist as the judge, a cadaverous-looking man with a widow's peak of dark hair, put the rifle down and began conferring with his clerk.

"I have a date open on the fourteenth of October," the judge said as he flipped pages on a desk calendar. "Could we start jury selection at that time?"

"Your Honor, that won't work for me." Burt studied the

appointment book he had open on the defense table.

"What do you got, another polo game?" sneered Teddy, standing beside him.

He'd lost even more weight in the weeks since the operation. The skin under his chin and around his eyes was hanging off his face like loose crepe paper streamers.

The judge looked at his clerk and flipped through more pages. "How 'bout November second?"

At the prosecution table, a trim young lawyer named Nevins, who had shiny auburn hair and black horn-rimmed glasses, clicked his pen and stood up abruptly. "Your honor, we may need a little more time."

"And why is that?"

"It's hard to be definite."

"I will not have you wreaking havoc on my docket." The judge looked like he was ready to pick up the rifle again. "What do you have in mind, Mr. Nevins?"

"Judge, it's not for me to say at this point."

"Are you planning to bring a superseding indictment?"

"Well." Nevins hesitated and looked down at his co-counsel, a young woman with straight dishwater-blond hair, who was busy scribbling on a yellow legal pad.

"If you are, then I want you to give notice now what the additional charges are going to be," the judge demanded.

Teddy and Burt exchanged nervous glances. The young prosecutor swallowed hard.

"Judge," he said, clicking his pen several times. "As I believe Mr. Ryan knows, the grand jury has been considering adding homicide charges as they relate to the DiGregorio situation. And they might supersede the simple racketeering indictment you have before you."

Burt Ryan took out his asthma spray. Teddy cursed, winced, and delivered himself of a belch that sounded like something out of a county fair.

"Your Honor," said Burt, taking a long shot from the

spray as he prepared to feign outrage. "I want the names of these cooperating witnesses right now. I'm going to need a chance to prepare for cross-examination."

Nevins approached the bench with a light bounce in his step. "Judge, I couldn't possibly release any names," he said. "It would seriously jeopardize the safety of a witness whose cooperation has not been fully secured yet."

"Why don't you wash your hair, you faggot?" Teddy said to the prosecutor.

"Your Honor," said Nevins. "Will you please direct Mr. Ryan to tell his client to keep his invective to himself?"

The judge nodded as Teddy leaned over to whisper in Burt's ear. Two paralegals rustled papers behind them.

"Judge, we want the name of that witness." Burt put away his spray. "And we want it now, so we can begin our preparation. I have appointments in New York City later today and Mr. Marino has almost an hour's drive back to Atlantic City for his dialysis."

"And I'm sure you will get the name in due time," said the judge, rubbing his forehead. "But at the moment, charges have not been filed and I see no reason to pressure Mr. Nevins any further."

At the defense table, Teddy was quietly raging. So there was a Judas after all. Maybe even someone who'd stood alongside him when he was battling it out on the streets and spilling the blood of real men. Here it was all being settled in little brown rooms and corridors by men with shiny hair and asthma sprays. Another hot flash from the medication washed over him and he found himself on the verge of tears. It was those goddamn female hormones they were giving him. Bad enough he couldn't get it up anymore, but now he was finding he could barely control his emotions.

"Fuck this," he erupted. "I can't face my own accuser? This is worse than the Nuremberg trials."

The judge leaned over the bench. "Mr. Marino," he said. "Are you comparing yourself to Nazi war criminals?"

Nazis? What the fuck? Teddy looked down at his shoes. "I meant those Rosenbergs," he mumbled.

What was the difference?

"Mr. Marino," said the judge, "I understand that you're not feeling well, but I won't tolerate another outbreak like that in my courtroom."

"My client understands, Your Honor." Burt patted Teddy on the back.

The judge flipped a few more pages in his calendar. "I have a date open right after Thanksgiving," he said, checking one more time with his clerk. "Is that all right with you, Mr. Nevins?"

"Yes, it should be," said the young prosecutor.

"And how about you, Mr. Marino? Can you live with that?"

"Do I have a choice?" asked Teddy.

52

"Fuck, no!"

Three and a half hours before the fight, Frank Diamond was trying to get me to put on a white sweatshirt with the letters B.U.M. stenciled in blue on the front.

"It's part of the endorsement deal," he patiently explained. "This is one of the major sportswear companies in the country right now. And our agreement was that everyone in Barton's corner would wear one."

"You're just trying to make me look like an asshole."

He grinned and ignored the obvious rejoinder. "Fine," he said. "Don't wear the shirt. But then you won't be allowed into his corner during the fight."

So I went along and put on the B.U.M. shirt, even though I suspected Frank didn't have an endorsement deal and was just doing it to embarrass me.

In fact, I was going along with most things he said that day, because I knew he had so much to teach me.

I was rushing around the hotel suite like a little dog, yapping at Frank's heels, trying to absorb all this information while I had the chance.

"So when am I going to get my advance?" I asked. "We agreed you'd give me a third of the money up front."

"All good things to those who wait," he said calmly, resting a telephone against the side of his shaved head. He made a call downstairs. "Darden, bring up the briefcase from the cage. Mr. Barton's distinguished manager is here."

I guess Frank was annoyed about having to deal with me at this level, but what could he do? I had leverage on him because of what happened with Rosemary and his fighter.

"So let me make sure we have this straight," I said, slipping on my suit jacket over the B.U.M. sweatshirt. "You're going to give me five hundred thousand dollars now and a million later?"

Before Frank could answer, there was a knock at the door and in walked a local manager named George Rollins, who had a fighter in one of the preliminaries. George, a heavyset black guy with wet eyes and a nasty scar on his chin, started pounding the glass coffee table and demanding more money for his fighter, thinking he had Frank over a barrel because he was coming to him on such short notice.

But Frank just draped himself over one of those elegant velvet couches and crossed his legs like Prince Edward as he sipped his tea. "Why George, I'm absolutely astonished," he said languidly.

"Well, that's the way it gots to be." George was chewing

tobacco and for some reason, pouring Oil of Olay lotion on his hands. "I ain't lettin' my boy fight for no twelve hundred dollars."

"But you're coming to me at the last moment with this proposal." Frank tilted back his bald head and his steam-shovel jaw, looking down his nose at George with obvious disdain. "I'm afraid I'll have to give your spot on the card to Anthony here, who has his own stable of fighters."

I just smiled, going along with the story.

George began sweating and chewing his tobacco double-time, realizing he was about to let his fighter's one shot at national TV exposure slip away. "Well, maybe we could work it out another way," he said, putting the bottle of Oil of Olay back into his vest pocket.

"Yes indeed," said Frank, not missing a beat. "In like circumstances, I've heard of promoters actually forcing managers to pay to put their fighters on a bill. But, you know, I wouldn't inflict that on you. Let's just say we'll call it even."

In other words, the fighter would now be getting in the ring for free. George left the suite quickly, before he felt the breeze telling him he'd given up his trousers too.

"That was amazing." My mouth was hanging open. "You cut that guy in two without spilling a drop of blood on the carpet."

"It's just standard negotiation." He couldn't be bothered to smile.

Again I was reminded there wasn't that much difference between these so-called legitimate people from Wall Street and the wiseguys like Teddy and my father.

"I hope you're not going to try the same thing with me." I tried to close my jacket so it would cover part of the B.U.M. on my sweatshirt.

Frank said nothing and made another phone call. Twenty minutes later, one of his aides arrived in the

suite, carrying a briefcase with the name of the casino
embossed in gold on the front. He handed it to me and I
felt my heart swell, almost like the veins and arteries had
erections.

But then I popped the briefcase open and saw it was
filled with chips from the casino.

"What the fuck is this?"

Frank covered the mouthpiece of the phone and glanced
over at me with total indifference. "It's a tradition I have
with local managers. I always like to take the pre-fight
payment directly from the casino's cage. Don't worry. You
can go downstairs afterwards and have it converted."

He went back to his phone conversation with somebody on the Japanese stock exchange. I quickly counted
there was only three hundred thousand dollars' worth of
chips; as Elijah's co-manager, I was entitled to just twenty
percent, or sixty thousand. Barely enough to cover my
debt to Teddy. There'd be nothing for my wife and kids,
either. Forget Danny Klein and Rosemary.

"Where's the rest of it?" I stood up and took a step
toward Frank.

"Yoshiki, let me call you back," he said into the phone.
"Yes. *Do mo arigato*."

"There's only three hundred thousand dollars here." I
pointed to the open briefcase. "We agreed to five hundred
thousand up front."

"Right. You lose a third off the top to taxes."

"That still leaves about three hundred thirty thousand."

"Of course," said Frank with huffy impatience. "And
some of that goes toward the accrued expenses that managers are expected to share in. Scoring judges, cost of
printing tickets, overhead for keeping the arena open."

"What about the million you owe me after the fight?" I
heard my voice cracking.

"We'll see how much of that is left." He stood up and

walked across the room to a silver tea service on the marble-topped bar. For a big man, he glided gracefully in his Gucci loafers. "Remember, you have to pay for the legal fees, the attending physicians, and the cost of laying cable. I wouldn't expect the back end to be more than one hundred and twenty thousand dollars if I were your fighter. Subject to taxes, of course."

"I'll sue your fucking ass, Frank." My take for the night was going to be eighty-four thousand dollars, thirty-six thousand short of what I owed.

"You and your lawyers are welcome to review my accounting practices," he said, making himself a fresh cup. "They will stand up in court. Naturally, if I were you I'd want to avoid legal proceedings, especially given your background."

Now I was the one feeling the breeze where my pants used to be. "Oh my God. This is outrageous. How am I going to pay my people?"

"Out of the advance I'd give you if I decided to take an option on Elijah's next fight."

"And what would it take to get you to pick up the option?"

"A strong showing tonight," Frank said with a faint smile. I noticed he held his pinky out when he sipped his tea, like a dainty English maiden.

I felt dampness on the inside of my thigh and hoped it was sweat. "You mean Elijah has to win before we get paid the full amount?"

What was left of my world was collapsing. Elijah was an old man who'd been knocked out sparring the month before. He didn't stand a real chance against Terrence. At his age, just climbing through the ropes was an achievement.

"He doesn't have to win," Frank told me. "He has to go the distance and do it in credible fashion. Not just holding on in the clinches. He has to put on a real fight."

"In other words, he has to have the shit kicked out of him and remain standing?"

"Something like that." Frank rang a bell for a servant to come and take his tea service away. "But I'd never say he had to win. That would be unreasonable."

53

"We got one rule," said Teddy as the car sped along the Garden State Parkway, "whenever we find a rat, we kill him. No ands, ifs, or buts about it."

Joey Snails, the ex-junkie with the oily skin and the crevices shaped like seahorses in his cheeks, was driving. He raised his eyebrows and the seahorses got longer. Tommy Sick in the seat beside him giggled moronically.

It was almost dusk. Tall stark pine trees stood on either side of the road like elongated shadows.

"Way I figure it," said Teddy, the collar of his shirt creeping up toward his jaw as he sank down in the passenger seat, "they have to have somebody who can put me in onna conspiracy for killing Larry and his son, even though I wasn't there. You know?"

"The only ones who was there for both of them was Anthony and Richie," said Joey, sniffing.

"That's what I was thinking too. And I know Richie ain't no rat."

The Le Baron hummed along quietly. Not bad for a leased car, thought Teddy. But who wanted to be driving a leased car? The thought never occurred to him before. What'd he have to show for himself? A leased car, insurance forms, and a bunch of lawyer's bills? Another hot flash gave way to a sudden chill. His life was getting smaller and smaller. If he wasn't sitting in some lawyer's office, he was going for his radiation. Or he was stuck at home, hooked to his dialysis machine. It was worse than prison. He started getting angry all over again.

Joey took Exit 38 and swung the car onto the Atlantic City Expressway.

"All right," said Teddy. "Then we have to get Anthony to come in and talk to us."

"I wouldn't come in if I was him." Joey wagged his head as he reached into his pocket for change to pay the toll. "I'd be afraid we'd try to whack him."

"Heh, heh, that's sick," Tommy Sick said with a machinegun laugh. His forehead bulged unnaturally, and he scratched a septum that had been deviated since his father broke his nose for trying to get into the bathtub with his sister at the age of seventeen.

Joey pulled up at the toll booth and took a good thirty seconds to figure out that a dime and three nickels were worth as much as a quarter. He gave the girl in the booth the change and a look that made her back away from her window.

"Maybe you're right," said Teddy as they drove away. "That's the whole problem with getting people involved who don't belong to this thing of ours. They don't have that blood loyalty. Fuckin' mutts. They deserve to die."

"Every one of them," said Joey.

"Heh, heh," said Tommy Sick.

Three lines appeared on Teddy's brow. "I told Vin to get that kid away from me. But he kept after me, 'Just gimme another chance, Ted, just gimme another chance, I'll straighten him out.' " He threw up his hands in disgust. "So first I gotta tolerate him putting nothing in the elbow, when he owes me his life. Then I gotta see him running around on my niece. And now look at the mess we're in. The kid Anthony's talking about us to the feds. He's a rat."

He was silent for a couple of minutes. Atlantic City was visible at the edge of the horizon. The red names of the casinos burned like bonfires in the darkening sky.

"You know who I blame for it?" Teddy said in a sullen voice. "Vin. It's his fault for not controlling this kid. I love the man, but I gotta tell you, Joey, I feel like he betrayed me. He told me he'd take care of it, and then he sold me out for this son of his, that isn't even his son. While I have to suffer with the memory of my own boy. I'm sick about it, Joey. I'm sick."

"Heh, heh, that's my line, Ted," said Tommy Sick.

Teddy leaned forward and punched him in the back of the head.

Traffic was starting to slow down. They were stuck in a long, long trail of cars arriving early for the fight at the Doubloon.

"What're you gonna do about it?" asked Joey. "Anthony ain't gettin' anywhere near us."

"If you can't get to the rat, you get someone who's close to him," said Teddy, as though it had all been decided by some great force beyond him.

Joey frowned and wiggled his buttocks uncomfortably in his seat. "You're not talkin' about whacking Vin, are you?"

Teddy's expression did not change. "The rules is the rules," he said. "You got any idea what he's doing tonight?"

"I don't know." Joey shrugged. "I talked about coming over and watching the fight with him tonight. But you ain't serious, Ted. Vin loves you."

"Have him stop by the Marvin Gardens house," Teddy instructed him firmly. "Tommy, you go to the fight and keep an eye on Anthony. We'll kill two birds, one stone."

"But, Ted, we're talkin' Vin," Joey protested.

"He's gotta go," said Teddy, tightening his face like a petulant child. "He's gotta be taken out of the way so we can whack Anthony without any problems afterwards. Otherwise, we'd have Vin coming after us for revenge."

Tommy Sick was silent. Joey stared at his fingers on the steering wheel. "Jeez, Ted, you're gettin' to be kinda a hard-ass, ain't you?"

"Just paying the cost for being the boss," said Teddy, staring straight ahead.

54

The angry red orb of the sun had sunk behind the silver casinos.

Frank Diamond had me in a true balls-to-the-wall situation. If Elijah didn't put up the fight of his life tonight, I was a dead man.

But I decided to enjoy my night on the verge. Damn it, I'd come this far, I wasn't going to quit. That whore called respectability was about to lift her skirts and let me have a go at her.

At half past eight, I went down to the lobby to watch all the celebrities and high rollers arrive. They'd set up the porte cochere entrance so that each VIP had to walk past a gauntlet of fans and photographers once they got out of their limos.

At first I didn't recognize anybody. It was just needle-nosed guys with big Brillo pads of gray hair and taut laugh lines around their mouths wearing tuxes with ruffled shirts and velvet bow ties, accompanied by flimsy-looking young blondes spilling out of their gold lamé dresses. Then came the old crones collapsing inside electric-blue evening gowns and the sclerotic old men in business suits with heavy wattles and features small enough to fit on a postage stamp. Soon the faces became more familiar. Here was a former vice president and the head of a credit card company. There was an actor who always played the stud in his movies, but when you saw him with his little hands and his twitchy butt, you knew he'd never touched a woman. He was with an actress who had to be about fifty but still giggled like a Betty Boop doll. They were followed by a former junk bond king and a famous dress designer.

Looking at them, you'd think the standard wasn't how much jewelry they wore but how much plastic surgery they'd had. Paulie Raymond would've loved it. There were tit jobs, dye jobs, face-lifts, hair plugs, people with the fat sucked out of their cheeks, cellulite scraped off their asses. You half expected a second division to come along, made up of the cast-off parts.

Still, you couldn't deny the excitement in the air. All these famous people had come to see a fighter managed by me. The only disappointment was not having a father around to see what I'd accomplished. But Mike was long gone and I could never speak to Vin again.

Instead I saw Dan Bishop, the Vegas casino owner, getting out of a limo, and I went running over. Frank Diamond was standing there to greet him as he climbed out of the car. Bishop was heavier than in the pictures I'd seen and there was more gray in his hair. He'd had plastic surgery too.

I sidled up to Frank and stuck an elbow in his ribs. "Introduce me, you sleazy fuck," I murmured.

He ignored me for a few seconds and began talking to Bishop until I elbowed him again. Then he turned with a glacial smile and guided my eyes toward Bishop's.

"Dan, I'd like you to meet Anthony Russo," he said in a low reluctant voice as the blitzkrieg of flashbulbs went off around us.

This was a moment I'd dreamed about for years. Meeting Dan Bishop. Who'd started off running numbers down in the Inlet and wound up getting invited to the White

House. I wanted to tell him how much I admired what he'd done, and how maybe one day soon I'd be out in Vegas and we could talk about some opportunities. But before I could get the words out, I realized he was staring down at my shirt. His eyes began to narrow and his lip began to curl. I realized I was still wearing the B.U.M. sweatshirt Frank made me put on.

"Nice shirt," he said.

Almost as an afterthought, he shook my hand. His grip was weak and cold. I'd been dismissed before I'd been introduced.

"Talk to me later about Terrence," he muttered to Frank as he went by. "I think I got something you might be interested in."

He signaled for a tall black bodyguard and a stubby redhead in a chiffon dress to lead the way. I noticed his tux looked a little tight in the back and the hair on top of his scalp was too shiny, like he might've been wearing a piece as cheap as Larry DiGregorio's. And what I kept thinking was: He blew it.

The great Dan Bishop. I finally got to meet him and all he had to say to me was "nice shirt." Well screw him, I thought. He was on the way down anyway. He could've taken a second to talk to me about the future. But instead he blew it. Someday he'd realize he'd made a mistake. All I needed to make him see that was a miracle out of Elijah.

55

"So I hear that kid's been calling you 'old man' again. That's beautiful."

P.F. was in the dressing room a half hour before the fight, watching Elijah trying to tie his sneakers.

"Who this?" said Elijah, missing the loop on the right lace a third time.

"The kid you're fighting tonight. Terrence. He said, 'Old man oughta go back to the old man home.' I heard it on TV."

"Oh." Elijah missed the loop a fourth time. "Perhaps tonight I ask him to call me by my proper name."

He went to work on the left lace. Pathetic. The man couldn't tie his own shoes and he was going to fight a kid half his age and twice his strength. P.F. wondered if he'd let someone beat his brains out for a million dollars. But then again, he'd sold his soul to Teddy for a couple of TV sets, so who was he to judge?

Eventually Elijah's cut man Victor Perez came over to help him lace up his shoes.

"You know, I ain't fightin' this fight for respect anyway," said Elijah in an already haggard voice.

"Oh no?" P.F. fixed the special security badge on the left side of his blue Doubloon windbreaker.

"That's right. From now on, I fight for one reason and one reason only, M-O-N-E-Y."

The dressing room had plain white walls and a red carpet with bits of brown woven into it. Terrence Mulvehill's ancient white trainer Ben E. Schulman came by to watch Elijah get his hands wrapped. A young man from the cable TV outfit hugged a clipboard and took deep breaths. Two other guards stood near the door, regarding the scene reverently.

A waitress came in with a bucket of ice water and then left. Elijah muttered something to the guards about not wanting to see any more women between now and the time the fight started.

"I gotta get the meanness started inside me," he explained. "I can't do it if I see women around."

The young man from the cable network got on his mobile phone and began whispering nervously.

"You know in Vegas they're taking odds on what round you'll get knocked out," P.F. said.

"Yeah?" Elijah lay on his stomach to get a back rub. "And what kinda odds are they gettin'?"

"Five to one that you'll fall in the first round."

Elijah smiled.

Victor the cut man slathered him with baby oil and began pulling his shoulders like they were lumps of soggy clay.

"Yes, sir," said Elijah. "I only got one rule anymore: Be comfortable."

"If you say so." P.F. held up his palms.

The sound of the crowd cheering one of the preliminary bouts bled through the walls. It sounded like a nation entombed.

"How you fixed, man?"

"What do you mean?"

"I'm asking where you got your money."

P.F. looked at him blankly. "I dunno, in a bank."

Elijah shook his head. "Somebody oughta take you aside, talk to you, man. You gotta get yourself into some triple tax frees and mutual funds. Can't just leave your money in some insured money market. You gotta make it work for you."

P.F. wondered why Elijah seemed so comfortable here, talking to him like they were old friends. Maybe it was just a way of loosening up before the fight. In any case, it wasn't bad advice, especially coming from a man who was supposedly punch-drunk.

"You know what the secret is?" Elijah stood up and began to shadowbox. He wore just a pair of socks and a black protective cup over his genitals. "You never put all your assets in one place. I remember when I was just a child I used to hide my money in the flowerpot. Now I don't put all my money in one bank. I don't put all my

money in two banks. I don't put all my money nowhere.
If the bank falls down today and takes everything I have
in there, I still will be able to survive. Because I got…" It
took him an eternity to settle on a word. "Reserves," he
said finally. "I got hidden reserves. Ain't nobody knows
about 'em."

He threw a right cross at the mirror on the wall. For a
moment P.F. thought he'd actually break the glass and
bloody his knuckles. He missed contact by less than half
an inch.

"Yup, that's the only reason to do anything," he said.
"For the C-A-S-H."

Pigfucker just looked at him.

"What? You still think I gotta do this shit for my self-
respect?"

P.F. didn't answer.

"Man, fuck that." Elijah threw a hard left jab that jerked
a muscle in his shoulder. "I don't have to do this to live. I'm
forty-three years old, man. I already been the champion
twice. I defended my title six times. I don't need to come
out of retirement to earn my self-esteem."

Elijah scowled at the mirror and saw P.F. watching him
from behind.

"I don't wake up in the middle of the night worrying,"
Elijah said, feinting with his left and throwing a stiff right
at the mirror. "I got a beautiful wife, a beautiful son, three
beautiful grandchildren. I'm proud. I started with nothing.
I grew up in a shack out in the Inlet and I became middleweight champion of the whole wide world."

The room was completely silent.

"I ain't got nothin' to be ashamed of," Elijah said, firing
two more furious punches at his reflection. "Just because
some punk hit me with a lucky shot when I wasn't ready
and I hadn't trained. That may be how some other people
remember me. It ain't how I remember myself."

P.F. finally looked away as Elijah stopped throwing punches. He'd heard more convincing declarations from swindlers and con artists in the back of the squad car.

Dr. Park, the boxing federation's physician, came into the room smoking a cigarette. A rail-thin Korean man in a navy pinstripe suit. Anthony Russo followed him in, wearing a dark suit and a B.U.M. sweatshirt. He seemed nervous and unsure where to put his eyes.

There was still something about the kid that made P.F. profoundly uneasy. Maybe it was just their common history with Teddy and Mike.

Dr. Park was shining a light in Elijah's eyes. P.F. thought he saw the pupils respond a fraction of a second too slowly to its movement.

"How you feeling?" the doctor asked.

"Like I could dance all night."

The doctor stepped away and Anthony moved in front of the fighter. Clicking his heel on the carpet and jiggling his knee. He was like a raw nerve in a good suit. You would've thought he was the one about to get in the ring. P.F. rubbed his eyes and swallowed a Tums.

"Look," said Anthony in a bitten-off voice. "I don't have to tell you your business. You've been in the fight game a lot longer than I have."

Elijah made a low virile sound, but he wasn't looking at Anthony. He was staring at some distant spot, miles past his shoulder.

"I'm not asking you to lay down your life tonight," Anthony said. "I'm not asking you to risk permanent injury. All I ask is that you fight like a man among men."

A man among men. He said it with such great feeling that Elijah's eyes flicked over and locked on to his.

"That's all I ever done," he told Anthony.

Anthony shook Elijah's wrapped right hand, made a note in his Filofax, and walked out of the room with the doctor.

"Hurt my hands." Elijah stared down at his fingers. "Every man comes in, thinks he has to show how strong he is by giving them a squeeze as hard as he can. They don't know this is delicate instruments."

"He's just scared, that's all," said P.F.

"Scared, huh?" Elijah began dancing in place. "You know, I used to be scared too. Scared of dying."

"Yeah, so what happened?"

"I don't know. I got over it."

He threw an abrupt head fake as though an opponent had suddenly materialized before him. "Only thing that scares me now is not knowing how it gonna turn out," said Elijah.

John B. returned from the other dressing room, where he'd been watching Terrence Mulvehill get his hands taped.

"Punched a hole in the wall," he told his brother. "He just reached out and punched a hole in the wall. You can see the lights from Pacific Avenue in his dressing room."

"He punch through the concrete or plaster?" Elijah wanted to know.

"I think it was plaster."

Elijah looked slightly disappointed and went back to dancing. There was less than fifteen minutes until the fight began. Elijah hopped back up on the training table and John B. began rubbing his shoulders.

"The Lord have a way," John was saying. "The Lord will find a way."

The smell of liniment oils and leather gloves began to fill the air. Elijah wasn't talking or moving. He bowed his head as if reaching down deep inside himself.

And from then until the moment the opening bell rang, P.F. only heard him say five more words.

"We can never really know."

56

Teddy and Joey Snails were in the stash house apartment in Marvin Gardens, trying to get ready for their guest.

"I was going to buy almonds," said Joey, putting on his red-and-blue Gore-Tex windbreaker. "You want anything else from the store?"

Teddy was lying on the black leather couch, still exhausted from his dialysis. He slowly raised his eyes. All six of the stolen digital clocks in the room said it was 9:53.

"Does he eat almonds?" he asked.

"Last time he was over my house, he ate the whole bowl," said Joey.

"That's funny," said Teddy. "Whole time I've known him, I've never seen him eat almonds. Forty-five years. It's unbelievable. You can know somebody and not know them at all."

He raised his head and looked around the apartment. The bar was crowded with untaxed bottles of Chivas Regal and Canadian Club, but he couldn't drink any of them. He didn't even have the strength to move the swag and stolen carpets in the next room to the car downstairs.

Joey looked at him with vacant eyes and a slack jaw. "What else you want me to get?"

"Get me some fruit," said Teddy, clutching his side as his eyes glistened. "Where you got that gun anyway?"

"In the bathroom. Where I always keep it."

"That the one you're gonna use?"

"Yeah. You got a problem with that?"

"Just don't fuck around. He carries one in his waistband."

"Don't worry," said Joey, grabbing the doorknob. "I ain't gonna shoot the place up."

"That ain't what I'm concerned about," said Teddy. "You aren't careful, you'll get us both shot. He's a tough old man. I know him."

"Yeah, I know him too."

"Where's Richie?"

"He said he'd stop by later."

"Tell him to hurry. We ain't gonna be here all night."

Joey sucked his cheeks in concentration. "Maybe I'll pick up some chink food while I'm out. I ain't had any dinner."

"Yeah," said Teddy, "and don't get too many of them almonds. They're hard on my stomach the way it is."

57

It was hopeless, I thought as I walked through the tunnel under the stands. Elijah was too old, too slow, and too sad to keep up with Terrence. My only solace was that Teddy would probably have me killed before I'd have to watch Elijah carted off to a home for the mentally disabled.

Just then, Rosemary came tottering toward me on high heels, wearing a tight red sequined outfit with bird feathers on her butt and holding a huge plumed head-dress. I'd gotten her a job as one of the round-card girls as a show of good faith that I'd pay her the money she was owed. But here she was with one of those four-alarm-chili, boiling-mad looks on her face.

"I have had it with you. Understand? I have had it."

"Why, wha, what's the matter?"

She pulled on her tail feathers like they were itching her. "It's bad enough I have your father abusing me in my own dressing room, but now I have to deal with your wife?!!"

"What are you talking about?"

"She had a gun in her bag! She was like Al Capone! She was going to blow my head off!"

I looked at her like she'd lost her mind. "Just put on your fuckin' bird outfit and start acting normal. I don't have time for this."

I heard the swelling murmur of the crowd above us. Elijah would be coming out of his dressing room at any moment.

"I don't have time either." Rosemary clutched at the zircon necklace around her throat. "After tonight, I never want to see you again."

"Very nice," I said. "After I went and got you this job tonight, so you could be a star."

"A star?" She looked like she was about to throw the plumed headdress at me. "Anthony, stars do not walk around in fishnets carrying numbers. Just give me the money you owe me and let's forget about the rest of it."

"All right, all right. Meet me in the parking garage after the fight. Section E 16. One o'clock. I'll give you the whole breakdown."

Though I didn't know how I'd tell her that Frank had rooked me out of the full amount. I'd already turned over two hundred forty thousand dollars' worth of chips to John B. The other sixty thousand were in the hotel safe.

"You better have the whole breakdown." Rosemary started to walk away from me, going out the exit into the main arena. "Or else."

"Or else what?" I ran after her.

"Or else…"

The rest of the sentence was lost in the crowd noise, as I followed her down the aisle toward the ring. We were in the lion's den, surrounded by fifteen thousand people, twenty-five tons of jewelry, and a small river's worth of cold sweat and adrenaline. A bank of colored lights was suspended over the ring. Various television cameras and news photographers jockeyed for position along the periphery.

I turned and saw Elijah and his entourage coming down the aisle from the dressing rooms, hands on each other's shoulders, like the world's most macho conga line.

Over the P.A. system, they were playing his theme song, the Commodores' "Brick House." The crowd cheered like they were greeting an old friend. Elijah climbed through the ropes and began sauntering around the ring with that drunken sailor gait he had. His blue-and-white robe looked like a cardigan somebody's uncle would wear. I began to worry about him all over again.

The worry turned into a snake in my guts when Terrence didn't show up for another five minutes. It was clearly part of some psych-out game meant to tax Elijah's patience and concentration.

But instead of just standing there dull-eyed and slack-jawed, letting it get to him, Elijah turned the whole thing around. He began working the crowd like an old revival-show preacher. He looked at his wrist like he had a watch on. The crowd laughed and clapped appreciatively. Then he tapped his foot. When that didn't produce Terrence, he grabbed the American flag off one of the ring posts and started waving it around in his gloves.

The place went nuts. By the time Terrence finally made it into the ring, skipping around and forcing his seconds to chase him to get his robe off, the crowd was a hundred and ten percent against him. Boos rained down like a pestilence. I still had this awful feeling, though, almost a premonition about what was going to happen.

I looked up toward the mezzanine section and thought I saw Tommy Sick standing there by the railing, wearing

a red shirt, red pants, and a blue blazer. I remembered
Tommy once telling a story about shoving a gerbil up the
ass of a guy who owed Teddy money, all the time laughing
and shrugging: "What can I tell you? I'm sick!"

There was no two ways about it—there was barely
even one way. I needed to have Elijah go the distance. If
he didn't, my life was over. They'd be hanging parts of me
from the telephone lines on Florida Avenue and feeding
the rest to a gerbil. My future was riding on every punch.

The Marine color guard came into the ring to hold up
the flag while some girl group from Terrence's old neighborhood in the Bronx lip-synched the national anthem. I
stood and sang every word with my hand over my heart.
The land of the free and the home of the brave. But I still
wasn't sure if being brave was what set you free.

The referee called the fighters to the center of the ring
to give them their final instructions. Elijah had this soft
half-smile on his face and his eyes were shining like buffed
marbles. Goddamn it, I thought as I climbed the steps
into his corner. They must've given him painkillers in the
dressing room. The fighters touched gloves and went back
to their corners. The bell rang.

Terrence moved out first. He was all spring in the legs
and coiled strength in the arms. Elijah plodded out after
him, his stomach jiggling like pudding. They met in the
middle and Terrence snapped my guy's head back with a
jab like a cobra out of wicker basket.

"STICK AND MOVE, CHAMP!" I heard John B.
shouting, "STICK AND MOVE!"

But Elijah just kept lumbering in a lazy circle, his right
leg dragging behind him as if it was caught in a bear trap.
Terrence was prancing from foot to foot, rocking his shoulders, bobbing his head. Like he couldn't wait to get this
over with so he could go chase girls at a disco. He lunged
forward and hit Elijah again with a right like an M-80

rocket. Elijah fell back a few steps and I saw his mouthpiece turn sideways. My jaw ached, like I'd been punched
too.

"YOU GOT 'IM NOW, CHAMP!" John B. yelled. "YOU
GOT HIM ON THE RUN!"

Terrence planted his feet and hit Elijah with a left cross
that sent him spinning into the corner diagonally across
from us. Oh shit, I thought. Here's where the beating be-
gins. Terrence chased after him and for a few seconds all
I could see were his shoulders and elbows, pumping like
a couple of pistons. The crowd kept going "ooooh" and
"aaah" like they were taking the shots with Elijah.

But when Terrence moved to the side a little, Elijah
didn't look that shaken. He must've been blocking more of
the punches than I thought. Terrence was breathing just
a bit harder as he danced back to the center of the ring.

Elijah moved after him slowly and reluctantly, like an
old groundhog being forced out of his cave. Terrence
lunged at him again, ready to throw the left jab. But this
time Elijah grabbed him with both arms and pulled him
close, like a father grabbing an unruly son. Terrence
squirmed and tried to get out of the clinch, but Elijah had
him in a headlock. The crowd began to boo. They'd been
spoiled by all the action so far. Finally, the referee pulled
them apart, giving Elijah some extra warning about holding
on to the back of the younger guy's head.

"WORK THE BODY, CHAMP!" shouted John B.
"WORK THE BODY!"

Terrence squared off and hit Elijah with a short left
jab and a hard right hook that dug into his rib cage like a
Bowie knife. Every time John B. yelled something en-
couraging to his brother, Elijah would get hit with a worse
shot.

A strong left-right combination by Terrence drove
Elijah into the corner right above us. I looked up and saw

Terrence's eyes get a little wider as he came our way. I thought of a rabid bull charging a matador. He was swinging harder now. A body shot doubled Elijah over and a right uppercut snapped his head back and showered us with bloody droplets and sweat.

The crowd was screaming and people were rising to their feet. Minutes before they'd been cheering Elijah, but what they'd really come here to see was blood on the canvas. Terrence hit him with a roundhouse right and a chopping left as the place almost began to vibrate. Elijah was getting jolted from side to side in the corner like a big rag doll. With each shot, the crowd got even louder, until the sound was like a hundred thousand monkeys shrieking in a steel cage.

And then abruptly the sound changed. Without any warning or advance movement, Elijah reached up and put a lightning bolt into the middle of Terrence's face.

The punch seemed to come from nowhere. I didn't even see Elijah winding up. He just threw a long right hand and Terrence fell back like the word of God had descended on him. He didn't just look surprised. He looked astonished. Like he'd never considered the possibility that Elijah might hit him back.

The crowd's roar had more bottom to it now—more of a satisfied noise. Like they were finally seeing something worthwhile. And instead of standing back and marveling at what he'd done, Elijah began advancing on Terrence, like an old World War II Army tank. A fat left hand smashed the side of Terrence's head. A right caught him on the bridge of the nose. I'd seen him throw these kind of long loping punches in workouts, but they never had this much force before.

They butted heads and when Terrence backed away, I saw he had a small cut on his left upper eyelid. Instantly, Elijah went to work on widening the seam, like an expert tailor in reverse. A right, another right, and then a powerful left hook brought more blood flowing.

And for the first time I found myself thinking: Hey, this fat old son of a bitch might actually win.

58

"You know," said Teddy in a ravaged voice. "I was thinking. Every day I read in the paper about the Sicilian Mafia. These guys got balls. Every day they're blowin' up a judge or some fuckin' politician. They even got to a guy in the middle of a motorcade and put a bomb under his car. So I was thinking. Maybe we could get one of their young guys to come over here and work with us. You know. Start all over again. Like a new beginning."

Vincent Russo shook his head and looked grim. "It wouldn't work."

Three of them were in the stash apartment in Marvin Gardens, watching the Barton-Mulvehill fight on cable TV. Teddy was on the black leather sofa with a can of diet soda in his hand. Vin was sitting in a chrome-and-leather easy chair, drinking his fourth beer of the evening and eating almonds out of a cellophane bag. Joey Snails stood in the corner, sniffing and scratching the side of his face. There were racks of men's suits along the wall and dozens of steel lamps by the door to the swag room. Joey excused himself to go to the bathroom.

"Why wouldn't it work?" said Teddy, shooting a look at Joey over the top of the couch. "We get a couple of these zips off the boat working for us, it'd be just like the old days. We could take over everything."

Vin crushed an almond shell and the remnants fell into the cuffs of his trousers. "This ain't the old country,

Ted." He balanced the beer on the arm of his chair. "It's the land of opportunity. We brought a couple of them Sicilian boys over here, they'd be listening to fuckin' rap music and talkin' to their brokers on car phones in two months. Tradition don't last in this country. You can't bind people by the old codes. They just melt away."

Teddy grimaced and touched his back. "I still say we could get a couple of them zips and rule this town again," he grumbled. "It'd be like starting the twentieth century over again, only we'd do it the right way."

On the 27-inch-wide color TV screen, there was a re-play of Elijah Barton shocking Terrence Mulvehill and the rest of the arena with that sudden right hand. As the screen showed a close-up of the deep cut above Terrence's eyelid, Vin sat up too quickly and spilled some of the almonds on the shag carpet.

"So what'd he say to you?" Teddy asked, yawning and stretching his arms as his face turned florid.

"Who? Anthony?"

Joey Snails came back in the room and Teddy just looked at him. One of the stainless steel lamps buzzed and vibrated above Vin's head.

"Well, you know, I talked to him," said Vin. "And, and, the kid's got an awful lot of confusion in his mind. You know what I'm saying, Teddy? You can understand what kids can be like after what you went through with Charlie."

Teddy was silent. Vin finished his beer and crushed the can with his fingers.

The second round ended and the two fighters went back to their corners. The camera focused on Elijah Barton sitting on his stool, breathing heavily as his brother squeezed a wet sponge over him and his cut man smeared more Vaseline on his face.

"Again," said Vin, taking a fistful of almonds and shoving them in his mouth, "it's this, this, you know. He don't understand what it was like starting off the way we did. You know. This, this is a different generation. I never got my first blow job from a woman 'til I was about forty years old, just got out of jail."

Joey and Teddy were staring at him. Vin was babbling on, fueled by the beer and the hour. "I remember it was right by the Steel Pier," he said, chewing almonds. "Right where they used to have the horses diving in the water. I still remember those horses and her mouth on me. I'll never have a day like that again."

Joey Snails was still staring at him without saying anything.

Vin's eyelids got heavy and silvery-looking. "I guess what I'm saying, Ted, is maybe we shoulda had more babies of our own if we wanted them to stay loyal with us," he said. "They say it takes the edge off a man…But like you said before, the gun wasn't loaded. I didn't have enough of them sperms. What could I do?"

He let his head hang down. Teddy's attention had drifted back to the television set. He coughed and put a hand to his mouth.

"He's not gonna give us anything. Is that what you're telling me, Vin?"

"I guess—well—yeah. He don't want to do anything right now," Vin said, trying to stay awake. "He don't want to make any deals. But I'll talk to him again."

"He should come in and tell me all this himself," Teddy said sharply.

"Yeah, yeah, I know Ted. But he ain't gonna do that right away. He's gonna go away awhile, clear his head."

Teddy glared over at Joey. Joey excused himself to go to the bathroom once more.

"What's the matter, you getting a small bladder?" Vin called after him. He turned back to Teddy. "I used to be able to drink beer all night and only have to go once. It's all this espresso they drink now. They spend half their time in the can."

"Things change," Teddy told him in an exhausted voice.

"Hey, Joey!" Vin shouted toward the bathroom. "Grab my comb if you find it, will you? I been looking all night."

On the TV, the round-card girl, who wore a red feathered headdress and an uncomfortable-looking sequined swimsuit, finished circling the ring and climbed through the ropes as the bell rang. The two fighters left their stools and touched gloves.

"I don't know, Ted," said Vin with a sigh. "I don't know how you keep up."

Joey Snails came out of the bathroom with a nine-millimeter Browning handgun and blew the back of Vincent Russo's head off.

He went around to the other side, put the gun in Vin's mouth, and fired another shot through the top of Vin's skull.

Teddy looked irritated. "What happened to the silencer?" he said.

"Couldn't find it. I thought you said you left it in the kitchen."

"It's the drawer where we got all the corkscrews."

Teddy looked past his shoulder and saw a purplish red bloodstain spreading on the white shag carpet. Vin's Ace comb was lying nearby. It had fallen out of his pocket earlier in the evening.

"For Chrissake, who's gonna clean that up?"

Joey looked abashed. "Maybe I shoulda thought to lay newspaper. I'll move the couch over it."

Vin's body gave a sudden jerk and slumped down in its seat. At least seven separate tributaries of blood were flowing down his face. It looked like someone had poured a jar of red molasses over the remains of his head. His mouth was open and twisted. The empty cellophane bag was lying sideways on his lap. Unshelled almonds were scattered by his feet.

Joey shot him a third time in the chest and Teddy jumped.

"Jesus Christ!" he yelped. "Why'd you have to do that? Can't you see the man's dead?"

"Hey," said Joey. "What do I look like, a doctor?"

59

By the fifth round, Elijah's strategy had become clear. He was going to stand in the corner and let Terrence hit him until his arms got tired.

"YOU'RE BREAKIN' HIS HEART, CHAMP!" John B. shouted. "YOU'RE BREAKIN' IT IN TWO!"

In the meantime, Terrence was hitting him with every punch in the book: body shots, double hooks, battering rams, more rattlesnake rights, slithering lefts, jabs that came out like crocodiles to snap off little pieces of Elijah. At one point, Terrence stood back in the middle of the ring and looked at him, like: "You sure you wanna do this, old man?" But Elijah just pawed the air with a beckoning motion as if to say, "Come on and fight. This is what we came for."

All that kept Elijah up was his ability to take a punch. His arms were like picket fences and his gloves were big meaty loaves for absorbing punishment. When a blow did get through, he knew how to move his head just a fraction of an inch to lessen its impact. Like John B. said, he'd learned to take three for every one he gave back.

But still Terrence kept coming. Jab. Jab. Jab. Each shot a little brushstroke of pain. Finally, toward the end of the round, Elijah dropped his hands and Terrence smashed him in the mouth with a devastating right hand. Just the sound of it was terrifying. You could almost hear the ocean breaking in Elijah's head. Blood sprayed over us like water coming over the side of a boat.

And for the first time all night, John B. stopped talking.

Elijah fell against Terrence and staggered out to the center of the ring, trying to hold on to him. And just when I thought he was about to collapse, the bell rang.

He came back to the corner and sat on his stool. Dark red blood was gushing from the back of his mouth.

"Somethin' the matter," he mumbled. "I can move my jaw with my tongue."

"Might be broken," said Dr. Park, the ring physician, who'd climbed up the ring steps.

There were five of us clustered around Elijah. Me, John B., Victor the cut man, the doctor, and this cop Farley working for the boxing commission.

There was less than half a minute until the next round began. Elijah's face was mashed almost beyond recognition. His lower features were so lopsided that they no longer matched with the upper ones. John B. was looking back and forth, unable to make a decision. Victor the cut man was busy with a cold-iron trying to reduce the swelling in Elijah's jaw. The doctor hung back, maybe waiting for someone to promise to pay him off later.

I looked up at the spot where I'd seen Tommy Sick before. But he wasn't there. I wondered if he'd moved down to a lower level to be closer to the action.

Elijah spit more blood in the bucket.

"He's gotta keep fighting," I said.

"You gotta go out there again," I told him.

"He's hurting," John B. said plaintively. "I'm gonna throw the towel."

"No, no, don't take it away from him!" I panicked. "Let him decide. If he quits now, he's through forever."

The rest of them just looked at me like I'd suggested putting his head under an eighteen-wheeler.

"Brain damage last forever too." John B. stared through me.

But no one could make Elijah do anything he didn't want to do. The way he'd fought so far proved it.

"You all right to do this?" I said.

Elijah pushed himself off his stool and somehow managed to stand again.

"Just point me in the right direction," he muttered through his wreck of a jaw. "I'll find him."

60

As she ducked through the ropes to begin her promenade around the ring with the ROUND 10 card, Rosemary heard the assholes down in front make that "alley-oop" sound again.

A thousand dollars a seat and they behaved like the morons back at the club. CEOs, heads of insurance companies and law firms, for God's sake. Men who'd built successful businesses. You'd think they'd never seen a half-dressed woman before. It didn't help that her sequined red swimsuit was riding up her butt again and giving her a wedgie in back.

The television cameras swung past her without much interest. Her arms ached from holding the giant card and the hot lights were melting her makeup. The ring smelled from sweat and desperation. When she'd first agreed to put on this ridiculous costume, she'd somehow convinced herself it would impress Kimmy watching on TV at home. Not like being a soap opera actress maybe, but something for her daughter to be proud of: "My mommy

was on TV." But now she was starting to accept that she
looked like a cheap Vegas showgirl. Hoping Kimmy was
already in bed, she affected a hotsy-totsy walk like her
pussy was a bowl with boiling soup threatening to spill
over the sides.

She passed Elijah Barton's corner and saw Anthony.
Would he be around later to give her what he owed her?
She wondered. She finally understood that nothing he'd
ever told her was true. The run-in with his wife the other
day had finished it forever between them. Forget it.
Kimmy had enough stress without strange women lurking
around her front door. When this was all over, Rosemary
would take whatever money she could get and move to
the West Coast, whether she could afford it or not. If she
could put up with this headdress, she could survive on
food stamps. Whatever. She looked back at Barton's corner. The fighter literally looked dead. It was as if someone
had scraped out his insides. All that was left was a husk.
The cut man shoved wads of cotton into his nose and took
them out all violet and wet with blood.

Is that what being a man was all about? Taking physical
punishment? Forget that too. She'd caught a few beatings
in her time and the pain was nothing compared to child-
birth. Men talked about blood and guts and going to war,
but having a baby was more than that. It was war in reverse. Shoving all your guts aside to make room for the
life and vital organs fusing, pulsing, and growing in your
belly. What was the pain of losing a fight compared to the
pain of losing a child?

But pain wasn't the point of it, she was beginning to
see. It wasn't enough just to get by. The point was sur-
viving with some part of yourself intact. And making it.
Making it for yourself. Making it so your kids wouldn't
end up giving blow jobs in the back of Honda Preludes.
She looked over at Terrence's corner and saw his father

and trainer Terrence Sr., trim and graying, kneading his son's shoulders like he was trying to mold him into some exact replica of himself. Perhaps that was the main difference between men and women. A man was always trying to teach his son to be as tough and brutal as he was, so that one day he could turn around and say the kid just didn't measure up. Leaving women to try and protect their daughters from these ferocious, frustrated boys.

What had she said to Anthony's wife, that sad girl with the gun in her bag? You couldn't depend on anyone else to rescue you. Rosemary had known that before. But she was only truly feeling it now.

She crossed one foot in front of the other and felt the muscle stretching from her hip to her thigh go as taut as a fishing line. She hoped she'd shaved high enough so there wasn't any pubic hair showing at the bottom of her outfit. A couple of guys in the fourth row were pumping their fists in the air and making ape noises, so she wasn't sure.

Fuck them. She was a survivor. She bared her teeth and jutted her hips out. Not even caring if her stomach bulged anymore.

She was coming up on Terrence's corner. She wished she could climb out through the ropes right there, but then she figured he was too busy to notice. After all, he hadn't said anything up to this point. His father was still giving him orders. Terrence had his mouthpiece out and his head turned half away, as though he wasn't really listening. He was looking right at her now and his eyes narrowed a little.

She was sure he couldn't really be seeing her. He had to be thinking about the fight and what was going to happen next. But she still had an eerie feeling like he was about to jump off his stool and come charging after her for the way she'd set him up. His father put his hands on the boy's shoulders to get his attention, but Terrence kept glaring at her, even drawing his own lips back to show he still had his teeth. And when she was directly in front of him, he said something to her. At first, she couldn't hear it above the crowd noise, and she hurried the rest of the way around the ring to get out sooner. But by the time she climbed out through the ropes, she'd put it together in her mind.

"You and me after this is all over, bitch," he'd said. "We gotta go another round in the sack."

61

Joey Snails brought the car to a full stop right outside Anthony's house on Texas Avenue. There was a roll and a thump in the trunk and Teddy, sitting on the passenger's side, gave a look back. Then he reached around to unlock the back door and Richie Amato, who'd been waiting for them on the sidewalk, got in.

"I can't believe you whacked Vin," he said in a dazed voice.

"I can't believe I carried the body downstairs by myself," Joey Snails whined.

"Will youse two shut up?" Teddy admonished them. "You sound like a couple of Girl Scouts, for fuck's sake."

"Yeah, but this was Vin!" Richie protested, sliding in behind Teddy. "He lived and died for you, Ted."

"He hadda go," Teddy said numbly. "He kept sticking up for that mutt. Hadda go. It was the only way."

He sounded like he was trying to convince himself as much as the two younger men. A couple of brown leaves fell from the trees overhead and brushed the windshield. The three of them fell silent for a minute.

"You shouldn't have done it," Richie murmured. "The

old man was the best thing that ever happened to you."

"Oh, what are you?" Teddy turned around. "You gonna be a rebel too? Am I gonna have to discipline you, Richie?"

"No," Richie pouted.

"All right." Teddy faced front again. He let out a deep breath and sagged back in his seat.

The downstairs lights in Anthony's house were still on. Through one of the front bay windows, Carla could be seen putting the kids to sleep.

"I think I'm gonna go inside and sit with my niece awhile," he said in a weary voice.

He looked back at the trunk. "You all right to take care of this thing?" he asked Joey and Richie.

"Yeah, I guess." Richie swallowed hard. He still seemed to be in a state of shock.

"Come back later to pick me up, after you get rid of him," said Teddy. He was on automatic pilot too. His instructions were without thought or inflection. He rolled down the window and spit in the gutter. Then he put his hand over his stomach as if the effort had cost him too much.

"What if Anthony comes back here?" Richie tried stretching his arms, but wound up punching the car's ceiling.

"He probably ain't coming back until this fight's over. And if he does come back, he'll have Tommy Sick with him."

"And what happens if he don't have Tommy with him?"

A car swept by and its headlights shone in the rearview mirror. Teddy barely recognized his own eyes, looking small and furtive.

"You shoot him right in the face, so there's no question," he said, feebly making the sign of the gun with his hand. "Don't worry about him giving you any problems. He ain't half the man his father was."

62

"Three more minutes, champ, and you got 'im," said John B. "Three more minutes and you got it won."

Elijah turned on the stool to face his brother. His eyelids were so swollen they looked like pursed lips.

"Three minutes," his brother repeated above the crowd's ceaseless noise.

"That bullshit," Elijah somehow managed to say through a grotesquely swollen jaw. "I gotta knock him out."

John B. shook his head and squeezed another wet sponge over his brother. "Say, you better not talk so much, bro. You liable to hurt your jaw some more."

It didn't matter, P.F. thought as he came up the steps to the ring, using his security badge to get access. For the last five rounds, Elijah had taken a relentless pounding, interrupted only by the occasional low blow he'd dealt Terrence. Even if his jaw wasn't actually broken, he'd been behind on points most of the night, and as he prepared to go out for the twelfth and final round, it was obvious he'd need months of reconstructive surgery.

He stood slowly, as if he was reconsidering how he'd spent the last forty-three years.

The crowd's din, merely deafening before, approached a new unbearable pitch for the last stage of the slaughter.

"You can still quit," John B. told his brother just before the bell.

Elijah didn't bother looking back. He staggered forward and touched gloves with his opponent one last time.

Terrence began the round the way he'd ended the last one, trying to unhinge Elijah's jaw from the rest of his face.

Only this time there was a difference. Elijah was talking to him, taunting him, challenging him.

At first, all P.F. could see was the jaw opening and closing slightly. But as the fighters moved nearer to his corner, he began to catch a few of the words.

"You ain't nothin'," Elijah somehow growled in a muddy, distorted voice.

Terrence, breathing heavily, with the first-round cut closed above his eye, reared back and hit Elijah with a jab that would've put the lights out on a pinball machine.

But Elijah merely bounced into the corner above P.F. and the others. "You ain't hurt me yet," P.F. heard him mutter.

Whomp. "Fuck you," said Terrence, hitting him with the jab again.

Knowing ringside microphones would pick up anything they said, the fighters began to talk more and punch less.

"You a pussy, Terry," said Elijah, miming the part of a punch-drunk fighter with wobbly knees, getting a laugh out of the crowd.

Terrence came back with a furious left hook. Elijah deflected it with both gloves.

By all rights, he should have been down four rounds ago, P.F. thought. It was only a thin membrane of humanity that kept him standing. And P.F. wished that in his own moments of weakness he'd had a fraction of Elijah's fortitude.

"Shut up, old man," Terrence said. His uppercut caught the tip of Elijah's nose and seemed to drive the bone a little closer to the brain.

Elijah turned his head just enough for P.F. to see he was smiling through the blood. Maybe a demented reflex.

"Who you think you fighting?" he glowered at Terrence. "What's my name?"

WHOMP. The jab tore into bone and nose cartilage again.

"Ah, that ain't nothing. What's my name?"

Whomp. A body shot drilled into Elijah's right kidney.

"WHAT'S MY NAME?!"

Whomp! Terrence opened up and hit Elijah with the right cross again, but the old fighter countered with a left hook that drove the kid out into the middle of the ring. The crowd was on its feet.

"WHAT'S MY NAME, MOTHERFUCKER??!!"

By now they'd both abandoned any semblance of defense or strategy. They were standing head-to-head, trading blows, like beasts battling in a primordial swamp. Each shot went straight to the head, a brandished club finding its target each time. The crowd was caught up in the blood mania, its sound ricocheting off the walls and filling P.F.'s ears, like voices coming from inside his own head. Terrence clapped Elijah on the ear with a muffled right hand. Elijah punished him with a driving left under the chin. Terrence countered with a twisting right to the midsection. Elijah mashed the kid's eye socket with a left and a halo of sweat exploded from the back of Terrence's head.

"THAT'S WHO I AM! THAT'S WHO I AM!" Elijah kept saying every time he hit him. "THAT'S WHO I AM!!!"

And just when it seemed they'd finally exhausted themselves and couldn't go any further, the bell rang.

Elijah immediately began to drop where he stood. Whatever spirit had been animating his body was now gone. His brother John rushed forward and caught him in his arms just before he hit the canvas. P.F. never had a chance to help him. Though he weighed less than his brother by some thirty pounds, John hoisted Elijah onto his shoulder and as tenderly as a mother holding a child he began to carry him back to his stool in the corner. As he turned, P.F. could see John crying uncontrollably as Elijah hung limply over him.

Above the cresting roar of the crowd, he could hear John's voice saying, "I love you, my brother. I love you."

63

As soon as the final bell sounded, I was on my feet, trying to shove my way through the crowd so I could stand beside my fighter in the ring. For years I'd thought someone like Frank Diamond or Dan Bishop would show me how to rise above and act like a man among men. But it was Elijah who'd done it. All I wanted at that moment was to shake his hand.

But as I began to climb the steps to the ring, I happened to glance over my shoulder and see Tommy Sick coming up the aisle toward me. I pictured him working me over with an acetylene torch and giggling, "I'm sick! I'm sick!" At the last possible second, though, a security guard grabbed him and started to escort him out.

I hoisted myself through the ropes and went looking for Elijah. The inside of the ring was like a slaughterhouse. Blood was splattered on the blue beer-company emblem in the middle of the mat. The rest of the canvas was still slick from whatever other juices Elijah and Terrence had spilled.

Now all the celebrities and VIPs came flooding in. It was like a billowing yeast of people. Here was the junk bond king, there was the movie star. I found myself pressed up against a United States senator from the West

Coast. We were all hemmed in together like cattle in a small pen. And for a split second, I felt like I finally belonged. Because of Elijah, I'd been elevated into the company of winners. We weren't going to get the decision tonight, but the fact that he'd gone the distance was enough. Frank would have to give us a rematch and money for the options. I was finally respectable.

I caught a glimpse of Elijah and John B. through the crush of bodies and began moving toward them. There were twice as many people as there should have been in the ring. Reporters, high rollers, board chairmen, and various other hustlers and con artists. Their dry, pampered smell was already drowning out the sweat that came off the fighters.

The microphone began to descend from the ceiling as I tried to squeeze between Sam Wolkowitz, the cable TV guy, and Eddie Suarez, the bagman for the boxing federation. I saw John B. still hugging Elijah and trying to pull the robe over his shoulders. I heaved myself toward them as a voice to the side of me asked to see what kind of access badge I was wearing. I turned and saw a security guard with huge pockmarks on his face. In the confusion, I'd lost the badge, but screw him. I'd earned the right to be here. When he reached for my shoulder, I gave him a shove and kept moving forward.

And then I got hit.

I never saw the guard frown or even draw back his fist. He just walloped me. The punch caught the right side of my head and rattled my brains. I went reeling sideways and fell against the senator. He stepped neatly out of the way, and I hit the floor hard, landing on the back of my head. For a few seconds I blacked out. When I came to, I was staring up at the colored lights and florid faces. I felt like I'd been shattered into a thousand pieces and put back together the wrong way.

Someone grabbed me by the arms and someone else got my legs and before I knew it, I was being carried out of the ring. They deposited me on one of the ringside press tables. I lay there stunned and paralyzed, like a deer strapped to the top of a station wagon, while the ring announcer read the judges' scores and shouted: "THE WINNER AND STILL CHAMPION TERRENCE THE MONSTER MULVEHILL!!"

The crowd's cheers made the blood swirl in my brain. I closed my eyes again. It could have been for two minutes, it could've been ten. I was vaguely aware of hundreds of people climbing over me, and occasionally treading lightly on a limb.

By the time I opened my eyes again, the arena was mostly empty. There were already maintenance men in orange uniforms sweeping up. It was as if the circus had just left town. I struggled to sit up and figure out how to use the rest of my body again. Everything seemed strange and unfamiliar. I looked at my hands, trying to remember what time I'd said I'd meet Frank in the dressing room to get the rest of the money. All I could think of, though, was Vin holding out his arms and saying "I been your father" on the Boardwalk. But that was part of another life. I couldn't go back to that anymore.

The clock above the ring said it was ten to midnight. An old black janitor with a face as withered and sad as the fall leaves outside was mopping the canvas. I got slowly to my feet and looked around for the red exit sign that would lead back to the dressing rooms.

64

"How is that?" said Teddy, looking at his niece's swollen belly.

"How is it?" Carla took the teakettle off the stove and tapped her foot. "I'm fed up, that's how it is. It's almost two weeks to my due date, I feel like I'm about to burst, I'm thirsty and tired all the time, and I have to go to the bathroom every five minutes. Now I think I'm getting hemorrhoids. I want this thing out of me."

Teddy was half reclining on the Spartz couch. He closed his eyes as if he had to concentrate to get the air in and out of his body.

"I'm thirsty all the time too," he said with a shrug. "But I ain't having any baby."

"Fine." Carla poured him a cup. "You wanna trade places?"

"You wouldn't want to be where I am."

It was just midnight and they were both watching the door. Richie would be back at any minute. After that would come Anthony, if Tommy Sick hadn't taken care of him. Wind blew against the windows and crazed the leaves on the trees outside.

"It must be something," he said. "Carrying around a life inside you. Taking a life, it's nothing. It's bullshit. Any moron can pull a trigger."

That gurgling sound came again from down in his throat and that deep pain squeezed his guts again. "Jesus." He sat up on the couch and waited for it to pass.

"You want I should call a doctor?"

"Nah, fuck it. It's all right." He put his head back on a cushion.

Then suddenly he propped himself up on his elbow and examined the couch. "Hey," he said, stroking the fabric. "Where did this come from?"

"Oh." Carla regarded him absently and went to the kitchen to get herself a glass of water. "I bought it from Spartz, the furniture store."

Teddy's mind flushed red with rage as the medication made the sweat pop out of him again. All the things he'd provided for these two and this lousy Anthony couldn't even buy a couch for them. He was too busy ratting them out to the feds and making money he should've been sharing with Teddy. It was worse than a disgrace, it was an *infamia*. Teddy had a mind to go wait for him on the sidewalk. To deliver a good beating, slamming Anthony's head in a car door until he fell lifelessly into the gutter. But the wide ache radiating down his sphincter and up his dick reminded him that he barely had the strength to close his own belt buckle. He'd leave all the heavy lifting to Richie and Tommy.

What was it that black kid Terrence kept saying before the fight? Old man, old man. "Old man oughta stay in the old man home." The words echoed in Teddy's mind and he knew all at once, he was going to die. He would go through with the radiation and maybe even the chemotherapy, but the cancer would kill him, no matter what the doctor said. Terror seized his heart and shriveled his lungs.

Suddenly he didn't want to leave this life. It was too soon. What did he have to show for himself? There was no son to inherit what little wealth and respect he'd accumulated. His daughter couldn't even understand he was a boss. And with Vin dead, there wasn't even anyone to share his twilight years. Why had he killed the one friend he had left? Out of a code? Out of vengeance? For what? Vin having a son when he didn't?

His mind began to collapse in on itself. Who would remember him after he was gone? There was Carla, standing pregnant over by the refrigerator. But she was only a girl. Teddy had an urge to go running into her children's bedroom to wake her son Anthony Jr., just to see if there was any family resemblance between them. Some small trace of Teddy to pass on to the next century.

But it was late and he knew he'd be out of energy before he had one foot on the floor.

And now the spreading warmth around his lap told him he'd given up the bag to hold his urine too quickly. He'd pissed on the couch. He started to tell his niece what he'd done, so she'd get him a towel and a blanket. But shame overcame him and he began to cry.

"Uncle Ted, what's the matter?" she said, coming over to take his hand.

"It's nothing." He choked. "Lemme be."

A grown man pissing and crying on a couch. You began this life like a baby and you finished it the same way. But in the end, you were alone, with no one to care for you. Especially if you didn't have children to look after you. Maybe Vin was right. They all should have made more babies.

He buried his face in his hands as his niece put her arm around his shoulder. "It's all right, Uncle Ted," she said. "I'm with you."

But she wasn't with him. And she never would be. She'd married that mutt Anthony and they were all poisoned by his tainted blood. Everything Teddy had done in his life amounted to nothing, and the dream he'd once had of controlling all of Atlantic City, the entire neon forest, was gone now.

He reclined all the way back on the couch again and closed his eyes.

"I think I'm just gonna sleep awhile," he said. "You get me up if anybody comes in."

65

"I don't see why you find this so unusual," Frank Diamond said.

"It's not unusual, it's irregular," explained the F.B.I. agent named Wayne Sadowsky.

"Look," said Frank. "You've been my case agent, investigating me for six years and you've never found anything. I'm a law-abiding citizen making a valid complaint. I'm entitled to have you investigate it and take action, as you would with anyone else."

They were standing at the back of the room during the post-fight press conference. Elijah Barton was not present. His brother John stood at the microphone, explaining that Elijah was upstairs with his doctor trying to determine whether any of the blindness or hearing loss would be permanent. Terrence Mulvehill was half slumped over on the dais, wearing a black baseball cap with a white towel draped around his neck. He had a large ice pack pressed against the side of his face.

"All right," said Sadowsky. "Run it by me one more time."

"The charge would be fraud and extortion. Mr. Russo set my fighter up with this girl I was telling you about."

"And why didn't you file a complaint before the fight?"

"I have certain fiduciary responsibilities," Frank said evenly. "If I'd had Mr. Russo arrested beforehand, I might've endangered the bout and cost my fighter a payday. I had to protect his rights."

At the front of the room, Terrence was standing at the podium as the photographers snapped flashes at his bruised eyelids.

"And you-all want us to pick this Anthony up tonight?" Sadowsky asked, looking and sounding only slightly incredulous.

"Why not?" asked Frank. "You shouldn't have any problem getting a warrant. I've seen a half dozen federal judges standing by the roulette wheel upstairs."

Sadowsky threw back his shoulders, as though he was ready to go twelve rounds himself. "Well, I suppose we could pick him up for questioning," he said. "Have you already paid his people for their part in the fight?"

Up at the podium, John B. was smiling with the innocence of a holy fool with a gold-capped tooth and saying his brother could claim a moral victory tonight.

"Of course, they've been paid part of the advance," said Frank, picking up a champagne glass. "But I can find at least five places where they've violated the spirit and letter of our contract."

Sadowsky inhaled and rolled his eyes. "You drive some hard bargain, Mr. Diamond."

"Well, what do you expect?" said Frank. "The object of this sport is to knock the other guy out."

66

A half hour later I was still in the empty dressing room, waiting for Frank. I was beginning to wonder if I'd gotten the time and the place wrong. Everything seemed out of sync since I'd gotten the stuffing knocked out of me by that guard. Doors opened and closed too quickly, footsteps were too loud on the stairs.

I dug the Filofax out of my jacket pocket and double-checked. "12:15: Pick up balance of payment from Frank D." Where was he?

I started tearing apart the dressing room, looking for some kind of note from him. He couldn't have just skipped out on me. He wouldn't have the nerve. I looked under the training table, which was covered in dried blood and sweaty towels. I searched through the box full of bandages and rolls of tape. I even lifted the red carpet at the corners. But nothing.

I was beginning to panic. I ran upstairs to the casino, hoping the guards hadn't let Tommy Sick back in the building. My vision blurred and then split in two. I saw two sets of Japanese businessmen jamming the baccarat pits; two sets of yuppie couples at the craps tables, hollering like it was divorce court; four sets of young black and Chinese dope dealers in expensive running suits throwing thousands of dollars at the blackjack dealers.

Something about watching two guys beat the shit out of each other made people feel like gambling, as if they were the ones taking the risks.

I blinked until my vision came together again and then walked the length of the casino floor, past the jangling bells and twirling slots, heading for the lobby. I wanted to at least get the sixty thousand dollars I had out of the hotel safe.

As I came down the escalator, I heard the old song "California Dreaming" playing on the P.A. system and wondered if I'd ever make it out there.

I got to the front desk and asked the clerk, who was dressed as a pirate, to go get my briefcase. He took my registration number and hurried away, twitching his butt in his tight brown britches. While I was waiting for him to come back, I caught sight of a tense, disheveled guy in a wrinkled jacket and dirty sweatshirt in the nearest smoked wall mirror. And then I realized I was looking at myself. My nose began to bleed as the clerk returned and handed me the briefcase across the counter.

"Sir, before I can let you take that, I need you to sign this book for me." He brought out a huge gilt-edged ledger book used to keep track of property in the safes.

I took a fountain pen from the green baize-topped counter and found myself struggling to remember how I spelled my last name. "Say, you haven't seen Frank Diamond around, have you?"

From his side of the counter, he studied my upside-down signature and licked his lips. "You are Mr. Russo?"

"I think so."

"Could you wait here one minute?"

He disappeared into the back office again, twitching his butt. Everything seemed wrong. I grabbed a Kleenex from the counter and tried to stanch my nosebleed. Two dozen losers wandered out of the casino, heading for the Boardwalk. Then I heard someone in the back office asking, "Hey, Tim, is that F.B.I. guy still here?"

That was all I needed. I bolted across the lobby with my briefcase and the sixty thousand dollars' worth of chips in my hand. And ran straight into John B., who was standing by the elevators, holding a silver ice bucket.

"Hey," I said. "What's going on?"

He looked at me once and started moving away.

"Hey John," I chased after him. "I asked what's going on?"

I caught him by the elbow but he wouldn't look at me.

"Come on, man. Let go my arm. I can't have anybody see me talkin' to you."

"Why the hell not?"

"Police came by the dressing room looking for you, man."

"Ha?"

A wave of static engulfed my brain.

"Said they wanted to talk to you, man."

"What'd they want?"

"I don't know." He shook his head furiously, disavowing everything. "F.B.I. man said he wanted a few words with you. Got nothing to do with me. Except only now we can't get paid for the fight."

I glanced across the lobby to see if anybody was watching us, but the only people around were other losers feeling sorry for themselves.

"The fuck is going on?" I said, trying to keep my voice down. "John, you better not have said nothing to them. I got you into this fight and gave you this opportunity. You wouldn't be anywhere without me."

"Fuck you, man," said John B., his jaw jutting out to challenge me. "My brother's upstairs and he can't stop the ringing in his ears. They gotta take him to the hospital and see if he's got a skull fracture. He don't even know me. He's on Queer Street. And now we can't get paid, because of something you done. You best get a good lawyer."

"Yeah, but what'd I do?"

"I don't know, man. All I know's I didn't have anything to do with it. Maybe your old lady dimed you out. I just know it's not my concern."

I went charging up one of the escalators, back toward the casino floor. My mind was boiling over. I looked up and saw "$17,901,873" in yellow digits on the giant Progressive Slots tote board. There was a crowd of gamblers six-deep around the nearest craps table. I went over and tried to lose myself in it. Some Wall Street girl with red hair was trying to convince the dealer to take her pearls in lieu of cash while a Vietnam vet in a wheelchair tried to throw his dice over the side. An announcement came over the

P.A. asking an Agent Sadowsky to report to the front desk. Then they went back to playing music. Only instead of "California Dreaming," it was "The Logical Song" by Supertramp.

So I tried to be logical. Why would the feds be after me? It could be only one thing. The fact that I'd killed Nicky. I knew it would catch up to me. But who could have told them about it? The closest thing to a witness was Richie Amato, and he was too much of a loyal dog-ass mob wannabe to even think of talking. So who else knew about it? Teddy and Vin. Forget them. Vin would protect me to the bitter end, and Teddy couldn't speak against me without implicating himself. That left Rosemary.

She'd been threatening me about Nicky ever since that night in her dressing room. What was it she said? "I know about you." And what about tonight? What was that business about paying her "or else"? Or else she'd go to the feds and tell them about Nicky? But then I'd never be able to pay her. It didn't quite make sense. Especially considering I was supposed to meet her in the garage in ten minutes.

I listened to the steady winding tick of the roulette wheel and the constant *bong, bong* from the slot machines. And I remembered how she'd acted that night at the club when she thought I'd betrayed her with Vin. She'd gotten so mad she practically raped that drunken idiot in the ring. She had the temper to do it. So maybe she had the temper to send me to jail, regardless of the consequences. That was the thing about having too much anger. You usually ended up hurting yourself.

67

The yellow neon sign above the row of slot machines said
REDEMPTION CENTER.

But why would anyone come here for redemption?
P.F. wondered. All casinos were good for was taking your
money.

The high rollers all flocked to the table games, leaving
the slot machine games like *Magnificent 7*, *Break the
Bank*, and *Aces High* to the old men and women who'd
be here on a regular night anyway. These were people
who'd spent their days in front of conveyor belts and video
terminals and their nights in front of television sets. And
now they expected a machine to give them something in
return.

The men seemed more resigned to losing. They put
their money in, pulled the levers, and watched the dials
tell them something they already knew. But the women
were full of hope and determination. Some played two or
three machines at a time. When they pulled a lever, they
put a lifetime of frustration into it. And when they hit a
jackpot, they celebrated like it was the birth of a grand-
child, jumping up and clapping their hands with glee.

Their joy was contagious. Between watching them and
seeing Elijah fight on past his prime, P.F. felt oddly elated.
What was the phrase his father used when P.F. discovered
he was having an affair at the age of seventy-seven? Never
too old to be bold.

He even felt encouraged seeing Wayne Sadowsky and
two other beefy F.B.I. agents striding down the aisle of
slots with great purpose.

"So what's the good word?"

"You-all see a gentleman name of Anthony Russo around here?" Sadowsky asked briskly.

"Why? What do you want from him?" P.F. found himself feeling defensive about the kid. Especially after the talk they'd had about Mike Dillon this afternoon.

"That's not your concern." Sadowsky scratched his upper lip with his bottom row of teeth. "Do you know this young man?"

"Maybe I do, maybe I don't."

The agent drew himself up to his full six foot two inches. "Detective, this is a federal matter. Your cooperation would be appreciated…"

"Beautiful. Tell me another one. Last time I cooperated with you, I found out you'd been the one telling the casino people all this bullshit about me and Teddy. Why should I help you now?"

The left side of Sadowsky's face twitched. "Because I will not hesitate to swear out a warrant against you if you impede a federal investigation," he drawled.

P.F. went belly-to-belly with him like a sumo wrestler. "Fuck you twice."

One of the other agents stepped between them. "Come on, Wayne. This scumbag doesn't know anything. We're wasting time here."

Sadowsky backed away slowly, shaking out his arms and rotating his head, like he was ridding himself of some taint. P.F. belched defiantly.

"I just hope you're not protecting this individual," Sadowsky said. "Because if I find out that's the case, it could make your life very complicated."

"My life's already complicated."

The three agents brushed past him, with Sadowsky jabbing an elbow into his ribs. As P.F. watched them cross the casino floor and disappear down an escalator, he wondered why he'd had the brief urge to protect Anthony. He'd felt some paternal stirrings during their talk that afternoon. But no, to hell with that. He didn't know where the kid was anyway. He'd only had the fight with Sadowsky because they hated each other and would do anything to screw up one another's cases.

He turned to go out the Boardwalk side exit and saw that he'd previously misread the sign above the slot machines. It didn't say REDEMPTION CENTER. A glass chandelier had been in the way. It was a COIN REDEMPTION CENTER, a booth for changing quarters into dollars. There was a waiting line of sallow-eyed gamblers grasping pink change cups, with their pants hiked up to their armpits.

Things were what they were, he told himself, moving toward the escalators. Only a fool would make too much of them.

68

I hid in the darkness for ten minutes, watching Rosemary wait by my car in the garage. I wanted to make sure she hadn't brought any cops along to arrest me. The world still seemed skewed. All the cars were tilting the wrong way. The casino lights beyond the concrete lip of the garage looked like dots of blood against the black sky. And the pain in my head was like a throbbing supernova.

From twenty yards away, I saw Rosemary lean against the rear fender, cross and uncross her legs three times, and then fire up a cigarette. She looked nervous, maybe even desperate. Maybe even desperate enough to turn me over to the feds, if it suited her purposes. She sucked down a lungful of smoke and held it with all her might. I wondered if I'd be desperate enough to kill her if she was the only witness against me.

I waited another five minutes until the rest of the cars on the fifth floor flared red and drove away. Then I came walking out of the darkness with the briefcase in my left hand.

"Get in on the driver's side," I told Rosemary.

"Why, are we going for a ride?"

"You tell me."

She got in and I slid in beside her in the passenger's front seat. The dashboard clock said it was 1:27 in the morning. My eyes were bloodshot in the rearview mirror. The gun I'd used to kill Nicky was still in the glove compartment. I'd had it there for weeks, perhaps because I felt guilty and thought I deserved to get caught. But now that I was backed into a corner, I was thinking of using it again.

"That thing you said earlier tonight. 'Or else.' What'd you mean by that?"

She looked confused for a moment before her mouth pulled the rest of her face to attention. "Oh. I was just saying I wanted you to keep your promise."

"But you said 'or else.' Or else what?"

"I don't know." She shrugged. "Or else I guess I'd have to talk to somebody about it."

"Yeah, like the police? What would be the point of that?"

She looked at me the way you'd look at a ringing alarm clock. "Listen, Anthony, I'm tired," she said, rubbing her eyes. "It's one-thirty, I gotta get up with Kimmy in the morning, and my arms are killing me from carrying the round cards all night. All I am asking is if you brought the money. If you didn't, we can talk about it tomorrow…"

"No! I wanna talk about it now!"

I slammed the dashboard with my fist as my voice

bounced off the windshield and stayed compressed in the car. Rosemary became very still.

"Well, if you don't have it, you don't have it." She glanced down at the briefcase on my lap and reached for her door handle. "There's nothing else for us to talk about."

Which meant she was going downstairs to call the F.B.I., as far as I was concerned. That was the reason she'd come to meet me. My head pulsed once more. She'd been waiting to see if she could get the money out of me before she threw me to the lions. I reached across her body and pulled her door shut with my left hand. With my right hand, I popped open the glove compartment and pulled out the gun.

"Just sit there," I said, aiming it at her head. "Is this how you wanted it to end? Like this? Don't you know I've been trying to get away from this all my life?"

Even in the dimness of the car, I could see her turning pale. "Anthony, what are you talking about?"

"I know you already called the police about me."

"That's not true."

"Don't you lie to me, Rosemary! I heard enough lies to last the rest of my life!"

Right at that second, I felt I was capable of killing her. After all, I'd killed Nicky and nothing had happened to me. That was what Teddy and Vin had understood all along. There was no difference between right and wrong. It was just a matter of what you could get away with. And now I was sure I had that same coldness in my heart.

"I never talked to any police officers," Rosemary said feebly.

"Bullshit! Why should I believe you?" The car rocked on its springs beneath us. I raised the gun right to the level of her eyes.

"Please don't do this," she said.

"Why not? You tore my fucking heart out. And now you're going to send me away for the rest of my life."

"It's not right."

"Yeah, you tell me about what's right. You come all this way with me and then you stab me in the back. You call that right?"

"I have a daughter," she said calmly.

"Yeah, so?"

"So do you want her to grow up the way you did? Losing someone she loved?"

Somehow when she said that, it was as if she'd flipped a switch and turned off a generator in my head. All the current began to cycle down and the energy that I would've used to kill her left the car. I couldn't do to somebody else what had been done to me. Probably that was my great failing in life. Even if I had been born Sicilian, I wouldn't have made it in Teddy and Vin's world.

I stuck the gun in my waistband and opened the briefcase on my lap. Sixty thousand dollars' worth of Golden Doubloon casino chips. I stuffed half of them into the five pockets of my jacket. Then I closed the briefcase and gave the rest to Rosemary.

"Go on, get out of here," I told her.

"What's this?" she said, balancing the briefcase on her bare knees. "A bunch of chips. How many are there?"

"Just get the fuck outa here! And don't let me see you again."

She snapped to it, realizing I was letting her get away with her life. She put the briefcase under her arm and reached for the door. But before she opened it, she hesitated and looked back at me.

"Yeah, what is it?" I said. "Didn't you get everything you came for?"

"Take care of yourself, Anthony."

69

She climbed from the car and went staggering across the slanted concrete floor in her high heels. She looked back and saw his silhouette through the rear window. Had he really meant to kill her? For some reason, she didn't quite believe it. Even with a gun in his hand, he still seemed like a lonely, frightened boy. She switched the heavy briefcase from her right hand to her left as she rounded a corner and headed down the ramp to the fourth floor.

A black Acura roared by, narrowly missing her. She heard the echo of the young men inside laughing as they raced downstairs. But she no longer cared. She had money in her hand and the city lights still blazing below.

Again, in spite of everything, she'd survived.

70

What can I say? It was a night for long shots coming in. She was somebody's mother, for crying out loud. I couldn't kill her.

I just sat in the front seat for a few minutes, overlooking the lip of the garage. Down below, traffic was rolling out of town slowly, the losers' wagon train. If I'd had any kind of mind, I would've followed it. But I had accounts to settle and debts to pay, and I wanted to see my wife and kids. I'd done wrong by them for so long that I couldn't leave without saying goodbye.

I decided my first stop would be Vin's house. I'd give

him the money I had and tell him to divide it up between Carla and her uncle. I had it all worked out. The eventual pay-per-view receipts would go to my kids. But when I drove over and rang Vin's door, there was no answer. I should've been glad to leave it at that, but after our talk on the Boardwalk the other day, I felt like there were things I wanted to say to him.

I drove over to the stash house, hoping I might find him there. As I went up the stairs, I noticed I still had blurred vision and the ringing in my ears. This was what they meant by somebody punching you into next week. My eye sockets were sore and my skull felt swollen.

I was so tired I could barely get the keys out of my pocket. The place was quiet as a tomb inside. I tripped once and fell into something wet and sticky on the floor. I got up and turned on the light. There was a smell of beer in there and another odor harder to identify. Paraffin, maybe, but mixed in with something much worse. My eyes began to adjust. I looked down and saw dried lumps of blue and red at the foot of the black leather sofa. Not huge lumps, but little bits with what looked like gray hairs mixed in between. Somebody had made a small effort to clean up the mess before shoving the couch over most of it.

It took me a good minute to realize I was looking at part of someone's brain.

My stomach heaved its contents up toward the top of my throat and I started to gag.

They must have whacked a guy in here earlier tonight. I had to get out quick before someone called the police. I tried to remember if I'd left fingerprints anywhere. The stainless steel lamp. I needed something to wipe it with. I looked around for a cloth or a rag, but all I saw were un-taxed liquor bottles on the bar and racks of men's clothing along the wall. I started to step over the bloody mess to get some toilet paper out of the bathroom.

But then I looked down and saw something that made my heart literally stop.

A long, brown Ace comb at the edge of the spill. Five or six greasy hairs were still caught in its teeth. It was Vin's, no doubt about it. All the circuits in my head blew out and I felt the floorboards giving way underneath me.

The thought of Vin dead didn't make sense. It was like a green sky or blue apples. I sat down at the edge of the couch and buried my face in my hands. All my life I'd only been sure of one thing: that he was this indomitable force that would always be there for me. If he was gone, nothing added up.

I started to cry, thinking back on that last talk we'd had on the Boardwalk. What had I said to him? Had I thanked him for bringing me up? Had I told him I loved him? What had he said to me? I looked down at the carpet, trying to remember and hold a picture of him in my mind. But instead I got a thousand little things. I could see him walking me through the schoolyard. Teaching me how to play boccie. Telling me I had to be a man among men.

There was no question that Teddy was the one who'd done this to him. And the reason probably had something to do with Vin standing up for me. That was the train running underneath our last conversation. Vin had been a loyalist all his life, and that was how he ended it. So now it was clear what I had to do.

I stood up, making sure I still had bullets in my gun. I stepped on an almond shell and noticed the cable box on top of the television was set to Channel 38, the pay-per-view station. They must have been watching the fight when they killed Vin. Just two hours ago, I'd been ringside, thinking my life was about to change. But pride and ambition were no match for seven hundred years of tradition and the lessons Vin had drummed into me. If you're brought up a certain way, you can spend your whole life denying it, but eventually some part of it's going to come out.

I went downstairs and got back in my car. Half of me was fighting it and asking myself: Why me, why now? Had I come all this way and done all these things just to fall back into the cycle? But in another part of my mind, I was calm and accepting of what had to be done. It had all been decided a long time ago, anyway.

I drove slowly through the side streets, avoiding the main thoroughfares that were still jammed with people leaving the casinos. All the houses seemed to be low, gray, and falling apart. No matter how much I'd struggled and hustled, it seemed I hadn't really gone anywhere. Every turn brought me back to Florida Avenue, or Georgia Avenue, or one of these other ugly little blocks.

Since my house was on the way to Teddy's, I made up my mind to stop there first to give Carla the rest of the money and see my kids one last time.

I reached Texas Avenue just before two in the morning and cruised around the block once to make sure there weren't any surveillance cars in the area.

A perfect yellow moon was hanging over the water. The jagged casino buildings on the skyline reminded me of the teeth in an animal's jaw.

I parked across the street and walked up those crooked wooden steps, trying to think of what I'd say to Carla. But when the door opened, it was Richie Amato standing there. Blinking and squinting as if he'd just woke up. I was so surprised I couldn't speak for a couple of seconds.

"Don't be here," he said.

"What?"

"I said don't be here. If you know what's good for you, you'll get outa here."

"Fuck you, Richie. I wanna see my wife and kids."

"They're all in bed," he said.

On the couch inside, Teddy was beginning to stir. He'd been having a dream about Vin. The two of them were trying to chase some mangy old dog out of the house, but it kept showing up under the sink and in the broom closets. Teddy was about to tell Vin to get a gun and kill it, but then he decided to take matters into his own hands. He pulled out his own Ruger and shot through the bathroom door, trying to get rid of the dog once and for all. But when he opened the door, it was Vin lying there dead. A sob choked Teddy's chest. But before he had a chance to grieve over what he'd done, Anthony's voice woke him up.

"What the hell's going on here?"

I couldn't understand what Richie was doing on my porch. But then I remembered he used to go out with Carla and I felt a surge of jealousy. I still had the gun in my waistband.

"Keep it down." Richie held up his hand. "Teddy's in there."

"Yeah? What's he doing?"

"He's been looking for you. He'd like for me to put a couple of holes in you."

"Oh yeah?" A shot of adrenaline ran through me.

"He thinks you ratted him out for killing Nicky D. and his father. He's about to get indicted for it."

"Not me," I said, still smelling the stench from back at the stash house. "Someone else must be the stool."

Richie just shrugged.

Now that he knew Anthony was out on the porch, Teddy sat up and looked for his gun. But Carla had taken it away with his wet trousers, leaving him stranded on the couch in his boxers. He tried to remember where Vin had hid the gun in the house all those months back. He'd put it somewhere in the kitchen during a late-night talk they'd had with Carla. Gripping the arm of the couch, he slowly got to his feet. His lap and legs were cold because he'd pissed himself hours before. The canisters, he remembered. Vin had left the gun in one of the canisters on the kitchen counter.

"Enough of this," I said to Richie. "I've got something to tell Teddy myself."

I pushed past him, went through the front door, and found myself face-to-face with Teddy in the living room. He looked even worse than the last time I'd seen him. His pants were off and his knees were trembling. His skin was gray and scaly. He reminded me of some frail old elephant on his way to the burial ground. But I knew he was still dangerous. My hand went down to the gun in my waistband.

"The prodigal son," he said. "You got some fuckin' nerve showing your face around here."

"I was about to say the same about you."

I could see he was afraid of me.

"What'd you come back here for anyway?"

"I came back here to give you what you gave my father and what you gave Vin."

Teddy's eyes roamed over my shoulder to Richie in the doorway behind me, as if asking how I could have known a thing like that. But Richie just looked dumbfounded.

"I don't know what you're talking about." Teddy started to back up into the kitchen. "Where's my fucking cut, you punk?"

"You want your cut?" I dug the casino chips out of my pocket and started throwing them at him. "There's your cut, you pig. Go get it."

The green, red, and white discs bounced off his stomach and clattered across the kitchen floor, rolling under the refrigerator and the stove. They were for Carla and the kids anyway.

Teddy looked at me with so much hate I could almost smell it.

"*Minchia,*" he said. "If I ever get a chance to meet God, I'm gonna ask him how he could take my only son and let a piece of shit like you live."

"Well, you might get the chance to talk to him soon." I took out the gun and pointed it at his heart.

With a heavy cough, he fell against the kitchen counter and began rummaging through the red canisters, like he was looking for a cookie. I looked over my shoulder once and saw Richie was gone from the porch. I wondered how long it would be until Tommy Sick or the cops showed up.

"Come on, let's do this outside. I don't want to wake the kids."

Teddy was still looking through drawers along the counter, like he was expecting to find something useful. "I always told Vin you were no good," he muttered. "I said you can't teach someone to love you. It's either in the blood or it isn't."

"You're a stupid old man," I said.

He looked at me blankly, still not understanding he was about to die. Then his face seized up like he was suddenly in great pain.

"Go ahead. You don't have the nerve." His eyes weren't as brave as his voice.

For a split second, he might have been right. I didn't have the nerve to kill him in the house where my children were sleeping. There may have even been some spasm of conscience telling me I couldn't just shoot an old man in cold blood. But then he suddenly stumbled toward the folded-up trousers on the breakfast table and pulled out a Ruger that had been tucked in there.

I shot him before he could aim it. The sound echoed

off the dishes in the cabinet and he fell to one knee. A dark worm of blood started to seep out of his belly. He cupped his hand over the wound and looked up at me in shock, like he couldn't believe my manners. I shot him again, this time for Mike. The bullet caught him in the windpipe and a purplish red arterial spray gushed out. He fell sideways, gasping for air, trying to dig the bullet out of his throat with his fingers.

Somehow I'd thought killing him wouldn't be this hard—I was going to take away from him what he took away from me by killing Mike. But it was monstrous, unbearable. The lack of oxygen was turning his face blue. A horrible sucking sound escaped from his chest. I felt myself suffocating, thinking about the paramedics who'd come and stick useless tubes down his throat. Each second watching him was agony. So I shot him once more, hitting him mercifully between the eyes.

He fell backwards and died looking up at our unpainted ceiling.

I just stood there for a few seconds, feeling like I'd landed on some dark uninhabited planet, cut off from everything I'd known and loved before. I backed into the living room. The couch, the television, and the Ninja Turtle toys were all where they were supposed to be. But I wasn't. I didn't belong here anymore. I turned and saw Carla standing in the doorway, her face a map of every betrayal I'd put her through. By some miracle, the children didn't wake up. That was one thing to be thankful for.

I tried to say something to her, but the words wouldn't come. How do you apologize for ruining someone's life?

71

Forty-five minutes later, I was still in shock as they put me in the back of the squad car.

"You probably did him a favor," said Detective Farley, sliding in next to me as another beefy detective got in the front. "He was dying of cancer, you know."

Great, I thought, as the car started and pulled away. I'd thrown away the rest of my life to kill a dead man.

As the old house receded in the distance behind me, I thought about what I'd done to the kids. At least I'd left something for them. Thirty thousand dollars in chips wouldn't go far, but once I got a lawyer, I'd get after Frank for the rest of the advance and the pay-per-view receipts. There had to be at least another hundred thousand coming.

Besides, I thought, they were better off without me, though it broke my heart to know I'd never see them again. All I ever did was hurt the people I loved. Little Anthony and Rachel would have to grow up without an old man around.

The driver started to make a left onto Atlantic Avenue and ran straight into a line of cars with their taillights glaring like a row of bloodshot eyes. More cars leaving the casinos at three in the morning.

"Fucking traffic light's broken on Missouri Avenue," he said. "It's only letting through six cars at a time."

"Atlantic City," Farley sighed. He turned and looked at me. "We gotta take Route 40 out to Mays Landing so we can book you. You got any ideas how we can get there faster?"

I sat up as the handcuffs dug into my wrists. "We could take the Boardwalk."

They looked at each other and lifted their shoulders. Why not?

They hit the siren, cut through an alley, and went up a ramp onto the Boardwalk.

With the window down a little, I was able to feel the salt breeze on my face one more time. It was a cool fall night. There were still a few stragglers out in front of the pizza joints and fortune-tellers' storefronts. On the beachside, the last of those red-and-white-striped tents were shivering and the gulls were circling.

"You get yourself a good lawyer, you could be out in five years," Farley said.

"Less if you can prove self-defense," the detective behind the wheel added.

I knew they were trying to soften me up to sign a confession. I kept my mouth shut. The way Vin would've wanted me to.

"Plus you got extenuating circumstances, don't forget that." Farley leaned over, pushing his shoulder against mine as if we were suddenly the best of friends.

"Like what?"

"You know. You could talk about losing your father and all that crap. Psychological distress."

"Yeah, right."

I stared straight ahead through the windshield at the lighted casino towers shimmering in the distance. Vin never really got inside them and Mike never lived to see them. And now I realized I didn't belong in them either.

"Did I tell you before that you look like him?" Farley asked.

"Who?"

"Mike. Mike Dillon. He was classic. Years ago, he tried to get me to invest in some crazy scheme where he was going to buy up land along the Boardwalk and build another of those grand old hotels. He was always a dreamer, Mike. It must have been something, having him as your old man."

I shook my head as we passed the Doubloon and its blinking TAKE A CHANCE sign.

Because when I thought back about being a kid going for those long walks on the Boardwalk, it was Vin's hand, not Mike's, holding mine. I remember him hoisting me up on his shoulders and telling me that someday the whole town would be mine. Vin showed me the way of the world and taught me that only the strong survive, though in Atlantic City, even that's not a sure thing. And when the time came, I acted like his son by reaching for a gun to avenge his death. That was what was in my heart, and it couldn't be any other way. I once thought I was something different or maybe even something better than him, but now I finally understood that what he was was also a part of me. And that in spite of everything, I would always love him.

"My father's name was Vin," I said.

A cold wind was whipping around the island. Probably a storm on the way, or at least a light rain. Sand rose off the dunes they'd piled up to keep the Atlantic from overtaking the beach.

"Have it your way." Farley shrugged.

I took one last look out at the ocean. A full moon was shining on the water and pulling on the tide. The ripples caught the broken pieces of light and threw them back up at the sky.

THE
END

Get Hard Case Crime by Mail...
And Save 50%!

☐ **YES! Sign me up for the Hard Case Crime Book Club!**

As long as I choose to stay in the club, I will receive every Hard Case Crime book as it is published (generally one each month). I'll get to preview each title for 10 days. If I decide to keep it, I will pay only $3.99* — a savings of 50% off the standard cover price! There is no minimum number of books I must buy and I may cancel my membership at any time.

Name: _____

Address: _____

City / State / ZIP: _____

Telephone: _____

E-Mail: _____

☐ **I want to pay by credit card:** ☐ VISA ☐ MasterCard ☐ Discover

Card #: _____ Exp. date: _____

Signature: _____

Mail this page to:

HARD CASE CRIME BOOK CLUB
20 Academy Street, Norwalk, CT 06850-4032

Or fax it to 610-995-9274.
You can also sign up online at www.dorchesterpub.com.

* Plus $2.00 for shipping. Offer open to residents of the U.S. and Canada only. Canadian residents please call 1-800-481-9191 for pricing information.

If you are under 18, a parent or guardian must sign. Terms, prices, and conditions subject to change. Subscription subject to acceptance. Dorchester Publishing reserves the right to reject any order or cancel any subscription.